# The Last Roar

Craig S. Whitmore

In the Interest of Peace

This book is dedicated to the following:

The National Park Service *Perry's Victory and International Peace Memorial*, Put-in-Bay, Ohio
The *Flagship Niagara* and the *Erie Maritime Museum*, Erie, Pennsylvania
Parks Canada *Fort Malden National Historic Site*, Amherstburg, Ontario
The officers and men who served under Robert H. Barclay and Oliver Hazard Perry.

The officers buried on South Bass Island:

Lt. John Finnis, Royal Navy, killed aboard the *Queen Charlotte*
Lt. James Garden, Royal Newfoundland Regiment, killed aboard the *Queen Charlotte*
Lt. John Garland, Royal Navy, killed aboard the *Detroit*
Lt. John Brooks, US Marine Corps, killed aboard the *Lawrence*
Midshipman John Clark, US Navy, killed aboard the *Scorpion*
Midshipman Henry Laub, US Navy, killed aboard the *Lawrence*

# CONTENTS

Acknowledgements

"The last roar of cannon that died along her shores was the expiring note of British domination." –Washington Irving on the Battle of Lake Erie

## To the Reader

This is a work of fiction. It is not intended to be the definitive history of the *Battle of Lake Erie*. Historical references abound concerning the engagements fought on the Upper as well as Lower Great Lakes, and readers should reference these to learn this particular period in the *War of 1812*. I have consulted both primary and secondary sources in telling this story. Many of the events portrayed in this narrative are accurate portrayals of the historical characters' own recollections. Where history is silent or at least vague on an event's details, the narrative is entirely from the author's imagination.

As a beginning National Park Ranger many years ago, I was intrigued with Daniel Dobbins's story of his escape via a canoe across Lake Erie. When I read more of his life, I realized that he had three versions he told. I chose the one version that was the most dramatic and intriguing to me. I also realize that even with original sources, the participant's memory fades over time. Then one is left to wonder, what *is* the truth?

As in all historical fiction, the characters are thrust into actual events for one purpose: to tell a story. Any resemblance of these fictional characters to real persons is coincidental. For historic fact regarding the battle, the building and manning of the fleet, read any of the many scholarly writings on these events. Particular attention should go to the works of Gerard T. Altoff, Robert Ilisevich, Robert Malomson, Max Rosenberg, and David Curtis Skaggs, among others. These are well-researched historians and biographers who have done the scholarly study required to promote an understanding of the period. They will help fill in the blanks.

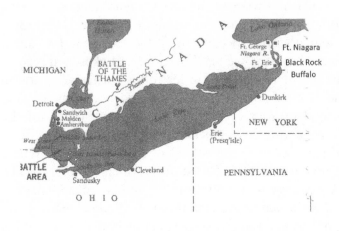

## PROLOGUE

Some modern historians have called it Britain's Vietnam – an unpopular war waged to protect interests in a distant land. After the American Revolution, many unresolved sensitive issues between England and the American states had festered into open sores. Even Benjamin Franklin is said to have observed, "We may have won our revolution, but we have yet to win our independence." The issues of free trade and sailors' rights became pawns in an increasingly tiring diplomatic game of words. On both sides, those who desired war pushed the heads of state to the brink. Napoleon desired the United States' help in creating a diversion from the European theater of the conflict. Through his own careful misinformation regarding trade embargoes, he drew America into acts of trade which were deemed aggressive by Great Britain. The British counteracted with measures of their own that amounted to piracy.

On June 1, 1812, President James Madison asked Congress for a declaration of war against England. Days of debate followed. Pro-war speakers led principally by Henry Clay of Kentucky demanded reprisals against England for her impressment of American sailors into the royal navy. They argued that England also had to be stopped from encouraging hostilities between the Indians and settlers of the western territories of Indiana, Ohio and Michigan. The War Hawks proposed an invasion of Canada to allow for American expansionism. They coveted these lands north of the Great Lakes, and the repeated cry was, "Canada, Canada, Canada!" Congress voted and sent a declaration of war to President Madison for his signature on June 19, 1812. Many loyal Americans opposed this action, ironically none more than in New England, the breeding ground of the American Revolution. Nevertheless, a war was declared which became known in some areas as the Second War for Independence.

Madison dispatched three separate volunteer armies to invade and control Canada. All three failed. One of these, under the leadership of General William Hull, surrendered at Detroit to an inferior force on August 16, 1812. This embarrassment left the British in complete control of Lake Erie. Ships carrying men, supplies and munitions sailed unmolested between Ft. Niagara on the eastern end of the lake at the Niagara River and Ft. Malden (Ft. Amherstburg) on the western shore at the Detroit River.

General William Henry Harrison, engaged in continuous military operations against Chief Tecumseh and his younger brother, Tenskwatawa, called the Prophet, and the British forces at the western end of the lake, wrote to Secretary of War William Eustis. In his letter, he implored Eustis to build a fleet capable of seizing control of Lake Erie. In September of 1812 three men met with President Madison to discuss the plan for construction. One of these was a merchant from Erie, Pennsylvania. In July 1812, unaware of any hostilities, Daniel Dobbins had been piloting the schooner Salina to unload trade goods and munitions at Mackinac Island. As he prepared to leave, the British schooner Caledonia captured his vessel and he was taken prisoner along with the small crew. Pardoned after having his goods confiscated, Dobbins was permitted to leave with his ship to sail to the British garrison at Ft. Malden. Instead, he pulled in at Ft. Detroit and became part of the fighting force there. When General William Hull surrendered the American army at Ft. Detroit, Dobbins was again taken prisoner. At Ft. Malden, he was identified by a British junior officer there as the ship captain released at Ft Michilimackinac. Twice captured, he was therefore sentenced to death for his parole violation. The British laid a price on his head if he was to attempt escape, and their Indian allies could return him to the British garrison dead or alive for the reward. Death on the run at least gave him a slim chance against the inevitable gallows at Ft. Malden. Dobbins had been granted what amounted to a free "get out of jail" pass from a British fellow Mason that would allow him to take a sailboat to Cleveland, but before he received it, he escaped again.

# PART ONE – A MONUMENTAL TASK
## Chapter One
## Detroit River,
## Monday, August 17, 1812

He had to admit it. He could've chosen better places to hide. For the better part of the day, the August sun had steamed the inside of the old wreck, intensifying the rotting wood's musty smell. The ship's hull was an oven, and he was baking like a rye loaf. George needed water, and he needed it soon. His escape had been anything but gallant. He merely walked out of Fort Malden's front gate, circling past the gun emplacements where the 32-pounders guarded the Detroit River toward Grosse Ile. The guards even nodded to him. As a civilian prisoner of war, in a matter of days he'd receive his release in the customary prisoner exchange. Or maybe in a few weeks. George hated waiting. So, he casually walked on, circling past the King's Navy Yard, onto the dirt road leading to the little village of Amherstburg less than a mile from the fort, and down to the river's edge. Nothing unusual in that. Villagers did it all the time, and he passed for a villager. In a remote area close to where the river widened and flowed into Lake Erie, he saw the old deserted wreck of a gunboat, keeled over on its side. A fire had ravaged the stern and she grounded near the shore to allow the crew to escape. George had scanned the shoreline and the rocky banks. No footprints nearby. As remote a place to wait for night as a man could want. Out in the open, yet by its very nature, secluded. Warily, he had entered the water downstream and worked his way back in neck-deep water, losing his footprints far below the wreck. He had slipped slowly down the slanted steps, surveying the hold. No rats, a prerequisite for this temporary refuge. To avoid suspicion, he had carried no haversack of food with him.

Now he regretted he had also brought no water. And as the heat continued to build, he regretted it more and more.

George focused his mind on other things – Polly, that smile that always charmed him, his job as a house carpenter, the home in Ohio he had planned for the two of them once he could free himself from Erie, his— thirst. It hit him again. Water. Maybe he could slip out unseen, steal back into town, get water and walk back. Might as well paint a sign on his shirt: ESCAPD PRISNER – PLEAS HANG. He lay on the steps, drinking in any air that trickled down into his steamy sanctuary.

The river's current propelled small ripples to lap the sides of the hull, embedded in the gravel and muck some fifty yards from the shoreline. He could hear the gentle thump, thump, thump of the waves against the gunwale, and his eyelids grew heavy. Normally he would take comfort in the sounds of the lapping water. Often it carried him to sleep back home at Presque Isle. Yet the drowsier he became, the more he fought the sleep creeping in. Thirst does peculiar things to the brain, and George knew that the parched sensation had some tie to the weakness he felt. In his delirium, he heard the guards' muskets firing at him as he ran from the gate and along the riverbank, then the roll of drums as he approached the gallows, arms held tight by the chafing ropes, the executioner's feet shuffling on the thirteen steps. He saw the head staring straight at him, the hand reaching forward with the small rope looping in front of his face. His eyes felt heavy, his lips thick and parched, the tongue sticky, and his hot face dripped the last of his sweat onto his shirt. The hand held out the rope, but attached to it was a canteen. One last drink before death. He snatched at the canteen in the air before him.

"Slow down there, friend," the voice said quietly. "It's not necessary to finish the thing in one go."

Pulling the wooden hole to his mouth, he drank long and hard, and the water brought a quick rush of cool to his face. He choked, the water hitting his throat, quickly spewing back into his mouth, snorting out his nose.

"Easy, friend," the voice said quietly.

"Thank you," he gasped. His eyes tried to focus on the man before him, but the sun's angle spotlighted into the hatchway, silhouetting the figure in an orange glow.

"George? George Armstrong?" the man's voice said quietly.

"Yes."

"You could've chosen a better place to hide," the man said.

"How – how did you know I was here?"

"I didn't. I chose poorly too." He moved to allow the late afternoon sun to shine into the depths of the ship. George recognized the smiling face.

"Mister – Dobbins?"

"It is, lad. Now I'll have a taste of that too. We have a long wait ahead of us, and we might as well prepare ourselves for the heat."

Dobbins took a long drink from the canteen, offered more to George and then laid it on the rotted steps. George leaned back quietly, for the moment refreshed, and he listened to the river lap the hull. Minutes passed, and no words passed between the two as they rested, drawing slow, easy breaths in the stifling heat. They tried to breathe deeply each time a breeze wafted down the hatch and into their refuge. These came too infrequently. Then in the distance, faint low voices carried across the water. Quietly Dobbins rose and peered through a crack in the hull. For a moment, he stared silently. "Shawnee," he whispered. No other words were exchanged.

George impulsively curled up, watched wearily through a crack in the hull. The war party was definitely Shawnee, and they covered the shoreline, intently searching the mud and sand. One short, stocky brave pointed to the wreck, shouted to the others, and stepped into the water, wading two steps toward their refuge, then hesitated. He wore leather breeches and a US sailor's blue wool waistcoat. His shiny top hat sported what appeared to be two long turkey feathers from the sideband, and in his hand he carried not a tomahawk, but a ship's boarding ax. Even in the heat, George felt a chill seeing this dress he undoubtedly removed from some poor unfortunate. Yet he couldn't take his eyes off of the Shawnee and watched him with a fascinated curiosity. Another voice called the warrior back, and the brave followed, glancing back repeatedly at the wreck. George felt the Shawnee's stare, and for an instant he knew they had made eye contact. He held his breath, afraid any exhale might expose his location, felt a cramp growing in his right calf, gently stretched his leg. The Indian shouted something to the others. George could not see their location from his position but waited, straining to hear the return of the search party. He turned his head away cautiously and rested against the hull, massaging his calf, closed his eyes and waited to be discovered. The river continued its swirling rhythmic slap at the sides of the wreck, and he drifted off.

The sun had disappeared behind the distant treetops when the two fugitives finally risked looking out. Twilight had nestled in on the river, and crickets had begun their evening serenade. No sign of the searchers. It was time.

"I know of a place where we can get a boat if you are well enough to come with me."

Armstrong didn't need to think twice. "No doubt they'll have a price on my head. I prefer your company to that of his majesty's soldiers."

"I think we're both important commodities to the Shawnee, and they won't allow us to live long enough to see the Redcoats. So George, you and I'll be of valuable assistance to each other. I know of a Frenchman a fair distance from here I've traded with. He may furnish us some sort of transport to get across the lake."

The light had fast faded, and the crickets and frogs silenced their chorus as the two escapees waded along the shoreline, leaving Amherstburg far behind them. Grateful for the cool evening air, George opened his shirt and let the breeze dry the sweat as they walked, stretching his cramped legs. By the time they approached a trader's cabin along the shore, the evening stars had begun their night vigil, intermittently veiled by high drifting clouds. Bear, raccoon, deer, and mink pelts adorned the cabin's front wall while a warm yellow glow seeped out from behind the closed shutters. A maze of stumps, woodpiles, discarded wagon wheels, animal traps, rolls of hemp, and hand tools seemed to block every blind step they took. Armstrong stumbled on some unseen object, caught himself, and kicked another object that clattered in the darkness before catching himself on Dobbins's shoulder.

"Well, there went the element of surprise," he whispered to Dobbins.

"Then, why whisper?"

"Who is dere?" the French accented voice spoke from the cabin door.

"Rinaud? Are you there?"

"I am, and who is dere in dis blackness?"

"Daniel, my friend. May I see you?"

The cabin door swung open to the silhouette of a burly, bearded man in buckskin pants, bare-chested, holding a pistol. "Monsieur Dobbins? Well, my old friend, to what do I owe dis great honor of your visit, eh? You maybe want my help, eh?"

"Actually, yes."

"Uh huh. Someone is after you, eh?"

"Yes again."

"Someone who wears dat red coat?"

"Rinaud, you know more than you're willing to share. Can you help?"

The Frenchman embraced Daniel in a muscular hug then grasped him by the shoulders. "But of course, my old friend. You pay me well for furs. I help you." George was grateful the man and he were still strangers.

The Frenchman held the door open wide, and Dobbins and Armstrong entered to a warm cabin. A low cooking fire had nearly burned out and the embers cast an inviting glow on the hearth. Several oil lamps lit the room. Rinaud pulled on a linen shirt and grasped a chair from behind a table for Dobbins who sat down wearily. He set out two mugs of water for the men, and after draining his, George stood, uncomfortably leaning against the door frame and listening intently to the crickets in the woods beyond.

"I escaped from Malden late this afternoon, and I must get back across to the States. I was to be hanged for breaking parole, and there's a price on my head. I never signed any agreement, but I think the army wants to make an example of me. They have their scouts out looking for me – probably for a bounty."

"Yes, I know, my friend. Dey was here before nightfall."

"Will they return?"

The Frenchman shrugged his shoulders. He laid his hand on the hilt of a large hunting knife sheathed at his side. "How much is dis bounty?" He laughed a dark laugh, quiet, but from the gut, and Armstrong got the feeling the Frenchman wasn't being funny at all.

"Enough to keep you happy for only about a month," Dobbins replied.

Again the laugh. He shrugged, folded his arms across his large chest. "Is not enough. Tree months dey offer me maybe, and den I bargain wit de soldiers. But I don't talk to de Shawnee. Dey give me bounty, and dey come back and slice my scalp while I sleep. Den dey take bounty and buy whisky."

"Do you have a boat? Can you take us – my fellow escapee and me?" He indicated Armstrong standing at the door.

Rinaud studied George. "Your friend nervous?" he asked.

"Tired," he lied. "He hid in the hull of that old gunboat south of the fort and was nearly dead of thirst when I stumbled upon him."

"Hey, Daniel's friend, you have a price on your head too?"

"I s'pose so. No, I probably don't." Armstrong hid as much emotion as he could. He didn't trust this Frenchman whom he'd never met, and he thought it better not to give out too much information. Why lay temptation out before your patron?

"Don't say much, eh?"

"The heat," Dobbins said. "So, what will it be? Can you help me or no?"

"I can help. De best I have, my friend, is a canoe. You have a long way to paddle, no?"

"Yes."

At the word "paddle" George felt the weakness in his own arms already, and he could see the fatigue in Dobbins's eyes as they exchanged looks.

"Ah, but a canoe is less seen den a sail in de moonlight, eh?"

"Much less, thank you, my friend. It appears even the clouds have sided with our cause. Very dark out there now."

Outside in the darkness, the crickets suddenly stopped their chirp. George listened intently at the door. A clatter of metal, and a curse sounded in the darkness. The Frenchman reached for his pistol and handed a rifle to Dobbins. Armstrong grabbed a long iron rod at the fireplace and returned to the door. Rinaud slowly opened the door.

"Hallooo," the voice sounded in the dark.

"Who is der?" the Frenchman stood partially out of the door, pistol drawn.

"Rufus Reed," the approaching voice called out.

"Rufus?" Dobbins appeared at the door.

"Daniel? Oh! I am pleased I found you," he said entering the clearing. "I have something that will be of importance to you. Read this," Reed said, holding out a folded paper.

*"Permit Daniel Dobbins and Rufus Seth Reed to pass from hence to Cleveland on board of boats dispatched with prisoners of war."* Signed by: *Robt. Nichols, Lieut. Col., Q. M. Gen., Detroit, Aug. 17, 1812."* Dobbins looked up, speechless.

"It appears you left too early," Reed laughed. "The colonel tried to do you a favor, being a fellow Mason. But since you're not on a dispatched boat, you are now an escaped prisoner, my friend. And since I chose to leave early when I couldn't find you, that makes me an escaped prisoner too, I think."

Dobbins turned to Rinaud, "I think we'll need another canoe."

"I have one more dugout not far from here. We better go soon," Rinaud said, turning back into the cabin.

The three escapees quickly ate what little bread and dried meat Rinaud had ready and packed more dried meat and biscuits into two haversacks, collected several bags of salt, three canteens, and paddles from the cabin and, along with their new partner, soon began a winding journey in the dark following Rinaud. George listened intently for any hint of the Indian war party that might still be in pursuit. Rinaud led on toward the lake shore, pausing at times to listen to animal noises – then continued, satisfied that no one had tracked them. At a small cove, they uncovered the dugout canoes, carefully searched the shoreline, and launched them into the water, paddling quietly and steadily toward the safety of the American coast. Rufus and Daniel glided mutely in their dugout with George and the Frenchman leading the party across Lake Erie.

Rinaud whispered to the others, "We will make for de Bass Islands first."

The four moved south across the calm lake, leaving an indiscernible wake under a moonless dark sky. Though paddling into the vast darkness was intimidating, George welcomed the darkness to aid their escape from the Shawnee. He knew they would not give up on the promise of bounty and whiskey, and would soon be in their own dugouts in pursuit, sweeping down from Grosse Ile and along the southern Canadian shore. The four intently searched the shoreline behind them for any threatening silhouettes as they moved steadily south.

The hours passed in weary strokes until the rising summer sun cast its bright orange glow across Lake Erie. The sunrise tinted the remnant clouds in violet swirls, just as the four reached Pierpont Edwards's Gibraltar Island which sheltered the harbor at South Bass Island.

They slipped their canoes into the inlet of Put-in-Bay, using Gibraltar to shield their movements, beached and dragged the canoes along the gravel shore, hiding them in some brush. Collapsing in the tall grass, they quickly fell asleep, exhausted and temporarily free from British pursuit.

## Chapter Two
## Lake Erie
## Tuesday, August 18, 1812

The noon sun blazed overhead when the party once again pushed the dugouts from the south side of the island into the flat waters of Lake Erie and toward the Ohio coastline. With each stroke of the paddle, George again cautiously scoured the waters behind him, fearing he would hear the war cry of his pursuers. Nearly two hours had passed when they reached the islands off Ohio's coast. As the four entered the bay on the south side of Catawba Island, they saw the scurry of soldiers, Ohio militia, rushing to meet them at the Sandusky River shore, muskets at the ready.

"Thank God, soldiers. Hallo!" Dobbins called. "Can you give us aid here?"

"Just keep yer hands on those paddles where we can see 'em and come this way," the answer came.

"Not too friendly are they?" asked Reed.

"It's war," George said. "They'll see everyone as a threat."

"Just stay calm. They'll see the truth of who we are soon enough," said Dobbins.

They paddled steadily and faster, gaining momentum to run the canoes onto the rocky shoreline. Two of the militia laid their muskets aside and pulled the canoes onto the shore. George and the others rose stiffly and stretched.

"Thank you," Dobbins offered. "May we have some water? We've come a long way."

A short, bearded militiaman took command immediately, "Sergeant, get these men some water."

As the order was passed, the four escapees rested on a fallen tree trunk. The militiamen gathered around them, studying the four fatigued travelers.

"Forgive me for not standing just yet. I am Daniel Dobbins of Erie. This is George Armstrong, and this, Rufus Reed. We've come from Amherstburg. What have you heard of the fall of Detroit?" Dobbins asked.

The bearded militiaman stood perplexed. "Captain John Morris. You said Detroit has fallen?"

"It has. I see the word hasn't reached here yet. We escaped from Fort Malden and need to get to Cleveland. Can you get us passage there? A boat perhaps?"

Morris stood dazed. "Detroit has fallen?"

"General Hull surrendered the fort nearly five weeks ago," George said. "Is General Harrison nearby? He needs to hear of this."

"The camp isn't far, but he may be at the Parsons Blockhouse at Danbury by now."

"We need transportation to Cleveland," Dobbins repeated. "You must send someone to notify Gen'l Harrison of this capitulation. We have to get to Erie as soon as possible."

"I'm sorry," said the officer, "but we have no sailing vessels here. You'll have to go by foot or continue in your canoes."

The men took their fill from the offered canteens, looked at each other in silent agreement. "We ought to leave at once, Daniel."

"At once, Rufus," said Dobbins. "You will kindly relay our compliments to Gen'l Harrison and inform him of the surrender and that we four are leaving to get the word back to General David Mead at Erie."

"And who is your fourth escapee?" asked the sergeant.

"This is Rinaud. He's a friend who gave us the canoes for our escape."

The sergeant looked at Rinaud warily. "American?"

"I should hope not!" said Rinaud.

Dobbins choked back a laugh. "No. He's French Can— He's French." He studied the sergeant, saw the distrust. "*And* he is my friend and trading partner," Dobbins continued.

"Well, seein's how the belligerents are British *and* Canadians, I think we must hold your Canadian friend here for awhile until we can be sure that he's no spy. You three, however, may be allowed to continue to Cleveland *and* beyond unmolested."

The order resonated with a tone of sarcastic finality, like both judge and jury had passed sentence. Daniel interrupted, "I don't think you understand the importance of us *all* getting to Cleveland. He's no spy, and we need him and his canoes to get us there since you have no other means of travel for us."

"Then maybe you *all* need to remain here under guard until Gen'l Harrison returns."

"And when will that be?" George interrupted.

"*When he returns,*" the sergeant emphasized.

George immediately recognized a militiaman with far too much self-importance to debate the point. Reed stifled a curse. Rinaud shifted his feet and looked for an easy way of backing away from the confrontation. Looking behind him, he saw three militiamen going over the canoes and rummaging around for something, nudged Reed.

"May I help you?" called Reed. "You need some tobacco? Salt perhaps?"

This seemed to suit the men. Salt would be at a premium if a war was expected. Reed and George walked quickly to the militiamen who had left their muskets aside at the prospect of receiving anything for free. Reed searched through the dugouts and retrieved three small bags of salt. He held them out. "Here, take these." At the same instant, George grabbed the muskets and stepped back, aiming one loosely at the men's knees.

"Hey! You can't just take...."

"But I already have. Now kindly sit where you are. The salt is yours to keep."

Captain Morris began to draw his sword. In one quick motion, Rinaud slipped the long bladed hunting knife from his side sheath and quickly held it to the officer's throat. "Be careful, monsieur. Dis ees very sharp, and you may wish to keep dis beard, eh?" The colonel slid the sword back into its scabbard, and the men sat gravely.

"We have no quarrel with you, but you haven't been cooperative, and again, we must leave," said Dobbins. "Please give General Harrison my regrets and tell him that with the British now in possession of Michilimackinac—"

"Mackinaw too?" asked the colonel.

"Yes, you fool. We tried to tell you that the entire—"

"George!" interrupted Dobbins. "Colonel, the fort under Lt. Porter Hanks was surrendered too. The British have the entire Michigan Territory under their guns now. Please let Gen'l Harrison know this, and we must beg leave of you. And as we can't have you preventing us from delivering the word to Cleveland – Rinaud, take his pistol."

Rinaud took the pistol from the man's belt, dumped the powder from the flashpan, and carried the weapon to the water's edge. There he submersed it into Lake Erie and tossed the fouled gun onto the sand. George followed along, soaking the muskets in the lake water and then tossing them onto the beach. The militiamen stood quickly, stepped toward George. Rinaud pulled a tomahawk from his belt and held it menacingly across the front of his body, the men immediately backed away.

The four climbed into the canoes and pushed them out into the lake, and the three militiamen quickly retrieved the useless weapons from the sand, upending them to a stream of water from the barrel. "Please tell General Harrison!" Rufus called out as they pulled at the paddles.

"No doubt of that! You bastards!" Colonel Morrison yelled as he watched them paddle away into the northeast's dimming light.

George put all his strength into the paddle. "He'll have General Harrison's men on us soon enough."

"Not likely," said Dobbins. "He didn't even know where the general was. By the time he does find him, we'll be too far out for them to do anything."

"Yes, but when they do—" George started.

"George, the general and I have known each other since he first took command out here. *If* the general catches up to us, he'll understand the need for prompt delivery of the news to General Mead. But we couldn't depend on those four to let us go in enough time. In any event, I doubt they'll catch up to us."

The men paddled past the outlying Cunningham's Island, spying the British Union Jack flying from the topmast of a distant ship near the island's southeast shore. Tentatively they watched and stroked on, expecting the vessel to turn toward them and cut them off from their escape. The waves began to rise noticeably, driven by an east wind. The men pulled harder, into the stiffening breeze, mindful of the British ship in the distance.

"They haven't seen us yet, have they?" George called.

"Don't know," yelled Dobbins. "At least they're not giving chase."

"She is aground," said Rinaud.

"Certain?" asked George.

"Oui. Look dere. She has driven onto de rocks."

They could see the ship swaying slowly, impaled by the bow on some concealed glacial boulder. The strengthening winds out near the island pushed her stern and the ship pivoted on its impaled bow, then a gust caught the main sail, thrust the mast hard, and she keeled over on her starboard side. The men saw no sailors scrambling from the ship, in fact saw no movement of any kind, suggesting that all had abandoned the ship long before they had discovered her. Whether they were all on the island by now, had drowned, or had been rescued by another British ship was equally uncertain. The men watched the wind-driven ripples approaching from the northeast, marginal whitecaps building behind the approaching wind. The four pulled into a steady rhythm, the dip of the paddles hauling against the building waves, pulling each bow into a rising swell that splayed over and around the dugouts. The subtle late afternoon breeze now was a more ominous herald of an approaching storm, blowing in gusts, driving the waves against the men, and they knew Lake Erie's fickle winds would imperil anyone foolish enough to risk riding it out. The skies darkened with ominous deep gray water-laden clouds out over the northeast, the lake roiling into deep blue-green swells.

"We must get close in to'rd de shore before de storm comes," Rinaud called loudly back to Dobbins and Reed, who now had fallen off the pace and struggled in the waves.

"Where?" yelled Dobbins.

"To dat break in de trees dere," Rinaud shouted and indicated the gap with his paddle tip.

The men toiled at the paddles and turned the dugouts toward the shore, the building waves slapping harder at the larboard side, threatening to capsize them. They quartered the waves, diagonally angling the canoes across the whitecaps, riding up a swell and gliding down the other side. They struggled with winds, now switched easterly, driving directly into their faces. George's arms strained against the waves, the pain across his shoulder reaching into his neck. Fear drove the men on, straining for their lives with each stroke of the paddle. With the last of his strength, George pulled hard to the shoreline, the wind swelling the surf and carrying the dugout onto the beach, another wave lifting it high and bearing them further onto the beach. As the wave pulled back, George tumbled out of the dugout and pulled weakly at the bow. Then another wave lifted the canoe, ripping it from his hands and tearing at the flesh on his wrists. He fell to his back, watched the canoe freed from the sandy grip and propelled onto the beach. Rufus Reed stepped out of his dugout and vainly tugged at the bow just as another wave pitched Dobbins's vessel onto the beach, leaving Reed sitting spraddle-legged in the water.

"This gale could last awhile," Dobbins yelled above the wind. "Let's get these into the brush!"

The men dragged the canoes into the shoreline brush and upturned them to form shelters. Now a heavy rain drove across the lake, pushing its telltale spray ahead and bearing down on the shore. The air turned cold, the menacing sky changed to a deep purplish black, and the men huddled under the dugouts while the tempest drove on in a torrential assault that lasted late into the night.

The sun rose warm and bright on Wednesday, revealing scattered limbs and leaves, and columns of earthworms strewn about their shelter, a reminder of the night's onslaught. The men divided the meager food from their haversacks, finishing the water from the canteens given them by the militiamen. It would still be a long journey by water to Cleveland. The growing village was inhabited by only about two hundred souls, but there would at least be food at the stockade. The men had risen stiff and sore from three days of paddling Lake Erie, damp from the wind-driven downpour, but their urgent duty required them to start at once. They pushed off from the wet sand and once again fell into a steady rhythm of paddling.

"We'll need to be alert as we pass the Huron River. The Huron tribes must know of the defeat at Brownstown and the British possession of Fort Detroit. They'll be emboldened to take the war to any settlers in the area," said Reed.

George looked at the water ahead of them tentatively. "Would we get help at Huron Village at least?"

"Doubtful," said Dobbins. "If anyone is still in the area, they may shoot at strangers trying to land. We have to assume they've already moved east to join the settlement in Cleveland. No, our best chance is to pull for Cleveland. They'll be suspicious, but at least Gen'l Wadsworth may be in the area. He knows me."

"We could maybe stop at John Reid's trading post at Mout' of Black River. John and me, we have traded for de furs and salt. He will help me," Rinaud offered.

"If he hails us, we will. But I see no reason to slow our trip. We've a long way to go to reach Cleveland," said Dobbins.

The men pulled at a quicker tempo, making faster progress, the waves now flattening into a mirror surface out on the lake. They saw no threats as they passed the mouth of the Huron River, and pulled steadily on past Mouth of Black River, Reid's trading outpost barely visible in the distant woods. They saw no one around the trading post, and without a word of command they pulled faster. It was possible Reid had abandoned the outpost and headed east, or that the hostiles had set upon him already. Yet he was too well known among the tribes, especially the Wyandot, and would certainly pose no threat to them. The men ventured that he undoubtedly had moved on until he was sure that he could differentiate friend from foe. They could see no sails of any vessels, American or British on the lake. No canoes in pursuit. Rather than calming them, it merely raised their anxiety. Anywhere along the shoreline warriors could lie in wait, and the fear of the unknown drove them. They pulled on, the sun now slipping toward the waterline behind them. They left the distant Bass Islands now turning dark against the yellow-orange mirror of Lake Erie. A faint glow on the shoreline ahead raised their spirits with the settling night. As the sky stretched out its blanket of stars, the high hill marking Cleveland emerged, and none too soon.

"Dere is de village," Rinaud spoke in a hushed voice.

"Shouldn't we make some noise so they don't think we're a war party," George said.

"In two canoes?" asked Reed. "A war party? Not likely."

"Still, George is right. No sense in startling anyone with an itch on his trigger finger," Dobbins said. "But we don't need to raise an alarm either. Just keep paddling and don't be too quiet about it. We are on a mission, after all."

The men pulled hard toward the shoreline, and at a hundred yards a sentry standing on the rocky outcrop challenged them. "Hello! Who is there?"

"Daniel Dobbins of Erie, with friends. We need your help!" he called.

The word relayed, and before the men could paddle to the rocks, a half dozen militiamen armed with hunting rifles had descended the hill and stood at the ready. George saw three of them sighting down their barrels at him in the faint light. Several met them at the shore, held the canoes steady as the travelers climbed wearily from their confinement.

George watched the guards warily. "Who's in command?" he asked.

"No one at the moment," answered a tall clean-shaven young man lowering his rifle. "Major General Wadsworth was here several days ago. He's over at Canfield now, but we still maintain this post. Until he sends our reinforcements, the order stands for the militia to continue our drills and keep watch over the lake for any marauders."

"You'll need to do more than drill now," said Reed.

George blurted out, "Detroit has fallen."

"Detroit?" asked the young man.

"And Michilimackinac," added Dobbins. "We've escaped from Malden and are trying to reach Erie to notify General Mead."

The word passed quickly and straight away a gathering of militia came to the shore with lanterns held high to escort the men up the hill to the encampment.

"Get these men some food and water," said the tall man. Three of the militia hurried up the hill toward a soft-glowing campfire where several pots hung simmering. As the travelers reached the cabin, a crowd of curious militia and citizenry gathered around the cabin's front porch to hear the men recount their story and watch them shovel down the presented food. The soldiers gave them leave to a house nearby. The owner, a builder named Samuel Dodge and his wife Nancy, greeted them, and they entered to the first beds they had slept on in days.

Later, as he lay on the straw-stuffed mattress, his spine popping with each stretch, eyelids resting heavily, George heard Daniel recounting his escape to the men in the main room. He listened to the murmur of voices outside his window, found comfort in finally resting free from the enemy, began to drift off and heard Dobbins say, "...and that is where I found George Armstrong, in the wreck...."

Chapter Three
Cleveland, Ohio
Friday, August 21, 1812

Early in the morning, the men woke to the sweet smell of smoked bacon slabs frying outside the cabin. But the sizzling was muted by the commotion of the community, their horses, cattle, wagons and carts painting the air with a haze of dust. For weeks after the declaration of war news reached the settlement plotted by Moses Cleaveland on the banks of the Cuyahoga River, they believed General Van Rensselar, commanding the Niagara Frontier, would gather a large enough army of militia. Then they would join General William Hull in the west and invade Upper Canada to protect northern Ohio from invasion. The militia had continued to drill, but they all assumed the war had little chance of reaching their village. Now this new rumor of Detroit's surrender and Hull's capture had unnerved the entire surrounding community. Some of the residents believed it was just that, a rumor. Yet many took no chances, and as the travelers rose to the smell of breakfast, the confusion and animated conversation on the dusty street verified that sentiment.

"General Hull was defeated?"

"No, I heered they was massacreed!"

"Yer both wrong. He surrendered."

"How is that possible? He had thousands with him when he marched on Upper Canada!"

"Well, I heard that he was drove back from Canada. He settled in Fort Detroit and then turned over the whole business to the British and Indians and that devil Tecumsey."

"He's a coward! He had them outnumbered and they tricked him. Colonel Cass was even one of the captured."

"Hey, Dobbins! What's true? Were you there?"

Daniel Dobbins looked up from his breakfast at the table beside their cabin. "It's true. Detroit surrendered. We thought we could hold out, but General Hull was offered terms and he surrendered all. We lost the brig *Adams*. They also took the *Mary*, and I lost my ship, the *Salina*. I can only hope they'll use them both to parole the prisoners."

"Hull is inept!" yelled one angry citizen shaking his musket defiantly.

"Yes," said George. "That's what Colonel Cass said."

"Is Cass well?" asked another.

"He is," said Dobbins. "I expect he'll be released with the other prisoners. I decided not to wait."

At the end of the dusty street, a dissonance rose as a rider galloped in from the west, calling to small groups the news he carried. The news was indeed grave. George and his comrades were right. Hull had in fact surrendered his entire force to General Isaac Brock and Tecumseh, leader of the Shawnee. The *Cuyahoga Packet* had been captured earlier by the British ship *General Hunter*. Needed supplies never reached the three companies of Ohio militia, and all the dispatches sent from Cleveland on that ship fell into British hands – and eyes. The British already knew Hull's numbers and his tactics, knew that he feared the Shawnee tomahawk and knife more than he feared the British soldiers' muskets. American troops at Brownstown in the Michigan Territory had walked into an ambush before they even knew a war had started.

"Even Mackinaw was surrendered, and the Indians gathered there numbered in the hundreds," said Dobbins. "They allowed my ship to continue, but I was present at Detroit along with my comrades when Hull surrendered."

"It's true," said the rider. "And I was told at Huron that two ships were spotted out on the lake near there last night. I rode early in the morning to get here. I saw no ships, but the settlers are preparing."

Down below the hill a shout carried up. "Sail, Ho!"

A small detachment of thirty or forty militiamen rushed to the hillside to look down on the white sail about two miles distant. The alarm spread, and the scurrying confusion erupted into near panic. The roads transformed into dusty chaos. Those who had already decided on moving further east to the security of Euclid or even further east to Canfield had hastily packed what meager belongings they could collect and now hurried by. The drivers whipped at their oxen and horses, all laboring under the burden of wagons of house goods, chaise carts, anything the settlers might load and not leave to the British and Indian invaders. A wagon passed with a featherbed in it, iron pots and pans rattling and clanking, the driver laying his gad to the back of the straining ox. George saw a woman riding a horse with one child on the front of the saddle and another seated behind her, each holding tight to a burlap bag stuffed full, he assumed with clothing. A strong line of defiant men formed about thirty yards from the landing place, and forty-two muskets and rifles now clicked into half-cock as the vessel came steadily onward. The tall young militiaman who had aided the four escapees now assumed full control of the militia.

"I need three fast riders to take messages out at once. We need help from the army immediately!"

"I'll go, lieutenant," yelled a lanky young boy whom George thought could barely climb on a horse, let alone ride one.

"Thank you, Ephraim. Where's your pa?"

"I'm here, Mr. Dill," Jonas Clark said. "Ephraim's all right. He can ride your message. I'll stay here with the soldiers."

"Thank you, Mr. Clark. Ephraim, you know the road to Canfield?"

"Yessir."

"Ride it as fast as you can and tell General Wadsworth to come to this place with all possible speed. We expect the enemy here soon. Can you remember that?"

"Yessir. Here with all possible speed. Enemy is coming." And he rode off, cutting between the carts and wagons clogging the road. *He sits the saddle very well for a young boy*, George thought.

The young lieutenant looked for two other riders, saw two women in the ranks. "Mrs. Walworth, you and Mrs. Long should be moving on too for safety."

The young wife of Dr. Long drew herself up. "Lieutenant Dill, we are not in your militia! And we are not leaving our husbands. Furthermore, if you face a determined foe, you'll need nurses. We stay." Two other women behind the standing company of men spoke out. "We'll help you."

"Very well," said Lt. Dill. "Please set up a treating room in Mr. Murray's store there."

The four women assented and scurried off to the white clapboard-sided store, prepared to treat their friends if they should fall before the first of the invading Canadian forces and the Shawnee.

"Someone will ride the same message to East Cleveland. Tell them to come at once. We need all the ammunition they can bring. We'll need someone also to ride south to Newburg and get help from them. I need volunteers."

"I'll ride to Newburg," called one old man, and he handed George his rifle. "Get one for me, son," he said with a wink. He limped away and disappeared behind a house beside the blacksmith shop.

"My son is in East Cleveland," said another. "I'll ride and get him and any others we can." The man slung his musket across his chest and returned up the hill.

"Thank you, Mr. Ogden," called the lieutenant.

The line of men appeared determined to make a stand of it, and George felt a quivering in his legs. He *did not* want to be here. He had decided contrary to his faith and had reluctantly accepted the musket, but there was no powder in the pan, and undoubtedly no ball in the barrel. *What good am I with an unloaded gun*, he thought. His first decision was to break ranks. He was, after all, in the back and could easily slip away at the first volley. He looked to the ground. Nothing to stumble on. Good. He looked to his right. No one to impede his flight should he choose to deploy to another part of the town. He looked to his left. Rufus and Daniel had joined him in line. No muskets in their hands, but determined and defiant, nevertheless. He didn't want to be shamed in front of these men who had helped him escape only days before, but the safety of Presque Isle shouted louder than shame could. Inside, the conflicting choices battled. And still the vessel came on. Behind the men, the rattling of a gun carriage sounded on the gravel, and several men wheeled a six-pounder into a position overlooking the beach below. A wagon drove in next, and the driver jumped down and rolled six cannonballs off the wagon bed onto the ground. Several bags of black powder perched on the edge of the wagon's open gate. The men turned the menacing smoothbore toward the lake. The wad man sank the sponge rammer into a bucket of water, pulled it out and spun the handle, flinging water about. He sponged out the barrel, and the rest of the crew stood to their posts around the field piece waiting for the order to load.

The sailing ship had thus far showed no aggression and the men grew more and more uneasy. *This could be a trap*, George thought. The British had in fact attacked Mackinaw without any warning. They had driven Hull back from the Canard River. They were a determined foe, and the

Shawnee, the Ottawa and Wyandot all fought by the ambush. The men no longer just watched the ship. Several broke off from the line and began to move toward the road, declaring they would post a defense by the road in case an attack came from that quarter. No order was given, and George suspected that those men had no intention of guarding any flank. No commanding officer was actually in charge of this militia, and without leadership, the forces sheepishly began to dwindle against the young lieutenant's attempts to organize them.

Dobbins smiled, stepped out of line, walked toward the high bank and gazed out at the approaching vessel. "It's the *Mary*," he called.

The ship now lowered a sail and drifted into hailing distance. A sentry called out from the lower bank. "Hallooo. Who are you?"

"American vessel *Mary*," sounded the reply, "with paroled prisoners of General Hull's army."

At once a shout of *huzzahs* rose from the ranks. The men ran and cheered down the hill and threw hemp lines to the ship to haul her in to the common dock. The joy of seeing the returned prisoners was tempered by seeing the extreme condition of many. They separated the wounded, and a party of militia formed to carry the worst of these up the hill to Murray's store for treatment. George and Daniel noted the weakened state of these sick and wounded.

"They have had one rough go of it."

"Dey look far worse den we do, Daniel," said Rinaud.

The men who came up from the ship cursed General Hull and prayed sundry blights and cruel afflictions on his head. To all in earshot, they told of several officers who had broken their swords in contempt for the surrender, how they had even contemplated replacing Hull right then and there for even entertaining the idea of surrender. Others had gone so far as to bend their ramrods and destroy their muskets, slamming the locks into trees and boulders inside the fort before they would give a working weapon to the enemy. The indignation that turned on this "coward," as they called him, astounded the militiamen. The disgust exceeded any hatred they had of the British and their native allies. The Cleveland militia listened intently, couldn't understand this hatred of the commanding officer, especially the one that could very well have been commanding them. Then dissension started among the men and tempers rose, some defending Hull, others joining the call for his head. Lt. Dill called for order among the defenders, singled out several wounded.

"How could they take an entire fort?" asked Lt. Dill.

"We were surrounded for a few days," said one soldier, his arm pulled tight against his chest with a long bandage. "They marched around us, stayed mainly in the trees and brush on the perimeter, and we could not see how many there were. They fired a few shots from their cannon, but at first none reached the fort. They moved some cannon closer and fired into the fort. Lt. Hanks was killed. Most of the wounded here are from the fight at Brownstown, and at the Canard. We were pushed back and pummeled there, but we thought we were at least safe inside the fort until reinforcements could arrive. General Harrison was out there somewhere to the south. General Brock, oh, he was a cool one. He sent this message." The soldier handed the message to Lt. Dill who read it to the gathered militia:

*The force at my disposal authorizes me to require of you the immediate surrender of Fort Detroit. It is far from my intention to join in a war of extermination, but you must be aware, that the numerous body of Indians who have attached themselves to my troops, will be beyond control the moment the contest commences.*

"General Hull, that overstuffed baboon, believed him and turned over the entire fort," the soldier said.

Lt. Dill looked to Daniel and George for confirmation. They nodded their agreement with the report. "Hull had asked for three days to consider the terms. General Brock gave him three hours," said Dobbins.

"Did you see any ships set sail with you?" asked Lt. Dill.

"Yes, the *General Hunter* and the *Salina* followed us out of the Detroit River."

Dobbins stepped forward. "Captain McGill is it?"

"Yes?"

"Dobbins. I trust you remember me. I saw you at Detroit. My boat? You saw the *Salina*? Where is she?

"I'm sorry, Mr. Dobbins. She didn't follow us long. When we passed the Bass Islands, she was sailing east with the *General Hunter*, probably to Long Point for supplies. The *Salina* is their packet vessel now, I would imagine."

Dobbins was indignant. He swore, and George could see the determination in his whole demeanor, his jaw set, neck muscles straining, fists clenched. He would avenge the loss of his schooner. For his part, George was relieved no British had thus far invaded, and he resolved to continue home to Erie as soon as he could get passage, putting as much distance between himself and Fort Malden as he could. He handed the musket to another militiaman, walked up the hill. Lt. Dill followed the long procession of returned prisoners up the banks and toward the store.

"Sergeant," he said. "Keep a sentry posted at all hours and inform me of any new ships in sight. I'll see about organizing a defense until General Wadsworth returns."

"Yessir."

"Rinaud, I think we have need of your canoes a bit longer. We need to make for Erie at once," said George.

"I am afraid not, my friend. Dis war, it is coming here, and I need to be home. Dough I have no love for de Redcoats, Canada is my home. I must, at all hazards, return."

"Well, you've done more than I can ever repay," said Dobbins. "When this business is done, I hope to see you more and continue our trade and our friendship."

"I will look forward to dat time, my friend," he said.

"You're not leaving," a voice from behind them spoke up.

"Yes, I am," said Rinaud. "I must return before any British ships appear."

"You don't understand. You are *not* leaving." The order was firm – and totally unexpected.

Reed, extended his hand, spoke up. "I don't believe I have had the pleasure—"

"Sergeant Moss," said the man ignoring the outstretched hand. He carried a primed and cocked pistol. Though pointed down, its intention was unmistakable. "This man is Canadian. If he leaves now, he can report our strength and our defenses to General Brock. He must remain here until he can be paroled by the proper military authority. That would be General Wadsworth."

"Well, Sergeant! We must leave *now*. And we are *not* waiting for the general!" George felt his anger burning and no inept sergeant of the militia was going to keep *him* from getting home.

"No one is keeping you here, mister. Only him. Come with me." And with that, despite their protests, he led the dejected Frenchman toward a fenced stockade where common criminals and rowdies were kept on the south perimeter of the village. Rinaud looked over his shoulder, his eyes pleading to Daniel and George. Daniel laid his hand against George's shoulder, restraining him.

"Now what?" asked George.

"He'll be safe. Let 'em go and we'll tend to him later, but first we must find horses or other transportation to Erie."

The men sought out anyone with a horse and offered money, which they did not have, for any animals sturdy enough to take them the final 100 miles to Erie. However, anyone who had horses was reluctant to let them out for the journey. They might need them themselves for a retreat or any other military operation, they argued. Time and again they were refused. When they asked one blacksmith, he suggested sailing. They had already come this far in dugout canoes, and at least a sailboat would be faster. A brother-in-law was to bring his vessel in soon from Erie and would probably lend it, or at least afford passage. Out of options, the men agreed to meet this smith's in-law on his arrival, and they began gathering what food stuffs they could find, helping themselves to victuals they found in abandoned homes. Riders steadily came into the village from the surrounding farms and villages, and the army of Ohio militia steadily grew during the afternoon, many of them settling in the vacated houses. Several regulars from the 41st Regiment of the United States Army arrived with a wagon, carrying ammunition for the lone brass cannon. These men had been dispatched earlier by General Harrison to assist the militia until the force at Erie could receive more regulars. While George and Daniel gathered supplies, Rufus Reed loitered near the stockade, taking note of the comings and goings of the militia, noting also who served at guard duty and when the guard would change. He reported all of this to George and Daniel.

That night the militiaman's brother arrived with his sailboat from Erie. After they had settled on terms of travel with him, they discussed all options over supper of a venison stew. The plan they agreed on was reckless, but the risk could be minimal with forcefulness. And George knew Dobbins could be especially forceful when the occasion arose. In the morning they would ready themselves to free Rinaud from his guards and depart for home. A gnawing doubt about their scheme kept waking George most of the night. He slept fitfully, and once when he tossed himself uncomfortably in his hammock, the source of his anxiety abruptly revealed itself: *could any of the guards read?*

Chapter Four
Cleveland, Ohio
Saturday, August 22, 1812

The sun rose strong with a hot south breeze onshore and no threats on the horizon, weather or invader. Reed had already been up and about, had met with their benefactor, and already hired out the boat to Erie. George met him before the cabin.

"Is all well, Mr. Reed?" asked George.

"All arranged. The vessel's waiting at the docks below, and our pilot receives his money when we're safely in Erie."

"What about the canoes?" asked Dobbins.

"Rinaud's dugouts are there along the bank," Reed said quietly, indicating with a subtle nod down the hill.

"Daniel," said Reed, "the guard changed fifteen minutes ago. It's about time."

Dobbins handed George a rifle. "I have all the papers here. Let's go about our business."

"Mr. Dobbins, I trust this time the rifle is loaded," George said smiling.

"No, it isn't. We don't need to draw anyone's attention because a weapon discharged. Just act like it is, and you'll be fine."

That didn't comfort George, but Daniel was right. These militiamen, after all, were not the enemy, and he wasn't predisposed to shoot at anyone anyway. Reed began the walk down the bank to the sailboat where the pilot waited for his passengers to board. He started clearing away the hemp lines, preparing to get underway. Once

George and Daniel saw the preparation start, they took the nervous walk toward the stockade. Daniel greeted the men on guard duty, now caught up in their card game at a small table. They barely looked up, and one even waved to the two as they passed. Dobbins selected the first windowless building inside the gate, knocked softly on the door.

"Rinaud?"

"Yes?" The door opened and Rinaud stepped out. He was fully dressed, and he appeared to George to be in anticipation of a journey.

George grinned at the Frenchman. "I guess I need not ask if you're ready to leave now."

"Oh, no. I love dis place. Make a fine home for me." He turned back inside to reach for a blanket and haversack.

"Well, if you'd rather—"

"Enough joke. You get me out, oui?"

Dobbins stepped in beside George. "Get your possibles together."

"Dey hang me, Daniel."

"No, they won't, my friend. Detain you probably, but not hang you. Keep your hands in front of you just like you're tied. And keep the blanket over your hands. George, you follow and have that muzzle pointed down but in the general direction of his back, and we'll look like we fit in."

"Uniforms, Daniel?"

"No uniforms, George, we're militia, same as them. Now walk straight for the gate. And Rinaud, don't stop."

"Oui, monsieur."

Rinaud led the way. George kept the rifle lowered and pointed indirectly at the prisoner's feet. As they approached the gate, he could feel the eyes of the guards on him. From the corner of his eye, he saw one rise and start to button his tunic. Dobbins pulled out a white paper stamped with what appeared to be an official seal. He flashed it in the general direction of the guards still seated at their game.

"General Harrison's orders," he said quickly and never missed a step.

The soldier, another regular with a US regiment, finished buttoning his tunic and sat down to scrape a pile of money on the table over to himself with one hand while the other hand waved the escapees toward the gate. Beyond the gate, George stopped and looked back incredulously. He stared ahead at Dobbins and Rinaud who continued to walk.

"It's that easy," Dobbins said over his shoulder. "Come on, keep up."

George shook his head and fell into line. *Could they be that simple-minded? No wonder we lost Fort Detroit. This could be a long war— or a very short one.*

The three crossed the village green and started down the hill to the dock where Reed and the boat captain waited. George shouldered the rifle and tried to look as much like a militiaman as he could. *These people don't know how vulnerable they really are*, he thought. At the edge of the water where they first landed lay Rinaud's dugout canoe upside down and unguarded. The second canoe lay in the high brush nearby. Rinaud flipped over the canoe and pushed it into the water. George tugged the other out of the brush and tied its rope to the back of Rinaud's canoe. Two soldiers on the dock at the sailboat watched them, and George was aware of them animatedly pointing at the canoes. They began to close in on the three.

"Trouble," he whispered.

Rinuad climbed calmly into the canoe. "Au revoir, my friend. It may be dat I was not to see Presque Isle dis time."

"Rinaud, how can I ever thank you for your help?"

"You already help, my friend. But you may help me once more and push dis boat out to de lake. And please to do it quickly." He winked and nodded in the direction of the two soldiers who now quickened their pace, a third now joining them from his guard post. Rinaud shouted good naturedly, "No, George, you keep de rifle. Now push!"

"Yes, thank you," shouted Dobbins casually as they pushed Rinaud into out into the lake. "And bring more furs. Those pelts will bring a good price. See you soon," he shouted and waved with a flourish. Three strong strokes and the Frenchman had cleared himself from the sandbar and propelled west toward the open lake.

"Who was that?" asked the first soldier as he confronted George.

"A trapper friend of Mr. Dobbins here," he stalled.

"Who are you," the private asked, studying Daniel's face.

"His name is George Armstrong," Dobbins said.

"Not his, *yours*!" he shot back.

"Daniel Dobbins, Erie Pennsylvania. I don't believe I have had the honor of meeting—"

"What're you doing here, and where's *he* going?"

George spoke up, "Well, I'm planning to go fishing, and this man—"

"Not you! *Him*!"

"Which him?" George continued to delay.

The private, now sufficiently worked up, spoke into Daniel's face. "What're you doing down here at this dock? And where's that man out there in the canoe going?"

"We are under orders from General Wadsworth to go home. To Erie. We are to report directly to General Mead and then move on to Washington City."

George's admiration grew as he watched Dobbins prolong a verbal joust with what he hoped was another pea-wit, while Rinaud glided safely out of musket range.

"General Mead, you say?"

"No, *General* Mead," he said sarcastically.

The militiaman nodded knowingly as though in reverence of the general's name.

"I have orders from General Wadsworth himself to report to Washington City – to President Madison. That man in the canoe helped me make it this far, and you, Private, are holding up official business," he said, holding up the official-looking paper he had flashed at the guards earlier. George noted the seal on the front bearing General Harrison's signature.

"Lemme see it," the soldier said, reaching out.

Dobbins pulled it back. "It's for *President Madison*, Private. And although I've not had the pleasure of meeting his Excellency yet, from what I hear, he is much shorter than you. So I'll wait for an individual of smaller stature."

George snickered, coughed, cleared his throat.

"I'll have a look at it anyway," said the private.

"Very well, but it is official business for the President," Dobbins sighed, handing the paper upside down to the soldier who inspected it, lost in thought and equally oblivious of the document's position.

"See?" Dobbins said helpfully. "It says here I am to go to Washington – *that* word is Washington, and it gives safe passage for my friend *here* – that's him in the canoe out yonder – *here* on this sentence to proceed directly to the fort on the Maumee to wait for further instructions." He now condescended as to a small child. "George and I – that's *his* name there – are to proceed by *that* sailboat with *those* two sailors," pointing to Reed and the captain at the dock, "to Erie and then on to Washington. That's Washington – *our capital*."

George could barely contain himself. Suppressing a laugh, he turned his back on the three to look out on the lake at the fading canoe, avoiding the gaze of the other soldier who now displayed a curiously reverent countenance. *We're deities*, he thought.

"Sir," the soldier spoke up. "If you need to be there faster, we kin he'p you by just gittin' horses o'er at the stable. You kin ride to Erie, it'll be faster. C'mon Jake. Gen'ls orders."

"But we have a boat," said George.

"We'll be right back," said the first private. "No need to take a boat. Wait right here," said the guard. And the three sprinted up the hill.

George admired Daniel's coolheaded parley. He had known him from the town, had never served with him on any vessel, but now felt bonded to this man who had first offered him a drink of water and helped him to escape the trackers. Not only was he beholden to him, but the more he observed him under pressure, the more he recognized that this was a man to follow. He had a way about him, the self-assurance of a man who wanted his own way and would do what was necessary to get it. God help the man who stood in his way.

"Imbeciles!" he said when the men were out of sight.

"Did you say something, George?" Reed chuckled as he untied the lines from the dock.

"They're imbeciles. How can we win a war with rabble like that defending the Northwest Territory? We might as well concede Michigan Territory, *and* Ohio *and* Pennsylvania and not waste any more blood. You've just talked us past soldiers and militia who don't care about this country, only whether they get paid this month's wages."

"George, that's not *our* concern. We leave that to the generals to handle," Reed said.

"Like Hull handled Detroit?"

"Many officers are better than Hull, or even Dearborn," Dobbins answered. "Rufus is right, though. It's not our concern. We need to get to Erie, and we'd better do it now. Now get in and shove off before those men bring back horses for a party who no longer has need of them."

The men pushed the sailboat away and, using the sweeps, rowed away from the dock until the sail filled. The southerly wind pushed them out into the open lake and they turned east toward Erie and the safety of home. George looked back on what they had left. Another sail was coming toward Cleveland, an American ship by her looks.

"Daniel –"

Dobbins looked back, recognized the paint scheme. "The schooner *Thames*," he said.

"What would she be doing there?" asked George.

"Possible that more prisoners, returned from Mackinaw and Detroit, are on board."

"At least that's two vessels returned," George said.

"Useless. They'll be required to burn them, destroy them in some way. That's part of the price for letting the paroled prisoners return. Now we'll need more ships to control the lake. Many more ships."

George looked about him. "Do you know where we can get any? We seem to be in short supply."

"Daniel," said Reed, "the *Salina* is with the British, they took our only brig the *Adams*, and add to that the *General Hunter, Queen Charlotte,* and *Caledonia*. That's an impressive fleet."

"What about the *Camden*? I saw the ship at Malden," George said.

"I saw her too, George, but she didn't look too fit. Still, if they make any repairs, that's still another vessel for their fleet, and we have no presence at all."

"We'll need superiority, that's for sure, and I intend to get it. I want to press General Mead to ask for ships on the lake. We may have to re-outfit any merchant vessels we have left, but it'll be a sufficient start. Then we'll need brigs, gunboats, anything big enough to command the lake and confront the British," said Dobbins.

"Where do we get brigs?"

"We build them," Dobbins said.

"Where?" asked George.

"Presque Isle."

"Erie? You're joking," George laughed.

"Not at all. It's a perfect harbor. You know the sandbar. It's so shallow there that a fleet would be protected from any threat of bombardment. Unless you know that channel, you'll most assuredly run aground trying to navigate it. I've no doubt that'll keep any curious British ships away."

George grasped the full meaning, "You *are* serious."

"Quite serious. I need only convince General Mead of the logic of it. No finer oak grows on Lake Erie's shores than those surrounding Presque Isle. And we've sufficient wood in those forests for any ships we need to build."

"And who would build them, Daniel?" asked Reed. "We appear to have a shortage of ship's carpenters too."

"I would think many will come to our aid once they're aware of the gravity of the situation. Allowing the lake to fall under control of the British and their savage allies will be a disaster beyond compare," said Dobbins. "We have some framing carpenters. You, George, can assist there. We simply have the house carpenters apply what knowledge they already have of working wood to the building of vessels."

"You make it seem so easy, Mr. Dobbins," George said.

"It'll be far from easy, George. In fact, it'll be the most monumental of tasks, but we must keep positive and persevere at all hazards."

"Provided General Mead is in agreement, that is," said Reed.

"He must be. Our very survival depends upon it."

They fell silent, contemplating the mission ahead, the south breeze slowly carrying them toward Erie and the safety of Presque Isle Bay. The passing shoreline was green and welcoming; the lake reflected the afternoon sun with sparkles on the tranquil waves, a false serenity that for the present reassured George the war had remained behind them. George never had wanted any war, had in fact fell into deep anxiety when captured from the *Mary* on the Detroit River, tactlessly sought a chance to escape, and made good on it. But since that impulsive choice, he lived under the fear of being hunted. Nearly a month had passed, and his only concern of getting home to Polly was overshadowed by the oppressive reminder that he had been drawn into a war that few wanted, he most of all, even apart from his family's Quaker sentiments. Any future plans he had for Polly and himself now seemed to tread so much water. And as the vessel carried him on into the evening hours, he worried on whether those plans would drown or swim.

Chapter Five
Presque Isle
Monday, August 24, 1812

Rising from the indigo of night, a pale yellow-green sky spread its welcome banner as the weary crew arrived at Presque Isle, its long sandbar peninsula curving from the mainland like a scythe blade cutting a safe harbor into Erie's waters. A light fog lay within the harbor, the cool water touched by the humid late summer morning air. George immersed himself in the stillness and breathed in deeply. He was home. The vessel's pilot deftly navigated the sandbar's narrow opening. Turning hard to larboard, the pilot slipped past the submerged sand that would obstruct any attacking British ship ignorant of its depth. *As safe a harbor as we would ever want*, thought George. The men broke out the sweeps and began to row the vessel through the light fog. The pilot dropped sail, swung the tiller, bringing the vessel about and turned toward the dock. There they saw a frenzy of activity. Many armed civilians rushed to the banks and secured observation points where they would be sheltered from any attack. George understood that everyone here expected an imminent assault from the lake.

"Daniel, be careful, they think we are attacking," George said.

"In a sailboat with three people? Hardly a credible invasion force."

"Maybe we can tell them that after they take a few shots at us."

"The assumed threat of invasion is real enough, though. Just like Cleveland, they'll all be wary of anyone they don't easily recognize," said Dobbins.

"Then we must find General Mead at once," said Reed.

"That won't be hard. Isn't that him?" George pointed out the officer standing with a telescope on the bank, now with a gathering group of militia around him. The fog continued to lift, and at the dock several men who had recognized the returning travelers waved them in, helped to tie up the sailboat and welcomed them safely home. General Mead greeted Dobbins.

"Welcome back, Daniel. We didn't recognize you at first. Where's your ship?"

"In the hands of the British. I'll tell all of it as we go, but there's alarming news from the forts west."

"Yes, we've heard rumors to that effect."

The men relayed all that happened to them. George had been on the merchant ship *Mary*, carrying supplies to Fort Detroit. The ship was seized and all of the crew taken to Fort Malden, the British fort guarding the entrance to the Detroit River, there to be released – after they helped unload the goods for the British and Canadian militia. Dobbins, Reed, Reed's nephew, and a dozen other men from the town had been surprised by the British at Michilimackinac. When he realized Lieutenant Porter Hanks could not defend the fort, Dobbins tried to sail away. The British had blocked the river with the *Caledonia*. There they captured him, along with Reed and the others from Erie who were aboard. The soldiers tried to force them to take an oath of allegiance to the British and not take arms against them. "This I refused to do," Dobbins said. They were paroled and allowed to sail the *Salina* away, minus her cargo, to Fort Malden. Instead, he landed the ship's passengers at Fort Detroit. He joined in with General Hull's men along with the Ohio militiamen and took part in one minor skirmish south of the fort. Lieutenant Hanks had been released and allowed to accompany the soldiers to Fort Detroit. Hanks faced a potential court-martial as punishment for turning over the fort.

"General Hull tried to attack Amherstburg by crossing the river. The army advanced as far as the Canard River, but they were forced to return for lack of reinforcements and artillery. We settled into Detroit. Then it was just a matter of time. Supplies ran low. I believe we could have held out, but Hull caved in to them too easily."

"Surely he knew his position was untenable?" asked Mead.

"We outnumbered *them*!" Reed interjected.

"What?" David Mead stood in disbelief.

"It's true— at least two to one," said George.

"We saw the surrender order ourselves not two days ago," said Reed. "He made Hull believe the savages would murder everyone in the event they had to attack."

"So we have lost Mackinaw, Detroit, and I assume by the incompetency thus demonstrated, now they have control of Fort Dearborn too."

"So much for the plan of taking Upper Canada in just a few days," said Mead.

"Yes. What was it Jefferson said, 'a mere matter of marching'?" Reed said sarcastically.

Mead was indignant. "General Hull had said we would need control of the lake for any invasion to succeed. He asked for it, and the government responded by ignoring us!"

"Well, they can't ignore us any longer! We had no idea we were at war, and the British seized the initiative," said Dobbins.

"And all the forts," added George.

"They had captured Michael Dousman and held him. He was detailed with trying to carry a message to the British commander on St. Joseph Island to find out what was true and what was not. He wasn't even a combatant," Reed said. "It was from him they found out the strength of Mackinaw. When they released him, he came back to let us know about the war declaration."

"And that's when we set sail. Didn't get very far," said Dobbins.

"No, it appears you didn't," said Mead.

"After Detroit's capitulation, we were all taken to Fort Malden."

"And now we're here," said George.

"General Mead, we have to wrest control of the lake if we are to take back any of the forts we have lost. To his credit, General Hull had already seen the need."

"Daniel, you don't have to convince me. I've believed all along that control of the waters is crucial. But we've no ships. The *Salina*, the *Mary*, the *Thames*, the *Cuyahoga Packet*— all are gone."

"Yes, we discussed that on our trip here. You can add to that the *Adams*," said Dobbins. "And with the *Caledonia* and *General Hunter*, and *Queen Charlotte* they have undisputed control of the Lake. Any thoughts of attacking Canada are futile."

"But they may attack *us* at will, and it could come soon. We need a fleet for the upper lake, and time is of the essence," Reed insisted.

"Then you must travel to Washington at once. I will give you personal letters of introduction. Meet with Mr. Eustis and Mr. Madison as soon as you get there. Insist on their promise of a fleet for the lake," Mead said.

"I will also insist on it being built here. Look at it, David. It's the perfect harbor to build. We'll have to get the entire town committed to this. I know we don't have enough ship carpenters, or enough of anyone yet, but we'll get them. I've thought of nothing else since I left Malden. When we have the authority, we'll recruit anyone who will work on the vessels."

Reed, ever the businessman, saw an opportunity. "Bringing workmen here will bring business to the village as well. We must get the word out at once."

"Daniel, the people are already aware of the capitulations to the British. We had messengers arrive on horseback yesterday with the news. You've only confirmed the messages we already received. These people are fearful about the possibility of attack. We even had word that a British fleet of several ships was sighted off of

Cleveland. Another rider told us that the Huron and Ottawa were attacking settlements around the Sandusky River. And they're expecting more savages near Buffalo too. The entire north coast is on watch. I think bringing more men here to work and to defend the area will help to calm them," said Mead.

"At least no British ships are here at this end of the lake," George said.

"None we can swear to. Several people said they saw a small group of British ships northwest of Presque Isle, but that is uncertain."

"Does the village have an adequate defense against the enemy while I get the orders from Washington?" asked Dobbins.

"Governor McKean has appointed me to command the Sixteenth Division, all of the northwestern district. John Kelso has the militia brigade of about two thousand, though they're scattered in several areas to defend the city. It was hard to round up enough militia for defense, but when news of the declaration of war got here after you had left, we received many volunteers. But, Daniel, these are militia, and they'll be available only until their commitment expires."

"When I left with the *Salina* we only had sixty with Captain Forster," Reed said.

"Well, we have twenty times that many now – for as long as they last," Mead said.

"We should be relatively protected here, so if you'll allow me some time, I'd like to visit with my family and then I'll be ready to ride to Washington City," said Dobbins.

"I'll have the letters of introduction ready for you. I'll see you in the morning. My temporary quarters are on State Street, number seventeen."

Dobbins, Reed and Armstrong, followed by the pilot of their escape vessel, made their way through the clutter of boxed supplies gathered above the shoreline for distribution to the defenders. They climbed the hill leading to Front Street, headed east and parted ways at the intersection of Peach Street. The pilot closely followed Reed to receive his compensation.

"Mr. Dobbins, Mr. Reed, it has been an adventure."

"George, I'm glad we've all made it safely. Give my regards to your mother and that girl of yours," Dobbins said.

"Polly. Yes, I will. Thank you." It felt good to finally stretch his legs and walk to the familiar streets and houses of Erie. George felt the burden finally lifted and immediately quickened his pace, heading to the town center and his home.

Sara Armstrong, a slender, curly-haired brunette of forty-four, had settled in Erie with her husband William in 1796. His acquaintance with Seth Reed who had settled Presque Isle two years prior led him to seek land and fortune in Pennsylvania. The much disputed Western Reserve lands had finally been sold to Pennsylvania and the Erie Triangle had opened up to settlers moving west. Upon Reed's invitation to "come forthwith and consider" the lands around Erie, William sold what could not be moved, packed the family's remaining meager fortunes and made the arduous journey from

Massachusetts to the shores of eastern Lake Erie. William and Sara began their new life with high expectations of what Providence had provided. But the second winter there on the lake ended all of their dreams. William contracted pneumonia and died in 1799, leaving Sara to care for seven-year-old George and his younger brother Seth. The following winter, Seth fell ill with scarlet fever. His death drove her into a deep depression which nearly brought about her own death. At only eight years old, George was forced to grow up quickly to help care for his mother, and as a result, the two were seldom separated. She had him apprenticed at twelve to a local house carpenter and intended that he would marry and settle in Presque Isle to fulfill his father's dream of having his own business in Erie. George had other plans. He had listened to the stories from trappers of the Ohio Territory, and when it was admitted to the Union, he set his sights on making his wealth in that state. Training also to be a ship's carpenter allowed him to sail Lake Erie with any of the merchant captains who could use another deck hand. In turn, he searched the northern coast by spyglass when he sailed, or he inquired of anyone coming back from Ohio what opportunities lay there for an enterprising young man like himself. From all the reports, he settled his ambitions on the growing village of Ashtabula. The river entrance there made a good harbor, so travel to the lake for trade went unhindered. Opportunities abounded for a young carpenter with determination and the skills needed to help build a growing community, and chafing at the binds he felt in caring for his mother, he yearned to break free.

Sara's sister had settled with her husband in Genesee County, near Buffalo. She also had one son, Jesse. Though the distance between the two towns of Erie and Clarence made visits too infrequent, Jesse became like a brother to George. Five years younger than Jesse, George had looked up to him to replace the brother he barely knew. Both sisters had insisted their boys would grow up learned men and taught them reading and writing, and maintained that they would practice those disciplines. As the boys grew closer, they traded letters as often as they found time to write. Finally Jesse had come at George's request for a lengthy stay to look at options for work in Presque Isle. He also looked at Polly. Competing for the affections of Polly Freer with his own cousin kept George diligent about finding suitable work, "making his fortune," as he called it, and looking to move west. Separation from her company for these few months made him uneasy. He wanted to rush to find her well— and alone— at the Freer house, but duty to his mother came first. *I'll make a very short stay*, he thought.

Sara saw him from her window and rushed down the front steps to embrace her son. "George! Welcome home. Let me look at you. You look tolerable alright." She repeated the hug and held him tight. "They said you was captured, but I knew you'd come home to me. I never gave up hoping," she gushed.

George welcomed the embrace but, as always with him, felt embarrassed by his mother's ramblings. Even now as he tried to separate himself, he saw over her shoulder several residents on their ritual stroll.

"Mornin,' George."

"Mornin,' Mizz Armstrong. I see George is returned to ya'."

Sara was oblivious to the greetings and George wanted to hide. He strained to loosen himself politely from her grasp.

"Mother, I need to tell you what all happened. Can we sit?"

"Well, of course, dear boy," she said and reluctantly released him, taking his hand and escorting him to the front porch, pausing only to nod proudly to neighbors who shouted their greetings.

As briefly as he could, he told of his capture, his escape, meeting Daniel Dobbins and Rufus Reed, and Rinaud. He advised her of the situation on the lake and that a war had started.

"I know all about that, George," she said. "We've had messengers coming here from the East for weeks bringing news about the war. They say we may be in danger here, but I doubt that."

"Mother, things will change here. That's for certain. Many workers will come here if Mr. Dobbins can convince the government to build ships here. This will make us a major target for the British and their mercenaries. None of us wanted this, but it has been thrust upon us."

"What will you do, George?"

"I've thought about that often in the past few days, Mother. I don't know. You know my belief about war—"

"The same as your father's was," she answered.

"And you thought he was right?"

"He was my husband as well as your father. I let him speak his own mind. Your grandfather fought in our revolution and never wanted William – or any of his sons for that matter – to go to any war. He had seen enough of that and raised William so. William wanted that passed down to you, and I think he did it. Our faith teaches us that warring is wrong, but I also see that at times we must defend ourselves if we must. There your father and I disagreed."

"Mother, I wanted to go to the Ohio country and settle there. You've always known that. I can't settle with Polly knowing that you're here where you could be attacked at any time. I— well, I just don't know."

"Have you asked her mind on the subject?"

"Mother, I just returned. She doesn't even know I am alive after all this time. And if Jesse—"

"Go to her. She will most likely know by now you are safe. Go to her. She has news to tell you." Sara's tears crept to her eyes and George saw the distress. His mind turned images over like so many sketches and he tried to hide the worry he felt.

"Mother—"

She forced a smile, "Go to her. It'll be all right. I'm just so happy to have you back home and safe."

George walked to the Freer home on State Street and every step troubled him, thinking about this news that so disturbed his mother. She had insisted that he allow Polly to tell him, and his fear surged inside. *Jesse married Polly. No, he couldn't. She wouldn't. Polly would break off their courting with him first. Ridiculous assumption.* His mind spun.

He saw her at her front gate talking to a villager, wanted to run to her, checked himself and tripped on a rock, sending it tumbling along the dusty street. Polly looked up, puzzled, and then broke into that wonderful smile he loved. She tossed a quick good-bye to the visitor and hurried to meet him. She wrapped her arms full around him and held him tight, not what he had expected.

"Oh, George, I'm so happy you are safe. Welcome home."

It felt good to hear her say it and he wanted to hold her, but his mother's words still weighed on him. "It's good to see you too," he said. "I stopped at home. Mother is well. She said you have something to tell me?"

She stepped back, holding his outstretched hands. She paused, the smile fading, and took a deep breath. "After you left with the *Mary* to go to Detroit, Jesse came here to Erie."

"Yes?"

"He said he too was traveling. He shipped onboard the *Commencement* from Buffalo."

George felt a new twinge of fear. "Where is he?"

She paused. "The ship was taken off of Buffalo. They had just cleared the Niagara River and were approached from Fort Erie by the *Queen Charlotte*. The British boarded her, and they took everyone, and the cargo. Some were paroled, but they held him and some others." Her voice broke. It's *impressment!*" She cried, "He will never be back!"

"Stop. When was this?"

"It was the 27<sup>th</sup> of June. We hadn't even heard about the war starting, and in fact he didn't either. Oh, George, it wasn't even a gunboat he was sailing. It was a merchant sloop. They were only carrying salt!" she sobbed.

George's face flushed. "This is what they did to us on the Detroit River, and what they did up at Mackinaw! No one can stop them. They've taken *every* unarmed ship they can lay alongside and hold for the cargo. And now taking American citizens here on the lake to serve their ships! It *has* to end!"

"How? We have so few ships left, and people say the army isn't even a real army."

"The army is *not* a real army, I can testify to that. From what I witnessed we'll be fortunate to keep any of our lands. But Mr. Dobbins and Mr. Reed believe that a fleet can be built to regain the lake. Mr. Dobbins is going to Washington to see that it's done."

Polly studied his face. "And you? Will you leave again to help him?"

"No," he blurted out. "I've had enough of war already. If I could, I'd leave this place and go to where there is no more war," George said. "But you're here, and mother's here, and – no, I'll stay here in Erie and do what I can to earn my living. Whatever happens, I'm finished with seeing wars, and I want to just – just *live*. I leave it up to those who love to kill to handle the lake."

"And Jesse? What about him?" she asked.

"I don't know about him! If I could free him I would. All of the merchants and sailors were paroled on the Detroit River and were to be carried home. Maybe they'll even release him."

"He's been gone for over two months, George. He's a captive on some British ship, out there," she said, swinging her hand out to the horizon across Lake Erie, "serving on an *enemy* ship! He's already gone for two months, George. He will not be paroled! You know that as well as I."

George had no control over these events, was helpless in their onslaught and he turned his anger on Polly. "And what can *I* do about it? I am *not* a soldier. I will *never* be one! I'm not even a good sailor. I'm a carpenter, Polly. There's nothing I can contribute to Mr. Madison's war."

Her tears streamed freely now. "And what can a carpenter do that a soldier cannot? I love you, George, but more than that, I trust you. And I believe in you. You have a skill that many lack. How will you use it? Everyone can do something to defend Pennsylvania. What is the something that you can do?"

She turned away from him, crying, hurried back to the house. George tried to speak, looked helplessly after. Her words struck him. *She loves me*, he thought. *Me. What can I do to answer that love? She was right, I can work wood. Wood. Yes, I can do that. But I will not fight.*

Chapter Six
Presque Isle
Tuesday, August 25, 1812

From his second-floor window, George watched the commotion in the streets, the war fever spreading through the community. Fear of imminent invasion dominated every conversation. They knew they had to prepare, but they lacked leadership, someone who knew anything about military preparedness. As he walked to Peter Williamson's carpentry shop, he saw John Kelso working with a nominal force of militia. From the troops George had seen since Detroit, he was not heartened by even this display of training. Polly and his mother and all the other families would have to depend on an untrained meager band of farmers and merchants with muskets and hunting rifles to oppose the Shawnee and Ottawa and the crack British regulars. It went against his character to suppose anything was better than lying prostrate before the invaders, yet he couldn't reconcile himself to joining their fighting force.

At the Williamson barn, he met Dobbins and General David Mead just taking leave of Peter Williamson.

"Good morning, Mr. Dobbins."

"George, it's good to see you looking well this morning."

"Thank you, Mr. Dobbins. I feel much better, more rested than I've been the past few days."

"Indeed. George, General Mead and I have concluded that our defenses are lacking here and desire much effort to bring them to a state of readiness."

"No doubt of that."

"Peter has accepted the responsibility. I am leaving for Washington City within the hour to press our request for the fleet of ships at Presque Isle. I'd like you to accompany me and report your viewpoint on the consequences of the surrender."

"Mr. Dobbins, I can give them no more information than you can, and will add nothing of value. I prefer to stay here. My mother needs my help."

"I thought as much, but I did want to offer. David and I hope that you'll agree to supervise the rebuilding of the blockhouse on the High Banks above the water's edge. As you well know, it's in need of repair. I believe you're the man to handle this affair."

George heard the urgency in Dobbins's voice and saw a compelling trust in his face. *Dobbins*, he thought, *will always find a way to get what he wants*. Yet this was a chance to use his skills, and Dobbins believed in him.

"Well?" asked Mead. "You have Mr. Williamson's trust too."

"Yessir," George said. "I'll do my best."

"We know you will, George. Then I'll take my leave, men. I can't lose anymore time in informing the President of our situation here." Dobbins mounted his horse and turned to the street leading south toward Pittsburgh.

"Godspeed, Daniel," said Williamson.

"George," said Mead, "I can give you a half a dozen men to assist until you can get enough skilled carpenters to build the defenses."

"Not necessary, General. I know of several men I can get to start as soon as practicable. I'll go straight away and find them."

George walked to Richard Graham's home and discovered him already loading his cross-cut saws, auger drills and wood boring brace bits into his sulky. *Dobbins has already been here, or at least he has sent the word here. He knew I'd give in, and he's already started laying the groundwork.* George chuckled to himself. *Oh, that man is indeed persuasive.* Together they rode in the cart to several friends' houses, recruiting the young men who had helped them with two houses the previous spring. The workers gathered at the blockhouse on the bluffs overlooking the entrance to Little Bay, Presque Isle. Most of the wooden walls had fallen into a state of rot and the roof had caved in. One well-placed cannonball would immediately turn it into a powdered mass of splinters. This relic of the French and Indian wars had seen little use since the village was founded, except as the gravesite of General Anthony Wayne, whose bones had been removed by his son eight years earlier. A stone marker beside the blockhouse testified to the place where the general's boiled flesh had been re-interred after the skeleton was removed. A solemn and, some thought, haunted ground, few ventured near the blockhouse — night or day. Now it was needed as an observation point and command center for the militia and other defenders when the dream of a fleet might become a reality. George and his men immediately began clearing away the collapsed roof and the rotted door. Four trees stood on the bank north of the blockhouse. These they cut down for needed lumber, and the clearing also gave the defenders an unimpaired line of sight over the harbor entrance. From here, the militia would have a perfect view of the entrance to Little Bay and further out to the lake beyond Presque Isle. Once the men could reinforce the blockhouse's site with artillery emplacements, the cannon would direct their fire as needed upon any approaching invaders. It was a satisfactory tactical position, and the men labored through the day to ensure its completion.

Late in the afternoon, the bi-weekly deliveries from Meadville arrived. The familiar wagon also carried copies of the *Crawford Weekly Messenger*. The headlines were bold and the message did nothing to allay the Erie citizens' fears. Polly read the newspaper upon its delivery to the general store and immediately rushed to the blockhouse where George was nailing boards on the roof.

"George," she called.

"What is it?" He looked at her face, saw the worry and climbed down the ladder to her. The headlines effectively shouted the warning: *Enemy on Our Frontier*.

The fear rose in her voice. "They're near here already," she said. "Look, it says they want every man '*capable of bearing arms to march forthwith.*'"

He read on through the news story. "But there's no mention of Detroit's surrender here. They don't even know yet. Polly, these may just be rumors they've printed. We saw no British soldiers, no Indians, nothing that threatened us during the whole journey – except some inept Ohio militia. I would put little stock in this."

"Many people do believe it, George. I've never seen the town so troubled."

"People will always believe what they want, whether they heard it from a neighbor, or they read it in the news. I read once that President Adams had said 'facts are stubborn things.' I think he meant the facts will stubbornly survive when all the rumors die out. The fact is this: we've seen no British ships. There was a schooner near Cunningham's Island, but it had wrecked. That's the only enemy ship I've seen since we left Fort Malden. We have to prepare a defense, but we can't be out chasing ghosts. You'd do well, Polly, to try to calm anyone you meet with what I've said."

Polly smiled, kissed his cheek, and took the *Messenger*. George watched her go, hoping she could allay some fears. A terrified village would birth irrational acts, and he wanted anything but confusion, for his mother, for Polly, and for himself. There was work to be done. Thoughtful organized preparation was one thing, irrational panic was quite another.

## Long Point, Canada

Long Point bustled with activity after word of war reached the Canadian villages. At Port Rowan, the British ships, now in full control of Lake Erie, easily loaded flour from the local Backus Mill and delivered it to Fort Malden and the newly recovered Fort Detroit. With no American ships to threaten their supply route, almost daily sailing supplied the outposts and villages along the Canadian south shore. One of these ships, the *HMS Caledonia*, a three-gun brig of 90 tons had been built in 1807 for the fur trade. At the war's start, the Provincial Marine used her to protect the south shore. The duty thrust upon *Caledonia* also included transporting artillery pieces to the battle at Mackinac Island. When Fort Detroit fell, *Caledonia* and the captured vessel *USS Adams,* rechristened the *HMS Detroit*, now plied the waters of Lake Erie transporting British soldiers to the western frontier for General Isaac Brock's needs. *Caledonia* augmented her crew of twelve Canadians with ten American prisoners, two of which now served under impressment. Jesse Harris had served as a pressed sailor in the Royal Navy for nearly a month, and never a day passed that he didn't look for some avenue of flight. Early after his kidnapping from the *Commencement*, he had taken a boat from shore without permission and attempted to row across the lake toward Presque Isle. He had gotten no further away than half pistol shot when a small sloop, maneuvering around Long Point, came bow to bow with the deserter. A grappling hook cast into the small vessel immediately hauled Jesse's boat to the ship's side. A dozen lashes across his back reminded Jesse that the consequences of his actions might go heavier the next time. From that event, he resolved to flee at the next opportunity. As he often did, he now stood gazing toward the water, and his daydreams worked out a magnificent escape plan.

"Mr. Harris!" The voice shocked him back to his reality, and he turned to face McDonough, the Provincial Marine sergeant who persistently dogged him. "Continue about your work on this deck, if you please! I want to see the blood from those boards scrubbed clean, or yours will mingle soon with it!"

And he paced away, slapping a belaying pin into the palm of his left hand. It had its intended effect and Jesse dropped to his knees, pulled a stiff brush from the water bucket, scoured in a circular motion.

"Fish guts and fish blood, that's all I clean from this deck," Jesse muttered to himself. The men had caught enough fish to dry for the entire crew twice, and he was once again left to clean all of the innards from their morning's work from the deck. The most menial tasks had been poured on his back to continually demonstrate to the crew that this young American, now a British subject, could not be trusted. The crew ridiculed him at every turn, but never interfered with his task, happy it was him and not them performing it.

When the *Caledonia* sailed to intercept the *Mary* and the *Salina* on the Detroit River, Jesse wasn't aboard and so knew nothing of George's demise. He had hoped by now that news of his own capture had reached George. After a hurried good-bye to Polly and his Aunt Sara, Jesse had ridden back to Buffalo for his duties on board the *Commencement* and its transport operation to the Maumee River and then on to Chicago and Fort Dearborn. He regretted not having seen his cousin George long enough before

George sailed up the Detroit, regretted too that George hadn't received news of the war before he too had left. As he scrubbed the brush along the wood grain of the deck, he wondered if George was safe, or was he also captured with the reported ships and forced to serve on one of Britain's sloops or brigs on the lake. *Maybe he's been taken to Ontario to serve with Admiral Yeo to control that lake. Ironic*, he thought, *that the two of us would serve the British navy in a war that we both hate.*

"Mr. Harris!"

*McDonough*, he thought. "Yessssir?" he hissed.

"We will be needing your help in loading cargo soon. Move it along, if you please! You may dream of home at night. But for now, His Majesty requires your service."

"Yes, Sergeant McDonough. As you say, Sergeant McDonough." The sarcasm was not lost on the sergeant, and he drew menacingly close, now holding the cat, its waxed, knotted ropes dangling before Jesse's kneeling frame.

"Sergeant!" a voice shouted from the forecastle.

"Aye, sir."

"Report to Master Irvine, if you please," said the voice.

"Aye, sir. At once." He rolled the rope tails tight around his fist and slapped his leg with the red handle. "Keep at your work, you," he said darkly.

Robert Irvine had been a sailing master in the Provincial Marine and master of the *Caledonia* when the war began. With a shortage of experienced naval officers, the Royal Navy had assigned him to continue command of his ship as primarily a transport vessel. However, it was now armed with two extra 24-pound long guns for defense, or offense, as the mission required. Since Jesse had been taken onboard, he had found Irvine to be evenhanded in his discipline and boldly energetic in command. But he questioned why Irvine would allow a sergeant such unbridled control of the ship. The man was callous and relished his chance to punish any hint of misconduct with the lash. Thankfully, Irvine had sent for him, and Jesse took advantage of his absence to rise from this crawling about on the deck and stretch his legs a bit. He walked to the stern of the ship, looked out to the docks where Canadian laborers were stacking it with boxes, no doubt for the *Caledonia* to deliver to some outpost in the west. The boxes carried flour, ground at the local mill, packed to provide food for the soldiers and Indians at Fort Malden, or at Fort Detroit. Maybe even a journey further north to Fort Michilimackinac. He had made two such voyages to the western end of the lake already. *Another trip across the lake,* he thought. *More miles away from Buffalo. More miles away from home.* He saw no method of escape here, and could only wait to go about his work aboard ship until she returned to port again. Then he would try again for the American shore. He observed the *General Hunter* anchored only a few yards away, had been there for two days after the soldiers disembarked and rowed to the shore – reinforcements for Fort Erie or beyond.

"Why you lazy—" the menacing voice started behind him. Startled, he scurried down the steps.

Another voice, "Sergeant McDonough!"

"Aye, Cap'n. And then in a quieted voice, "Mr. Harris. Finish the deck, if you please!"

"At once," Jesse said. And he knelt down to scrub the deck, pleased that the captain had interceded. *Bide your time,* he thought. *This won't last forever.* And he set to work resolutely scouring the fish blood from the pine planking

Chapter Seven
Presque Isle
Wednesday, September 2, 1812

Many of the rumors regarding the invaders on the shore of Ohio and Pennsylvania had finally faded. The defenses continued to build around Erie with members of the 147th Pennsylvania militia among the first to respond to the call-up. Yet no officer had assumed command. A dubious feeling of safety kept the townspeople uneasy but not incapacitated in fear. The mere presence of these few members of the ill-trained militia was enough to calm most and allow some normality to return. The finished blockhouse had been established as the rallying point or command center, if the need arose. Members of the militia had brought into the town a nine-pounder brass cannon for the heights overlooking the sandbar entrance to Presque Isle Bay. Private John Silhammer of Bellefonte, Pennsylvania, directed its placement, and as the men blocked the wheels of the carriage and positioned the caisson to its rear, he determined it a worthy defensive position.

"This should put a stop to anyone entering the harbor," he said. "But we'll need more artillery if we face a full scale assault."

George had just returned with a wagon load of cut timber to reinforce the gun emplacement. "Your militia has more, don't you?"

"Not at hand. But we've asked General Mead to see about getting more for the town. When he went to Pittsburgh, he had suggested he'd try for guns there. I believe he'll find enough to defend this position."

The men unloaded the timbers from the wagon and stacked these to form a wall with earth piled behind them for a functional parapet. The labor lasted all of the afternoon, and by evening the fortress was sufficiently prepared. George still waited for Daniel Dobbins's return and a positive report on the fleet of gunboats. General Mead had agreed to it, General Hull had requested it before his ill-fated invasion of Canada, and General William Henry Harrison had agreed to the strategic necessity even before his victory against the Shawnee at Tippecanoe. General Wadsworth had asked for enough gunboats to control the Lake Erie shoreline and repel any invasion. Indeed, it appeared that all were in one accord. Yet, to date the Secretary of the Navy had desired that Lake Ontario be first fortified with a small armada, and afterward, turn to defending the Atlantic coast from British ships, the greater threat being perceived as the Eastern seaboard. The earlier news coming to Erie by way of the *Crawford Weekly Messenger* confirmed the necessity of reinforcing Lake Ontario. In July the New York militia and a few sailors under the command of Colonel Bellinger and Captain Camp had repelled a British attack on the *USS Oneida* and the American naval yards at Sackett's Harbor, New York, with nothing but cannon and courage. Commodore Isaac Chauncey had seized upon the victory to strengthen the Lake Ontario positions all the way to Black Rock. This heartened the townspeople of Erie as they prepared for their own threat. The paper also reported the first major victory in the war as the *USS Constitution* had defeated *HMS Guerriere* off of Nova Scotia. The paper had even dubbed the American ship "Old Ironsides" because of the oak planking that glanced off the British cannonballs. If the carpenters could only build a ship like that on the lake, the British should have no choice but to retreat to a defensive position across the lake. But with Lake Erie still an enemy objective, and no worthy ships between the American coast and the thirteen British ships now plying Erie's waters, time was running out. George determined to use that time, as Daniel had instructed him, and he recruited any able-bodied men, from the carpenters who helped reinforce the blockhouse, to the house carpenters he knew from Meadville and the hamlets in between. For several days he visited with friends, and relatives of friends, imploring them to send the help he needed. Many had implied they would consider it, but with no actual order to begin construction, and no word from Dobbins either way, the workers, to a man, hesitated to leave their families for something that may turn out to be merely chasing straws in the wind. Many of them were like George, not yet persuaded on Mr. Madison's war and the resulting hardships it was creating. But they affirmed they would come to the country's defense *if* they saw Pennsylvania threatened.

George returned from Meadville on September 15, disheartened, unaware that on that very day, Daniel Dobbins had already received a direct commission as a sailing master in the US Navy and authorization to leave Washington City, return to Erie and build his fleet of four gunboats. George had done what he could. But the waiting, as it always did, wore on his patience. If he could, he'd start building a ship. Any ship. The families he asked were not willing to part with their trees without some compensation, and if he could provide no proof of payment, they would not give him permission to take an ax to any of their standing timber. George paced anxiously before the defensive bulwark, watched four militiamen playing at cards by a cooking fire. Two doves, spitted on a long iron rod, dripped their fats into the coals and hissed. Rolls of wheat dough sat by the edge of the coals, slowly browning. Polly walked at his side.

"Be patient, George. Mr. Dobbins will return and you'll know then what's to become of the ships. You said yourself he could convince two dogs to share the same bone. So, you know he'll get the permission to do it."

"It's the waiting, Polly. I'm sure— I think— he'll get the order. It's just that there's so much work to do once we start, and it's already fall. You know these roads are like a marsh in the winter. When the lake freezes, we can't use the water to bring any supplies here. And we have *no* supplies. Only wood."

"But the British can't attack either. Right? Am I right? No one can sail that lake when the ice sets. So they can't capture any supplies either. It seems we've a very good position here."

"But Polly, we'll have to build through the winter. You do understand what that means?"

"George, I know you better than that. When have you ever shirked a challenge? I would think you have more confidence in yourself than that. I certainly do."

"I don't think it's self-confidence, Polly. I'm one man and can only do so much. I couldn't get anyone to commit to coming here to work. And the militiamen who are already here—well, you've seen 'em. They're useless as carpenters. Most of 'em have no carpentry skills and no one to command them. They drill, they watch the lake, they eat, they play at whist, they argue. Then they drill some more. They're getting bored, and it won't be long until they use their furlough to go home permanently. Even those that don't desert are only waiting for their terms of commitment to be up, and they'll leave too."

They walked from the crest back down toward the town and met Rufus Reed coming from the general store.

"Afternoon, Mr. Reed."

"Ah, good afternoon, Miss Freer. Afternoon, George."

"Mr. Reed," George nodded.

"George, I was looking to find you. Do you recall that British schooner we saw off of Cunningham's Island as we passed her?"

"I think I should, why?"

"Word reached us that the Ohio militia burned her. It seems after we passed, a Lieutenant Allen and the militia were gathering what supplies they could from the abandoned Lower Sandusky farms. They saw the vessel stranded and canoed out to see what supplies were left aboard her. After helping themselves to the provisions, they burned her to the waterline."

"Well, that's one less vessel to sail into battle, isn't it, Mr. Reed?" Polly said.

"Indeed, Miss Freer."

"Too bad they couldn't have captured her and brought her here. That would've been one more for us," George said.

"We'll get there, George. We'll get there. Daniel will convince the President, and we *will* get there," Reed said.

"Need more help, though, Mr. Reed," said George.

"I have business friends in Pittsburgh that will help when called upon. When Daniel returns I'll go there and recruit whomever I can. They have a vested interest in Erie, with our port for their shipping. Oh, and the report on the British vessels is that they sailed from Port Dover on the tenth of September."

"Did anyone say which vessels sailed?"

"They identified *Queen Charlotte* and *Caledonia* along with another small schooner, possibly the *General Hunter*. Oh, no worry. They were not headed toward the United States shore. They sailed west, probably more transport to Amherstburg and Detroit. More supplies for the King's Navy Yard."

"Not worried about them coming here. The last word that we received was that my cousin Jesse is aboard the *Caledonia*. Sailing to Fort Malden can mean only one thing: their fleet is continuing to build. When I escaped, I saw the keel for another ship being laid up at the naval yard. They've probably made much progress by now, and we've no way to stop them, or even to threaten them," George said.

"It appears the army has given up on that for the present anyway. Another of the many rumors is that some of the men from the army of General Dearborn have been sent to the Niagara with General Van Rensselaer."

"Invasion?" Polly asked.

"It could be. There are more ways than one to attack Canada, you know. They're gathering at Lewiston."

"But if the rumors have reached us, they've surely reached Canada too."

"There are spies all about, George. No doubt you're correct," said Reed. "So it's important for them to gather enough of an army to complete the task. Overwhelm them. That'll keep Buffalo and Black Rock safe. Capturing Fort Erie is paramount to any action on the Niagara River."

"But the west? What about out here? When we were captured at Detroit, we understood that having the lake from Detroit all the way across to Long Point will allow Tecumseh and his men free passage to anywhere in Ohio and after that, Pennsylvania."

"Would they come this far?" asked Polly.

"Across Ohio? Not likely," Reed said. "They'd have to eliminate any forts along the way. Fort Meigs is still a stronghold. At least we've heard nothing to the contrary. Fort Stephenson and even Fort Wayne out in the Indiana Territory are good defenses. Ohio militia will defend against any further encroachment."

"Do you really believe that, Mr. Reed?" George asked. "How easy was it for us to get past them? Do you really believe they're disciplined enough to stop the Shawnee, the Potawatomi, the Delaware, the Wyandot?"

"Yes, George. I do believe it." Reed was more trusting than George, but as Reed left, George thought on it. *He may be right. But it'll take a much larger well-trained force to defeat the Canadians and British. Building the fleet will demonstrate our resolve, true; maybe even buy time for an army to gather for the northwest invasion again.*

"George, Mother said she had talked to Mr. Dobbins before he left. He said as part of his parole by the British, they had asked him to sign an agreement to not take arms against the king. He refused to do it. Is that true, George?"

"I wasn't there at Fort Michilimackinac, Polly. I don't know. He says so."

"Did you, George?"

George hesitated. He had signed the agreement, but he was not willing to share that fact. He wasn't proud of it.

"Did you?"

"Polly, when I left here, I wanted to make enough to set aside so that we could marry and start a family. You know I'm against the war. I've always been against it – any war. There are many out here who didn't want it, and it's been dumped on us. I didn't even know we were at war until the attack on Detroit."

"George, did you sign the parole papers?"

He blurted it out. "I did. I would've done anything to get back home. But when the British delayed our release, that's when I escaped. I knew I wouldn't fight against the British, and I wanted to make sure I wasn't put on any British ship to fight for them either. I would've signed anything to get away from there. Now, if they come here, and I'm found fighting, I'll hang. So will Mr. Dobbins. So will Mr. Reed, anyone who was returned here. We'll all face death."

"Then how can you remain passive? You must defend yourself, defend all of us. We need you and every able man to stop the British and the Indians who will surely come here. It's a clear decision, George."

"It's not all that clear, Polly. Our faith doesn't permit us to engage in warfare. You know that. I'll not take up arms against another human being. And why do you want me to go against my principles?"

"You're willing to build warships."

"It's a fine line, I know, and I struggle with it. If I can build something to keep people safe, I'll use my skills for that purpose. But taking a gun against another person – it's where I must take a stand."

"You must help. They are so short on defenders. Jesse would not duck from his responsibility," she said. Now it was out. She was holding him to her view of Jesse, a comparison that repulsed him.

"Jesse is not here! Alright? He's not here! I'm not Jesse! What Jesse does with his convictions is his own choice. If you wanted Jesse, then maybe you should've let him know before he left, convinced him to stay. Or you should've let me know so I would not have returned!"

"George, can you actually think that?"

"Yes, I can!"

She stood before him, studied him. George defiantly held his ground. "Then you don't understand me at all, Mr. Armstrong! Good day to you, sir!"

King's Navy Yard
Amherstburg, Ontario, Canada
Friday, September 25, 1812

Jesse had finished loading the last of the bales of furs into the ship's hold and lost himself in the crowd of sailors now leaving the docks to refresh themselves in Amherstburg before *Caledonia* set sail. He followed a French-Canadian trapper named Rinaud who had received a note of receipt to present to the quartermaster for payment for furs. He noted where the soldiers had gathered to board the *Caledonia* and the captured *HMS Detroit*. The *Queen Charlotte* rested in the harbor, not designated to make this return trip to Port Dover. For the past week, Fort Malden had been busy with new troops gathering from Mackinaw and Detroit to sail to the eastern end of the lake as reinforcements for General Brock's campaign on Lake Ontario. Jesse had recognized the mercantile *Friends Good Will*, belonging to William Lee. He had met that trade ship several times before the war when she came to port. She too had fallen victim to the war. Now pressed into service, she wore fresh paint and carried a new name, the *Little Belt*. A company of soldiers had disembarked from her in the afternoon and moved to the high grounds of the fort. Jesse noted the number of soldiers encamped along the lower hill between Fort Malden and the Detroit River had grown to a sizable force. An encampment of Shawnee under the leadership of Roundhead had also joined the growing presence around the fort, a fighting strength of perhaps a thousand. What he could accomplish with this information, he didn't know, but in the chance he returned home, he wanted to get the information correct. Soldiers loaded cases of powder and musket balls onto small push carts, traversing down the path to the docks. The musket balls were obviously not for the cannon but were army supplies on way to the Niagara Frontier. *General Hunter* was already loaded, and it looked like the *Hunter* was part of a planned campaign against the American forces somewhere. More soldiers stacked muskets near the longboats destined for the *Hunter,* and he could tell no one of the buildup. No way to get the word out.

"Harris!"

Jesse turned toward the voice. It was Lieutenant Rollette, commander of *General Hunter*.

"Yessir?"

"Mr. Irvine has asked for you. Report to him at once, if you please. He is in the supply room."

"Yessir." Jesse had been watched from the time he'd been pressed into service three months ago. All newly assigned sailors on the lake were watched, and the British made no secrets of this practice. He assumed that on the oceans it was different. There was no place to escape to in the open waters – no need to watch over someone who was unlikely to risk the water. Most sailors couldn't swim anyway. One just waited until he reached a friendly port, and then at an opportune moment, slip conveniently into the populace, the press gangs notwithstanding. On the lake, it was a different story. No friendly ports availed themselves to any sailor. The British who might dock on American shores would receive anything but friendly greetings. No. His chance had to come by acquiring any vessel, by any covert means, to carry him to safety. But first he had to escape the watchful eyes of whomever the ships' officers had assigned over him. As he turned toward the supply building at Fort Malden, that eerie feeling returned that someone knew too much, and he would soon find out *how* much. At the supply building he knocked at the open door.

"Enter," a voice called. Several officers and men stood or sat in various stages of business. He recognized Lieutenant Irvine at an inside doorway going over a ledger with a sergeant of the 41st Regiment of Foot.

"Sir? You wanted me?" Jesse asked.

"Yes. That will be all Sergeant. Oh, and Sergeant, I want an extra check on that ledger with the executive officer aboard the *Queen Charlotte*."

"Yessir."

"Mr. Harris, follow me. A word with you."

Jesse could feel it coming, and began to prepare any words of defense to counter what was about to fall on him. He followed the lieutenant onto the parade ground, crossed to stand under the Union

Jack hanging limply from the pole, far from the hearing of anyone. *Odd*, he thought.

"Mr. Harris, I have had occasion to observe your actions onboard the *Caledonia* in the past month, and I am surprised."

"Sir, I have never—"

"And I also wish to commend you for the way you have conducted yourself in your service to the King. I know you did not ask for this service, but recently I have seen that you have accepted your lot in life and have performed well. I also recognize that Sergeant McDonough has been overly heavy-handed upon you during that time."

"To say the least!" A pause, then, "Uh, sir."

Irvine smiled. "I understand. I know much of his action was unwarranted. Therefore, I have recommended that you be transferred."

"Transferred, sir?"

"Transferred. You will now report for duty with Lieutenant Thomas Stokoe aboard his majesty's ship *Queen Charlotte*. I believe this should be sufficient in keeping you and the sergeant out of each other's way. You have become a responsible sailor lately, and I commend you and your service to his majesty's ship. You will find the *Charlotte* a suitable vessel for the lake. She's larger than the *Caledonia*. She's faster, and she's better armed. You haven't been trained to work in the loft and on the sails yet, but learning under Lieutenant Stokoe will only improve your abilities in that situation. I will sail the *Caledonia* tomorrow. I wish you well." And he shook Jesse's hand.

Jesse was dumbstruck. Praise from his commander, no reprimands, and a transfer. No more of the lash of McDonough. As happy a tiding as he had heard in a long time. But he realized this also meant with the *Queen Charlotte* anchored at Amherstburg, he was farther from Buffalo. They *must have* observed him. This was just an attempt to keep him at the opposite end of the lake where he could not affect an escape. *Irvine was complimentary*, he thought, *but he's surely used it as a ruse to get me further away from freedom. All right*, he thought. *I'll take it. No one aboard the Charlotte knows me, and I can watch for my opportunity. With no routine habits, no one will be the wiser. I will get free.*

In town, the tavern would be busy with soldiers, sailors and Provincial Marines. It seemed as good a place as any to hear useful information, and rum often loosened the tongue. Through the gate, past the 24-pounders and toward the village he strolled with a new purpose.

Chapter Eight
Presque Isle
Saturday, September 26, 1812

Word didn't take long again to spread. Daniel
Dobbins had returned from Washington late Friday
evening. George pulled on a wool overcoat and
walked to the church where the meeting was
scheduled. Out on the lake, the autumn winds blew
in from the northwest and Lake Erie had turned into
a choppy gray-brown torrent. Waves crashed on the
beach out on Presque Isle and along the exposed
section of shoreline. The weather had turned
considerably cooler that day and although rain had
not set in, the high waves on the lake threw mist
into the air with each gust. Upon his return from
Pittsburgh, General Mead had asked for every man
available to gather to hear the recent news from
Washington and to be ready for work soon after.
George joined the growing procession of men
traversing Sassafras Street to the meeting. Dobbins
stood outside, greeting familiar faces and even some
unfamiliar ones with a business-like appearance
about them. Rufus Reed glad-handed every
merchant who approached him, faces George did
not recognize. Financing would be needed, and
George saw that Reed was selling a fleet before the
announcement was made. But these men gathering
were not of Erie. He overheard snatches of
conversation indicating Meadville, Waterford, even
Pittsburgh businesses represented here. *Not enough
craftsmen to build anything of value for a navy*,
George thought, *but plenty of backers who wanted*

*the reassurance of what they might receive for an investment.* He heard no monetary commitments in those brief moments, but guessed something would come of that later. *Mercenaries, all of them.* George weaved through a group of men standing under an oak tree, its rustling, yellow-red leaves scattering with the fall wind.

"George," Dobbins called.

"Mr. Dobbins, welcome back, sir."

"I hear you've been busy while I was away. The men did very nice work on the blockhouse. You're to be commended."

"Thank you, sir. I had enough help to make a decent fortification there. What is wanting though are more defensive structures. Possibly out on Presque Isle by Little Bay."

"Indeed, we will. Have you done as I asked and enlisted any more carpenters? We'll need them."

"Mr. Dobbins, I've asked as many as I knew and sent the word out to anyone who had acquaintances with carpentry experience, but I've received very little except promises, for whatever those're worth," George said. "Wait. You said we'll *need* them?"

Dobbins smiled at George.

"You got the orders!"

"I did. That's why we're having this meeting. Come in and let's see who's with us."

Dobbins and George walked into the church building, today doubling as a town hall. Several lit pipes glowed under the draw of puffing men, and the swirl of gray smoke clouded the air., Already at the pulpit, General Mead awaited Dobbins. Rufus Reed followed the pair into the church and readily greeted two men standing at the back of the building. Shoulder clutching, back slapping, hand shaking – he was a master at working the crowd.

"Order! Ladies and gentlemen, order!" The crowd grew quiet with Mead's call. "No doubt you all understand the purpose of this assembly, and have attended today to allow us to clarify what's expected of everyone entering this enterprise. Mr. Dobbins has returned from Washington where he has already met with President Madison, with Secretary Eustis, with Colonel Lewis Cass, and the Secretary of the Navy Paul Hamilton. The government knows that losing both the lakes – Erie and Ontario – will be catastrophic to the war effort. As it stands, and you all know this, we have *no* naval presence on Lake Erie to impede any invasion. *None.* Mr. Dobbins has been appointed by the President to begin work here on vessels to do just that, and he has also been awarded the rank of sailing master in the United States Navy."

Applause and congratulatory cheers erupted in the building. Daniel Dobbins was not at all displeased with the notoriety, seemed to stand a little taller, tugged down on his lapels, smoothing his new blue navy uniform, picked non-existent lint from the gold trim, nodded smiling to those close by who slapped him on the shoulder. He had traveled to Washington, had gotten what he wanted, and now the rank of sailing master only added the weight of authority to his resolve. General Meade continued as the crowd quieted.

"Commodore Isaac Chauncey, recently of the Brooklyn Naval Yard, has been charged with overseeing the completion of two fleets of warships and gunboats, one for Lake Ontario and one for Lake Erie. He's been ordered to Sackett's Harbor, and will be the commander of all our efforts. However, other than the six merchant ships at Black Rock, which will be refitted as warships, we must provide more of our own. This is where Presque Isle Bay comes in. Sailing Master Dobbins has brought these orders. Please listen: *'You are to return to Erie, Pennsylvania, and there contract for, on the best terms in your power, all the requisite timbers and other materials for building...'"* Here he paused for emphasis, and the assembly held its collective breath: *"'...**four** gunboats agreeably to the dimensions which you will receive.'"* Having let the declaration of this task take its effect, Mead continued. "Daniel has already received the dimensions of the first gunboat, and it is to be forty tons. We will begin at once in building this vessel, followed by three more like it, and this is where all of you come in to this enterprise. We have few artisans here in Erie, but you all know of someone in the surrounding communities who may come to our aid. Work will progress at once. The government has authorized a sum of money to be spent in this endeavor, and Daniel will work with Commodore Chauncey in portioning out the compensation as necessary. The artisans will be paid by the government, and anyone who joins us in backing this project with their own financial commitment to the glorious cause will receive repayment as well. It is an investment gentlemen, an investment in the future of Pennsylvania, the future of our country."

A murmur of approval among the assembly, which had begun under the announced words, now erupted into applause, and soon the crowd discussed among themselves the aspects of this immense project – both the good and the bad. Questions immediately arose about the town's defenses against the British threat. Surely the enemy would not stand idly by and allow a US fleet's construction to go unchallenged. How would the town be protected? George's immediate work of restoring the blockhouse, the subsequent building of the emplacement for the single cannon overlooking the mouth of the harbor would slow but never repel a landing party. The town was in imminent danger, and they all knew it. Maybe not today, for even the Canadian Merchant Marine would not venture to sail in these gale winds, but Lake Erie is fickle and could go dead calm within a few scant minutes. Soon the British would make an attempt to stop them. General Mead had already sent dispatch riders to request reinforcements from the state militia. He'd also requested General Dearborn to assign a force of regulars to the town's defenses. But then would come the winter. Today's cold winds were a reminder that fall had reached the north coast and soon the winter ice would accumulate on the lake. Some accepted this to be a provident blessing. Ice would surely obstruct any British ships from reaching Presque Isle. Yet for others, especially those workmen who entertained an idea of joining the construction, the hardship of building ships there through the dead of winter gave them concern. They acknowledged it would be a difficult job indeed. But the consequences of losing the war for *not* beginning the job would be more than difficult, it would be disastrous. Each man had to settle the idea for himself whether or not to join the construction. And for those who did come, they would expect some lodging. Would the town have enough to house the influx of workers? Seth Reed's Presque Isle Hotel would fill first, and with only enough room for six or eight laborers, the task of housing the rest was immense. Even the question of feeding such a large assemblage must be addressed. These were all considerations, and the answers to their shouted questions in the meeting room were as distant as the fleet itself.

As the assembly dispersed to their own homes and businesses, George met Dobbins in the yard outside. Several men had already given their names to him and Reed had assigned Giles Sanford to write these in a ledger, the business element now underway.

"Add my name too, Mr. Reed," said George.

"He already has, George," said Dobbins. "We know your abilities. Peter Williamson recommended you for the blockhouse work and was not disappointed, so there will also be work for you on the ships."

"Mr. Dobbins, you actually met the President?"

"Yes, and Secretary Hamilton," Dobbins said.

"What was he like?" George asked.

"Mr. Madison? Short."

The men laughed. "The President was determined to add to our defenses here. He understands the urgency. Secretary Hamilton too, though I don't know how much longer he'll be of use to anyone. He doesn't hold his brandy too well. I saw him twice, and on both occasions, it seemed to me that he was an embarrassment to the President. From what others told me, he won't hold that office beyond this year."

"So, you got your appointment into the navy just in time," Reed laughed.

"None too soon," Dobbins grinned.

"When do we start?" asked George.

"Now. Follow me."

They left the yard and walked to the wagon nearby. Dobbins revealed that he was only authorized $2,000 for the work on the fleet. A meager sum, given the task before them, but he did not protest, thankful to at least have something. Payout would be only one dollar for each tree cut from private property, so they would have to select wisely and use every tall tree they could find. George climbed into the wagon with two other workers, newly arrived from Waterford. Leaving town, they passed a dozen other workers intent on gathering tools for the work ahead, and they drove through the dense forest at Massasaugua Point on Presque Isle. Daniel searched intently into the woods on either side of the trail as they drove on. Soon they pulled over by a small clearing. Daniel got out, grabbed an ax from the wagon and walked into the woods a few paces, pushing through the briars, the men following close behind. There stood a tall black oak, slightly bent, its growth shaped by its search for adequate light. Dobbins said nothing, surveyed the tree from bottom to top, considered it from three different angles. Then he removed his sailing master's blue coat, brushed a twig from the buff-colored collar, laid it carefully to the side on a fallen splintered log, spat on his hands and swung the ax, imbedding the blade deep into the trunk. The ker-thunk, ker-thunk continued unabated. George remarked quietly to the other men how determined Daniel's focus was. He must have chosen this tree long before he had returned from Washington, maybe even before he had *arrived* in Washington. Chips of bark and wood splinters flew about Dobbins's feet, but no one spoke, no one offered any kind of assistance. This was his solitary mission, an initiative he must do on his own, no help, no advice – his personal defiant revenge for the loss of his ship to the British. He was beginning to rebuild the *Salina* right there on the edge of that forest on Presque Isle. Those splinters tossing about were forming the timbers of a warship – a splendid thing of reprisal that he would personally sail into the fray if necessary. Minutes passed and the trunk began to sway slightly. Finally, he spoke.

"Stand away."

Dobbins set the ax aside, resting the handle against another black oak. The tree stood silent, resolute against the lake wind, and then Daniel approached it slowly, pushed against it. The groaning crack echoed, and he stepped back once again to watch the oak in a slow arc crash into the limbs and brush, and with a resounding *harrumph*, bounce on the ground. Then silence. Dobbins wiped his brow with his shirt sleeve, picked up his uniform coat, swiped away an insect on the breast, put it on, and fastened the gold buttons, tugged down on the sides to smooth any wrinkles. He looked at the men, stood erect, smiling.

"That'll be the first keel."

A cheer arose from the men, and they set to work with a peeling spud and stripped the bark from the tree, hacking at the branches with hatchets until only a bare log remained. The Presque Isle sawmill would soon see the first of many native trees turned into ships' timber. As the workers began to pry and heft the log onto the wagon, they heard the rattle of other wheels, the steady clop of hooves, and before long oxen-pulled wagons began to stream onto the lane on Presque Isle. Dobbins instructed each wagon-load of workers passing by to cut black oak and white pine from the forest, and the men at once began to mark trees suitable for cutting.

"We'll need more axes, Mr. Dobbins," said one man.

"We'll make them here. I sent Giles Sanford to Meadville this morning early to acquire steel to be delivered here. We'll set the blacksmiths to work on the axes as soon as the steel arrives," Dobbins said.

Dobbins and George drove the wagon to the sawmill and unloaded the first oak log there with the operator, along with the dimensions needed for the first boat keel. At the blacksmith's they submitted the initial order for a hundred ax blades with the Meadville steel. In one day, the entire town was turning into a manufacturing community, and soon the arrival of the first artisans who had attended the morning meeting created an immediate need for housing. George and Daniel drove the wagon into Erie, stopping by the largest homes and asking citizens who were able to provide hospitality for the workers until suitable long-term housing could be arranged. Those that could do it agreed. The Presque Isle Hotel along the main road had limited rooms, and these filled first. They would soon need to build housing of some kind for the laborers. Winter's coming required necessary warm shelter, and George decided his house building skills could be used for lodging. He volunteered his services to Dobbins. Riding along the bluffs, George looked down to the bay below, scanning the beach for a suitable location to build. Protected by Presque Isle, the calm bay showed small rippling, the only testimony to the winds out on the lake. At Sassafras Street he dismounted the wagon and walked past the houses there, picked his way through the red cedar and ash trees towering above the precipice and stood on the edge of the bluffs, the wind directly in his face. Here, Lee's Run meandered down the steep bank and emptied into the bay. The road that traversed the bluff crossed a small bridge over the creek where it descended the hill just as it began its eastward slope in a gentle incline away from the cliffs. The road led to the beach near the protective sandbar that thrust out into the bay. This was the only easy access road on the northeast face of the bluffs close to the bay's entrance that teams of oxen might use to pull wagons of supplies to the beach. Above the beach, and well away from the precipice stood the blockhouse, guarding the beach and the bay's entrance.

"Mr. Dobbins, I think we have the location for our dockyard."

"Indeed? Where would you suggest, George?"

"Look to where the road winds down to State Street. Wagons can use this, and then they can turn back to a point directly under here." He pointed down to the beach below the bluffs. "There, where Lee's Run enters the bay. It's open ground, not many trees to fell, and the dock is already available to bring in what supplies we can from the lake. It's not ideal, but—"

"But it's close!" Dobbins cut in. "It's the site I had thought about too. This is where we'll start as soon as I notify General Mead. We'll need the men to transport the cut timbers from the mill here whenever they're ready. Climb in, George." The men turned up Peach Street and drove to Dobbins's house.

"I'll leave you here, Mr. Dobbins. After dinner tonight, then?"

"All right, George. My respects to your mother and to Miss Freer, and I'll see you this evening."

George started toward home, but Polly's angry farewell had weighed on him for the better part of the day. He couldn't let the irritation continue to prick at him, and he decided to walk first to Polly's house, ask her exactly what feelings she had for him. It had been understood that they would marry. Or maybe only he understood the idea. He should've had the discussion out earlier. Maybe weeks earlier. He felt guilty for not listening to her feelings. But even as he turned to walk her street, he envisioned scene after dreadful scene and each ended with him losing her. Losing her to Jesse of all people. His fears were irrational, he thought, and he was never an irrational person, took pride in his logical thinking. But her attraction to Jesse was unmistakable. He stopped before the Kaylor house, sat on a stump in front. She had been distressed to report Jesse's impressment to him, wanted him to abandon his beliefs, to be like Jesse and fight. Yet she had declared her love for him. Maybe it wasn't him that was confused, it was Polly. If she was confused, it wouldn't do any good to discuss it with her. She would have to get her feelings right in her own mind. No. It wasn't his place to try to placate her anger with him. He must give her time to think about her feelings. It was entirely up to her. George rose from the stump, looked down State Street in the direction of her house, decided not to deal with emotions tonight. He still had to meet with Dobbins and the others later and he turned toward home.

## Fort Malden
### Monday, September 28, 1812

For three days northwesterly winds had whipped up the lake, and the British fleet still lay anchored at the King's Naval Yard awaiting favorable weather. *Caledonia* had been loaded with supplies and a large fur cargo, the munitions already aboard the *Detroit,* and still they waited for orders to transport the infantry to Port Dover and the Niagara Frontier.

Jesse had accepted his new post on the *Queen Charlotte* as a minor but valuable disruption, and he used the time to gather information on British plans. He watched as the shipyard finished outfitting the enemy schooner *Lady Prevost* for the forces on the upper lakes. Though the ship had been in service for over a year, Jesse saw the Canadian Merchant Marine had recently increased the schooner's armament. The vessel now boasted thirteen guns. Added to her ten carronades were three long guns, one on a swivel mount to support either side of the ship in attack. Along with the heavy guns of the *Queen Charlotte* and the *Detroit*, the addition of the extra guns on *Lady Prevost* gave the fleet immense firepower. Jesse couldn't halt the preparations himself, but he understood what information on the fleet's guns would mean to the American side. On the docks he had used his time to strike up a friendship with William Bell, the designer, and asked many questions, pretending to be a sailor assigned to the *Lady Prevost*. He hoped she'd be a good vessel for him to serve on, he said. Indeed she would be, he was told, sturdy and well-armed. Jesse memorized everything he thought might be of value to the US Navy.

In Amherstburg, Jesse had soon befriended Sara Hall, niece of Commodore George Hall. General Brock had rewarded Hall with his current rank after his part in the attack on Fort Detroit. The *Queen Charlotte* not only had ferried soldiers across the river to attack Detroit, but had used its guns to shell the city, inflicting little damage but making a strong enough demonstration of power to sway General

Hull into accepting General Brock's terms. Hall awaited his appointment as the new superintendent of the Amherst Naval Yard, a post to be awarded as soon as more British naval officers could arrive to relieve him of other duties. Then he would relinquish command of Jesse's ship, *Queen Charlotte*. Only three days had passed since he had met Sara while she waited for the commodore near the fort. He liked Sara right off, liked spending off-duty hours with her, liked walking along the docks or before the walls of Fort Malden with her. Yes, he was dishonest with her, had moved quickly closer to her warmth and frankness, had charmed her for the sake of information. He understood that drawing close to Sara made him a spy, and his discovery would not end well, regardless of her uncle's position. All right then, a spy he would be. Until the *Queen Charlotte* sailed for the eastern end of the lake, he would use their relationship to glean information. He never intended to return to Malden again as soon as he could get free of the ship, so it was of little consequence what she might think of him in the future. He learned her weaknesses, her sympathy for anyone facing unjust treatment. She had a sympathetic ear and listened to him mourn his impressment. The more she reacted to his story, the more he manipulated her feelings. The act was fruitful, and her attraction to him grew, waited casually for him to pass her and meet as if by coincidence. And when he saw her, he poured charm on her like honey.

This day he accompanied her home from the small general store in Amherstburg, carrying the small bags of ground meal, and of salt.

"How long did you say you've been with the Royal Navy, three months?" she asked.

"Three long months since I was taken," Jesse said.

"I know it must be hard for you, but I am glad you're here in Upper Canada," Sara said.

"Why?"

"Well, you must know the United States will lose this war of aggression against the crown, and you are here, part of the navy now. You may decide to live here, eh?"

"That's presumptuous on your part. I mean no offense, to you Sara, but remember I was taken against my will. I serve on these ships because I'm required to. I don't like the treatment. And I must say I don't see how the regular tars can enjoy this life the way they're treated."

"But it won't be forever, Mr. Harris. You may find that you like it here."

"What are you saying, Miss Hall?"

"Hmm.... I'm just saying that you might find it to your liking here and wish to stay, that's all. When the war ends, what will you do?"

"I only know sailing. I have worked the merchant ships until the war, out of Buffalo. I want to sail the lakes again with the merchant fleet."

"Well, who knows? Our two countries may continue trade and you will get to sail again."

Jesse kicked at a stone on the street, thought, *oh, I will sail again. I will sail against this navy that kidnapped me. I will sail against every soldier and sailor who showed me the cat on my back, or mocked the floggings. I will definitely sail again!*

"Yes, I will want to sail again," he said pensively. "And you, Miss Hall? What do you plan?"

"I make no plans, sir. I take every day one day at a time. Whatever comes my way, I accept it and live for the moment." She was quiet for a time, thinking. "Although, I don't pretend that I don't want to see more of you," she said. "So maybe that is a plan. With the war going on, though, maybe that is too much to expect."

"You sound confused, Miss Hall."

"I suppose I am, Mr. Harris," she smiled. "But I also have optimism."

"Well, I find it hard to have much optimism at the moment, Miss Hall. How could I not? One day I'm sailing with a merchant vessel carrying nothing more than salt, and that same day I'm captive and sailing a foreign ship. I'm grateful that at least it's not the *Caledonia* anymore. There were certain soldiers aboard I prefer to never sail with again. So now I'll sail on your uncle's ship, but I don't know anything about it. I suppose it's a fast ship."

"Oh, my, she is fast! Uncle says she's also the best armed ship of any in the fleet. He has had a glorious command with her."

"Best armed? How many guns?"

"Seventeen! I've counted 'em."

"Is that a fact? And when did you count the guns?"

"Oh, Mr. Harris. I've been on board the *Queen Charlotte* several times. I even sailed up to Mackinaw with Uncle once. Of course, Aunt Angelica wasn't happy about my going, but I enjoyed the voyage thoroughly." Her eyes lit up with pride that she, a mere girl, had been sailing on a warship of the British navy. None of her friends could say the same, and he was sure she flaunted that air of satisfaction before them.

"I'm sure your friends also disapprove of your sailing on a warship. That would be *positively scandalous*."

"Oh, to the contrary! They are *positively green* with envy. It does me good to see them suffer so. They've even been watching you and me walk these past two days, and they turn their heads so."

"I hadn't noticed."

"I have."

"That gives you satisfaction, does it, Miss Hall?"

"Oh, indeed it does! They were unhappy that Uncle George received the ship, unhappier still that he will command the navy yard soon. They didn't speak to me for weeks after he received command. Jealousy here on the frontier is rampant. Everyone pushes in for a better station in life. I let it be known when I was sailing on the *Charlotte,* so they could see me off at the pier. It was my moment of triumph. And now, well, that's twice!"

She laughed a self-satisfied giggle that Jesse would've found unappealing in any other girl. It didn't matter. He would eventually be free of that arrogance as well.

They continued past the fort and arrived at the commodore's home, the parlor warmed with a low cooking fire already started. Angelica Hall, wife of the commodore, worked at a long table, preparing the noon meal.

"Sara, you've finally returned. You do have the foodstuffs I asked you to bring?"

"I have them. Or, rather, Mr. Harris does. Mr. Harris, you may come in here," Sara called.

Jesse stood at the doorway and surveyed the room. The commodore was not inside. He brought the two bags in and laid them on the table.

"Thank you, Mr. Harris."

"Your servant, Ma'am," Jesse said and bowed slightly, looked over his shoulder back toward the door nervously.

"You needn't worry, he's not here," Sara said.

"Oh, I'm not worried."

"If you say so," Sara laughed.

"I guess I'll be going, Miss Hall. I will see myself out," Jesse said backing toward the door.

"Nonsense," said Mrs. Hall. "Sara, you see this young man to the front gate."

Sara tucked her hand around Jesse's arm and escorted him outside and along the walk to the surrounding white picket fence. They stood quietly, awkwardly at the front gate.

"Think on what I said, Mr. Harris."

"What?" Jesse asked.

"Think on remaining here."

"That would be impossible. I'm assigned to the *Queen Charlotte*, and I'll sail when she sails. I can't get free of that duty."

"We shall see," she said meaningfully.

Jesse did not like the secretive look about her and it disturbed him to think she knew more of his future than he did. She continued to look into his eyes, drawing closer to him.

"What have you planned?"

"Why, Mr. Harris, I told you I never make plans."

He glanced away, avoiding her look, saw the commodore approaching in his carriage, discreetly stepped back, his hands clasped behind his back.

"Your uncle," he said quietly. "Good afternoon, sir," he called too eagerly. *Be careful not to seem anxious*, he thought.

"Good day," the commodore called. "Mr. Harris, is it?"

"Yessir," Jesse saluted.

Commodore Hall returned the salute. "Are you leaving?"

"I am, sir."

"Sorry I missed you. When you return to the ship, please remove your effects and take them to the fort. Report to the executive officer in the supply room. He will have your billeting assignment for you."

"Am I being imprisoned, sir?"

"Ha! No. To the contrary, you are being reassigned to shore duty as needed. I want for good men to help with inventory, and this will get you off the lake for a rest. Men with wits like yourself are in short supply and you will serve me well at the naval yards. I don't think you'll find the new position disagreeable, Mr. Harris. I dare say my niece will find the position agreeable to the both of you."

And he kissed Sara on the forehead.

"Thank you, Uncle George," she said.

"You may join us for dinner some evening soon, but for now, report to the *Queen Charlotte* for your personals."

"Aye aye, sir." Jesse tried to hide his gloom, forced a smile to Sara, and began the long depressing walk to the skiff that would carry him out to the ship in the harbor. Not only was he to stay at the western end of the lake, but he was to be landlocked at this most remote wilderness outpost of Upper Canada, surrounded by hostile Shawnee, Ojibwa and Ottawa. Likelihood for an escape was now as remote as ever. She had schemed up this duty for him to keep him close, and she had used her uncle to get her way again. He had gambled with her emotions, and he was in danger of losing the game.

At the pier, Jesse boarded the skiff along with six redcoats for the *Caledonia*. The markings on their coatees indicated members of the 41st Regiment of Foot. He spoke to no one, but listened to the soldier complaints: food, sleeping quarters, pay, officers, the things that were part of the grievances common to all soldiers. Headed to the Niagara River, joining up with General Brock and moving to Fort Erie, then on to Queenstown. It will be a cold winter there. Jesse thought, *humph, maybe US regulars can warm it up for you.* The soldiers climbed aboard the *Caledonia*, and Jesse saw Lieutenant Irvine passing his commands to the sailors who were making ready to sail. Several of Jesse's shipmates were Americans like him, pressed into His Majesty's service on the Great Lakes. Still under the watchful eye of Sergeant McDonough, they toiled at the lines. He saw them, wished he was sailing with them. Lieutenant Irvine came to the larboard side of the ship. Their eyes met, Jesse saluted, and Irvine nodded, touched the rim of his hat, then back to ordering the men. *Good, fair man, Irvine. As Canadian officers go, he is admirable. Hope that the men avoid McDonough's lash.* Jesse rode the skiff that approached the *Queen Charlotte*, and he prepared to go aboard, saw the *Detroit* under sail heading down the Detroit River and toward Lake Erie. *Can't go this trip, but some day.*

Below deck he gathered his clothes bag, haversack, canteen, and his oil-coat, said a quick good-bye to his mates, returned to the skiff and sat down for the trip back to shore. He watched the *Caledonia* hoist the anchor. Orders shouted, she set her sails and turned to follow the *Detroit.* His means of escape now showed her stern to him, and he felt the anguish rising inside. Some of that crew were impressed American sailors too. Few of them spoke to him of escape, but he knew all wanted any way off the ship. He wished them success. On impulse, he stood, waved to the departing *Caledonia*. A sailor on the topgallant's yard waved back.

Chapter Nine
Presque Isle
Friday, October 2, 1812

Dawn rose on the town of Erie, and with it rose the clamor of clopping hooves as teams of horses and oxen dragged fallen oak and ash trees, pine and red cedar to the sawmill. The saw blade over the pit had begun at dawn, another demanding day of squaring off logs, splitting them into boards and turning the wet wood into a ship. No provision was made to dry-cure the timber. This was to be an armed fleet of green-wood ships that would require sailing Lake Erie for only one battle. Just long enough to pulverize the enemy's ships and re-take control of the upper lakes. George rode out to Presque Isle to assist at the saw mill and met Joel Thompson from Waterford. A blacksmith by trade, Thompson had arrived on the weekend with the promise of higher pay for working on the ship construction. A good smith could earn the high wages of two dollars per day, much more than he'd make in Waterford, and he had already sent word back informing laborers whom he knew that they could work as strikers in the forge. Of course the men earned less money than he did, but sixty-two cents per day was a very good wage, and the men eagerly responded.

"George, good morning!"

"Mornin' Joel. Has the steel arrived?"

"It has, though we're still waiting for our load of iron for nails and bolts. We have steel enough to keep making axes 'til Rapture, but what the men cut can't be nailed together. They're fixing to use the locust trees to make trenails for the ribs."

"That'll have to do for a start. The cutting they've done up around Erie can't be easily brought here, so the men have started hewing the timber with the axes you've made. It'll take long to do it that way, but it'll take less time than dragging timber here. I've come to drive that wagon-load of lumber over yonder back to the beach. Can you help me lift those last two timbers onto the load?"

Two workers joined Joel and George, hefted the two massive timbers up and onto the wagon, trussed them up with a length of rope. George felt a sharp pain in his hand, instinctively put it to his mouth and bit the soft skin carefully. Joel climbed atop the wagon and cinched up the rope, knotting it.

"Have you seen Dobbins today?"

"Not yet," George said. "Why?

He swung himself down from the timbers and turned seriously to George. "Stay out of his way. He's in a mood this morning! Cursing the commodore and the navy to beat all hell. Something really got his goat 'cause the men say they never seen him this riled up before. I'd say, just stay upwind of him and you'll fare well."

"Oh, I've seen him riled up before, but I'll heed the warning. Thank you."

George took the reigns, stuck the ox with his goad, "C'mon, now. Git up!" And he began the long trek back up the hill to the bluffs overlooking the construction site. Piles of lumber lay about the beach below him. Not one ship's frame had been started, and the shoreline was cluttered with lumber, planed and waiting to take shape. He could make out Dobbins below in an animated exchange with General Mead. George saw no way to avoid it. He had to pass by the pair to deliver the timbers to the site, and he hoped he wasn't the target of the loud tirade.

"He's never been here! How could he make that judgment? Answer that! I might have known when I didn't hear from them straight away that this would happen!"

"Daniel, did you write to Secretary Hamilton about it?" asked Mead.

George pretended not to listen, couldn't help it. The rock facings amplified the voices. Even the workmen stopped stacking boards to eavesdrop. Some casually walked over to George's wagonload of wood, feigning to unload so they could get closer to the fuming Dobbins.

"George!"

*Here it comes*, he thought. *No way to escape.* "Yes sir, Mr. Dobbins?"

"Do you mind when I sent that letter to Commodore Chauncey about our undertaking here?"

"Yes sir?"

"Did I not specifically say we were *ordered* to start construction of the fleet at once?"

"Yes sir. You said you had already signed contracts with the men to cut and work the timber for the four vessels." He was not sure he wanted to get any more involved, but it slipped out, "Why?"

"Commodore Chauncey *never received my communication*!"

"But I saw the post take it by express. The mail *must* have gotten there, Mr. Dobbins."

"Oh it *went* to Black Rock! It *arrived* at the naval yard at Black Rock! It just never got to *Commodore Chauncey* at Black Rock! The commodore was at *Sackett's Harbor*. Lieutenant Elliott received the instructions instead!"

"Is *that* the problem?"

"No! *He* is the problem!" Dobbins raged. "The good commodore left Lieutenant Elliott in charge of affairs and my instructions went to *him instead*. I had hoped for Commodore Chauncey to send me more artisans and more shipwrights to assist, but instead *Elliott* sends me *this*!" He held up the communication which bore the wrinkles of Dobbins's angry clenched fist.

George stepped down from the wagon and took the letter, reading, *"...Lake Erie has not a single harbor calculated to fit our naval expedition."* He looked up, perplexed, felt his own energy drain. "Do you mean we've cut all this timber and brought all these workers here for nothing? Who is this Lieutenant Elliott? Does he have command at Black Rock? What about Commodore Chauncey?"

"Chauncey has delegated Jesse Elliott in his absence, and all communication has gone through him," said Mead. "He believes that Black Rock is more aptly suited to the fleet's construction."

"Why?" asked George. "Just because he's *there*?"

"*Exactly* because he's there," said Mead.

Dobbins interrupted, "And he will send *no one* to read the prints for the ships' construction! We have workers, we have timber, we have more laborers coming here from Philadelphia, from New York, even from Washington. Yet we have no one to read the plans that were drawn up by the Secretary of the Navy himself! We've sent notices far and wide about this project requesting laborers, and now *this*!" He grabbed the paper back from George, read in a rage, "*It appears to me utterly impossible to build gun boats at Presque Isle.*"

Silence. Then the men started to murmur among themselves. What about the work they had already done? What about the trip they had made to settle here? What about the pay that was promised? The grumbling crescendoed into angry curses and George sensed they may shortly have a mutiny growing, that these men would leave them, ride back to their businesses, to their farms, desert the enterprise if all the promises weren't soon delivered.

Dobbins continued to fume, read, "*...and therefore, I have no further communication to make upon the subject.*' Well, I have further communication to make upon the subject! And I will be heard! This Elliott thinks he can sit there at Black Rock and pass judgment on a place he has never visited? I intend to move forward with the construction, and I intend to use every laborer who arrives at this place. I have the *Secretary of the Navy's orders* to complete this project! And I also have as perfect a knowledge of the lake as any other person on it. I believe he would agree with me if he were here."

"But he's not," said Mead.

"No, he's not. I'll leave today for Black Rock and I'll bring back a shipwright or an architect or a trained gorilla, if that's what it takes. Even if I have to kidnap him and tie him to my wagon! I will not be delayed in this purpose!"

Everyone knew when Daniel had his mind set on a goal, he would not be deterred. Dobbins stomped across to his horse tethered to a lone tree near the road, grabbed the saddle pommel and swung himself up, spurred its flanks and rode hard up the trail.

"I believe he's going to Black Rock," a voice quipped. The men's laughter roared, easing the tension, and they returned to unloading George's wagon of lumber. Lumber that now had a dubious future. Rough cut, still needing ends trimmed to exact lengths yet to be determined. *Just unload it and stack it*, George thought. *Daniel gets his way, we'll finish the work.* He turned the wagon team onto the road and drove the oxen back to Presque Isle, reaching the sawmill at noon. By evening George had delivered four more loads to the cluttered beach, and the men returned to the village on the back of his wagon, weary and uncertain.

From the livery, George walked up Holland Street and saw Polly sitting with his mother on the porch, greeting workmen returning to town from the beach and the forests. A quilt lay across their laps and the two of them worked the cloth with needle and thread. October's chill had perched in the trees and the bright reds and yellows, orange and gold, now adorned the town as a giant patchwork quilt.

The women of the town loved the beauty of the town, most of all Sara Armstrong. This was always her time of year, as she had often said. Sitting with her favorite quilt wrapped around her shoulders, chatting with visiting neighbors was her passion in autumn. She was more at home near these colorful forests than any other time of the year. The settlers of the community saw the surrounding forests as the main source of income, that is, after the highly profitable salt trade. Many had first come to settle in Erie for the vast forests that would provide wood to build housing both here and in neighboring communities. Business opportunities abounded in the Western Reserve since it was first settled, and there was little doubt that this community would grow too. Traders, wagoners, trappers, carpenters, and some capitalistic entrepreneurs all had joined the budding community, and Sara readily welcomed the possibilities. George could make a profitable living here. He had heard it over and over. Planning out his future in Erie, Sara certainly attempted to influence Polly too. Every time she had spent a day with his mother, their evening courting conversation in the past had turned to his settling in Erie with her and to be on hand to care for Sara. He could only imagine the focus of their discourse was on him again, and the uneasiness grew as he approached home. For several days, he had let his presumptions die away, but had never yet put to rest his fears about her faithfulness to him. Every time he felt his courage grow to confront his worries, some obstacle stood in his way. This time, another barrier sat before him: she wasn't alone.

"Evenin', George," Sara called.

"Good evening, mother. Polly."

"Good evening, George." Her voice was unsociable, her eyes cast down to her needle work.

"You've been busy today. Esther and I rode past from our sewing circle meeting and saw the logs piled high. Mary Dobbins said the men couldn't start building yet. Is that true?"

"It is."

"There are so many workers here already. Why wouldn't they allow them to start building? Is it Commodore Chauncey's decision?" asked Polly, intent on her sewing.

"I believe it has to do with a power struggle between Mr. Dobbins and a navy officer, a Lieutenant Elliott. Mr. Dobbins left for Buffalo and Black Rock to see if he could persuade Commodore Chauncey to allow us a shipwright to draw up more detailed plans for the vessels. Apparently, he or his subordinates, this Elliott I imagine, think the fleet should begin at Black Rock. We have to wait until Mr. Dobbins gets the approval from them. In the meantime, we've harvested enough wood for at least one ship already," George said.

"Black Rock? They still have the merchant ships there, don't they? Jesse had sailed on them before he was taken. Couldn't they use those against the British?" Polly asked.

Again she had brought up his name and he wanted to explode, fought against his emotions with his mother seated there. "I reckon they can, but they have to outfit them as ships of war first. That's possibly what Chauncey has in mind, why he's reluctant to part with anyone to help us, I suppose. They need the fleet to protect Buffalo."

"What would the British and Canadians want with Buffalo?" Sara asked.

"I don't know. But it does have the naval yards. Maybe that's enough. Anyway, I'm glad I'm not there. I want to be no closer to the enemy than I was. Once in a lifetime was plenty for me. I just want to be free of the lake's threat," George said. "The further I can get from here, the happier I'll be."

"You mean because of the war," Sara said, studying his face.

"Yes." George understood her meaning, was unwilling to elaborate.

"But you're staying now, aren't you?" asked Sara.

"Mother, of course I am." He looked at Polly, thought it could be so simple if he just moved, never see Jesse again. *But she'll be at the mercy of invaders herself. I can't leave her defenseless. She won't leave her family either, not with the war going on.*

Sara, satisfied with his answer, excused herself. "I'll leave you two here. I have to straighten up for our boarders. George, we have two men staying in your brother's old room. They arrived from Pittsburg today and needed a temporary place. I said it would do fine for them to stay here awhile, and we can use the money they'll pay me for the rent."

"That's fine, Mother," he said. "You do what you must."

Sara returned to the house and George stood. "I'll walk you home, Polly."

"George, I heard from Buffalo today."

"Jesse, I suppose?"

"His mother said that a returned prisoner had seen him on the *Caledonia* and he was at Long Point, but then he sailed to Fort Malden. I hate to think of him on that ship as a prisoner."

"I'm sure you do. How was he? Was he well?"

"His mother was told that he was beaten several times. They all were. The British officers used a lash on him. He even tried to escape and they lashed him for that."

"This is why they need to kidnap sailors for their navy. No one would serve under that kind of discipline. But don't worry about him. Jessie will survive. He's strong, and he knows what to do to stay alive until he can get free. It's just a matter of time. Still, being at Fort Malden doesn't give him very good prospects. I've been there, and it's a long journey if he wants to get away."

"It's been so long since you escaped, George. Do you think he can? Will he come home?"

George couldn't find the words to give her hope. He secretly wanted her to despair, to turn back to him. "Well, he isn't an escaped prisoner or they would have said so, so no one will be searching for him. I know Jessie and he'll bide his time, do his work, and wait for an opportunity. He's very patient that way."

"Not like his cousin," Polly teased.

"No. He's not at all like me. Does that bother you?"

Polly looked at him, studied him seriously. "At times. Once in awhile I wish you were like him. You're so set on getting your way, and you have little regard for anything you imagine will interfere."

The remark was one more bruise, and it hurt that her opinion was so critical. "Am I such as that?"

"At times," she smiled. "I don't think ill of you, but I do see you drive yourself to do whatever you've set your mind on, and there's no one who can coax you away from it. A bit like Mr. Dobbins, I suppose."

"But Polly, I'm not like Daniel. He *wants* this war. I never did. If I could get out of here, and never see another war, I'd go today."

"None of us *wanted* the war, George. But now that we're in it up to our bellies, I'm proud of a man who will do what it takes to help win it. I admire what Mr. Dobbins has done to get the village rallied around the ships. You know Jessie didn't want the war either. I saw him before he sailed for the last time, before we knew President Madison had declared war. It was while you were gone, and he was willing to do what he could to protect Pennsylvania and New York if it came to that. He didn't want the war, George, but he was willing to help win it."

"What are you saying, Polly?" She looked away, studied the houses as they walked, looked at the stones in the street, avoided his gaze. "Polly? You want me to be more like Jessie?"

She stopped, looked at him firmly. "No, that's not it at all. You said when you first returned that you would work on the ships, but you wouldn't fight. I respect that decision. That's your faith – who you are – and I wouldn't have you be someone you're not."

"Then what is it?" George asked.

"It's your mother."

*Oh here it is,* he thought. *Now we are to the heart of the matter. This isn't about the fleet. This isn't about the war. They've been talking again.*

"And what about her?"

"George, everything you do is to get away from here, to get away from her. Do you wish to get away from me as well?'

"Polly, you know it's not like that. Since we've been together, you know I've set my heart on moving to Ohio. There's land there, and there are opportunities for a builder. The state's growing and I want to be part of it. I wanted you to be part of it as well. I had planned on settling there if we were to marry, and I've never hidden that from you. But mother wants me to stay here and live in Erie. I want to live in Ohio. It's that simple."

"But she needs you."

"She doesn't need me. Since father died I've had to care for the home. All right, I've accepted that responsibility. But that was just to get through the rough times. She's young yet. There are young men who want to court her, who would be good to her, and she has nothing to do with them. They have asked me for permission to call. I've gladly given my blessing, and she will have none of it. She merely wants things to remain the same. Things change. I've changed." Seldom had George so spoken from his heart to Polly. He felt he had crossed some line and that she would retreat now, that whatever affection she had was slipping away, that she may not want him. "I'm sorry to have spoken to you so. But this is what's been on my mind. This is what I'd set my heart on, what I was working for. That is, until the war began."

"She feels you'll desert her when you're most needed."

"She knows me better than that. Anyway, I can't leave now, not with the need for building ships. If my help on the ships can help bring Jessie home, if it can help end the war at least here on Lake Erie, then I'll do my part. If it keeps Ohio safe for you and me in the future, then I'm willing to build whatever it takes to defend it. But when this war is over, I will leave. Until then I'll do what I can to help her." Then a sudden thought, "And I will introduce her to every unmarried workman who comes into the town. That way she can never feel deserted." George smiled, waited for the smile to work on Polly. Her look was warmer than he had expected toward him, and he thought he saw trust in her eyes. He looked at her steadily, repeated, "Polly, I promise she will never have to feel deserted."

As he left Polly at her door, he thought on her. It wasn't his mother as much as it was Polly's insecurity about him. Maybe she needed to feel he would never leave her, maybe why she had grown closer to Jesse. It was his own actions that had misled her. He needed to demonstrate that better to her, resolved to do just that. Jessie still troubled him. She undoubtedly loved Jesse, maybe not as much as she loved him, but there might still be time. Something tugged at his insides, a nausea that he had carried with him for days. He began to secretly wish Jessie would stay captive to the British, at least until the war ended, or until he could marry Polly, settle down. Then he'd welcome him home, as a proper cousin should. He was as close a brother as one could wish for, and the dilemma troubled him. He unconsciously began to pick at his right hand, an itch earlier in the day that had now turned sore. Hadn't given it much thought until now. In the fading evening light, he finally examined it. A splinter had nestled between his thumb and forefinger. He scratched at it, broke the tip off, and the nagging prickling intensified.

By the time he arrived on Holland Street, the house's oil lamps were lit and his mother had prepared the dinner. A roasted beef and potatoes and carrots set in a pot by the table. *Not the normal dinner fare,* he thought. The two guests came into the room and promptly sat at the dinner table. He had seen them at the saw mill earlier in the day. *Good workers*, he thought. His mother wore a fresh apron, unusual that she had gone to such lengths for the evening meal.

"George, wash up please. Supper is ready. We have a very nice roast beef this evening."

Out of her character to announce with pride the evening meal. That she would make such a fuss pleased him, he paused and watched the two figures seated in the parlor and credited the new attitude to these two strangers.

"Well. Where did we get a roast mother?"

"You know very well, we had one in the smokehouse."

In fact he knew they had none in the smokehouse, and that she was trying to impress the two. The subtle stern look was enough.

"Oh! That one. Of course, I forgot. Well, mother, it does smell good. I'll be just a moment. And may I please have a needle? I have a splinter."

Out the back door, he went to the well and drew water. *I wonder where she got a roast for guests? Where did she even get the money to buy a roast? No doubt she is trying to make an impression,* he thought. *For which one? What does it matter? If she can be happy, my business is settled.* The thought was tantalizing. With light still shining just enough to see his hand, he dug the tip of the needle gingerly into his skin. The splinter moved, and carefully he drew it out, relieved. As he toweled off and started for the house, he decided to help Cupid along by sharpening his arrows. Maybe even string the bow for him.

## Chapter Ten
## Presque Isle
## Tuesday, October 13, 1812

The original surge of timber cutting had tapered off during the two-week period Dobbins had traveled to Black Rock and returned. Without guidance on the construction, the workmen could do little with the accumulating lumber. Carpenters from Philadelphia began to arrive on October 6 and the men were eager to build. Not merely ax men, these true carpenters looked to apply their skill to the fleet. Of course, the draw of good wages made them particularly willing. But with the lumber delivery at a near standstill, the men shortened their work hours voluntarily. They now looked for ways to occupy their idle time. Almost nightly, the townsfolk and workers held dances in the chill night air, bonfires lighting the sky, as fiddles, banjos and guitars filled the night with sounds of reels and jigs. Occasionally, British ships sailed well off of the harbor during the daylight to confirm their spies' construction rumors. The workers joked they should invite the enemy sailors into the harbor to join the nocturnal festivities. Then they could burn their ships to light the festivities while the British and Canadians were otherwise occupied. Imagine the embarrassment, they said, of reporting the loss of one or two or even three of His Majesty's warships while his sailors danced with American beauties. Some even thought seriously of pursuing the idea. More sensible heads prevailed.

The evenings' revelries had brought an unexpected but agreeable respite to George as well. During these occasions he watched his mother relish the rivalry developing between two Philadelphia men competing for her attention. She had regained a youthful heart and George encouraged her to not spurn their advances, to the extent modesty would allow. In short, he was happy that she was happy. Polly observed a quickness in her step that was not at all improper. She enjoyed accompanying her and grew closer to her, as close as she was to her own mother.

The three women had joined the sewing league of other ladies from the village, and over their community quilting, traded gossip and other news, but always looked to inventive ways they could assist the enterprise. The times spent with their cloth and needlework provided an interlude from the stress of anticipated British invasion and the busyness of tending to the needs of the many laborers housed wherever there was a room to let. The women displayed the products of these gatherings with pride and easily sold them for substantial money, for it could indeed be a cold winter on the lake. The gatherings regularly took place at Margaret Forster Stewart's home on East Fourth Street. With its substantial parlor and fireplace, Captain Tom Stewart's home was well suited to host larger projects. Ten to twelve women could entertain there comfortably. Sara had been friends with Dorcas Forster Bell, Margaret's sister, ever since Sara and William had settled in Erie. More than once she had introduced Polly as

"George's Polly" to the sisters and their friends. Welcomed into the circle, Polly listened and learned from the women of society. Polly had kept George enlightened with all of the intimate details Sara willingly divulged to her group, of course always under the strictest secrecy. Thankfully, no man had so far divulged the secrets of the fleet to the sewing circle of friends. News traveled through that group like water through a sieve, and often they heralded details of some event well before the newspapers reported it. Polly delighted in sharing any gossip with George. At times she appeared at his house, sometimes even at his work on the docks, bubbling with enthusiasm over some new report, and the people always anxiously awaited accounts of the war.

Then Lake Erie's autumn nor'easter returned, blowing heavy rains on the coast, from Presque Isle on east to Buffalo. For two days, foul weather besieged the community and the rain turned the roads into mush. Travel was cold, slow and hazardous, the news of poor travel all along the Niagara frontier reaching all of the communities by couriers. They also reported on General Van Rensselaer's gathering army in Black Rock, and General Smyth's regulars marching toward Lewiston, New York, an invasion perhaps. Finally the Americans would start their conquest of Canada, forcing Fort Erie to surrender, countering the loss of Detroit. The presence of over seven thousand soldiers and militia was a godsend, and the Erie residents found comfort in their relative safety. The fleet building would continue. But hampered by the muck of the roadways, the task of supplying the workers slowed to a crawl. On this day, one story declaring a glorious victory of a kind arrived in the community, and the women naturally spread it about. The news *was* true, Polly said. A rider had brought the message. The navy had captured a British ship. The women's group eagerly carried the information to the entire community, and Polly drove her cart through the downpour to find George. He and other workers stopped their muddy work, plodding through the quagmire of roads to gather together at the base of Cascade Creek to get the particulars of the event.

"Which ship?" asked George.

Polly didn't know which one, but the rider had said one ship was captured and another was burned near Black Rock.

"Maybe it was an American ship that was burned. The British navy could very well invade along the Niagara and attack without warning," a worker reasoned.

"No. It was definitely two British ships, and one was taken," Polly said breathlessly.

"Who will know the real story? When will we get real proof?"

"General Mead is getting the details, and he'll come here to the docks with the official report. George, I just had to let you know. Maybe it was Jessie's ship."

"Maybe. It's possible that he may have been rescued. We'll know soon enough. Then he'll be coming home – to Black Rock. His father will be happy with that."

"You will be too, won't you?" she studied his face for a moment. "Won't you?"

"Huh? Oh, yes, of course. Of course, I'll be happy too."

Then Mead arrived on horseback with the particulars of the event. Lieutenant Jesse Duncan Elliott, in temporary command at Black Rock, and Captain Nathan Towson had led a raiding party in two vessels, attacking across Lake Erie and boarded two ships anchored under the protection of Fort Erie's cannon. At 3 a.m. on this past Friday, October 9, the men cut *HMS Caledonia* and *HMS Detroit* from their anchors and took them. Elliott reported that it took only ten minutes for his boarding party of one hundred men to secure all the prisoners, run the topsails up, and have the ships underway. They floated downstream toward Black Rock because of unfavorable winds. The *Caledonia* had a considerable cargo of furs, and the prize would fetch a very good price.

"Prisoners? Who was aboard?" asked George.

"There were few. Two were killed and tossed overboard, the officer on board was slashed with a cutlass in the struggle, but he was released and set adrift in a boat with the other sailors. They took a few British prisoners, but rescued several American prisoners," Mead said.

George looked at Polly, saw her distress. "You said there were Americans aboard?" he asked.

"Yes. Lieutenant Elliott freed ten American prisoners and brought them back safely to port at Black Rock. But it wasn't without some adversity. In taking the ships, the crew sailed the *Caledonia* out of range, but when the *Detroit* followed, she ran aground at Squaw Island. The British sounded the alarm while they were still within range of the Canadian guns. The guns fired toward the ship all day, but the raiding party escaped. Lieutenant Elliott and his men came back later that night and stripped whatever supplies they could from the *Detroit*. But she was fast aground and in danger of the British recapturing her. He had no choice but to set her afire. She burned to the waterline. At least that's one ship that won't prowl our shores anymore. But the *Caledonia* – Elliott's men got away with all aboard and she's in our possession now, safe and out of the reach of Fort Erie's guns."

"What of the freed captives?" Polly asked.

"All are safe," Mead said.

"Do you have the names of the Americans?" asked George.

"I don't have their names, just that all are safely returned to Black Rock."

"George, we must go," Polly pleaded.

"I can't just leave here. If Jesse is among them, he'll come to us, or at least send notice to us. We'll wait and see."

"What if he was one of the men thrown overboard?"

"The men who died in the short contest were British soldiers, it was reported to me," said Mead.

"See? Jessie will be safe." George tried to reassure her, had little success, but Polly was willing to wait. She dejectedly drove her cart back up the hill leaving George's emotions as cold and bleak as the October sky.

"And one more thing, men. The ship's architect has finally arrived, and he is meeting with Daniel over the drawings for the gunboats."

"It's high time," said George. "Now we can get to work. How soon can we meet?"

"That's them coming now, George. Gather the rest of the men, so they can meet their new supervisor of building." George spoke to two men and the three of them separated to assemble the workers at the base of Lee's Run. The crowd trickled in, huddled against the wind and drizzle. Dobbins and the new shipwright waited for the assembly, Dobbins in a much better mood than George had seen him in weeks.

"George, we've finally received the authorization for two 60-ton schooners, and we must waste no more time. You workers here," he announced, "will report down to the dockyards within the hour." The men began to congratulate each other, smiling, pats on the back, finally ready to get to work on a real fleet.

Joel Thompson stepped forward, "Mr. Dobbins, didn't Secretary Hamilton order four gunboats built? We, that is, all of the workers, had hoped for four vessels."

"Indeed, he did. And Commodore Chauncey has allowed for just the two schooners. So, we'll start on the schooners first, and then we'll construct the other gunboats until we have the four that were ordered sitting on the stocks. We've worked too hard, prepared too much to set it all aside for the whims of a local commander who seems content to ignore our requirements. That's why I searched out the best shipwright I could find. Come here, sir." The short, wiry bespectacled stranger, stepped away from the cart where he had sat unassumingly, awaiting Dobbins.

"George, men, this is Ebenezer Crosby. Mr. Crosby has come all the way from Niagara County, New York, to aid us in this undertaking. He's a master shipwright and is highly recommended. Ebenezer, this is the George Armstrong I spoke of. One of our better carpenters. He's been invaluable to me in helping with organization, along with his assigned duties as a builder, driver, and jack of all trades."

"Your servant, sir."

"Pleased to finally meet you, George. Daniel tells me you've accomplished much here," said Crosby. The deep bass voice emanating from such a slight frame of a man caused the men to snicker amongst themselves.

"The accomplishment is only in the cutting. The men who've been laboring here are all eager workers. They'll work for patriotism as well as for profit, but they need guidance. We all do," George said.

"Men, I've looked over the plans the secretary gave Daniel and have made a few corrections for the shallow harbor and for the lake. If you men have the adequate timbers prepared, we can commence on the first gunboat at once," he announced. He looked up to the low rolling clouds. "Ah, perfect weather to build. Not too hot," he laughed.

The voice carried over the heads of the men now assembled, and had anyone in the back seen who had barked the orders, the raucous catcalls would've been hard to suppress. Most were none the wiser, for once he gave the order, the men poured over the shipyard with a level of activity not witnessed in weeks. Crosby surveyed the scene at the foot of Lee's Run. Dockyards built, lumber cut and stacked, and men congregating like ant colonies, ready to form work parties. Then Crosby took charge. Work crews organized, tasks assigned, and the general milling around ended. George and Ebenezer selected timbers from the cut piles. Workers laid out Daniel's black oak and the first keel took shape. Under Crosby's direction, workers methodically sorted, cut, planed, and fastened timbers, and like some giant resting mastodon skeleton, two ribs rose above the beach. Work parties swarmed over the skeleton, drilling holes, knocking in trenails, cutting and planing the ends smooth. The afternoon sped on. It was wet work. Green timbers, slippery boards and framing, and wind that cut through the woolen coats, yet George felt something different in the air. The men now had a sense of pride in this monumental task. The ships, no longer a dream, lay before them in crude wooden skeletal framing, two ribs rising on each side of the massive keel resting on immense wooden blocks. George stood on the wet sand and surveyed the work they had accomplished. *Yes*, he thought, *it's only a start. But it is finally a start.*

## Fort Malden, Canada

A foreboding hung in the air like so much lake fog, thick and oppressive. The news of the *Caledonia*'s loss to the American raiders subdued the usually positive atmosphere around the fort. Though no sense of immediate disaster to the western inhabitants of Upper Canada, Jesse sensed the winds of war had been knocked from the Canadian sails. General Brock had left with a contingent of men to prepare for the Americans moving against the Niagara forces, but had not arrived in time to thwart the raid. Probably couldn't have done any good even if he had been present. The supposedly invincible British navy and Canadian Merchant Marine had suffered a sufficient setback and the rumors of how they intended to deal with the losses became the fodder for table talk at the taverns. The talk was anything but boisterous. Jessie observed three sailors who talked in low tones, occasionally glancing surreptitiously about the room. He chose to position himself near these three sailors. Nursing a mug of rum in his hands, and adopting a morose air, he casually joined in the conversation, nodding his head drunkenly at each statement, and soon learning where hearts for king and country truly lay. These men were planning a way out, and Jesse wanted a way into it.

"Lieutenant Irvine was one that was killed," said the lean Canadian wearing a green foraging cap.

"Naw, Jack," said a tar, who Jesse observed was missing several upper teeth on the right side of his jaw. "He was slashed with a cutlass! He was saved by his men who wrapped his neck and shoulder. The Yanks cast them adrift in the boat, but they was all rescued at Fort Erie."

"Well, it was bold enough," said the Canadian, "and we are now short two vessels. Burned the *Detroit*, is what they say."

"Colonials never fight by gentlemen's rules," said a soldier near Jesse. "Isn't that right, sailor?"

"Oh, I wouldn't shay dat," Jesse slurred.

"You're American, aren't you?"

"Thash right," he said. "But dey do fight by their own rulesh, shometimesh. I've sheen 'em."

"See? I tell you when we get into the thick of it, we will not be able to stand up to them," said the soldier. "We might as well admit it and get the plan together."

The toothless sailor nervously looked about for anyone appearing to listen. "This is treason you speak of, John," he whispered.

"Yes, it is," said the soldier. "So we'd better be sure we're all together in this. We'll all be sailing with the *Charlotte* to Fort Erie. When the time comes, we can make our break there."

"What are you looking at, Yankee Doodle?"

Suddenly sobering up, Jesse asked quietly, "Are you men to be deserters?" He looked at the men hopefully.

Glancing about for any listeners, the three drew themselves together ominously, one large hand drawing a knife and holding it closed fisted on the table. "What's it to you, Yankee Doodle?" asked the sailor.

"Might mean plenty to me."

The Canadian studied him intently. "You don't look as drunk as you were. Something sobering you up?"

Jesse thought, *could be my only chance. Might as well go through with it and trust them.* "I'd say the thought of getting home would sober anyone," he said. He scrutinized the men, the suspicion evident in each face, "Listen, Jack, if you think I'll report any of this, then you've no appreciation for what a captive feels at all, do you?"

"Captive? What was your ship?"

"I was seaman aboard the *Commencement* when they kidnapped and pressed me into service over three months ago. I've served aboard the *Caledonia*, and I was assigned to the *Queen Charlotte*, same as you."

"We know all 'bout that," said the tar. "But you ain't with 'em now is ya?"

"I've been lately assigned shore duty by Commodore Hall. Have to work in Malden, but if I can get out of there, I'll go with you. Closer to Buffalo I get, the happier I am."

"Do we take him with us?" John asked. The men huddled together, whispering. "Either that or we kill him," Jack, the Canadian, said dismissively.

"Are you in with us, mate?" John asked with a threatening stare.

"How could I be otherwise?" Jesse asked. "Look, there are ways to go about escape. I've tried three times."

"Not very successful, are you?" the tar sneered.

"I've found three ways to *not* escape. But there are more chances when you get to Fort Erie than you'll find here. I've been there, and I can show you how. But I come with you, or I give you no help."

"You're assigned to the fort here, mate. How do you think you'll get to Erie? You plan on stowing away?"

Jesse hadn't thought of that. "I had planned to get myself assigned to a ship going east. But I'll take your suggestion under consideration too." He studied them again. No one spoke, considering whether to trust this American. Then he broke into a wide grin. The men laughed raucously.

"Alright, mate," said the soldier, offered Jesse his hand. "I am John Chapman, 41st Regiment of Foot. We will talk. Later tonight, we're meeting at the docks. Each of you bring a plan. Consider it well, for we risk much. We'll see which plan best suits our purpose. We're all in this, eh?"

The men all assented. One by one they casually left the table, leaving a few coins on the table to placate the tavern keeper, though Jesse observed no other drinks had been ordered than what they had brought to the table with them. They had covered every hint of suspicion. Jesse grabbed the sleeve of the Canadian sailor as he stood to leave.

"Jack, at what time?"

He scanned about the room. "Eight bells," he said softly and was gone through the door.

The Halls would want him early for dinner, but he needed to relay his apologies so he wouldn't miss the secret meeting. He considered this turn of tidings as he returned to the fort and his barracks, thought, *maybe at long last another chance for home.*

"Mr. Harris," a voice called.

At the gate stood Commodore Hall. "A word with you."

"Aye, sir," said Jesse.

Lieutenant Stokoe tells me you were drinking with four of the men assigned to the *Charlotte* today."

"I – uh. That is – I was sir. Is there harm in it?" The commodore was having him watched. What had he done to attract this scrutiny?

"There is if you want to court my niece." He paused, Jesse thought, *maybe looking for a chance to spring a trap on me.*

"Court your niece, sir?"

"Yes. I must say, a man of your background, an American who may indeed rise high in His Majesty's service, must be prepared to give up the life of the ordinary seaman."

"Excuse me?"

"I have plans for you, Mr. Harris. You may in fact one day captain one of the vessels after this war ends. I would like to see my niece well provided for, and if you use your indenture here to rise in the ranks, I daresay a captaincy would not be at all out of the question. You must learn to conduct yourself as a man training to be an officer and gentleman."

"Sir," I don't know whether to be flattered by— uh –" His words moved dangerously close to confronting the commodore, and he paused to summon his courage.

"Yes, Mr. Harris?"

"Sir – uh – I – uh – have –"

"You have what Mr. Harris?"

"A girl back home," he blurted out. Then the words tumbled out. "I had just been betrothed before I set sail, sir. Then I was pressed into service off the *Commencement*. And I haven't seen her since these past four months. Sara, I mean, Miss Hall is fine, I mean she's as pleasant a woman as one would choose – if one were at liberty to choose. But, sir, I'm *not* at liberty to choose. I've done nothing to lead her astray, on my honor, sir. I haven't tried to lead her into any – er – ill repute, as they say. I know you want the best for her and you're trying to help us both along. But sir, it would go against my own honor to treat this woman at home so dishonorably."

"You can say the woman in question knows your mind?"

"Oh, indeed, sir. She accepted my pledge just before I sailed."

"And do you know my niece's mind?" he said sternly.

Jesse saw thin ice, but now committed himself and hoped he wouldn't break through. "I'm not sure that I do, sir. I've held her in high regard. I've never tried to place her in any compromising position, that is to say compromising her own honor. But I've also not pledged myself to her or even broached the subject with her. Uh – Sir." He waited for the effect to settle and steeled himself against the impact he could face.

"Hmmm…." The commodore searched his face. "Is it your intention to remain a normal seaman in the king's navy and never rise to your potential?"

It was not his intention to remain in the king's anything for any more time than it would take to plant himself on US shores again. But this he hid.

"For the present, sir."

"And my niece? Is she to be without your company from this day forward?"

Jesse had to consider the fact that he was gambling now. If he missed an opportunity to escape with the three deserters, it might be months until he could return to the Buffalo region. But if he apologized to the commodore, he could stay here and continue to glean information. For whom? What more could he do than he had already done? He had information to pass on that could readily be used, but it was useless here at Malden.

"I don't know how to answer that, sir. Your niece, Miss Hall, is a fine woman and I am attracted to her, but I must remain faithful. Sir, I hope you understand the conundrum that choice places me in."

"Indeed I do. I will make it easy for you. I am relieving you as of this afternoon from your post here at Malden. You are to report immediately to Lieutenant Stokoe aboard the *Queen Charlotte*, where you will…"

Jesse heard no more of the speech. He couldn't believe his ears. In the manner of punishing him, the commodore had just issued him free passage from the base. The reality almost made him grin widely. He tried to focus on the commodore.

"…and you will serve aboard the ship for the rest of the war. While there you will…"

He blocked out the orders, absorbed in his plan. He could get aboard tonight, get his berth, and meet the three companions later as arranged. Now they would welcome his knowledge of the eastern end of the lake, and his assistance in escape.

"You do understand?"

"Sir?"

"You do understand the gravity of this assignment, Mr. Harris?"

He hadn't heard enough to draw any conclusion. "Yessir. I am sorry to have put you in such a position yourself, Sir. But I believe you will understand that I must do the honorable thing, regardless of my feelings for Miss Hall. Sir, if I have nothing else to bring to a marriage, I must bring my honor. Will you convey my respects to Miss Hall, and tell her I am sorry?"

"I will do no such thing! She will understand that you've been assigned to greater duty with the naval forces on this lake. She understands the navy's needs are paramount to her desires. And if you should survive any engagements with the enemy vessels, you may then consider speaking to her yourself. By that time you will see whether your girl, as you call her, has maintained her own honor and dedication to you. That will be all, Mr. Harris. Report to the barracks inside, retrieve your effects, and then report to the *Queen Charlotte* at once."

"Aye, sir," he saluted and turned militarily but with a quickness to his step that nearly betrayed his excitement at the prospect. Returning to Buffalo and freedom was a matter of setting sail at the next order.

The bell had tolled the eight o'clock watch and Jessie paced the deck of the *Charlotte*, watching the docks for the familiar figures of his intended rendezvous. In the shadows, one man casually walked down the dock, lantern in hand, stopped at the *Charlotte's* berth, took out a pipe, lit it, and then casually strolled back toward the shore. At the same instant, a lantern shutter opened and flared near the shoreline, silhouetting a face in its glow. Jesse recognized the foraging cap on his head. The figure walked down the shoreline and met the first man. Jessie checked about him for the watchman who had not reappeared on deck, swung himself over the side, grasped the large hemp line, wrapping his legs in a scissors about the rope, and hand over hand, eased himself out from the ship to the wooden cleat on the dock. He quietly and quickly joined the other two on shore.

"Where is our comrade?" he asked.

"I suspect he will join us soon," Jack said. "What are you doing aboard the ship? You endanger us all. We never said to go aboard," he said angrily.

"It was never my intention," Jesse said. "I was assigned duty aboard the ship just today. Apparently, I've fallen out of favor with Commodore Hall. I only reported this afternoon, not long after our conversation. It's just as well. Now I don't have to stow away."

The men looked about suspiciously. "Did anyone hear our talk? Has anyone followed you?"

Jesse was incredulous "Followed me? Followed you, you mean!"

"What?" said Jack.

"Over there," said Jesse, and he pointed to a stack of flour barrels further ashore where a figure stepped out of the shadows. A soldier of the 41st Regiment of Foot strode toward them, unslinging the musket over his shoulder.

"Good evening, Sergeant," Jesse said cheerfully.

"Good evenin', gents," he said. "What might you be about tonight?"

"Just taking a smoke in the night air, eh?" said Jack. "Care to join us?"

"Would take that as a compliment, gents, but no thanks. Must be about me rounds."

"Terrible duty," Jesse said sympathetically.

"Not at all. I appreciates me free time on duty. Gets to think and plan, and dream. Ahhh, there's dreams for the stealin' tonight, gents. I can have any of 'em I wants 'cause most e'ryone's asleep and there are many more floatin' around in the night air. You know what I mean?"

"Not really, no," said Jesse. An angry stare from Jack. "I mean, er, yes, I know just what you mean, Sergeant. Feel that way myself sometimes. Just lookin' for a dream to make my own. Why, that's what we was just talkin' about when you came out of the shad- I mean when you happened by. Dreams. Weren't we, boys? I was just sayin' I need a different dream. Had the same one for the past six months."

"Girl, I suppose?" said the sergeant.

"Exactly. My how clever you are! And she is lovely. Just got betrothed, I did. Well, we won't be disturbin' *your* dreams, Sergeant. We'll say goodnight to you."

"It is I who should say g'night t' you gents. Pleasant dreams. Ha ha ha." A boisterous self-satisfied laugh echoed off the water, and the three laughed uncomfortably in response. *Everyone in the harbor must have heard it,* Jesse thought. The sergeant strolled at a quicker pace still laughing quietly to himself.

"Pleasant dreams," he repeated softly with a laugh. "Pleasant dreams," shook his head at the marvelous quip he had made and once again slung the musket over his shoulder.

Jesse watched him leave and his companions peered uneasily into the dark along the shore. Another figure stepped out from behind the flour barrels. Jesse immediately recognized the gimp in his walk. Here was their third comrade. "A bit late wouldn't you say?" Jesse said.

"I'd say right on time," said the tar, tossing his head in the direction of the disappearing sergeant. "Did he suspect anything?"

"No," said Jesse brightly. "We even asked him to join us." He saw the sailor's jaw slacken, erupted in a laugh. "Not on our intended adventure, however," Jesse said.

"To the matter at hand," John said. "What is your plan?"

"I've been reassigned to the *Queen Charlotte* and I'll be joining you when we sail east. I've seen the orders myself in the supply room this morning for the goods to be loaded tomorrow. We're underway on the 17th and will stop at Long Point.

From there we pick up more supplies to take to Fort Erie. I'd expect we'll be taking more soldiers with us, so that makes disembarking a perfect time to wander away unnoticed. But we can decide the timing when we get to Long Point, or at any events, on our last voyage to Fort Erie."

"And then what?" asked the tar. "We're still on the Canada side of the Niagara. You expect we can just swim the rapids?"

"Are you a good swimmer?" he said sarcastically. "Look, there are always vessels we can hire."

"To take us to America? Are you mad? Who would risk that?"

"I would," a voice spoke from the shadows.

Startled, the men peered into the dark, the tar pulling a tomahawk from his belt. "Who is there? Be quick about it!"

"My name ees Rinaud. You must know dat if you plan to go to America, it would be best to not discuss eet so noisily. You never know who ees listening, eh?"

"What do you know?" asked the tar, his hand tightening on the tomahawk.

"What's your name, eh?"

"Alexander. Why"

"Well, Alexander, I know dat I will split dat skull of yours, if you don't put your weapon away, my friend."

The Canadian released his grip on the tomahawk and Rinaud slipped his weapon back into his belt. "You need a voyage to the States, eh?"

"Maybe," said Jesse. "We are to ship aboard the *Queen Charlotte* to Long Point soon. We'd prefer to see more of the world than that. Are you offering to help, or do you have more sinister motives?"

"What parts of de world would you like to – uh, visit?"

"I have always wanted to see Buffalo. I hear it has spectacular views of the cataract falls," said Jesse.

"Too far. Dat part of de world takes you to Fort Erie. I don't like Fort Erie. But, I have shown some men like yourselves parts of de world dey needed to see."

"What part of the world would you say one might want to visit before their time on earth is done?"

"I had one friend and his fellows go wid me to visit Presque Isle several mont's ago," said Rinaud, a hinted gleam in his eye.

Jesse immediately stiffened. Jack seemed suspicious, "Who was the traveler? Or shouldn't we be asking?"

Rinaud looked around, peering into the shadows, then, "A merchant friend you do not know. Name ees Dobbins."

"Never heard of him," Alexander said.

"Daniel Dobbins?" asked Jesse.

"Ahh, you do know him. He had two companions, fellow adventurers who also wanted to see new sights in de world. Man named Reed and one more named George."

"Was it Armstrong?" Jesse became more animated. "Did he say his name was Armstrong?"

"Oui, Armstrong."

"You know these men, Harris?" asked John.

*Best to keep the relationship to myself*, he thought. "I've heard of them. They've both sailed out of Erie before. Merchant ships, I believe," he said. "How far did these travelers go on their – er – voyage to see the world?"

"As far as de port at Cleveland. Too much risk with de storms on de lake to travel any furder. But I assume dey went to more parts of de world from dere. De world ees a big place – to de east, no?"

"East. Yes. Much, much bigger place," said Jesse.

"If one was to want to travel to see other parts of the world with someone, say, like you for instance, what would be the cost and when would a voyage like that take place," asked the soldier. "Not saying that we want to do this, but merely asking for future consideration."

"My passengers preferred to travel at night in canoes. Dey like de night, less chance of being hindered on de trip. It was a long journey, so travelers should always look to de skies for de choice of when to go. As to cost, dis ees open to barter," Rinaud smiled.

"And where may one find lodging before a trip to see the world takes place?" asked Jesse.

"Oh, I have been known to offer assistance dere in my cabin, sout' of de fort. From dere, a journey could begin as soon as de lake water ees favorable. You understand dat dis ees only for dose who plan to visit de world as a traveler and den return back here to deir own homeland?"

144

"Of course," said Jesse. "I wouldn't have it any other way."

"Good. Den when you are set to see de world and have leave to see new places, you come to see me first, eh?" The Frenchman left, scanning the beach as if expecting someone, but continued on the shoreline, following the Detroit River until out of sight.

"Can he be trusted?" asked Jesse.

"I don't know. I've seen him around the fort. He's a trapper and does well enough with the fur trade, seems to be respected. Knows the lake, comes and goes as he pleases," said Jack.

"But will he report our conversation?" asked Jesse.

"It seems to me he only wants money, so he'll take the risk for the British pound. I think he can be trusted," John said.

"I am not so sure," said the sailor. "He was too eager to help. He may be a bounty hunter."

"But we're not wanted, have done nothing to attract any heavy discipline, and he did know those men from the States he claims to have transported," said Jesse.

"Did he conjure that story for us?" Jack asked.

"I don't think so. He wouldn't just pull names out of his haversack – names that I've heard myself. These men are all from Presque Isle. I know of them. It could only mean he helped them escape from here and would do the same for us. I say we hear what else he has to offer and look for a time when we can start."

"When?" asked Alexander."

"It must be soon. The *Charlotte* sails to Fort Erie or to Long Point within days. It's now, if we want to venture it. We either join the Frenchman—" He paused, studying their eyes, "Or we sail."

Chapter Eleven
Fort Malden
Friday, October 16, 1812

Jesse and his fellow conspirators did their best to throw off any suspicion, worked with the other sailors and marines as needed on their assigned duties, continued to load the ships, *Queen Charlotte*, *Lady Prevost* and *General Hunter* with military supplies to equip an army. Powder and shot for the cannon, kept in supply at Fort Mackinaw, had arrived and they distributed these among the ships. This was no ordinary supply mission. Members of the 41st Regiment of Foot would soon sail on an operation that demanded extra rations, powder and ball, and extra flints to complement this artillery ammunition supply. In the few days since their night meeting, none of them had seen a trace of the Frenchman, and none of them had leave from duties to walk about or slip away to find his cabin. But communication with the eastern theatre of war came swiftly enough, and the report arrived of a great battle near Fort Erie at Queenston Heights on Wednesday. While Jesse and the men sat discussing over drinks in the tavern their intended desertion, the United States Army and New York Militia had struck at the Niagara Frontier. General Stephan van Rensselaer attacked across the Niagara River from Lewiston, New York. Though General Isaac Brock, in trying to rally his troops, had fallen in the conflict, hearing of the incompetence of the militia and their leaders, and over a thousand United States regulars and militia killed or captured sank their hopes.

"You still want to go through with it, mate?" John said, as they lifted a heavy crate of flints.

"Do you?" asked Jesse.

"Don't know that I want to run to the losin' side, you know?" he said wryly.

"You think the States will lose, do you?"

They carried the crate up the gangway past the officers checking off each box on the supply record and changed the conversation. "It's lookin' like we have the Americans on the run as far as invasions is concerned. Doubt that they'd come searchin' for trouble out this way neither. So, aye, I think they be thinkin' twice about the war."

Jesse looked around for listening ears, indicated an officer, "We may need to re-visit our talk later," he said quietly. They stacked the crate and returned to the shore for more crates.

Alexander feigned shifting a crate for lifting and looked around again for listeners, spoke softly. "What I am sayin' is that we haven't seen this Rinaud for a few days, and we now hear the US Army is nearly wiped out to a man, and we be thinkin' of makin' a break for the border to a nation that hasn't actually shown much of a will to fight. Now, why would I risk hangin' for that?"

"Maybe because daily treatment in the British navy is a worse fate than punishment for running? Assuming they even catch us, of course." Jesse suggested.

"And you, Jesse? Same reason?"

"I'm an American. That's reason enough for me."

"You two!" an officer called. "Get to work. I haven't got all night to wait for these crates!"

"Aye, sir," Jesse called. And they lifted a wooden box, *BISCUITS* inscribed on the sides and top. "We must talk later," Jesse said, indicating the top of the box with a nod. The morning continued with the four men passing secretive looks and nods as they passed each other, loading the ships in the harbor, anticipating their mealtime break and the next opportunity to settle on a course of action.

At noon they grabbed their trenchers, slopped on bits of meat and potatoes from the iron pots simmering before the gates at Fort Malden. Customarily, they ate before the Shawnee were permitted to eat, but this day, they were late and elbowed their way past the warriors who had gathered around the cooking pots. Two of the warriors there pushed back, and a shoving scuffle began. Jessie didn't want to attract undue attention to his comrades, immediately called for a guard to arbitrate the dispute. His Majesty's sailors got first rights to the food, and once again the warriors were relegated to wait until all were served – a slight that angered Tecumseh's leaders. Roundhead gestured with a war club to one of the officers who immediately pointed him in the direction of the building housing the commandant's office.

Jack watched the warrior storm out. "We've made a few more enemies."

"I would sleep with one eye open, tonight," Jessie said. "Do you still want to remain here at Malden?"

"The Frenchman's o' no use to us now, so we might as well prepare ourselves to sail with the fleet. Travel'll be easier when we get to the Niagara frontier," John said.

Jack shook his head, doubtful. "I'd put no stock in it being any easier there."

"No, I think Chapman's right," said Jesse. "We'll be just across the river from safety. As it is, we have a long way to travel if we take to foot from here. That trapper may be reliable, but so are Shawnee trackers. Better wait until we get to Fort Erie. Then plan it well, and at first opportunity we go cross river. There will be other opportunities for escape there."

"I trust our chances much better there too," Alexander said, nodding toward the Shawnee. Near the gun emplacement on the northeast front wall the warriors sat together, eating the bits and pieces left for them by the sailors and infantry, murmuring in low tones and tossing glances and angry gesticulations toward the men.

The three considered the warriors a moment, "Then we're agreed?" said Jack. "When we get to Fort Erie?"

The men assented and finished their meals, quickly returned to the docks. But as they worked to finish loading the supplies, Jesse noticed two Shawnee had taken a position where they could watch the men from the shore unhindered. Their patiently sinister manner made Jesse uneasy, and he worked a quicker pace, spent little time on the shore fetching boxes and returning them to the *Queen Charlotte*. By nightfall, the exhausted men had finished putting in the last of the provisions, joined the other crewmen aboard the safety of the ship, and fell asleep anticipating their escape.

With the early morning ship's bell, the men rose and prepared to get underway. Jesse took a turn out in the morning air, cold and crisp, a light fog resting on the Detroit River. On the bow of the *Queen Charlotte* he stood, nervous, awaiting orders, mentally saying his good-byes to Sara, thought he saw her standing on the shore, up the bank, there, near the 24-pounder gun emplacement. Just a figure in the dark. He was fond of her in only the three weeks he had known her. But his love was in America, and the sooner home, the better. Below the cannon, several Shawnee, carrying muskets walked slowly, a calculated step. *A purpose in their action,* Jesse thought. He fixed his eyes on them, fascinated with how they walked. Not walking, it was more of a gliding as they moved from tree to tree. Not hiding, but using the trees as though hunting. *But hunting for what?* Jesse thought. *They wouldn't dare take a shot at His Majesty's Ship Queen Charlotte, no matter how much they hate the sailors who elbowed in on their victuals. This is a show of their resolve as equals, if not superiors, a reminder that they're fierce allies, not to be cast-off.*

"Mr. Harris?" Lieutenant Stokoe called.

"Sir?"

"I might say I am pleased to have you aboard again."

"Aye, sir. It's good to feel the deck underfoot again."

"You may be pleased to know that when we get to our destination, we will have our captain back."

"Mr. Irvine, sir?"

"He is well after his scrape with the Americans that raided the *Caledonia*. Got an ugly slash with a cutlass, but is mending well, and has been reassigned to this ship."

"That's good to hear. He's a fair man – uh – sir, meaning no disrespect of you."

"Ha, no I quite understand. He is very fair. I have learned much under his command. Hope to command my own ship personally one day. He's the ideal tutor for the job."

"Yessir."

"You may beat to quarters, Mr. Harris."

"Me, sir?"

"You, sir."

"Aye, sir."

Jesse had never been given any authority before, a complete break from protocol but he welcomed it. He strutted to the aft where the ship's drummer leaned sleepily against the railing, thought, *who would give me this recommendation? Surely, not Irvine.* He hadn't seen him since he transferred to the *Charlotte* and Irvine sailed the *Caledonia*. *Had to be Commodore Hall. Hmmph! Still trying behind my back to train me to take a ship. Groom me for a marriage I don't want.*

"You, boy!" he barked.

The young man snapped to attention, brought his sticks up and across his chest ready to play. "Yessir?"

"You may beat to quarters."

The tattoo snapped in the air, echoed in the harbor, the cadence picked up by the *Lady Prevost* drummer. Jesse watched him smugly. *Well, then, if they want to give me some authority, I'll use it. Suspicions die when they will give me leave to take charge, however small that authority is. This suits my purpose.* The men had gathered to their stations, awaited orders.

"Mr. Harris!"

"Sir?"

"Man the sweeps!"

"Aye, sir!"

"Man the sweeps!" he passed the order.

The men at station in unison hauled out the long oars and dipped them into the water. "Hands to the loft!" Sail hands scurried up shrouds and stood to the yard on the mainsail mast. "Hoist anchor!"

"Sweeps!" The drummer began his slow cadence and gradually the ship turned to the river. Slow steady strokes pulled and the *Queen Charlotte* followed *Lady Prevost* out of the King's Naval Yard. The current caught the vessel, the order to haul in the sweeps passed and the sails unfurled. Jesse took one last look back at Fort Malden, glad to be rid of that burden, inhaled the wind of freedom filling the sails. On the shoreline, the warriors he had observed, stood resolute and watched his passing. The most fierce-looking of the two, a short stocky brave, wore leather breeches, and US sailor's blue wool waistcoat, a long turkey feather in his glossy tophat. His quiet stare met Jesse's eyes, and he seemed to mark Jesse in his memory. For now he was safely in the British Navy, sailing away from the threat, but he shuddered to think of facing that blue coat warrior in open combat.

"Mr. Harris!"

"Sir!"

"Well done, Mister. You are relieved and may go below if you wish."

"Thank you, sir. I'd like to stay on deck for awhile if I may. Just want to get the feel of my sea legs again."

"As you say, Mr. Harris."

Jesse stood on the aft near the tiller, watching the wake behind. He savored the sense of power he had over the men, his enemy, and the strange circumstance that had brought him to authority in the very navy that had kidnapped him only a few months before. Providence had smiled on him, and Jesse prayed that Providence would continue to smile right up until he was safe in Buffalo. The vessel came hard to larboard and the main sail was run up. The wind quickened, and the Detroit River islands faded behind him. Soon they had sailed to near the mouth of the river, and Jessie relaxed as the confines of Malden disappeared behind the ship. Walking to the bow, he looked out to the west where lay the Sister Islands, and directly off the bow, Lake Erie's Bass Islands. He loved sailing the lake, and he drank in the mist as it sprayed from the bow to his face.

"Jesse, you dreaming?"

"Yes, John, you might say that."

"You handled the crew well in your first command, I must say."

"Not a command. I believe I was being tested. For what, I have no idea, but I'm sure it was a test."

"You seem to have come through it well enough, though."

"Well, I got us out of the harbor. That's what can be said for that."

"No Jesse, I watched the men. They observe you, and they respect you. They know you were pressed into service and have been extremely cautious. But you have shown leadership."

"You flatter me. I'm not sure why a pressed sailor is given any authority at all. It's unheard of. I think maybe I'm being positioned for failure. Stokoe and Irvine wouldn't have done this of their own accord. I've been in this service – forced service, mind you – for only three months, and I'm to assume authority?"

"I wouldn't look this gift horse in the mouth, Jessie. Enjoy it. You've earned it."

"I still think that Commodore Hall has something to do with it. Look, John, I didn't ask for that assignment, nor deserve any of it. I have enough lash marks on my back to testify to that."

"The crew knows that too, but they'll follow a leader, whoever it is."

"What are you suggesting, John?"

"Jesse, are you sure you want to make a break for the States when we get to Erie? You could assume command of a smaller vessel eventually, maybe the *Chippeway*, or even the *Little Belt*, and then we could use her to make a break under sail at some other time."

"I know the *Chippeway*. She was Captain Martin's vessel before they stole her at Detroit. I couldn't take command of her yet. And I'm not willing to wait until that happens – if it should happen. I say we still go at the earliest opportunity, just as we planned."

"Then we're still with you, whenever that day arrives," John said.

Jesse had already decided to escape at the next opportunity, and training to command a vessel couldn't stop his goal. He'd just have to let the work serve as a cover, a diversion from the truth of his scheme, no matter who trusted in him.

## Presque Isle
### Saturday, October 17, 1812

The news of the disastrous invasion attempt slammed down like a mallet on the Erie community. They waited in anticipation of a counter-attack by the Redcoats and Canadian York militia, fueling rumors and paranoia. Some workmen had quit the boat construction to take up arms with the local militia, preparing for an invasion. Meanwhile, news had arrived that Commodore Chauncey was continuing outfitting the American merchant schooners sheltered at Black Rock. The *Amelia*, *Ohio*, *Catherine*, and the returned sloop *Commencement* lay at the harbor on the Niagara River as workmen converted them into battle vessels. Though Jesse Elliott's daring raid had safely captured the *Caledonia*, the loss of the *Adams* (*Detroit*) meant the building crews needed to build at least one more brig to match the armament of the *Queen Charlotte*. The maneuvering for firepower superiority drove the Black Rock workers to greater effort and deprived Presque Isle of the men and material they desperately needed to complete their own vessels. James Kerby's guns at Fort Erie across the Niagara trained on the Black Rock dockyards, and their intermittent firing drove away the workers often enough that some felt compelled to abandon the work for their own safety. Presque Isle still remained an afterthought to the Black Rock command, even though logically it was a safer location. Every report the crews received from messengers, news reports, friends and relatives testified to that fact. Elliott had risen in the esteem of the nation, and George and Daniel learned he was using his high standing with the government and his swaggering power to thwart their intentions at Erie. George returned to the town with the papers of the workmen who had requested their separation wages so they could leave the Presque Isle shipyards for militia duty.

"Mother read the newspaper this morning and told me that the Seneca nation held a dance in Lieutenant Elliott's honor at Black Rock. She says that even Congressman Clay has praised Lieutenant Elliott in Congress."

"Is that so?" said Dobbins, poring over a ledger.

"She says he praised his 'judgment, skill and courage' in the raid. That's a direct quote."

Dobbins didn't look up from his ledgers. "Well, I should think Congressman Clay would need to praise Elliott, somewhat. After all, the congressman is married to the lieutenant's childhood friend."

George laughed. "Cronyism."

Dobbins lifted his head, smiled, "Matrimonyism," returned to his work.

"Mr. Dobbins, these are for you. I'll just leave them here on the desk. We're losing a few more men today."

"Yes, I know, George," he said, a noticeable irritation in his voice. "I've asked for more workers to replace those who are moving on. We still have months of work ahead, and winter is soon here. My requests to Black Rock go unheeded. If we haven't been forgotten, then they're purposely ignoring us. The only consolation I have is that we're well defended in most positions. But we're lacking defense on the outer perimeter. If the British decide to land on the isle, we'll have little time to stop them. Our cannon on the heights can't throw shot far enough to repulse a landing there. We need a strong defense out on Presque Isle, and I need your skills to build a blockhouse on Little Bay close to the harbor's entrance. When the British see us progressing with the vessels, it'll only be a matter of time until they move on us. I asked General Meade to draw up these basic plans for you. You'll need to make them more specific at your discretion."

George looked over the drawing. "I can make a working drawing from these. I'll get to it at once."

"Thank you, George. We also need storerooms, a warehouse of some sort, out there apart from the blockhouse. If we must take supplies out, it's best to have a place to keep them from the elements. And, George, if you can spare a few minutes, find Rufus and inform him that I'll meet with him this afternoon here as we scheduled."

"I'll let him know."

George joined Peter Williamson at the shop, had him throw his eye over the plans, and together they began to turn out a detailed drawing for the laborers. It was a strong fortification, solid enough to repulse small bore artillery, and requiring good thick timber. The store room would be secondary to the defense, but they decided it could be finished in good order with the men and material on hand. By late afternoon, a plan in hand, George made for the dockyards to gather a few men to accompany him to Presque Isle. Here he met Rufus Reed.

"Mr. Reed, Daniel was to meet with you today."

"We have met already. I just left him and he has ridden for Black Rock again to see if he can get any substantial orders and help from Commodore Chauncey. I told him it was another wasted trip, but he insisted on following protocol."

"Is it intentional?"

"What, their ignorance?"

George laughed, "Well, yes, their ignoring of our requests. Daniel says he's asked for help on our work here again and again, and still they do nothing. It's one thing to be refused – it's quite another to be ignored."

"Commodore Chauncey believes the main threat is from across Lake Ontario. From his standpoint, sending aid here strips him of workers, weakens his position there."

George shook his head in disgust, "We're on the same side, aren't we? This Lieutenant Elliott appears hostile to the whole project."

"Oh, no doubt he is. I think he expected a command for himself at Black Rock, and Daniel's orders here stole his thunder. You see, it wasn't just patriotism and bravery that compelled him to attack the two ships under Fort Erie – it was bravado. A hero's welcome adds weight to his command. There is already talk that he embellished his report of the *Caledonia's* capture, even criticizing the captain who ran the *Detroit* aground. Most likely, much of that is due to jealousy, though."

"As I suspected, we have another enemy to fight, eh?"

"Not fight, George. But I'd say more likely to impede our progress. Understand this, George, if we fail in our efforts here, that failure gives Elliott support to his argument that a fleet could never be built and armed here at Erie. Winning that argument translates to power for his command. He not only will command the squadron, but he can claim ownership of its construction too. This war won't last forever, George, and the rewards are great for those who serve successfully – those who make a name for themselves. It's glory, George."

"But I don't see that in Mr. Dobbins."

Rufus smiled, "No, his rewards are much more personal. He does this for revenge. The commodore and the lieutenant have a larger goal – public recognition. After that, there's the inevitable promotion."

"What will that do to our efforts here?"

"I don't know. He can continue to suppress them, or he may join us. If it's the latter, he may assume command of the whole fleet."

"Elliott, commanding the entire squadron?"

"It's possible. Or at least be second, subordinate to Commodore Chauncey. Combine the ships he's outfitting at Black Rock with our gunboats, and he'll have an imposing fleet to fight the British."

"There's much at stake, Mr. Reed."

"To be sure. The whole northwest territory – not to mention the egos and reputations of the command."

A wagon load of workers from the shipyard pulled up, their destination, the point of land on Presque Isle nearest Little Bay. Peter Williamson sat on the bench with the wagoner, intently studying the drawing of the blockhouse. George climbed on board, sat in the back beside John Silhammer. The men huddled together against the cold air, wrapping woolen blankets around their shoulders.

"Winter's in the air alright," George said.

"We'll warm up when we get to work on the blockhouse," John said.

"But building the rest of the vessels through the dead of winter – the thought alone gives me chills. It won't be healthy."

"No it won't, but I'll be back at the forge when we get more iron supplied. I can take my turn at the fires at the shop. Looking forward to that."

"The rewards of smithing, eh?" George joked.

"It has its incentives."

Two workers on horseback met the men at the point and the seven soon had selected several trees for cutting. Axes resounded in the woods and the timbers fell. By the end of the day, the men had worked up a sweat, and the blockhouse's base had taken shape with the framing well underway. The team of men took care in forming a solid structure resistant to cannon shots. This position would serve them for only a few short weeks, but it was necessary. Soon winter ice would set on the lake, sailing would end, and that ice would protect the harbor from British vessels until the spring thaw. The returning wagon traveled along the shoreline, past the mouth of Lee's Run and the cascade. On the high cliffs above the men, the workers had at last finished constructing the abatis.

Joel Thompson stood and waved from the beam of the gunboat. "George!" he shouted.

"What is it?"

"Think we have a name for the first gunboat."

George laughed, "She doesn't even have a deck yet!"

"This morning when we came to work, we scared off a porcupine that had holed itself away from the cold in between some of the timbers. 'Twas a devil of a time to get him to leave. One of the fellas had to prod him along with a branch. He didn't take too kindly to it neither. Kep' bunchin' himself up and trying to stick us with his quills. So we thought, if he was that feisty and couldn't be driven off, we're just goin' to call this first ship the *Porcupine*. Mr. Crosby likes the idea just fine."

"It's a good name," said Williamson. "She'll show her quills to the British. Maybe stick a few of them in a fight."

"The *Porcupine*. A fitting name for her," George said.

The wagon returned to the livery, the men returned to their various lodgings, and George took the turn up State Street and the Freer home. A warm fire cast a glow over the parlor and welcomed George as he entered. Polly greeted him cheerfully, "I hear you started work on another blockhouse out on the bay. Let me take your coat."

"Thank you. Yes, we can have it all framed by Monday. Reinforcing it should take a couple more days. I think it'll be a good defense for the harbor. Did you see my mother today?"

"I did, my mother is over with her now, taking her some soup. George, her cough is not improving. She had chills most of the day, and when I saw her, her face was hot to touch. Doctor Barnes has visited and says she needs rest. But she must tend to the workers housed with you."

"Then they must leave."

"George, she's very fond of Mr. Dawes, the carpenter from Philadelphia."

"I know, but he's shown no further interest in her. I thought they'd develop a lasting friendship, but I think once he won her heart and found a permanent place to stay while here, he ceased his courtship. Nothing unseemly, but he's not whom I want to see courting her. Besides, he'll leave when his work is done here."

"Shouldn't your mother be the best judge of that? You're not just going to order those men out, are you?"

"I may have to. I just don't know. She's ill and they must know they're a burden. I can't be there to help her all the time with the work at the ship yard on-going. They'll just have to get lodging somewhere else. I'll look about tomorrow to see who has lodging. Some of the men have left working to serve in the militia duties. Others are leaving due to lack of work."

"Has it come to that, George?"

"Daniel hasn't been able to get authorization from Black Rock to continue the work on the four vessels. We have the one started, but the cold and lack of money has slowed everything down. We're putting most of the men to work on the fortifications just to keep busy until orders arrive. The abatis and the redoubts are finished on the heights. We'll have the new blockhouse done by next week. After that, there's little work to be done. And Daniel also told me the money he was given is nearly gone. He may not be able to pay the wages. Mr. Reed has contributed and has gotten a few investors, but it's not near enough for completion of one boat, let alone four. Please don't let anyone know that, it'll drive the workers away in force, and Daniel may yet have some promise from Commodore Chauncey when he returns Monday. But either way, when winter finally sets in, we're going to lose more workers to the weather, I'm sure of it."

"Oh, George. It was so promising for the town. Surely they can't abandon the work here."

"They may have no choice. Daniel's worked to keep the prices steady, but they've inflated so much that if there is no pay—well, what would you do? It's not a good situation, Polly. The timber already cut will sit on the shore and rot."

"But you and your friends will stay on the task, of course?"

"We will as long as we can. But we're limited as to what even we can do. With the cold and limited supplies, and not enough hands – well, it's frustrating.

"Tomorrow is Sabbath, George. Will you be going to meeting?"

"I'll see how mother is in the morning. But I may have to stay in house with her and deal with our tenants. May I call on you later in the day? I have some things that we need to discuss."

"Oh? Pleasant talk, I hope."

"I trust it will be. I'll say good-night to you then."

Polly helped George with his coat, and at the door, leaned forward to kiss him warmly. George welcomed the display and pondered her affectionate embrace walking home. The chill night air seemed to warm suddenly. *Almost winter*, he thought, *but it feels like spring.*

Chapter Twelve
Fort Erie, Canada
Wednesday, October 12, 1812

With General Brock's death at Queenston Heights, the command of the armies of regulars and the York Militia fell to Sir Roger Hale Sheaffe, a strict disciplinarian. General Henry Procter maintained command of the Detroit River forces at Fort Malden. The troops that General Procter had sent on Jesse's ship reinforced Fort Erie with the present soldiers to form a defensive force that would repel any other sorties against Lower Canada. But General Procter faced the very real threat of a growing army under American General William Henry Harrison, convinced its intent was to retake Fort Detroit. He kept as many forces with him as he felt necessary, buoyed by Tecumseh's warriors and the Six Nations tribes. The news was good for the Erie residents. In late September British General Adam Muir had attempted to take Fort Wayne and was driven back by General James Winchester, solidifying the American presence in the West. The Canadian Governor General Sir George Prevost now determined to fight a defensive action, forcing the invading Americans to waste time, men and material in fruitless battles. With his newly appointed position of authority, Jesse gained access to the officers' information of all the military strategies. The American command in New York could use this news about the defensive strategy to the war.

General Brock was laid to rest with full military honors at Fort George, and the throngs that gathered provided the perfect opportunity for Jesse and his comrades to sift into the crowds and disappear. That plan withered quickly when Lieutenant Stokoe chose the four together to remain at Fort Erie with the *Queen Charlotte* while he accompanied a contingent of soldiers and Provincial Marine as an honor guard to the ceremony. He left Jesse as the sailing master in charge of the ship, and the men used the occasion to prepare their escape.

"That skiff that's tied on the wharf below the fort has been there for three days. I've watched to see who's responsible for it, and it appears no one has any use of it. That should be our easiest way to get out. It only has oars for two, though. Chapman, how soon can you get two more sets of oars down to that boat?"

"I don't know, Jessie, maybe this afternoon, after I finish duties on board."

"You're a soldier first, so I'll have you reassigned to the shore, say, to check on some inventory of goods. Anything that'll get you down to the docks. When you leave, take the old fishermen's path down to the wharf. That's usually guarded by only two sentries, but they'll not bother you. Take the oars. Don't be secretive about it. Just walk fast and ask a question."

"A question?"

"Yes. That should throw them off from asking *you* any questions. Look about and see where you can stow away two more pair of oars on the bank.

You must keep them close to the skiff, thrown in at the last possible moment."

"When do we make the break?"

"Tonight. I have the watch. I'll slip off the ship and follow the shoreline without being seen," Alexander said.

"Jack, I've assigned you to shore duty tonight. You're to report to the armory to see about loading cannon powder aboard tomorrow. You will make a detailed list before you leave here. Once at the armorer's, leave the list with him and find a reason to return to the ship. Instead, you go directly to the skiff. I'll be there near the shoreline and will signal you by walking with a lantern if there's anyone prowling about. If you see no light, go to the skiff, untie and hold the lines. Alexander, at eight bells, you slip off the ship and get there as soon as possible. Now, once we cast off, we need to row quietly, get into the current and let it carry us down the river. We head for the Squaw Island and beach it there. Once we're ashore, we'll look for a way to get passage to Buffalo. If needs be, we row again, get across to Cornelius Creek, and work our way back to Black Rock. The current is stiff, and it's a dangerous undertaking. We all understand the risks?"

The three co-deserters all assented they knew the risks and vowed to implement the escape. The men parted ways, each to his feigned duty station, and Jesse reported to Lieutenant Stokoe, received his orders to assume authority over the ship as his second. He busied himself and nervously awaited nightfall. At the sound of the ship's bell at 7pm,

Jesse left the ship, climbed the bank to the fort and entered the gate. Chapman nodded to him and left the gate, walking down the bank. Jesse watched him disappear below the bank, and waited for the sunset out over the lake. *Beautiful*, he thought. *Tomorrow I can watch it from the American shore.* He leaned against the stockade wall, his mind obsessed with his imminent escape. This time he would finally be free of the British navy.

It was time. Under the darkening sky, Jesse slipped behind the barracks, found the unlit lantern hanging on a nail in the door, placed there to light the way to the privy. He felt for the tinderbox in his coat pocket. *Good. The flint and steel are ready if needed.* A shadowed figure leaning on a large oak tree by the parade ground stood alert as Jesse passed in front of the barracks. Aware he was being observed, if not followed, he decided rather than go through his act of escape, he would confront the shadow and determine who was stalking him. He walked swiftly and with as much of an air of confidence as he could muster. Just as he got to the tree, the figure stepped out.

"Mr. Harris? Fine night to be out and about, eh?"

"Sergeant McDonough. It is – a fine night – as you say."

"Yes, good you have a light for the night. Wouldn't want to see you fall off a precipice – drown or the like because you couldn't find your way back to the ship."

"I appreciate your concern. Always lookin' out for my welfare, eh?" Jesse said.

"Lookin' out for you? Yes, I suppose I am. Your welfare? That is another question."

"If you'll excuse me, Sergeant McDonough, I'll be about my business." Jesse tucked the lantern under his arm and started for the gate.

"And just what is your business?"

"*My* business, Sergeant."

"Where are you taking that lantern, Harris?"

"Why, back to the ship, Sergeant."

"That light does not belong to the ship, it belongs to the barracks."

"As you said, Sergeant, you wouldn't want me to have an accident – fall off a precipice – as you say."

"You think you're all high and mighty, in charge of the ship. No need to listen to me anymore, isn't that right?

Jesse knew he was being baited, thought, *disengage from him quickly.* "As you say, Sergeant, I'm in charge of the ship. So, I'll be about my business. Now, if you would be so good as to stand aside, I must be going. Good evening to you."

"Mr. Harris!" he called. Jesse dared not turn around but walked on across the parade ground toward the gate, heard again over his shoulder, "Mr. Harris!"

Turning, "Yes, Sergeant?"

"I should like to accompany you, if you please."

"But I don't please, Sergeant McDonough, and you're holding up my rounds."

"Then by all means I will not delay you. As you say, you have business, and I will see to it you are not delayed. I'll accompany you so you arrive at the ship in a timely manner."

"Don't bother."

"Oh, no bother. I have no other place to go tonight. Do you?"

Jesse looked for any way to free himself from the sergeant, picked up his pace, thought about the men now headed to the skiff to put out across the lake. He needed to light the lantern, warn them, fumbled for the tinderbox in his pocket.

"May I be of service, Mr. Harris?" the voice echoed in the dark, a few paces behind him.

"No, thank you. I believe I can light a lantern on my own," Jesse said and continued down the fishermen's path, stumbling on rocks in the dim light.

"That is not the way to the ship, Mr. Harris. Possibly you are confused with the dark. Let me guide you."

"Not necessary," Jesse called loudly over his shoulder and turned toward the trail leading to the wharf where the *Queen Charlotte* was moored. Possibly he could lead McDonough away from the shoreline, but if he lit the lantern now, the light could expose the men at the skiff, if indeed they had arrived and were now waiting for him. He dared not slow up to light it, didn't want McDonough within an arm's length of him. No telling what the man might attempt in the dark, no one to hear him, no one to find his body. If he could just get the turn on McDonough. Not enough time to take him and get to the skiff. He picked up his pace, kicking loose rocks and righting himself. Best just to lead him loudly away and hope the men would leave without him.

"Halt!" McDonough called. Jesse stopped in his tracks, tensed his muscles, waited for the blow. "Halt, I say!" A shot. Jesse started, fell to the brush, cowering there. Heard the sergeant running toward the fishermen's path. Jesse peered into the darkness, heard McDonough yell again. He had seen the men in the skiff! Jesse tried to light the lantern, struck a spark, blew into the tinder and clumsily lit the lantern, held it high overhead, waved it over his head, a warning, but by now too late. Another shot, further away. Sound of voices above him, alerted Royal Newfoundland Regiment guards began to run down the path, came upon him, muskets ready, a Brown Bess leveled at his chest. "The shot was down there," he yelled, pointing down the path. The guards continued down the path. In the confusion, nervous soldiers could wound anyone. He used the lantern, abandoned the compromised plan, prayed silently, swiftly for their escape, and sprinted for the safety of the ship. Another shot. Then a volley of muskets. Jesse didn't turn to look back, threw the lantern into the water. It hissed quickly and went out. He climbed aboard the ship, quickly reached the stern, clung to the ship's wheel, breathless, felt the shiver. He wasn't cold. The musket fire had unnerved him, and he listened intently, hoping for any sound that the men had affected their escape.

Jesse went about his duties aboard the ship, avoided talking to any sailors below deck. Passing through the men's quarters he brushed off questions about the gunshots fired along the beach. Probably soldiers hunting for meat. No, too many shots. Jumpy guards firing indiscriminately at shadows, thinking the enemy was attacking. Each of his excuses was disregarded. Decided to leave them to wonder what they would. He put on a coat for his night watch, returned to the gun deck. A hand appeared above the gunwale. Alexander, in a blood spattered torn shirt, pulled himself aboard, breathless, faced Jesse, his face intense, voice quiet but strained, "Where did you GO?"

"Here," Jesse said quietly.

"No! Before!" he whispered.

"I went to the fort, got a lantern. Sergeant McDonough confronted me, so I tried to lead him away from you."

"You mean you led him to us, don't you?"

"You think I would do that?"

"To save yourself, yes."

"Alexander, are you out of your mind? I led him away. He fired. I thought it was at me, so I ran. I lit the lantern, didn't you see it? Where are the rest?"

"No, I didn't see the light. I was busy dodging musket balls. The others escaped, I think. I didn't even get to the skiff. I ran into the brush and lost them when I climbed the hill to the fort. I came down behind them like I was just leaving the fort. No one saw me, and I came here."

"Who did they fire at?"

"All of us. Some took aim at me, but as you can see their aim was not all that good. Not a scratch." Jesse looked at his blood soaked shirt. "From the muskets, at least. But the brambles sure played havoc with my shirt."

"Hurry, get below, and get changed, Alexander. It won't be long before the soldiers will come here to look for the deserters. Unless you've been flogged recently, that bloody frock will arouse suspicion." Alexander started for the hatch.

"Alexander, did all of you get away?"

"Jack was hit. I saw him go into the water. I did not see after that." He went below deck.

Jesse peered out toward the hill and the fort above, torches lighting the front of the fort, and a detail of soldiers holding torches and lanterns down on the shore searched for the men. If they found Jack, he might give away their plan in order to save his neck. He knew Jack's skin would undoubtedly be flayed by the cat, but his neck would not stretch. Jesse did not want to face a flogging again, and he resolved to save himself from that misery, by whatever means he could use. He waited, tense, feigned checking the ship's ropes, carronades again and again. In a few minutes, the torches changed direction and began to string out in a line along the shore, coming toward the ship. As the column of men approached the wharf, Jesse saw they had one man in ropes. The lights fell on his face. Chapman. His soaked clothing clung to him, and he looked nearly drowned, his eyes met Jesse's and he hung his head.

"Ahoy, aboard the *Charlotte*!"

Jesse followed protocol, "Yes? Who is it?"

"Captain Whelan, Royal Newfoundland, we have a returned deserter under arrest. Will you have him aboard?"

"Bring him aboard," Jesse called.

The prisoner secured aboard the ship, and Captain Whelan satisfied in Jesse's accepting responsibility, the soldiers retired to the fort. Jesse had said nothing to the captain, but acknowledged receipt of the prisoner, took him to the bow of the ship, feigning to lash him to the foremast. Once they were out of hearing, "John, are you hurt?"

"No, Jesse, a might roughed up, but I am well."

"Where's Jack?"

"He didn't make it, Jesse. The first volley hit him square in the back and he was dead before he tumbled into the water. I couldn't row myself and Jack dragging half in the boat. I pushed him over the side, but they fired again. Struck the boat, and I surrendered. They got Alexander too."

"No, they didn't. He's below. He said he made his getaway through the brambles and circled back here. They know there were three of you. One dead, one captured, and one at large. They'll look for awhile, but he's safe here. I'll not report this to Lieutenant Stokoe, but when Jack is absent from roll, I have to say something. It's my fault that he is shot deserting. I suppose it'll be my back that takes the flogging for this. I'm sorry, John."

"Jesse, how did they know?"

"I don't think they did. McDonough had me watched at the fort, and I thought he had come for me, to kill me somewhere outside of the fort, but he saw you three and gave chase. It was McDonough who gave the alarm, but I don't think he recognized any of you."

"He was there when they fished Jack out of the water. He saw me too. If he recognized Alexander, he'll clap him in irons too. And you, by association with us, are in peril. He'll report this to Lieutenant Stokoe, and it will not go well with any of us."

"I'll do what I can with Lieutenant Stokoe. None of us will hang. They need every soldier and sailor to man these ships. When we have to use soldiers to man the guns, then you know they need every tar they can to handle the vessel. There's even talk of using some of Tecumseh's warriors on the ships. No, they won't hang any of us. John, consider yourself honor-bound to return to your berth below. I'll not place a guard on you. I expect to see you in the morning." He touched John kindly on the shoulder, cut the rope's knot and helped him to the steps.

"You're a good officer, Jesse. Even if you don't have the rank, nor the pay."

Presque Isle
Thursday, December 24, 1812

In November President Madison had won his reelection bid over De Witt Clinton in a close race which saw Madison slip by with just over 50% of the popular vote, and many perceived it as a mandate for the war's prosecution. As unpopular as the declaration of war had been, with the Democratic-Republicans given another four years, some saw profit to be made. The businessmen at Erie held to the fading hope that they could play a major part in the conquest of the Northwest Territory, and a dream of conquering and annexing Upper Canada. However, the New Year's anticipation in Presque Isle brought slim hope for any immediate victory on Lake Erie. During the month, the progress on the first gunboat came to a standstill. The fifty-ton *Porcupine* sat framed in the stocks, awaiting orders to continue. Her sister ship *Tigress* was on her stocks with deck timbers cut and laying about to rot in the damp weather. The last two of the commissioned gunboats lay in pieces on the shore, timbers cut and stacked, awaiting workmen and money. In early December, the winter freeze had turned the lake into its annual function as a roadway, and the horse-drawn sleighs, hugging the shoreline, now made the icy run from Erie to Buffalo in half the time it had taken on the mucky roads. But they brought no more workers, no more assurances from neither Lieutenant Elliott nor Commodore Chauncey that the work would even continue. Dobbins secured two cannon from Black Rock and brought these by sleighs, modified to support the weight. But one by one the workers who had started with glorious hopes of victory and visions of fortunes made in government shipbuilding had returned to their homes disillusioned and poor. The few workers who did remain completed blockhouses to repel an invasion that would not come, at least not during the winter. Beginning the last of November and into the first weeks of December, they had constructed a large barn as a barracks to hold scores of workers. The fifty men available in mid-November faded to as few as a dozen men most recently occupying it, and when the pool of money had dried up, George was left with four men to work along with him and

Ebenezer Crosby. Dobbins rarely worked on the vessels, using his waking hours to scrounge supplies and material for eventual outfitting. He was dogged in his determination, but the outlook remained as bleak as a north coast winter. The bitterest weather was yet to come to the town of Erie, and the constant vigilance against invasion had slacked to something short of nonchalance. Any invaders, whether British, Canadians, or painted warriors could be seen miles away across the frozen lake and the citizens of Erie knew they would not attempt it. From as far away as Cleveland, visitors had come to Erie to see the wooden saviors of the Northwest Territory sitting on the massive blocks, but had left disappointed. No one in the town recognized these visitors, and they suspected that some of them were British spies who would return to Canada, carrying the word that American plans to seize the lake had evaporated with the money and the manpower. The militia no longer drilled on the village green, now painted white with high wind-swept drifts, and many of these part-time soldiers had completed their terms and returned to their homes for the winter months. Some had stayed on for a few weeks to assist with the ships, but with no pay, their warm patriotism froze as solid as Lake Erie.

The frustration that Dobbins shared with anyone who would give him ear finally reached its tipping point. After repeated letters to Commodore Chauncey at Black Rock had gone unanswered, he summarized all his indignation in a scathing letter to the Secretary of the Navy. Though he was now a non-commissioned officer in the US Navy, he threw protocol to the wind, flouted the chain of command and demanded answers to the dilemma at Presque Isle. His original $2,000 was gone, and Rufus Reed consented to advance a loan for the project from his considerable wealth. However, he would do it only if Dobbins obtained official confirmation from the Navy Department that he would receive compensation from the government. Dobbins wrote to Secretary Hamilton, complaining of the lack of support from the command at Black Rock, but in his despairing words he left an opening for himself in his letter: *"I hope to have the gunboats ready by the time the ice is out of the lake, if required."* He had vented his frustration, assuming Chauncey, Elliott, and Lieutenant Angus had never intended to help the project in Erie at all. They were apparently satisfied with the naval station at Black Rock and had concentrated their efforts foremost on winning Lake Ontario as the precursor to an invasion.

"That's probable," George said. "Elliott said in his earlier letter that he didn't believe in our location as the place for a shipyard. Even when you went there, they weren't convinced."

"The site they've chosen for a shipyard is far worse, and I've told Secretary Hamilton so. The yard is within reach of the enemy's batteries across the Niagara River. Any ships that the commodore completes there will be cut to pieces in passing up the rapids to enter the lake."

"They're that close?"

"George, when I went to meet with Lieutenant Angus, I saw it myself. The workers ran like scattering rats when Fort Erie's guns pummeled the shipyard. Those men are scared to remain there. And frankly, I'm surprised he has any workers remaining at all. To continue that insane project will require them to capture the fort, and that prospect doesn't look too likely. We all know what a disaster that debacle at Queenston Heights was. I told Secretary Hamilton that too."

"Maybe we could entice some of those workers to come here to a safer location."

"I thought the same, and I invited them to join our enterprise, but like the rest who left us, they want a guarantee of wages. In the meantime, we must wait for authority from Washington City."

"I hate waiting."

"We all do, George. We all do. But tomorrow is Christmas, so maybe they'll be in a more charitable mood."

Charity took a holiday too. More days passed, leaving the workers awaiting further word from Secretary Hamilton. The men alerted Dobbins that they had seen a ship out in the lake. The lookouts had monitored it for two days where it appeared anchored for some reason, yet they saw no one aboard. The vessel flew the Union Jack, and the men finally resolved to venture across the frozen lake to where the ship was stuck fast and abandoned in the ice. Here they might find provisions and armament to steal for use on the gunboats. With no chance to sail the vessel to the Erie harbor in the winter, the men harnessed four horse-drawn sleighs and armed themselves with weapons for the journey. The expedition across the frozen lake kept the men on edge, watching for cracks in the ice, watching too for any hints that this was a trap set for them. But they saw no movement, no sign of British deception. As the men approached the ship, Dobbins stood quickly, focusing on the deserted vessel, let out a loud laughing war-hoop, startling them. Then they had all understood. For there in the ice of Lake Erie, destined to never sail for the British again was Daniel's old ship, the *Salina*.

"Merry Christmas, Daniel," Rufus Reed called from his sleigh.

"Merry Christmas indeed," he laughed.

The sleighs surrounded her on all sides, the men quickly climbing aboard, and in three hours' time, they had her stripped of every supply and accouterment they could pile onto the four sleighs. Rope and provisions, sailcloth and iron, barrels of black powder and furs for trade: the men packed all aboard the sleighs as their prizes of war. This was the chance Providence had given Daniel to get some satisfaction for the loss of his ship and his precious cargo. After overseeing her stripped of anything usable and portable, and resigned to the fact the ship would be stuck fast in the ice for months, Dobbins bid one last farewell, saluted her, and dropped a lit match onto the oil he had personally poured over the deck. The men drove the horses back over the ice toward Presque Isle, watching the *Salina* burst into an inferno that citizens and soldiers saw from both countries' shores. The smoke lasted until late into the evening. Then the charred smoldering hulk finally slipped below the waters. Days later her grave site was covered by a foot of Lake Erie ice.

Dobbins wanted compensation for the loss of his ship to the British and his forced immolation of the vessel, and he immediately wrote another letter to the Secretary of the Navy to urge Congress to entertain his petition. Unbeknownst to Dobbins or any of the dwindling workers at Erie, President Madison had finally had enough of Secretary Hamilton's public intoxication and had accepted his resignation, appointing a Philadelphia merchant and mariner to succeed him. William Jones assumed the duties and, knowing what the contracts could do for his home state, he immediately investigated the project at Erie, reward perhaps for Pennsylvania giving its vote to the President. New York, decidedly pro-Clinton, would have to wait its turn for attention. And since Buffalo and Black Rock fell under the intrigue of that political process, Dobbins remained hopeful for some support for his repeated requests of the Navy.

On the morning of January 1, the town finally saw the bright light of hope for the New Year. After weeks of waiting, wondering, frustration, and fussing, two surprise guests materialized. Commodore Isaac Chauncey arrived at Presque Isle with Henry Eckford, one of the most respected ship designers in all of New York. George had just finished nailing down slats to the shed roof, when the man in uniform approached him.

"Yes Sir?" George greeted him from atop the roof. "How can I be of service?"

"Young man, who is in charge here?"

"That would be Mr. Dobbins, sir."

"I know he's handling this project and I will speak to him later. I mean who's in charge *here*?

"Why, that man up there on the ship. That's Ebenezer Crosby. He's supervisor here on the shipyard, but he answers to Mr. Dobbins. And, well, Mr. Dobbins — er – he – uh – he doesn't know whom to answer to. Sir."

Eckford put his hand to his nose, scratched at it and quickly coughed to stifle a laugh. "These are the only two ships you have constructed?"

"Yessir. We've lost so many workers because the money's gone, and no one will tell us what to do next. We're not even sure if we're to finish these two ships. And we were instructed by the Secretary of the Navy himself to build four."

"Of this size?" asked Eckford.

"Yessir. Fifty tons each is what Mr. Dobbins was told. That one we call *Porcupine* because – well, we just call her *Porcupine*. And the one there, that which holds Mr. Crosby – that one is called *Tigress*."

Eckford walked about the ships, studied them and their profiles, shook his head in thought. "Commodore, these will have to do. Too late to change them, but the next two must be larger to contend with the enemy." George heard the word, and the realization hit him. This was Commodore Chauncey, here to inspect. It didn't bode well for Daniel, for sure, and equally for the rest of the town that these men had come unannounced. He needed to get away at once to report the guests to Dobbins, and he quickly scrambled down from the shed roof.

"Sir, I can get you Mr. Dobbins if you have more questions. I mean, I am sure he can— did you say *two larger ships*?"

Chauncey looked at Eckford, "If that's what you think will be needed, Henry, then by all means have the plans altered so the men can begin work on the next two large vessels as soon as practicable. And, young man?"

"George, sir. It's George Armstrong.

"Well, George, if you would have Mr. Crosby be so kind as to come down here, I think we can meet with him in a much warmer place than out here on this frozen tundra, don't you think?"

George soon had Crosby off the ship and in his wagon, driving the men to Dobbins's house. George expected a cold greeting, but Dobbins met the men, cordially invited them in, and stoked the fire at his hearth. Soon, tea and hot rum were on the table and the men turned to the task at hand. George remained long enough to glean information before retiring with his wagon to summon Rufus Reed to the meeting. His transport completed, he hurried to Polly's house and shared the news. Dobbins's repeated letters, badgering, pleading, even bucking the chain of command and communicating directly with the Secretary of the Navy finally paid off. The remaining ships of the fleet would begin construction immediately, albeit in the dead of winter. Henry Eckford, a famous New York ship designer was here, and he was going to draw up the plans himself to expand the next two gunboats to sixty tons.

"Not only that, Polly. Commodore Chauncey has ordered us to build a brig. A brig, Polly! It'll be nearly 300 tons! This isn't just some small coastal gunboat, but something that'll challenge the *Queen Charlotte*!"

Polly threw her arms around his neck. "George, I haven't seen you this happy in weeks."

"At last there'll be work. Hard work, but work nonetheless. Oh, I'm happy, Polly, but I tell you who is happier – Daniel. At last he'll get his fleet. You can see it in his eyes. Vindication. After all we've been through, he feels vindicated. I have to take the wagon home to tell Mother."

He rushed out the door, stopped on the porch, thrust his head back inside. "And Polly, the commodore also believes this is the ideal place to build a fleet!"

PART TWO – THE ROAR AND FURY

Chapter Thirteen
Presque Isle Harbor
Monday, January 11, 1813

With a renewed enthusiasm, Ebenezer Crosby, George Armstrong, and five carpenters from the town ascended the framed hulls on the stocks, fastening down the planking. Still lacking iron nails, the men improvised, setting about drilling, driving in trenails, and hammering them flush. Then they were back to the surrounding woods, taking the axes to the trees. Once again, the sawmill began cutting lumber for framing the two large gunboats. But as more trees fell, the work moved farther away from the mills, forcing the workers to turn to hewing the timbers at the construction site to save time. This in turn required more laborers to handle the increased burden. Though he never returned to the massive project at Erie, Commodore Chauncey saw to it that more carpenters were hired, with recruiting extending as far away as the Philadelphia shipyards. In three weeks' time the town again was alive with laborers, some returning, others newly arriving after reading the newspapers' advertising for the work and the wages. The government ordered cannon and cannonballs from the Fort Pitt Foundry in Pittsburgh to defend the fortifications George and his men had built in the fall. Finally the blockhouses and the redoubts on the bluffs above the shipyard would have the firepower to drive off an enemy when the spring thaw arrived. Joel Thompson had returned from Waterford to work in the blacksmith's shop, but lack of iron deliveries forced him to join the carpenters on the ships' construction.

George greeted him on the deck of the *Tigress*. "It's good to have you back with us, Joel."

"We were promised wages, and so we all signed on. The Waterford paper said that Commodore Chauncey and Sailing Master Dobbins have even sent out notices to Pittsburgh and Philadelphia for laborers. I read you need carpenters, builders and blacksmiths. That's why I came."

"We need more than that. Sawyers, joiners and caulkers. All of them will have work here, Joel."

"I want to return to smithing. Do you expect the iron shipments to arrive any time soon?"

"I only know that Daniel has already sent orders in to Pittsburgh and to Meadville, but with the roads as poor as they are, it'll be slow going for any wagons. It took a week for the first cannons from Pittsburgh to arrive, and that was done with heavy labor. But the roads are in much worse condition now. It'll be weeks taking deliveries of arms. Some of the iron we requested is for the anchors we'll need. Daniel said he's signed a contract with the Steam Machine Company in Pittsburgh to cast our anchors, but we still need nails and bolts. In fact, that's our biggest need."

"And sails, George?"

"Sails and hemp line for rope, both from Philadelphia. We're finally building the fleet, Joel. Can you believe it! And we have three more ships to build, including a 300 ton brig! That is, if we can get the manpower. Wages are good, but it's only temporary work and not many want to give up regular work for temporary."

"It's twice the pay. That's why I came, temporary or not."

Many workers had returned for the same reason. With assurances from the government that all would be paid, the town quickly surpassed the number of workers from their first effort. Finally, there was no Black Rock chain of command to hold them back. The lodgings soon started to fill, including the barn built as barracks. The two Philadelphia men who had lodged with Sara and George had returned to Philadelphia, and Sara actively sought lodgers for the income they would provide. At the shipyard, George recognized another arrival, Samuel Dodge of Cleveland. The promised wages had lured him to Erie too, and George eagerly offered him a week's free lodging in repayment for his hospitality at Cleveland on his escape journey. Dodge readily accepted and joined the others working on the gunboats. The enterprise was now limited only by the available supplies and the weather conditions. They needed coal to fire the blacksmith forge. Wagons navigated the road between Erie and Mercer County hauling the fuel from the Sharon mines. Their relatively close proximity to the Erie shipyard kept the delivery cost low, and Daniel was committed to keeping the project on budget. Consequently, he kept meticulous records, and George saw little of the man who had now more than ever become the driving force behind the fleet. But travel was slow-going on the winter quagmire of roads connecting Erie with all other communities.

The sail cloth and hemp, along with oakum for caulking the seams depended on transportation of several hundred miles from Philadelphia. Worse yet, some of the extra armaments required driving wagon teams over the bogged winter roads from Washington City. For Dobbins, it was a logistical nightmare. Yet when George did observe him, he saw a calmer determination in the man. Finally Daniel had what he desired, and he was resolute in seeing it through. This optimism passed on to all the workers. George's crew on the *Tigress* had also caught the vision. Daily they came to work uncomplaining, in the bitterest of conditions, braving the snow and wind to erect a shelter over the boat. The days began with shoveling away the overnight snow that had drifted over the stacked lumber, then climbing to the joists, and nailing rough-cut boards loosely to a makeshift roofing frame – a temporary house to cover the fifty-ton vessel. *Porcupine*'s hull was finished and ready to slip into the water whenever the harbor's ice thawed. As usual, George was impatient to see the finished project. The bitter cold grated on him. Chafed hands and face were his daily thorn now, and though he didn't complain around the fellow workers, he felt safe airing his feelings at home or with Polly. This night was no exception, and he complained unceasingly. Polly finally had her fill of it.

"Months ago, you said this would not be easy, and now all you do is complain when you visit me. It's become much too tiresome to me, George. I don't wish to be depressed or sullen with you, so if you can find your way back into the cold without my assistance, your mother may need your help this evening with her tenants."

"Polly, you haven't been out to work in this bitter cold. It's a nearly impossible task, even if we had the desire. Most of the men on my crew just go through the motions of building. It's all we can do just to stay warm enough to cut the boards. When spring comes, so will come the British fleet and we won't be ready. The delay the government forced on Mr. Dobbins has set us back, and the winter freeze is taking its toll."

"On whom, George? I've heard no one complain but you."

"I just don't think we can get the ships done before the thaw."

"Then you'll have to finish them *after* the thaw. George, sometimes to appreciate the warmth, one must experience some bitter cold. So just maybe Providence is teaching you that lesson here this winter. Maybe you should pay heed to that."

In these winter months Polly had become a stronger woman, and George had admired her for it – at least until she pointed out his shortcomings. His impatience always became a sticking point for the two of them. Since Christmas they had grown closer, but his intention to finally ask her parents for her hand was continually thwarted, and it was usually because of his own actions. Though he desired her and treated her with respect and was as affectionate to her as decency and modesty would permit, above all he still wanted to get out of the town, and he never hid that. He grew more restless and set on uprooting for the move to Ohio. He even entertained the idea of quitting his work on the ships before they were finished, packing all, and moving west.

"If you don't want me here with you this evening, then I can go. And I can leave Erie too."

"Oh, George, don't be such a child! You know that I want you here, but you must make up your mind as to what *you* want. Can it be any clearer? You have a duty that you undertook with the full trust of Mr. Dobbins, of Mr. Reed, Mr. Williamson. Even when the others faded away, you stayed – not just here in town, but you stayed on the job. You're a leader, George, whether you want it or not. The people here count on you, and those few workers who've remained with you, to show the rest of the country we accept this commitment solemnly and without reservation. George, it's our sacrifice here in Erie that will help us to win back the lake and keep villages safe. Do you understand the responsibility? I mean *really* understand the responsibility? If not, then give it some hard thought. You'll not only let the village and your friends down, you'll let me down." She watched her words sink in. "And more importantly, you'll let yourself down."

"Polly, you talk about letting people down when they trust someone. What about you?"

"What do you mean, George?"

"I'm saying that ever since I escaped last year from the British soldiers at Malden and risked my life to return to you, I've wondered if it was worth the risk I took."

"What on earth are you talking about?"

"When I returned to Erie, I wanted to be with you again, and I arrived to hear that Jesse had been here to see you after I was taken. The way you told me about his capture and how worried you were, well, to me it showed uncommon concern."

"How can you say that! He's your cousin, George. Aren't you worried about him?"

"Worried that he had decided to court you while I was gone and imprisoned, yes!"

"George! What on earth?"

"What am I to think, Polly? Answer me. What am I to think? That he wants to marry you and waited until I was in British hands to say it." It was finally out, and immediately he regretted the words. He waited uneasily for that door to slam.

Polly stared at him, astonished. "George, you can't be serious!"

"As serious as— as I've ever been in my life," he said hesitantly.

"This has been all about your jealousy? All this work on the ships was about your jealousy of me and your own cousin? Is that what has driven you?"

George refused to answer. He stood, defiant, arms folded across his chest. He awaited the answer, any answer. He read the anger in Polly's eyes, felt himself begin to weaken, but refused to give one inch of inner ground. After all, he had his pride, and he must defend it.

Polly was indignant. "George, I'm going to say something you may not want to hear, but it's for our own good. Yours and mine. Listen carefully, and then it's goodnight indeed. Yes, it's true Jesse came here after you had left. He wanted to visit your mother and you before he sailed out. He expected war to come and was worried about all of us here. He wanted to let us know that he'd decided to come back here and settle as soon as he returned from the mission with his ship."

"But he—"

"Stop right there! And please hear me completely and say nothing! He wanted to announce to you and his aunt Sara his engagement. Yes, George, his engagement. He's betrothed to a woman from Buffalo. Her name is Esther and I know little of her, but he was so happy to tell me and wanted you to share in his happiness. No. Don't say anything. I'm not finished. He wanted to come here and settle with her and possibly start in the carpenter's shop with you and have your own business together some day. He even talked about Ohio and that he could sail from there and you could build the ships. But, you see, their plans have been thwarted with his capture too. Only he wasn't as fortunate as you to escape. So, yes, I am worried. I want to meet Esther. I don't even know her last name, so I can't even go to her and comfort her. I know what I felt when they reported your ship taken, and I can't imagine what she's feeling for he's been gone far longer than you. So, if I seem to be overly sympathetic to her plight, maybe it's because you have no empathy yourself. You've been so self-centered and set on getting your way. If you want to move to Ohio and start your new life, then I won't hinder you. In fact, at this point I'll encourage you. Maybe finally being alone will give you time to reflect. Now, that is all I have to say on the subject, and I'll thank you to take your jealousy, and your selfish ways and return home. Some time well spent in caring for your mother might do you some good. I will thank you to not call on me, for I too must take time to consider my future! Good night, George!"

Fort Malden, Canada
Monday, February 8, 1813

The soldiers on the Canadian side of the lake fared no better than the Presque Isle citizenry as the winter cold took its toll. Sickness had run through the ranks, leaving few able-bodied seamen to man the ships, now locked back in the ice of the harbor. Supplies dwindled and the many mouths awaiting provisions at Fort Malden now depended on the slow-moving supply wagons following the King's Way across Upper Canada. General Proctor had many more mouths to feed when he returned with over five hundred prisoners taken at the Battle at Frenchtown on the River Raisin. That stunning defeat to General Harrison's command also brought US General James Winchester to Fort Malden as a prisoner of war. The American advance on reclaiming Fort Detroit was thwarted for the present, but General Proctor and Sir James Yeo understood that holding to both lakes, Ontario and Erie, was vital to the nation's survival. Without the supply ships, the warriors who had followed Tecumseh back from the River Raisin to camp near Detroit were at the mercy of the elements. And there at the King's Naval Yard stood the same perplexing task facing the Erie builders. The British had begun construction on a replacement for the large ship, the 490-ton *HMS Detroit*, and with few experienced carpenters to build her. Feeding the large body of men women and children surrounding and inhabiting the fort would burden the British cause through the war's end. Jesse Harris used the opportunity to get away from Fort Erie while the *Queen Charlotte* lay anchored awaiting the spring thaw. He volunteered to make the trek through the snow on the King's Way, a well-worn wagon road along the southern shore. Transporting flour from the grist mill at Long Point with other soldiers and Provincial Marine allowed him freedom from the fort and any of those assigned to keep close watch on him, if only for a few days. Though he had convinced Lieutenant Stokoe he knew nothing of the attempted desertion of Jack and the others, it fell under his watch. He fabricated a story that was convincing enough, putting all blame on Jack. Dead men tell no tales, and no one disputed that the others had merely wanted to help a fellow sailor night fish, unaware he was deserting. John Chapman avoided a court-martial and possible hanging, and Alexander dodged being tied to the mast for a severe flogging. A relatively minor punishment of two weeks of half-rations was laid upon Jesse with a stern warning from Lieutenant Irvine that this "should be a lesson to an officer in training to never again neglect his duty." Providence indeed smiled upon him, and he vowed to not be so negligent again. Next time he would plan it better.

At Fort Malden Jesse supervised the unloading of six wagon-loads of supplies. Hardly enough to feed the multitudes, but perhaps some little Canadian boy might arrive with two fish.

"You make light of our situation here," Sara said as she watched him check off the supply ledger.

"Not my intent, Miss Hall, but I do try to keep my humor when so much around us is humorless."

"Are you to stay for any length of time, Mr. Harris?"

"For awhile, Miss Hall. With my assignment to the *Queen Charlotte* and her supplies, I'm necessary to the Crown as a supply clerk of sorts for the continuing operations. Of course, I'm needed on the Niagara frontier, but this trip at least gives me some diversion. It becomes so tedious performing shore duty, don't you think?"

"So, that's why you left here without even so much as a 'by your leave' is it, Mr. Harris?"

"Your uncle must have explained to you that I was needed aboard the ship. That wasn't voluntary, I assure you. I didn't find out that I had been reassigned until the morning they placed me on board."

"But even a quartermaster can get leave for—"

"Assistant quartermaster, Miss Hall," he interjected. "And, no I can't get leave. Remember I'm an American, and a pressed sailor isn't permitted to ramble about. He may decide to not return to duty."

"You would return. I know you. Besides, you had freedom here."

"Miss Hall, I had freedom here because I was watched here. Never allowed to travel too far, I was under the orders that kept me tethered to the fort."

"Well, you may get to come here after all. Uncle said that they've offered him the fleet when it's finished. He's declined, of course, but he may yet have you assigned to the fort in the quartermaster building. That wouldn't be disagreeable to you, would it?"

"Yes, it would, Miss Hall."

"Sara."

"Yes, Sara," he said, "it would. I'm a sailor, and I want to be back on the lake as soon as I can. I'm just waiting for the spring thaw like every other man."

"But I don't want to see you go there. There will be a battle eventually. We've heard the reports of the Americans building in Erie and on the Niagara River, and it's just a matter of time until we go out to defeat them. I don't want you there," she said, her voice turning distinctly worried.

"If I must go, it'll be my duty to sail with my friends on the fleet. At any rate, there will be no movement for at least a few months, until the ice is off the lake. So I'll travel by wagon until then."

"And then you return to the *Queen Charlotte*."

"I hope to, yes. I respect Lieutenant Irvine and Lieutenant Stokoe, and they've treated me well enough under the circumstances. I've been given some authority, and I'm trying to not abuse it."

"Jesse, when they finally do battle with the American fleet, where will you be? A quartermaster must still fight the ship, no?"

"I haven't given it too much thought, Sara. That's a long way off and much can happen before we face them. My service in battle isn't a foregone conclusion. I'll go wherever I'm placed. Now if you excuse me, standing in the cold is making my feet go numb, and I see your uncle is watching us from the hill. I don't need to have him on my back either."

Sara cautiously looked up to where her uncle stood on the bank above the shipyard and then openly waved to him. "Jesse, when will I see you again?"

Jesse pretended to focus on his inventory, lowered his voice, "Tomorrow evening, Sara? At the tavern in town?"

"I will be there at 6," she said cheerfully.

"I'll be there at 7," he said and went back to his work.

Sara walked the snow-packed path up to the fort and joined her uncle. Jesse guardedly watched them and finished the last of the inventory, mounted the last empty wagon and rode toward Amherstburg. Captain Scott of the Newfoundland Regiment had orders awaiting the detachment when Jesse arrived. Three wagons carrying a detachment of soldiers were to start at once for the Niagara River and Fort Erie. The final three wagons would make the journey with ammunition on Wednesday. Jesse volunteered to leave immediately. Commodore Hall still had him watched and once again the further he could get from Malden, the better. He hated Fort Erie, couldn't wait to get free from its confines, but he hated Fort Malden where Hall and his niece had their spyglass on him. At least the week of travel between the two would make him a moving target.

The first evening of travel through Essex County was an uneasy one for Jesse. Once again he avoided Sara Hall and, though he knew Commodore Hall would undoubtedly approve of them not meeting, that gnawing feeling that in some way he had invoked the commodore's anger with this speedy retreat kept him on edge. He expected at any moment to hear horses following, carrying soldiers with orders to arrest him and bring him back to Fort Malden. Late at night, they reached the junction of the road leading to Point Pelee, and there they bedded down with blazing fires for warmth.

"Jesse," the voice quietly called to him.

"Here. Who is it?"

"Alexander. Can we talk?"

The figure stepped near the firelight and Jesse saw the worried look. He and Alexander had never discussed the failed escape attempt since the night it all unraveled. Both knew they were being watched, and they avoided all friendly camaraderie, even on the journey out to Malden, had even placed themselves in distant wagons to avoid any indication of familiarity. At Malden, they had stayed in separate barracks those three days of supply duty.

"Jesse, I don't know if you've abandoned the idea of escape," he whispered. "But I haven't. When we get to Fort Erie, I'm asking for transfer to Lake Ontario. If I can get to Fort George, I can make my escape there. I've been watched. You've been watched, and if we stumble in anyway, it'll be the lash again. I've settled it in my own mind. Will you come with me?"

"If we both try to transfer to Ontario, that request by itself will arouse suspicion. As soon as the command sees the appeal, it'll be denied. Look, if you really believe you can make your escape from there, don't let me hinder you. We may just make a better break of it going on our own."

"Jesse, I don't blame you for Jack's death. We all took our chances, but it's time for me to take my chance. I'm only asking that you assist me in my transfer. Put in a word for me wherever you can."

"I will. Don't be too hasty about it, though. When we return to the fort, see Lieutenant Irvine, and request it. But don't be surprised if he denies the request himself. You know the talk. The ships here on Lake Erie will need more men as soon as the ice clears. I don't believe they'll spare any men for Ontario."

"Then I'll waste no time waiting for them to keep me. I'll request it at once. I'm sorry, Jesse, you're a good fair man, but I need to do what I must to get to the States."

"What about Chapman? Is he going with you?"

"He is with the 41st. He knows they'll never transfer him. I guess his fate is yours."

"I understand, and I wish you good fortune. And if you get to the other side, let them know what's being built out here, the armaments, anything of value."

"You mean spy?"

"Well, yes, in short, spy."

Alexander grinned widely. "Happy to."

"And if you get to Buffalo before me, please get a message to Esther, the girl I told you about. Let her know I'm well, and I'll get to her as soon as I can find a safe way back."

"I will, but I have a half crown to bet that you'll be waiting for me in Buffalo."

"Make it American dollars and we have a bet."

"American dollars it will be."

Chapter Fourteen
Erie, Pennsylvania
March 1813

Henry Eckford's visit with Commodore
Chauncey to the shipyards proved fruitful. Not only
had Dobbins received the blessing of the
commodore, he had also received revised plans. The
order of a brig to counter the *Queen Charlotte*
spurred the men to begin with renewed enthusiasm.
Then came the order from the navy for a second
brig. What had started as a relatively large project of
four gunboats had evolved into a massive effort of
the original two gunboats, the *Porcupine* and newly
named *Ariel*, and now two large brigs of over 260
tons, with orders for two more ships. An entire
flotilla of six vessels was now underway at Presque
Isle. Scrutinizing the ongoing work at the mouth of
Lee's Run, Ebenezer and George selected the mouth
of Cascade Creek for the two largest ships, further
away from the harbor entrance, about a mile beyond
the village. The pilot boat *Ariel,* named after a
character in Shakespeare's play *The Tempest,* had
already been built on the blocks there and the new
naval yard afforded deeper water for the heavier
brigs.

A change was coming over George. His
concern for his mother and what had developed into
pneumonia burdened him. He thought little on
Polly, seeing her on occasion, but distancing
himself from her. She and her mother had continued
to care for Sara on those days when he worked at
the shipyard, keeping her comfortable until he

returned in the evenings. Her two tenants had moved to the recently constructed lodging. George had never liked staying at one project too long, his patience waning, pushing him to complete each assignment in as little time as possible. He consequently left the carpentry on occasion and drove wagons to solicit what very little iron trickled into the village. This kept him clear of any confrontations with Polly, and yet with his mother's prognosis unsettled, he returned to join the growing numbers of builders. He settled into the routine of the frigid work and supervised his crew's assembly of large shelters at Cascade Creek for the brig construction. By March 12 the keels were laid and ready for framing, at least partial frames. Early in the month Williamson assigned George's crew to build more barracks to house 250 workers. Many who had lodged with local citizens now moved to these barn-like structures. The old rundown French fort underwent rebuilding to help house the growing militia arriving to defend the dockyards. Lake ice still protected the town from attack, and the heavy snows repeatedly dumped on the roads between Erie and Buffalo, Erie and Pittsburgh, Erie and every other outside town and city. They were cutoff, and arrival of needed materials was at a near standstill. Dobbins frequently contended with the nearly impassable roads beyond Presque Isle to bargain for any supplies to build his fleet. But the men at least had the one critical item, a limitless supply of timber. In those quiet evenings after work, George kept his mother abreast of the progress, once remarking that they were working so fast that a tree standing in the morning had become a deck plank by evening.

Commodore Chauncey had hired a new supervisor of construction from a ship construction firm in New York. Noah Brown arrived with laborers and vast experience building US Navy vessels. Brown's expertise paid off, and soon he had complete control of the growing fleet. In due course, Daniel had relinquished all control of his project's manual labor, and concentrated on appropriating supplies, financing, armament, and recruiting, making several tedious journeys to Meadville, to Pittsburgh, and even taking sleighs on the ice of the Niagara to Black Rock to transport cannon. He was seldom seen. Noah Brown was a perfect match for the men's individual talents, and the workers thrived in the teamwork. George's crew readily faced the bitter cold with energy and vision, confident in the leadership. They liked Brown personally and did everything he asked of them. He was a genial sort, readily joking with the men and using all his contacts to draw in the best workers from as far away as Philadelphia and even in New York. But the fleet still needed a commander.

To Daniel's pleasant surprise, Lieutenant Elliott was transferred from Black Rock to Sackett's Harbor to command the vessels on Lake Ontario. He also found that Lieutenant Angus, who had rebuffed all his requests for men and materials, had been at loggerheads with Commodore Chauncey and received reassignment to Delaware to handle gunboats for coastal defense. At about the same time, a young master commandant from Rhode

Island had had his fill of commanding gunboats on the east coast and had requested a transfer. Using his political contacts through his wife's family, Oliver Hazard Perry wrote to the Secretary of the Navy for a position on the Great Lakes where he hoped to gain glory for himself. The secretary forwarded the request to Commodore Chauncey at Sackett's Harbor. Having no desire to journey to the Erie shipyards for the foreseeable future, Chauncey was overjoyed to get a man with experience in ship-building supervision. Perry's appointment would allow a Navy presence at the project and give Chauncey stricter control over those pests of Presque Isle while he tended to the more important duty of gaining control of Lake Ontario. He had authorized the transfer immediately. It didn't take long for word of the new appointment to make the rounds through the village. Few knew of the man, but Noah Brown had occasion to meet Perry in New York and was agreeable to his appointment, and he told his work crews so.

"He is a strict disciplinarian, but he is fair. He tends to lose his temper when he sees incompetence, yet he will encourage anyone pulling his own weight, anyone who's willing to work for the common end. I believe he'll be just the man for this enterprise."

"When may we expect him?" Williamson asked.

"At any time. Daniel left days ago for Black Rock to requisition more supplies and is to bring Captain Perry here by sleigh. He'll stay at the Dobbins home while here. Daniel's also gone to inform the commodore that we'll be fleet ready by the first of June."

"A bit optimistic, wouldn't you say?" asked Willamson.

"That's Daniel for you. Always looking for the bright side."

"Mr. Brown?"

"What is it George?"

"We have a crisis building at the dockyards, and I thought you should be aware of it."

"I have no desire for guesswork, so be plain, man," Brown said.

"For days the food has been running low. With the supplies arriving slowly, we haven't been able to keep up with all the workers' needs. With Daniel gone, it falls on your capacity. One of the crews asked me to come to you. We need provisions. The men made it plain that they will rise up if they don't get food – and soon. Mr. Brown, we may lose our workers and we can ill-afford the crews walking off the job."

"What provisions are near here that you know of? Any farms that would be willing to sell their cattle?"

"I know of two or three along the turnpike road toward Waterford. Everyone in the surrounding farms has already sold and slaughtered. Those sources have been exhausted."

"George, have your crew pulled off the *Ariel* and send them out to buy whatever cattle are still available, then drive them here. Peter, pull your crew and have them get their rifles and see what meat they can bring back from the forests. These workers deserve to eat, and I will not have the project halted for lack of food."

The men had welcomed the order and within the hour, they had saddled horses and spread into the outlying farms, buying all the cattle the families were willing to sell and they started driving them into the stockyards in town. The hunters of the group ranged into the plentiful forests. By that evening the current crisis was averted. Cattle began to arrive, and the hunters' travels began to bear fruit. In four days, the hunters brought in venison to add to the provisions. Noah Brown had gained the men's respect and they were now willing to do anything the superintendent asked of them. Brown himself was satisfied with the abilities of those first workers who had arrived, but to build all the vessels and have them ready to engage the British by summer, the government would need a massive influx of workers that Brown just did not have.

"George, I've never seen such dedication. Each of the men engaged in this operation appears as if he's on a mission of his own. I'm pleased with those we have, but we still need more. Are we certain that we've drawn from all the wells of laborers?"

"Mr. Brown, I don't know where else we can get workers. Daniel offered high wages, and we've recruited from the nearby towns and villages, but not many are willing to come here. The word of our halt circulated after we first had to cease the operation, and that still causes some reluctance. Many just don't believe they'll be paid. Others excuse themselves because of the conditions. Do you have any untapped resources?"

"I've written my brother in New York to send me men from the shipyards there. Those are fine workers, and when they arrive, they'll bring experience. But we still need more, and they'll be days in getting here. We also need shipbuilding tools, which they may bring with them. Your crews will soon exhaust themselves, and I can't have them constantly moving from one vessel to another. With fatigue comes mistakes, and we can ill-afford the time to undo any errors. Then, all the ships need to be ready at the same time. This fleet cannot engage the enemy piecemeal, or they'll be destroyed piecemeal."

"This Captain Perry that's to command here, he will bring men with him, won't he?"

"I would assume so, George, but we can't wait for that answer. Use any of your acquaintances and have them persuade anyone with experience to come to this place with all possible speed."

"I will, but no promises." One thought had burdened George, and he sensed the time had come to air his complaint. "Mr. Brown, most men that I've been acquainted with are craftsmen. House carpenters. If they do come here, they won't like rushing to finish the job. We all want to do our job properly, but we've been rushed. The men who might join will be reluctant since they don't like doing haphazard construction either."

"George, you tell them we don't want any extras on the vessels. Plain work is all I require. These ships will serve only one battle. If we're victorious, that will be all that is required of the ships. But if the British defeat us, well, then the work will be good enough to be captured."

A commotion rose from townsfolk out braving the cold in the town. A small crowd gathered along Peach Street in the falling snow, waving to a horse drawn sleigh. Word had spread, and their anticipation was finally rewarded. "Mr. Brown, I think there's our answer to how many men are coming."

Daniel Dobbins's sleigh arrived with the young master commandant riding huddled against the cold. A young boy, bundled in the back seat under several blankets and packed in by several trunks and bags, peered through a small opening in the cloth.

"Captain Perry, it's good to see you at last," Noah said.

"Mr. Brown, I'm delighted to be here at last. The journey was a bit demanding, heavy snow and all, but I'm prepared to do my duty here."

"Captain Perry, sir, I'm George Armstrong. Pleased to have you here."

"Thank you, George. Mr. Dobbins and Commodore Chauncey have informed me of what has been accomplished here thus far. I must say, you've had a rough go of it, but it will be worth it in the end. We'll bring glory to the country and to this place."

"And who is this in the back, sir?"

"This is my brother, Midshipman James Perry. James, it's safe to uncover yourself now."

The young boy climbed from the sleigh and stood beside his brother, a wool blanket still clutched around his shoulders. *Midshipman*, George thought. *He's younger than Seth would be, and he's assigned to a fighting ship. When the inevitable comes, I pray he lives through the conflict.*

"Will there be others coming here to work, sir? We still need many more skilled workers," George said.

"Commodore Chauncey assured me there will be workers following us here. In the past two weeks I've been with him at Sackett's Harbor. Those that can be spared are ordered to repair here at all possible speed."

"No disrespect to you, sir, but we've heard these promises before," George said.

Daniel Dobbins gazed steadily at him. George grasped the meaning in the look. He had rashly opened his mouth again, and he tried to explain away his frustration, none too successfully.

"I understand your apprehension, George. I believe with the arrival of a Naval presence here, our needs for this project will soon be met," Dobbins quickly interjected.

"I'll personally see to it," Perry said. "Let's at least go down to the shipyard so I can have a look at what you've accomplished thus far. I've no doubt you'll do your duty, and I'm confident we'll get sufficient help to complete the task before June."

The men walked down Peach Street, looked over the escarpment, and to the dockyards, bustling with activity. Perry was satisfied with the overall progress, vowed to pick up the pace with all the workers he could hire.

"The men are drilling holes for trenails? You have not enough iron for nails?"

"None," Brown said.

"We shall have to remedy that at once," Perry said.

"With respect, Sir, we've exhausted all supplies, have ordered more but to no avail."

"Then I'll personally travel to Pittsburgh if I must and see to it that we have all the iron they can scrounge brought here at once. I want nails, scraps, bars, anything that can be of use. What cannot be used on the ships' construction will be used in the cannon to tear down enemy rigging when the time comes. We'll also need cannon transported here soon."

"I've brought a few from Black Rock already, but Lieutenant Elliott didn't want to spare any more in the event he needed to repel attacks on his base," Dobbins said.

"Then I'll write Commodore Chauncey personally. Whatever he can spare from Sackett's Harbor will be brought here. We need to contract for cannon from Washington, from Philadelphia, and from Pittsburgh, Fort Fayette. These must be here by the time the vessels are ready for the lake. We'll also need them for defense," Perry said. "What provision have you made for repelling invasion?"

"Sir, I've had my carpenters build a blockhouse out by the Little Bay as a first line," he said, pointing to the distant peninsula. "We've repaired the blockhouse on the heights over there and have a position for our artillery piece," George said.

"One? You'll need placement for at least three more. Let that be a priority too. The spring thaw will come soon enough, and we must be vigilant. Strengthen the blockhouse and build redoubts. We'll need artillery out on that point of land there, near the harbor," he said pointing to the Little Bay. "We need more militia and regulars here too. General Dearborn can't spare us any at this point. He's gathering his forces for the attack on Canada as soon as the ice clears. Once they have Fort George in hand, we should soon have the soldiers we need to defend this station. Any other artillery the militia can bring we'll use on the gunboats if necessary. I'll get that request to General Meade immediately."

George whispered to Dobbins as Perry walked the escarpment and looked out over the harbor. "He certainly does grab the bull by the horns, doesn't he?"

"What do you mean?" asked Dobbins.

"He seems rather impetuous and somewhat impatient," he whispered.

Dobbins laughed quietly. "Then you two should get along handsomely."

A sleigh rapidly approached the men, and George recognized Polly sitting beside the driver and huddled against the cold, was happy to see her, but restrained any show.

"George, I need to bring you back at once. Your mother asked for you."

He needed no further explanation, climbed into the sleigh without a word. In minutes they had pulled before the house, and George rushed in. The fire had been stoked and the house was extremely warm. Sara lay on her bed, her favorite quilt pulled up to her neck. She was no longer flushed with fever, but pale and calm. Polly's mother sat at her bedside, clutching her hand, the doctor standing grimly at the washstand. She opened her eyes dimly, saw George, a smile on her lips. "George, thank you," she said weakly. "Be good to Polly." And she was gone.

In the parlor, George sat in his mother's chair, the one she favored when knitting, the one she pulled to the table when she laid out her cloth for quilting, the one she had sat in when she held him as a little boy. He sat. He stared at the floor quietly. Then he cried. For the first time since his brother had died, he felt the real sting of loss. Polly left the doctor in the bedroom and came up behind him, bent over and lay her head on his shoulder, kissed his neck and wrapped her arms around him. Then she fastened her coat and silently left. George was finally alone, and the feeling was not what he had expected.

Fort Erie
Saturday, April 2, 1813

Ice had begun to melt farther out on the lake, and a few warmer days had given the fort a respite from the heavy snows, the frigid winds, the monotonous gray skies. The orders had come from General Prevost, and Jesse went quietly about his work, checking ledgers, filling orders. The *Lady Prevost* and *General Hunter* were being loaded for an operation, and by the supplies that Jesse saw on the requisitions, it was to be a major campaign.

"Jesse, can we speak freely?" John Chapman stood at the quartermaster's door searching about.

"Yes, John, no one is here. What's happened?"

"I heard the rumors among the men. You know how rumors are, they always have basis on some fact. The men have heard that the Americans are planning an expedition against us across the Niagara."

He had Jesse's full attention, and he closed the door to any eavesdroppers. "Over the ice?" Jesse asked.

"No. They say that an army is building at Sackett's Harbor, and that can only mean one thing. When the ice is gone, they'll attack – possibly Kingston or even Fort George. This could be only a few weeks away. We have to defend the fort here, so the *Charlotte* will be prepared accordingly. We'll stay here unless we're needed there to repel a bigger invasion, possibly setting a blockade on the Niagara River."

Jesse dismissed the rumor with a wave. "That's nothing to be too excited about. We're always being readied for some perceived attack."

"There's more." Jesse saw the expression change. John became more guarded, lowered his voice.

"Well?"

"Three men deserted across the ice. One was Alexander."

"What? Did anyone know if he made it? Was he captured?"

"He made it to the American side. Apparently all three of them made it. At least none of us will be implicated in his desertion since he did it after he transferred to Fort George. This was entirely on his own, and you must say so if the command comes to you, Jesse. We were his closest friends, and the inquiry will surely come back to us," John said.

"We knew nothing of it," Jesse said firmly. He was angry that his opportunity had passed him by, but inwardly he was relieved to know Alexander had made good on the escape. He hoped Alexander would remember his promise to find Esther for him. He could have gone with him. No. It was better this way. More men involved in the conspiracy would have aroused suspicion. Maybe none of them would've made it. Still, three men had crossed to the United States, and he should have been one of them.

"I guess I'll lose my bet with him."

"What bet?" asked Chapman.

"Oh, just something we talked about once on a trip back from Malden. I'm glad for him, John. Maybe our time will soon come."

"I pray it does, Jesse. I haven't given up on our getting across to the states. I've been there twice before the war – near the falls it was. Lovely country, eh? And you? Where will you live once you get back to the States? New York?"

"That needs no thought. I'll return to Buffalo and find Esther, and when we're married, we'll move to Erie, Pennsylvania, where my cousin is. I had hoped to work together with him in our own business. Of course, my aunt says that George has his hopes set on a move to Ohio when he's married, so I may have to just settle for following him to Ohio. What about you? In New York, I assume?"

"Ohio sounds about as good as any land I know of. At least I'll know one person there. Maybe we can work together, eh?"

"George is a carpenter, and I had long thought about joining him, but I plan to sail merchant ships out of Ohio. Maybe deliver his goods for him," Jesse said.

"Then I'll sail along with you."

"I'd like that, John. Now, keep an ear to the ground for any more rumors. We'll soon know what's fact and what's not."

"And then?"

"And then we plan. We'll see what hand we're dealt and we'll play that. Maybe it'll be the hand that deals us to the Americans." He looked over John's shoulder to the opening door. "Ahh, Sergeant McDonough! Right on time as usual. How can I help you? Thank you, Private Chapman, I will take care of those supplies this afternoon."

The sergeant pushed open the door and strolled in purposefully, and John gave McDonough a wide berth and went for the door.

"Private!"

"Yes, Sergeant McDonough?"

"What requisition did you bring to this Yankee boy?"

Chapman stammered. "Uhhh… Requi…"

"Sergeant McDonough," Jesse interrupted, "it is none of your business what errand the officers send these men on. He may be in your division, but this man is assigned to the *Queen Charlotte*, and you're interfering with his duties. That seems to be a preoccupation with you, doesn't it?"

"You insubordinate little – I'll have respect from you if I have to flay you alive!"

"Now, Sergeant," Jesse smiled, "surely you forget that I'm now acting quartermaster in the Royal Navy, under Lieutenant Irvine's orders, and I believe, why yes! I outrank you. So, unless you have official business with the quartermaster, kindly take your intrigues out of my sight. You did have business here, of course?"

"My business has to do with you two. I know you're scheming, and I have watched you — you and your accomplice here. I know you have plans, and I will find them out. Then I'll personally command the firing squad that executes the judgment."

"Sergeant, surely you have better duties to attend to than following me around or eavesdropping on official business. If not, I can see that Lieutenant Irvine can have you reassigned somewhere else."

"Mr. Harris, you don't have that much power!"

"No? My dear Sergeant McDonough, Commodore Hall is planning to give me command of a ship one day. You had better hope for your sake you're not assigned to my ship. Oh, don't look so stunned. If we get back to Fort Malden, I shall introduce you to him and his niece. Sara would love to meet the soldier who gave her fiancé such a hard time," Jesse said.

"Fiancé?"

At the door, Chapman closed his eyes and shook his head. *You didn't just say that!* Jesse saw the look.

"Private Chapman, I didn't tell you of my betrothal?"

"No, sir, you didn't," John said. McDonough stared incredulously.

"Hmm… It must have slipped my mind. Sergeant McDonough, apparently my, er, friend here isn't as close as you had assumed. Surely, I would have divulged this to a trusted – what was the word – accomplice, wouldn't I?"

McDonough looked at Chapman standing at the door, who merely shrugged his shoulders. The sergeant turned, shouldered Chapman out of the way.

"Oh, and Sergeant! Close the door when you leave."

The door slammed. Jesse nearly doubled over stifling the laughter.

"Are you insane?"

"What are you talking about, John?"

"Don't you think he'll check your story?"

"John, he doesn't know the commodore, and if he were to meet him, he'll not be so stupid as to ask him personal information about the commodore's niece. He can't ask anyone else because no one else here knows about our engagement."

"But if we go back to Fort Malden –"

"John, when we sail back to Fort Malden, then I'll deal with that. But as you said, it doesn't look likely with the buildup on Lake Ontario. It'll be a long time until we go that way. And who knows?

We may not be here long enough to make the journey, eh?"

"I hope not, for both our sakes. But we know he's been watching us, and probably having others watch us."

"Then we must be discreet. 'Wise as serpents,' scripture says."

"Yes, or we'll have our heads crushed under their heels. Keep a sharp eye out, Jesse."

## Chapter Fifteen
### Presque Isle
### Wednesday, May 19, 1813

George leaned on his mallet at the base of the blocks, the *Porcupine*'s weight poised against the stays, ready to slide into Presque Isle Bay. Daniel Dobbins stood on the opposite side, mallet in hand. It was early morning, and it seemed the entire town had gathered at the dockyards or on the bluffs above to take in the spectacle. Here the culmination of months of work awaited the order. The murmur had silenced and with a collective breath held, they heard the order.

"Stand away! Gentlemen, if you are ready. One. Two. Three!"

George and Daniel each swung their mallets at the supporting stays, knocking them clear, and the screech of the wood on wood sounded across the silent harbor The *Porcupine* slid down from its wooden cradle and launched into the water. The crowd's cheer erupted with the splash, and the waves rolled across the harbor toward the Presque Isle peninsula. George saw the pride reflected in Daniel's misty eyes. Almost a year had passed since their escape, and here they finally witnessed the result of all the sweat, the frost-bitten bodies, the sleepless nights, the roadblocks, manmade and natural, rocking steadily in the harbor, ready for her rigging. Then Rufus Reed and Ebenezer Crosby took up their mallets, and to the applause of the crowd, sent the *Tigress* down her wooden rails and into the harbor.

The first step to completing the vessels for the coming operation against the British began in earnest. Samuel Hambleton had arrived along with the first of Perry's contingent of sailors, on orders from Rhode Island. These sailors were a remarkable lot, and George immediately admired their tenacity. Young and eager to show their daring against the British, they were few in number, yet experienced in ships of war, some having engaged the British already on the Atlantic. They immediately began the task of mounting the guns aboard the *Porcupine* and *Tigress*. Using block and tackle and straining at the ropes, the sailors lifted and swung one 32-pounder long gun onto the first vessel. George had helped to modify the carriage on the *Porcupine*, and the gun settled perfectly into place. Although she carried only one gun, the ship would be fast enough to chase down any British ship and hurl the 32-pound shot nearly a mile into its sides. Within the hour they had the first gun mounted, and then they advanced on the *Tigress*. The next 32-pounder long gun was lifted and swung into its cradle on the bow and bolted into position. Now they only had to wait for the next cannons to come from Buffalo.

With the arrival of another shipment of oakum, the caulkers immediately set to work making the *Scorpion* watertight. Though she was smaller than the *Porcupine* in length and tonnage, she was destined to carry two guns rather than one, a carronade on a swivel mount, and a long gun on a swivel. Sitting in the water, awaiting the next cannons to arrive, she looked to George as fierce a ship as he had ever seen. His primary duties had been varied and he had taken a measure of pride in the first two vessels. Though the *Scorpion* had been the product of another work crew, he felt ownership of this vessel too. In fact, all the vessels now floating in the harbor or on the blocks being framed were in some way his. He had been involved since the first day of tree felling and willingly shared that fact with the newly arriving seaman of Samuel Hambleton's party. He became obnoxious.

He stood on the shore, arrogantly smiling at the three vessels floating in the water, watching a 10-man crew heft the wooden masts destined for the *Scorpion*. A young black seaman stood beside him, arms folded, imitating his stance. George saw the mimicry, and he resolved to engage the young man.

"Quite a ship, isn't she?" he offered.

"She seems to float well enough. How will she take to the lake water?" the seaman asked.

"She'll hold her own, I warrant," George said.

"Hold her own? Ha! Will she hold men?"

George grew impatient with this man questioning his abilities. His cheeks flushed. "What do you mean by that?"

"I see she is holding the weight of the first gun. And after they finish mounting the second, will she be able to hold men enough for battle against the British squadron?"

"I built you a strong ship. She'll hold all the crew you can crowd on her deck, mister."

"You built?"

"We. I've been on this project since last September, and I and the workers who remained here when all others lost the vision, have built strong ships to face any enemy," George said.

"Have you sailed against an enemy?"

"I had the displeasure of being captured near Fort Detroit when my ship was taken last summer. What about you?"

The seaman looked into his eyes, ignored the question. "How did you like it when they fired at you?" the young seaman asked.

"They, uh, didn't fire at us. They just came aboard and took us all prisoner," George said awkwardly.

"So, they came with a boarding party? Tell me, how long did you resist when they thrust the boarding pikes, and bayonets, and swung the axes at your men?"

"Well, we didn't resist. We had no idea a war had started. They just boarded us and took the whole lot prisoner," George admitted.

The sailor stood an open stance, arms folded and looked George up and down.

"Look here, Armstrong, I'm sure you built a seaworthy vessel. I'm sure you put your entire being into it. And I can believe that this was your labor of resolve to fight British tyranny. But you've no idea what you're contending against when you get out into the fray. I've watched you. You know your way around wood. I've seen your supervision of the crews on the brig. You're a good worker, and the fellows in your crew respect you. But good workmanship is meaningless out there in the fight. What all this comes down to is this: You're not an entity just to yourself. We're all part of a larger mission. When these ships you're so proud of get out there in open water, they'll have to endure the pounding of cannonballs spewing from the smoke and fire of cannon like we mounted today. Did you see the size of the ball that comes out of those?"

George stood timidly and listened, avoided the seaman's gaze. He had indeed seen the size of shot they would fire. He focused on the ships in the harbor, looked to the brig on the blocks, nearly ready for her launching. He watched the crews busily caulking the seams and painting the wood, wood that would one day feel the iron impact thrown from British cannon.

"Did you?" the seaman repeated.

"No," he lied.

"No. Well, I suggest you see 'em. Take a long, close look at 'em. The men who crew these ships will have no time to think when the roar of the guns starts. No time to react. We'll all have to hope your ships will withstand the beating. And do you understand that they won't? I sailed on the *USS Constitution*. Cannonballs bounced off her sides. We'll have no such luck with your vessels. Iron, my friend, heavy iron will hit the sides of your Presque Isle wood and will shatter that wood into splinters. You ever had a splinter in your wood working jobs?"

"Yes," George said, understanding the meaning. "Many times."

"Ever had one the size of a spear run through your guts? I've seen 'em. That iron ball smashing into the ship will send splinters of all sizes, as big as a fingernail, embedding itself in the eyes, or a boarding pike, skewering you like a rabbit over the coals. Then we'll get in close, and they'll fire bags of scrap iron, langrage to cut our sails and rigging. But much of it will hit the men. That's what will become of your ships. Are they strong enough? For God's sake, I hope so, for I'll be on one of those vessels you're so proud of. And where will you be? Are you confident enough in your craftsmanship to dare sailing on one of these alongside us? Captain Perry will need men. Are you willing to trust your workmanship, to stand beside us on the deck and watch us fall? Friend, your arrogance will serve no function out there in battle."

George finally turned to the seaman. He had no words, knew the man was right. He merely looked at him and shook his head. The seaman slapped him on the shoulder, smiled affably. "Name's James Bennett," he said, and he walked toward the brig, climbed the scaffolding, disappearing over the edge, his head emerging above the gunwale to look down on George. "Good luck, Armstrong."

From down below, at this angle, the fighting deck looked much deeper, but the full realization came over George that Bennett and these other men would have nowhere to hide, to duck for cover when the cannons roared at each other. Their battleground was a deck 113 feet long and only 32 feet wide. His pride in his work on the ships faded, his selfishness replaced by a growing admiration for the men who would sail them into battle.

Admonished, George returned to the town, stopped by Wilkinson's shop, and saw General Meade leaving. The sail makers who had arrived weeks ago finally had cloth arriving, and the town hall had turned into a sail loft. The entire town organized for the project, and anywhere George went, he saw or heard of someone new joining the operation. Meade had just left Wilkinson with an order for more work. Before he left for Pittsburgh to speed up the delivery of more cannon and other supplies, Captain Perry had determined the defenses needed reinforcement and had sent his request to Meade. Wilkinson ordered his carpenters to strengthening the redoubts to repel an invasion. British ships, curious about the progress in the harbor, had ventured past the entrance several times and Perry had assumed they might be reconnoitering for a possible invasion. If the British gained control of this eastern end of the lake, the town was in danger. Of primary importance was the blockhouse on the peninsula out by Little Bay, their first line of defense. General Meade had ordered the militia to move in a battery of field artillery and set them on the low rise near the harbor entrance. The three guns would stall for time while defenders prepared to protect the heights. Meade had no doubt they would be overrun, had ordered the work only as a gesture to reassure the town that they would defend them. Wilkinson knew they could never stop an invasion if the British really resolved to take the town. But he agreed to the work, assigned George to get a detail and begin.

"Mr. Wilkinson, you know it's futile."

"Challenging, George, but I don't think it's completely futile. And even if I did, do you think

I'd allow anyone in the town to think it too? We don't need a panic here like when you first arrived."

"Wouldn't it be more prudent to let the folks know what we're facing so they can at least save themselves?"

"No, George. They'll need to make their own safety precautions when the time comes. But to allow the town to believe we can't repel an attack, will do more than incite panic. It'll embolden the British and the Indian allies. There are spies everywhere. It's a game of chess. They know what we're doing, and we know what they're doing. They already know we have ships, how many, and soon what armament each has. But we also know what the enemy has. Word travels very quickly, George. I know that not all those observers at the launch were the newspaper writers. It'll be a matter of only a few days until the British have our entire disposition. We already know they're getting a new commander for their fleet, a Captain Barclay to replace Commodore Hall. We know they're building a new brig at Malden, and Captain Perry thinks that could tip the balance in their favor. No need to let the townspeople know it too."

"What's he plan to do about it?"

"As soon as he returns, he and Daniel will leave for Buffalo to assist Commodore Chauncey. We hear rumors of an assault finally on Fort George. If they succeed, that'll keep the British on the defense while we continue our work here."

"Then we won't need the defenses?"

"We'll still need them, but they'll make a very strong wall against a smaller force. Sailing Master

Taylor has a small detail of seamen that arrived with him, and he'll be in command until the captain returns. You may use any of them for help with your construction if they're not assigned to rigging and sail duties on the gunboats."

"Not necessary, Mr. Wilkinson. The carpenters that worked with me on the blockhouse will be good enough."

"When that's finished to General Meade's satisfaction, you will strengthen the old French Fort. You see him about his needs for that. There'll soon be plenty of militia to help with that. George, you're a good worker, and I've given you much responsibility. Don't think it has gone unnoticed. I personally am grateful for your leadership."

George collected a box of his tools, stowed them in the buckboard and drove home. *Leadership*, he thought. *There it is again – that word that Polly used.* It was humbling to know that his work had done some good. But Bennett's words cast doubt in his abilities. He drove his horse past the Freer house, decided to take a chance on seeing Polly. He'd spoken very little to her in the weeks since his mother's death, had hoped to repair a shattered relationship, and knew he had to make the first steps. He tied his horse to the hitching post. Polly came to the front porch. "George, it's good to see you."

"It's good to visit with you again too, Polly. Have you leave for a while?"

"I have. Let me get a shawl."

An awkward silence passed between the two after she joined him on the porch, and they walked quietly. Words tumbled over in his head, and he kept checking himself on every thought that came to him. He didn't know her feelings anymore, and whatever they were, she seemed reluctant to share them. One idea had nagged at him all morning, and she was the only one with whom he could share it.

"Polly, I've given much thought to what I'm to do next."

Silence.

"These men gathering here will soon fight these vessels out on the lake. I've seen their preparation. The first of them seem well-trained, but there aren't enough of them. They'll need other volunteers if they don't get enough seamen from the Navy. I'm considering joining them."

Polly listened intently, stopped, and she looked deep into George's eyes, tears filling hers. George waited for her to speak. She said nothing, continued to look into his eyes. Then she put her head down, and walked on, George at her side. He too looked at the ground, hesitant.

"They'll face the *Queen Charlotte* eventually. A deserter arrived in Buffalo recently. By the reports we heard, Jesse was aboard the ship. He'd been mistreated but apparently has gained favor with some officers, and he's still looking for his chance to break away. If he's on board when they do battle, I want to be there to free him. If we fail and I'm taken prisoner, at least I'll know he's safe and we can chance an escape together. I listened to one of these black seamen who've been in conflicts. He's a free man but still wants to do battle. I still have no desire to kill, but I can't sit idly by while Jesse goes into battle, knowing that I might be able to help him. Polly, it's a frightening thing. He told me what happens to the ships, to the men. I don't do this recklessly, and I've no insane desire to throw my life away foolishly, but I think that honor commands me to help in some way. At least I can live with knowing I tried. Anyway, I needed to tell you that."

They walked silently on, passing through the town, circling past the heights where they watched work crews finish loading another cannon onboard the *Scorpion*. Polly paused, lost in thought, her hands clasped together in that meditative way of hers. George never knew her to refrain from speaking her mind, but she remained quiet, absorbed. Silently they walked back through town and returned to the Freer house. George mutely walked her to the front porch. Then he turned to leave.

"George." He heard her voice call as he untied his horse, "I'm proud of you."

He drove the buckboard out to the Little Bay on Presque Isle, stopping to pick up his friends from the work crew along the way. Few tall trees remained, and these soon fell by the ax, destined to strengthen the new blockhouse and the gun emplacements where three six-pounder cannon guarded the bay. A detachment of soldiers or raiding party of Indians could not gain a foothold here unseen. With no cover on the beach, friend and foe alike were now targets for a hailstorm of iron and lead. The men dug deep into the sand, burying the pointed logs, packing soil and sand between the abatis and the walls of the blockhouse. *That should help absorb the shock of a ship's cannon,* George thought. Defenders here would give a very good accounting of themselves. By nightfall the men had strengthened the position, had packed their tools, and gathered at the militia's cooking fires.

Erie, Pennsylvania<br>
Saturday, May 29, 1813

The men once again went to work with a determined will. Purser Samuel Hambleton brought more supplies from Waterford. Lieutenant Holdup went to Buffalo to bring in men and supplies, but for all their efforts, the required supplies still trickled in like a drying summer stream. Then, calamity struck the shipyards. Since the attempted launching of the first brig on Monday, it had been stuck on the ramps. A timber support had collapsed and wedged itself against the hull. Though the brig had slipped down the ramp about 10 feet, it was now solidly stuck. Noah Brown had sent word to Perry at Sackett's Harbor that they were ready to launch; however, this new report of the failed attempt did not reach them, for Perry was not there. A rider returned to bring other news.

"Fort George has fallen."

"When?" George asked.

"Yesterday. Commodore Chauncey's fleet bombarded the fort while the infantry landed. Captain Perry commanded one of the ships."

The news spread over the town in a wave of excitement. With Fort George fallen, Black Rock was safer. The residents of Buffalo could sleep easier at night. And now the fleet at Erie had only one nemesis left: the British squadron that kept an infrequent, but intimidating vigil off the harbor. They would disappear for several days, only to obstinately reappear just as the citizens began to relax their guard.

Fort Malden
Tuesday, June 1, 1813

Jessie and John loaded the crate of provisions aboard the *Queen Charlotte*, returned to the dock for another. And then another. Regimental soldiers joined the line of workers and the stacked crates on the docks dwindled steadily. A big operation was planned, and most of the men readily assumed they would be gone to the east end of the lake for a considerable time. Jessie hated being at Malden, could only anticipate getting away within the next few days. Soon the new commanding officer would arrive, and all anticipated a change. No one knew any rumors or facts about Robert Barclay other than he had battle experience, having fought with Lord Nelson. The esteem the officers had for Nelson added weight to the new commander's authority, and many of them eagerly anticipated having him as their fleet commander. Jesse hoped that Barclay would have a rough go of it against the American flotilla. The new ship, already christened *HMS Detroit,* was still on the blocks but needed sufficient workers to complete the outfitting. Wood arrived slowly across the King's Way. Though travel had improved with the coming of the winter thaw, a lack of skilled workers to build the ships put the British at a decided disadvantage. The best they could hope for was to keep Perry's fleet bottled up at Black Rock and at Presque Isle until an invasion could assemble. This new ship required armament. Repeated requests to Admiral Yeo for cannon to arm the *Detroit* went unanswered. Jessie believed that once again Providence had orchestrated the demise of his captors, this time by hindering *HMS Detroit* before she could even set sail. Though it was his nature to look for sun's rays peering through dark clouds, he no longer had to search. The sunshine of victory, it seemed, had already begun parting the clouds of his captivity.

"Jessie, I have an idea that's risky, but might be worth that risk."

"You have my ear, John. What is it?"

"I noticed crates in the supply warehouse this afternoon that were not being brought out."

"Food?"

"Better than food, Jesse. Flints for the cannons' firing locks. Just suppose they never get delivered to the vessels. No spark, no firing."

"That won't last long. They'll only need a spark of some kind."

"But that's the point, Jesse," he said smiling slightly. "They'll have to make an alternative for firing them. And unless we get supplied with a miracle of men from the Niagara frontier, we'll have untrained sailors and landsmen trying to fight a battle with no working firing locks for the cannon."

"I assume you have a plan for losing these flints, John?"

"Never gave it a thought," he beamed. "I leave that up to the quartermaster." He winked slyly.

"Then I'll have to give it a thought. A lot of thought," Jesse said.

Jesse made his way up the path to the fort, saw Commodore Hall in a heated discussion with Captain Barclay. Jesse avoided eye contact with the commodore, hurried on about his business, passing the men until he was inside the main gate. He rushed to the steps leading to the blockhouse. No guards on duty. *Good*, he thought, and in less than a minute found an unobserved place to glean information. He pressed his ear near a gun port and listened intently.

"Well, then send the requests again."

"Captain Barclay, I don't think you grasp the situation. Admiral Yeo must protect Lake Ontario. He has very few men to spare. The attack on Sackets Harbor must be a priority. The western basin of the lake is superfluous. We're merely branches. The admiralty and General Proctor believe the key to the war is controlling the roots and the main trunk. If the Americans get to the roots, to Quebec or Montreal, the entire tree dies."

"So, he'll sacrifice us, the branches?"

"You're not to be sacrificed, Captain. You're just not a priority."

"I need men."

"You are getting them, Captain."

"Did you see them? I have soldiers, sir. Soldiers. And I'll have to use warriors to man cannon that none of them have ever fired. How do you expect me to defeat the American squadron?

"You were assigned here because of your skill and because of your experience. I was passed over for this assignment, so it falls on your shoulders to carry the burden." Jesse heard the sarcastic tone in the commodore's voice. So, Sara had lied to him. Commodore Hall didn't turn down the command. He was ignored. The commodore was condescending, "This is a nightmare the admiralty has created at Malden, and the nightmare is now yours. We have over twelve thousand natives living in proximity, and they must be fed, or they'll turn on us as readily as they'd turn on the Americans. You wanted this command, and now you have it. You will bring honor to the flag, I have no doubt. The admiralty may yet get you whatever crewmen will be sufficient to defeat Perry's squadron. If not, you will have to use the hands available, even if some of those hands are red. But as it stands, they may not even get into the lake anyway. Presque Isle has a terrible harbor and the sandbar will hold them at bay."

"I understand it will hold us at bay too."

"Yes, Captain Barclay, but you have the lake. They don't. The status quo, Captain, you maintain the status quo."

"Could General Procter bring some of the army here to launch a strike on the ships at Erie? My fleet could transport them and help to make the assault."

"He's requested that more than once. Commodore Yeo and General Rottenburg will not weaken their hold on Lake Ontario. That choice will leave us perpetually insecure. You'll not get any help from that theatre, and it'll go badly for you."

"God help us if they launch into the lake," said Barclay.

"God help us indeed, Captain."

"Then we'll set sail on the morrow and keep Captain Perry bottled up."

Jesse had heard it all, peered through the gun port to watch the commodore head toward his home. *What the Americans might do with this information! Hall passed over for Barclay's command. So, this is how the Royal Navy disdains the Provincial commanders! Well, all the better. Dissension in the command is as good a weapon as any. Now, how to exploit it.*

## Chapter Sixteen
## The Niagara River
## Buffalo, New York
## Monday, June 14, 1813

George stood by the 32-pounder bow chaser, peered out into the fog, squinted his eyes, could not improve the view. This had been Jesse's ship when he was first taken, and now he was sailing in it back toward the enemy that had kidnapped him. He leaned over to John Silhammer, elbowed him. "I have a bad feeling here about this. Commodore Barclay's ships are out there somewhere waiting for us, and this fog is so thick we could be right upon them before we even know it."

"Relax, George. If we can't see him, he can't see us. At least the wind is with us this time, and we can just ease on past. This time we'll make it."

"Wish I had your confidence."

Marine commander Lieutenant John Brooks walked quietly along the deck, straining to hear any sounds in the fog bank, leaned over to the men, "Pass the word, quietly. Battle stations," he whispered.

The word passed from man to man along the deck. The *Caledonia*'s two 24-pounders were each noiselessly manned by six gunners, all crouched at the gunwale, peering into the fog. George looked along the deck, could barely see the seaman in the rear at the tiller.

"I can't see the tiller, let alone the gunboats behind," he whispered.

Seaman George Varnum leaned over to him, whispered, "Don't worry, Armstrong. That's one of the luckiest men you'll ever meet."

"Who? The captain?"

"Aye. Oliver Perry has the luck of Providence with him. You could do worse in battle than to be on his ship. Stick with him. I plan to crew on his ship when we meet Commodore Barclay. That man will get you through," he whispered.

The five ships sailed up the river, each man hoping, praying the fog would hold, but ready at their stations in case it should lift. Not a word was spoken aloud. Clammy-skinned men glistened in the dim morning light, stifled coughs, some showing the effects of on-going lake fever, yet manning their duty stations, listening intently for any sound of the British squadron. The river's swift current pushed against them, making the sailing painfully slow. George could barely see through the fog. The *Queen Charlotte* was anchored out there somewhere waiting to unleash grapeshot on his boat. Possibly Jesse was still aboard. The darkness was gradually fading, still too dim to see an enemy, but the fog would soon lift. *Maybe an hour or so until full light. Where are the ships? Likely waiting to spring the trap just as we're within carronade range, maybe even pistol shot range. They won't miss from that distance.* George gripped the gunwale, stared into the fog. His fingers hurt, noticed he had sunk his fingernails into the wood, chipping small splinters from the ship. *Annoying habit*, he thought.

Strung out behind the *Caledonia*, the *Somers* and *Trippe* still crept along, hidden in the fog. Far to the rear, Daniel Dobbins followed with the *Ohio*, finally getting his chance to bring a gunboat to bear on the enemy. George hoped the men on the *Caledonia* were equal to the gunners on the *Charlotte*. No, he was only deceiving himself. They were outgunned, helpless, struggling upriver against the current. Sitting ducks, all of them. He quivered at the comparison, released his grip, quietly walked barefoot across the deck. To the larboard side he could see the river bank, maybe 50 yards away in the mist, thought he saw a man in the half-light, midway up the bank, waving to the fleet. *If he can see us....*

Startled, Jesse rose from his hammock, stepped quickly into his shoes. Sitting on a round stool near the stairs, he stretched, rubbed the sleep from his eyes. He nervously glanced around, trying to grasp his surroundings. No longer acting quartermaster on this voyage, he had been relegated to the task of the normal seaman. He didn't mind so much. Less responsibility for him. But it put him back under the orders of the sergeant for the time being. Never mind. His time would come again.

"Make haste, it's your watch." The voice repeated, intentionally low to not disturb the sleeping crew. Still delivering his customary threatening tone, McDonough stood at the base of the stairs. Not yet ready to take his station with less than an hour until sunrise, Jesse rubbed his eyes again, tried to focus.

"Yessir," he muttered, and McDonough climbed the stairs, disappearing into the charcoal gray light seeping in from the hatchway.

Jesse tied his shoes, trudged up the stairs. *A year*, he thought. *It's been a year under impressment, and no closer to getting home.* He fought down the despair, the idea he could merely jump off the ship, have it done once for all, stepped onto the deck, cool morning air bathing his face and waking him to the morning's dim light. A fog had set in, laying a shroud over the fleet at anchor far from Fort Erie's guns. Here in the Niagara River, the British had the American gunboats of Black Rock boxed in at Buffalo. They anticipated a move to unite the vessels with the squadron at Erie. The small fleet of five vessels had already slipped up the river, towed from the shore by teams of oxen and horses and volunteer soldiers before the *Queen Charlotte* could intercept them, a miscalculation that they did not want to duplicate. If Perry merged the two elements, he could assure a victory. Their combined weight in metal would outgun the British fleet, so intercepting the ships was critical.

Jesse peered over the gunwale at what he perceived was south. Fog. Heavy, oppressive mist thickened the air like gravy. *Which way is the mainland? How close? Dunkirk is out there, just a mile. Maybe.* No one was near him. He could barely make out the top of the foremast of *Lady Prevost*, judged her to be a half-mile or less to the stern. *I can jump ship now, swim. But how far? One mile? Five? The splash will be heard. Then comes the seven-knot current. Drown before I get swept into the rapids, tossing my body over the Niagara cataract.* He feared the lash as much as he feared drowning, stared at the blue-green water below, lost in thought. Felt a hot breath on his neck. *McDonough.*

"Do you need help finding the topmast?" he snarled.

"No, Sergeant."

"Well?"

"Well, what, Sergeant?"

McDonough stepped before him, looked deeply into Jesse's eyes, searching again, it seemed, for any hint of disloyalty.

"I was – I was just thinking."

"Not about jumping, I trust. Would be a helluva way to go – over the falls, eh?"

"No, Sergeant, not thinking – not thinking about jumping." He paused. Collected his thoughts, the water beckoning below. Felt the urge to rush McDonough, push him to the edge, and leave him to fight the current, sweep down river. "I was thinking about how long this war might last, about when I can see my family again."

"You may have the captain deceived, you may have the lieutenant deceived, you may even have Commodore Hall deceived, but you don't deceive me. You're thinking about escape, as you always do. But for your own fault, you would have gone with those deserters. If it hadn't been for me, you would've gotten clean away. It was me – me who had you watched. I haven't trusted you since you were aboard the *Caledonia.* And I still don't trust you – you or your friend, Chapman. If we didn't need every able-bodied seaman aboard this ship, I'd throw you and him overboard myself. You may yet be of use when we face the Americans – your countrymen. And make no mistake, we will face them. Imagine the irony of it – you helping to man the *Queen Charlotte* against them." He laughed darkly.

*Only until the Charlotte gets in close enough for the Americans to board us,* Jesse thought. *Then we'll see who gets thrown overboard.* Jesse backed away from the sergeant, grabbed the ratlines and quickly climbed the shroud, distancing himself from McDonough's reach. Sitting on the sharpshooter's platform on the topmast, he was hidden from view in the low fog blanket. He couldn't see the deck. *Good,* he thought. *Then I can't be seen either.* Minutes passed as he relaxed, his back against the mast, and he scanned the haze toward the river. He imagined the Americans just at the bow, ready to free him. A mast crossing in front of him, some distance away. Then another, slowly making its way up river. Yes, they would now come save him. If only. He cleared his eyes, scanned again. They were gone. Then they were there again. It *was* a ship. And another, and another! Perry's fleet had slipped out of the Buffalo naval yards and was making sail, attempting to escape to Erie! He stood quickly, perhaps they would see him. He waved. If they saw him, they might open fire, and he was a sitting duck. He dropped his arms quickly, froze in place, scarcely breathing, his heart racing. He looked down, still no deck below. At least the guard had not seen his actions. He watched the sails stealthily creeping past. They must know he was there, avoiding any action. They were not prepared to do battle, or they would have engaged by now. They moved on. Another opportunity slipping by him. Momentarily in view, only to disappear in an instant, they were now perhaps a half mile away, ducking in and out of the misty clouds. Difficult to judge the distance in this fog. No chance of swimming in that current. He felt his heart sink as they glided farther up river, well out into the open lake. *I wish them well. Let them get safely to Erie. I'll join them at another time, but my time is running out.*

He sat back down on the platform, looking intently into the fog, the tips of the masts jutting above the fog bank like so many herons standing in a backwater swamp. Then they were gone. The air was thick and warm, and Jesse leaned again upon the mast, wiped the mist off his face with his neckerchief. Perhaps a half hour passed. An easterly breeze now ruffled the flag above him, the Union Jack slapped the air, and the fog gradually dispersed. He searched below. He could faintly see the deck. Standing quickly, he grasped the lines and feigned peering into the fog downriver. If they questioned him, he could swear to not seeing anything coming up the river. Blue patches broke through the cloud and disappeared again, lightening and then darkening. Once again he peered into the dissipating fog, this time to the west. The sails were just barely visible and well on their way to the safety of Presque Isle Bay.

"You at the masthead!" the guard below him yelled up.

"Yes, what is it?" Jesse called.

"What is it you see?"

"Fog," he lied, "but it's lifting now!"

"Any sign of the American fleet?"

"I've seen nothing down river at all. Perhaps they're waiting for the fog to lift!"

"Aye, that would be my guess. Well, keep an eye peeled for them!"

"I will. I'll keep watching the river and will call out if they come up it."

"Carry on," the guard called and strolled up the deck with his musket slung over his shoulder.

Arriving safely in the harbor, the American fleet anchored close to Cascade Creek while the citizenry marveled at the armada recently united with their squadron. The *Niagara* was nearly completed and ready to launch into the harbor. The first brig's caulking and final painting had concluded and had been launched.

The newspaper had reported a major disaster on the east coast. The *USS Chesapeake* in combat with the British had surrendered to the *HMS Shannon*. The loss of the frigate was bad enough, but the devastating news came that Captain James Lawrence had died of wounds suffered in the engagement. Noticeably distressed, Perry spent much time to himself. George watched the captain, usually driven to push the men to their limits, lapse into days of despondency.

Daniel Dobbins sat in his parlor, papers stacked in several neat piles across the massive desk. He rested his head in his hands, staring intently at one paper.

"Mr. Dobbins, sorry to bother you, but could I have a word with you?"

"Yes, come in George, what is it?"

"I can't help but notice the captain is not himself. Everyone has noticed. Is he well?"

"Much on his mind. We have word that our anchors won't be delivered here until mid-July. We request more men to handle the fleet, and none are sent. Except for the group that came with Mr. Taylor, we have only the militia volunteers. General Harrison promised that he'd release some of his Kentucky reserves to us, and we're waiting for them to come. But those aren't seamen, they're landsmen like yourself. Then there's the news of the *Chesapeake*'s loss. Did you know that Captain Lawrence was a personal friend of Captain Perry? Newspaper said that his last words were, 'Don't give up the ship.' And yet she was given up. Perry's taken it very hard."

Perry appeared at the door, and George swallowed hard, assumed the captain had heard their conversation. But Perry seemed preoccupied, gave no indication he had heard anything.

"George?"

"Sir?"

"Have you given any more thought to how you can serve? I need every man I can get. General Harrison has asked me to draft seamen to fight with us."

"Does that mean me, sir?"

"It means no one, George. I see drafting as equal to impressment, and that's the very action that we've gone to war to end. No. I'll take no forced conscription. I do hope many will join us for the prize money. That's somewhat an incentive. George, you may share in the prize money too after we defeat the enemy squadron."

"It seems mercenary, Sir."

"I don't see it that way. You're to be paid for your service. The prize money is for your service. All of these men can use the money to take care of their families."

"Providing they survive, Sir."

"Providing they survive, George."

"Captain, I want to serve, but I still struggle with what I can do. My father was Quaker. Until the day he died, he raised me to abhor fighting."

"Well, George, it may interest you to know that my family is Quaker too."

"Yes, sir. I've heard some men call your family 'fighting Quakers'."

"Not very flattering, I admit, but my father saw duty to his country as paramount to anything. We have freedom to worship, and it's only as free as we can make it by defending our country. That's why we all serve."

"Yes, sir, I understand your perspective. But I'm not you. I have no intention of killing anyone. I want to serve, but I ask that if I sail with you, I may not be required to fire a cannon. It's also personal, Captain. My cousin was pressed into service and serves onboard the *Queen Charlotte*, at last report. I can't fire a gun that might strike him down."

"Very well, George, you'll not fire a gun at the enemy. I warrant I'll have use for many others who won't need to service the guns. Mr. Dobbins, the first brig is to be named the *Lawrence* in honor of the late captain."

"Fitting, sir."

"The second is to be named the *Niagara* in honor of our victories on the Niagara frontier. Those few we have achieved thus far, that is. But if we are to engage her, I'll need more men. I've written to the Secretary of the Navy, and I've again urged Commodore Chauncey on this matter. I trust that will stir things up a bit."

"Knowing how the Black Rock administration has responded before, I believe things stirred is a foregone conclusion," said Dobbins. He held out an envelope. "You have a response, I believe. It came by rider today. Possibly you have stirred things?"

Perry took the envelope from Dobbins, read it over. George saw his complexion change, growing redder. *"Sailing Master Stephen Champlin has been ordered to report to your station. He will have at hand fifty men to serve in the squadron."* He threw the letter to the desk. "Fifty! I need five hundred and fifty!"

Lake Erie, US Waters
Monday, July 19, 1813

Just after noon Jesse stood at the bow and watched the Pennsylvania shore growing larger.

This time the fleet would make a spectacular showing, and the *Queen Charlotte* would lead the assault. The order passed, and the gun crews at their positions, waited the order to fire. He could faintly see the American flotilla safely back in the harbor and speculated on just how Captain Barclay and Lieutenant Finnis planned to get into the harbor. *I've sailed in and out of that harbor many times, and they have no idea where the safe water is. Should be fun to watch,* Jesse thought.

"Mr. Harris, fetch the lead line, if you please."

"Aye, Lieutenant."

The lead weight dropped over the side of the ship and soon touched bottom. "By the mark, five fathoms," Jesse called out. Again the weight dropped. "And three." The bottom rising quickly, in a minute they would be dangerously close to running aground. Finnis brought her hard over and turned parallel to the Erie shore. A flash erupted on the hill, a thunderous boom, and a plume of water shot up nearly four hundred yards off the starboard bow. *Well out of range,* he thought. The order passed. Answering shots fired by the gun crews. One broadside ineffectual. The gun crew swabbed the barrels, prepared to fire again. Another shot from a field artillery piece at a blockhouse on the shore. This too fell far short of the *Queen Charlotte*. Trading shots would waste powder, and the ship could ill afford using up its stores.

"Lieutenant Finnis!"

"Aye, Captain."

"It appears we will not coax them out this day. Captain Perry's fleet will attempt to cross the bar soon, and I'm confident they won't clear it without running aground. Let us stand off, and we'll anchor out in the lake for the night. Having them bottled up here is just as good as sinking them where they lie. If they should attempt to move out in the night, we will have them. But I think the commodore will be more sensible."

"Aye, sir. Secure guns!"

The men swabbed the guns, returned the balls to the shot garland, stowed powder away. The lone Provincial Marine guard on the sharpshooter's nest stood at the ready observing the fleet at rest in the harbor, then scanned the deck below. For a moment he entertained the idea of jumping into Lake Erie and take his chance at swimming to shore. But Jesse's critical position thwarted him. And he'd be a duck in a barrel, an easy target. Again, frustratingly close to freedom. It wasn't the courage he lacked. Cautious vigilance kept him open to opportunity, but prudence kept him free of suicidal decisions.

Erie, Pennsylvania
Friday, July 30, 1813

The village bustled with activity as more than fifty new personnel had arrived on Wednesday to man the fleet. George ended his meeting with Dobbins, satisfied over the wages he had requested for the house carpenters. These workers would be pleased with the generous payment Dobbins had negotiated for the men who had remained through the winter. *It's more than pay,* George thought. *It's a reward for staying on when others fell away.*

Though it took all of the spring to wrench the extra pay from Washington, Daniel had succeeded on behalf of the Erie men. It was now left to man the fleet and await the various shipments of iron and sail cloth which still trickled in to the village. Numerous letters written, still no sailors of any consequence had arrived from Chauncey. Perry had inspected the men who had arrived. He didn't hide his disappointment from Dobbins or Sailing Master Taylor

"Mr. Dobbins, did you see them?

"I did," said Dobbins.

"Mr. Taylor?"

"I did, sir."

"George, did you see these new men?

George hadn't been about the town long enough to see any of the new workers, only those he had passed on his way to work on Thursday. But he did see that vein on Perry's neck standing out again.

"I did not, Sir. At least not more than a glimpse."

A glimpse is all it would take," said Perry. "I asked for trained, experienced seamen. The commodore sent me dregs. They are a motley set, and I'll tell him so. I need men to fight a battle. He sends me blacks, soldiers and boys! He gleans off from his men anyone who is sick, or inexperienced, or troublesome and sends them to me! How does he expect me to win anything with them?"

Perry paused, collected his thoughts, walked to the window and gazed out. He seemed lost deep in his thoughts, plotting, scheming, strategizing, trying on scenarios for size to see their fit. No one spoke.

Taylor watched him expectantly, Dobbins, worriedly. George studied the faces. Who would make a company of fighting men from these men who'd been thus denigrated?

Perry paced the room angrily. "Well then, I'll train these men who have arrived to a high state of readiness before we do battle, and we'll commence with them today! I'll also let the commodore know what I think of his choices. I still have no officer to command the *Niagara*. What does he expect me to do? Very well. If I can't fight with a full squadron, then I'll fight with what I do have." Perry stormed out of the room, mounted his horse tied outside and rode at a gallop toward the shipyards.

Frustrated, Dobbins watched Perry through the window, turned back into the room. "George, if you're going to join the men in the coming battle, then you need report to Captain Perry this morning at the dock. Gun crew practice," Dobbins said.

"But, Daniel, I told the captain I didn't want to serve on a gun crew. If there's need, I'll do anything else aboard."

"Mr. Taylor, George here needs a position on the *Lawrence*. If he volunteers with us, what opportunity can he avail himself of?"

"George, how are your sea legs?"

"My sea legs?"

"Yes, can you maintain balance while running on the deck while your vessel is underway?"

"I should hope so, Mr. Taylor."

"Very well, then. You will be assigned to service the guns." George's eyes widened in protest. "You will not fire any guns. You, mister, are a powder monkey. You will run powder from those below deck to each gun crew to which you are assigned. You will keep the guns serviced or we'll be blown out of the water. And, George, to quiet your conscience, you'll not be killing, but you'll be saving the lives of your shipmates, and consequently, yourself. Now report to the skiff. We'll have gun drill today. Join the men rowing out to the *Lawrence*. That will be your ship."

George reluctantly reported to the skiff with ten other young men, some white, some black, and even the soldiers in the blue uniform of the 17th Infantry, all transported by four oarsmen to the *Lawrence*. Perry personally singled out each man for his job on the gun crews. Sailing Master Taylor led George to the hold and the steps below to the powder storage. There he helped him retrieve bags of cannon powder and brought them back to the deck. The men aboard sat, gripping the sweeps that thrust out through the square holes in the gunwale.

After rowing the first brig out into the middle of the harbor, the sailors stowed away the sweeps on the rack between the masts, tied off the skiff to the stern and took positions on the deck. They loaded empty barrels into the skiff and Marine Private James Bird and John Silhammer took the skiff out into the harbor, rowing to the sandbar. They pushed the six barrels into the water at intervals where they would remain as floating targets. Several miles distant, the British warships patrolled the lake, sails filled, watching the American fleet and their readiness. Private Hosea Sargeant of the US Infantry stood by, ready to fire the carronade.

"Private," George said, "They'll soon get a good show of the US fleet's firepower. Maybe scare them into a retreat?"

"We'll give them a good show. Whether they retreat, well, that's another story."

The skiff rowed away, leaving the barrels floating. When the boat had cleared the sand bar and the two men had beached it, the order came. "Gun crews, to your posts!"

The experienced seamen who had arrived with Taylor's contingent took positions at their respective carronades to demonstrate the action of a gun crew for the new arrivals. Each carronade's tompion removed, the barrels wormed out, the coiled spring pushing down the bore to scrape any residue clinging to the barrel. The sponge rammer shoved quickly down the bore, washing out the loose powder residue. Then the cry of "load." The cartridge bag loaded with black powder rammed into the barrel, seated deep against the breach. The long vent pick inserted into the vent, punched through the cloth bag inside, and a long powder-filled quill inserted into the vent. The gunners performed each step with precision then stood at their station. George watched the men execute the action, demonstrating for the others what their task would be. No cannonballs were loaded on this practice exercise. The efficiency of this crew from New England inspired the landsmen, and George admired the economy of movements.

The smoldering lintstock touched the vent. The roar of the cannon shook the deck and in an instant

George was knocked spraddle-legged onto the flooring.

"Mr. Armstrong!"

"Sir?"

"You will see to it that the deck is sufficiently covered in sand in good time. I'll not have lads sitting about in such fashion when the day's bloody business commences!"

"Yes, Cap'n." It was a reprimand, George knew, but Perry always had purpose behind his orders. He picked himself up and saw the men of the gun making sport of him. Sheepishly, he descended the steps to hurry more powder to the waiting guns. It was a rehearsal, but it would soon be deadly serious. As he retrieved two more bags of powder, through the white smoke that hung like a dense fog over the deck, he saw a crowd gathered on the banks. They stood holding their ears, intently watching the spectacle the fleet created in the harbor. The carronade re-loaded, this time with a 32 pound cannonball, the crew stood at the ready. The carronade roared to life, and in an instant one of the barrels near the sandbar exploded into hundreds of wooden splinters. An enthusiastic cheer from the citizens on the bank welcomed the hit. George looked long at the crowd, saw Polly standing with her mother, and his heart quickened.

Lake Erie, off Presque Isle
Saturday, July 31, 1813

"Mr. Harris, you will need to complete the inventory of the armaments today, and report that to

Lieutenant Irvine. When you have completed that, I need a full report on our provisions, including grog, and our freshwater."

"Aye, sir. I'll have it done by the noon hour. Uh, Lieutenant Stokoe, sir, may I have the assistance of Mr. Chapman?"

"You may. Just complete the inventories by noon."

Jesse went below and found Chapman resting from his night watch. Since their first attempt at escape, he and John claimed a much closer bond than merely partners in a failed flight. Chapman jumped at the chance to help Jesse, anything to move about and avoid McDonough. The *Queen Charlotte* was a larger brig, but the longer the two remained aboard, the smaller and more crowded it became for them. Not many places to escape someone's intense scrutiny. Though Jesse's willingness to assume leadership duties allowed him a bit more freedom, he was in all other respects still a pressed seaman in the Royal Navy. Daily he had fought a growing depression, the sense of gloom that he might not ever see New York again, except from the deck of this ship. During these bouts he sought out Chapman and his companionship.

They went into the magazine area, kept their voices low, checking off bags of powder against the tally sheet and trading stories of what New York and Montreal both looked like in the summers. And always they conspired on how they would visit each other's homes when the war ended. Inevitably the talk faded into quiet scheming. When could they see another chance to escape? It was an obsession with both men, and yet Chapman became more fixated on another attempt than Jesse did.

"Jesse, just how long do you think we'll have this blockade?" Chapman asked quietly, kneeling over bags of cannon powder.

"I have no thoughts on it, John. I just try not to let it consume me."

"If our supplies are low, we have to lift the blockade, eh?" Chapman whispered.

"But they aren't low, John."

"Yes, but the water supply is only adequate," he said deliberately.

Jesse looked around at the men relaxing below, spoke quietly, "More adequate than it will be."

With that, he stood, checking a ledger and walked to the provisions. Two casks wedged against the hull, masked by a cask of biscuits and another of salt pork, seemed likely targets. Chapman produced an awl from a tool crate and knelt beside the casks, began to bore into a seam near the bottom. Jesse stood in front of the casks, feigning a thoughtful calculation of the provisions. In a minute, a slow trickle of water began to seep into the bilge.

"They'll never see the hole until we get back to port. It'll look like a barrel damaged in transit."

"Thank you, John, I'll note the freshwater is low here. Even if it weren't, these biscuits aren't adequate for more than a few days anyway. But there's no harm in encouraging an early departure."

"No harm unless we're caught, Jesse."

They continued casually making their rounds through the provisions, checked the arms and accouterments, the racks of cannonballs, doing a quick estimate of their numbers, and slowly making their way to the deck. The sun blazed high overhead in a humid haze as they came up the steps. It was nearly noon. They allowed time for the freshwater cask to drop to a sufficient level to invoke interest. Then Jesse reported the leak, to immediately throw off suspicion.

"Sir, the stores of fresh water are nearly depleted. We discovered a small hole near the bottom of one of the casks, possibly damaged when we last loaded provisions. We would've put some pitch on it, but we have none aboard. We also have food for another day, maybe two, and we'll need to consider half rations on provisions and grog if we're to continue the blockade."

"Thank you, Mr. Harris, I'll inform the captain. Take the message across to the *General Hunter*. Inform Lieutenant Bignell of the situation. Ask how his stores are, and bring me his report."

"Aye, sir."

Jesse brightened at the opportunity. Here he was presented with a boat, permission to row to the *General Hunter*, and the chance to make a break for the American shoreline. His pulse quickened as he untied the rope from the railing.

"Mr. Harris!" The voice sounded immediately. "I'll be coming along with you. Hold the vessel."

"Sergeant McDonough. You're just everyone's ray of sunshine, aren't you?"

"Only yours, Yankee Doodle. Lieutenant Irvine would like me to accompany you on your mission."

Jesse searched his face. "Your idea or his?"

McDonough merely smiled, climbed down the ladder, handing Jesse his musket. *A dare*, Jesse thought. He promptly returned the musket to the sergeant who settled in the bow, draping the Brown Bess across his lap. McDonough pushed away and Jesse pulled at the oars, gliding toward the *General Hunter*. He felt the sergeant's cold stare on his back, stiffening his shoulders in preparation for any stroke across his back. None came. He looked off the stern at the *Queen Charlotte*, and beyond her, the distant ships of the Americans resting in the harbor. The invitation loomed behind him and suicide was his fate if he should attempt to escape now. He could never dispense with the sergeant quietly, could never row fast enough to escape musket fire, could never get away if the cannons trained on him. He fought the anguish setting in and continued to row until at last he came alongside the brig. He climbed aboard, went straightaway to Lieutenant Bignell.

"Lieutenant Irvine's compliments, sir. Food stores are low, sir. He asks how your supplies are."

"My compliments to Lieutenant Irvine. Tell him we have two days at most. Will await his or Captain Barclay's orders."

Jesse saluted and immediately crossed to the ladder, down to the rowboat, and grabbed the oars. McDonough once again pushed away and Jesse pulled hard for the *Queen Charlotte*. Minutes later he approached Lieutenant Irvine standing with Captain Barclay at the starboard rail. Barclay listened to the report, nodded his head.

"Very well. Thank you Mr. Harris. Lieutenant Irvine, we'll prepare to get underway after dinner. I want to cloak our movements with the night. We'll return to Dover, re-supply and continue our blockade upon completion. Of course, Captain Perry may attempt to escape while we're gone, but that will surely bring his demise. I expect we'll come back to find his fleet fast on the sandbar. We can dispense with him properly at that time. If we can't force him out, perhaps we can finally coax him out. And by that time we'll have the *Detroit* fully outfitted. I just pray Admiral Yeo will heed my requests for more seamen. If we get the necessary crews, we'll be ready to battle him right where he sits."

Jesse went below deck, found a hammock and climbed in to await orders. He didn't feel like joining the evening dinner, as meager as it was. Another lost opportunity to escape and another trip across the lake made another disappointment. Dining with his mates didn't improve his outlook. But he was patient, vowing to outlast his enemy. His day would come. In the meantime, he'd watch for the ideal moment when Providence would pave the way home.

He slept uncomfortably, waking to nearly every sudden sound. Finally venturing up to the deck, he saw the sun had slipped below the lake's waters and the deep red glow had faded to a deeper purple. On the Pennsylvania shore he saw the fires of hundreds of soldiers sparking in the drawing darkness. Once the surface light faded, he could no longer make out the forms of the fleet resting inside the protective harbor. The wind began to stir and the temperature drop noticeably. Jesse smelled rain in the air. Toward the east and the mouth of the Niagara River, lightning played across the sky, revealing thick clouds. Seconds later rumbles of thunder rolled in along the lake. A storm was brewing, and the fleet would have to raise the blockade soon and return to Canada.

Barclay stepped up on deck, passed orders and the signal flag ran up the halyard. The order to raise anchor sounded and Jesse joined the men at the capstan, trudging around the axle and leaning heavily into the bars. The anchor rose, and the men climbed the topgallant, unfurled the sails which immediately filled. The fleet slowly gathered speed, sailing east. Jesse presumed the Americans would see the ships, so Captain Barclay was leaving them guessing as to his intentions. The movement east, one could suppose, was to begin a night patrol, or to sail to the leeward of some land form and wait out the approaching storm. Soon the wind began to gust and the ship now wrestled the rising waves. Barclay put the helm up, the ships turned north, and in the wave-swelled darkness, they sailed for safe harbor at Port Dover.

Jesse peered deep into the darkness, watching the foam on the waves highlighted by flashes, and listening to the punctuation of rolling thunder. The storm continued unabated, the waves swelling, until the ship pulled into the shelter of Port Dover's harbor. The anchor fixed, the officers disembarked in the downpour and rowed for the shore in the long boat. Happy to be at anchor, Jesse climbed back into the hammock. One more patrol done, he would endure yet another day of indenture in His Majesty's Royal Navy. Another missed opportunity to escape. It had grown into an obsession. He tossed fitfully, attempting to sleep, knowing his escape options were dwindling with each passing day.

## Chapter Seventeen
## Presque Isle Bay
## Sunday, August 1, 1813

The night's storms had settled the dust on the Erie streets and puddles had formed. Sparrows flitted and flapped their wings, bathing in the standing pools. Robins hopped along the mud, casting their eye over the banquet. Grackles called noisily from their perches. Columns of night crawlers slithered through the mud, many unsuccessful in reaching the relative security of the wet grass. Limbs and sticks flung from the trees lay scattered along the yards. George drove the buckboard along Peach Street, saw Polly attempting to navigate the muddy street and offered her a ride which she readily accepted. He tried to start a conversation that would draw her back to him. She didn't take the bait. She was singularly focused on getting to Margaret Forster Stewart's house where Margaret's sister Dorcas Bell and several women of the town had gathered. *Lady's sewing circle*, he thought. Polly was less than reticent.

"George, I know you can keep a secret. Would you like to know what we've been doing these few days?"

"I assume it's more sewing to sell for raising money for the ship work," he said.

"It is for the ship – for the *Lawrence*. You can't come in, but we're sewing a battle flag for Captain Perry. He requested a flag to fly proudly from the topmast of his flagship. Mrs. Stewart has had us sewing together this past week, and no one is to know until he's ready to display it for the whole fleet to view."

"That's a great responsibility for all of you. When will you have it completed?"

"Tomorrow, I'm thinking. We have it near finished now. We're sewing on the letters for the standard today. Mrs. Stewart used black dress material. Isn't that clever? We sewed the cloth strips and hemmed it. Now we're sewing on white letters. It's a beautiful tribute to the gallant Captain Lawrence. It reads, 'Don't give up the ship.' His dying words, they reported in the newspaper. Isn't that a wonderful, inspiring message?"

"It is. Would that be Captain Perry's order?"

"Yes. He wanted Captain Lawrence's words to cheer the men's courage on to victory. But no one is to know, George. Only the captain and two or three officers have seen it. They stopped here after the dance party yesterday. I'm sorry you can't see it, but you'll find it inspiring too."

"I'm sure I will," George said. "It should keep everyone's courage up when we meet the British squadron. That is, if we meet the British squadron. It seems all they do is sail before the harbor and try to lure us out. The captain won't be baited out. He's waiting, biding his time. He can be so impetuous and yet he can be so patient. Polly, that man is such a mystery."

"They're gone!" the cry shouted down the street. George and Polly stepped out to the yard and looked for the commotion. Mrs. Stewart and her sister stepped out to the porch to listen. The cry repeated all along the shore, taken up by soldiers, seamen, militia, civilians. The news covered the entire town. The British blockade had lifted some time during the night. Nowhere in the dawning light was a sail, a mast, a spar, a flag. All had vanished in the dark of night. It had to be a ruse. Surely, Barclay's ships had sailed down toward the river only to wait to trap the Americans. Perhaps they had moved to the other side of the peninsula and deployed a landing party there for the expected invasion. The conversations were animated.

"I must go, Polly. I need to see what's happening with the ships. We may have use of the flag sooner than later. Polly, I don't know when I will—"

Polly shushed him. "We'll have time for words. You go join the men on your ship. I'll attend to my task."

The nervousness grew, the militia roused to defensive positions, and riders scattered along the shore line to the west and to the east, searching the horizon far out onto the lake, and down the Niagara River, but still no sign of the British ships. They had indeed deserted their blockade. The citizenry rose late to the commotion, began thanks-praising for this gift of Providence.

George was stuck dumb with the luck of it all. What would possess them to leave the American fleet unthreatened? Apprised of the situation, Perry wasted no time. He passed his commands to all subordinates. Do not tarry. All hands report to the shipyards at once. And within the half hour of the discovery, the entire expedition mobilized and took their stations. General Meade placed his artillerists and militia defenders on the heights, training their guns on the waters beyond the sandbar. The defenders out on the peninsula looked to their defenses and prepared to repel landings. Another battery of field artillery arrived at the shore line and positioned the guns to look out over the harbor. From above, from the beach, from the peninsula, the gunners prepared a stiff crossfire to meet any threat.

Then in the next hour, the fleet began to move. Perry ordered the smaller schooners out across the shallow sandbar. Normally drawing anywhere from eight to nine feet of water, the depth had shrunk to a mere four feet from the night's stormy winds. The small vessels slowly, carefully navigated the channel opening, skimming the bottom sand and silt, finally anchoring outside of the harbor, setting a protective perimeter before the entrance. Any British ships that returned to Presque Isle would meet with a token resistance, but at least it was a resistance. *Ariel* and *Porcupine* anchored away from the entrance, while the *Trippe* and *Somers* took their stations along the outside of the peninsula. At noon George joined the crew aboard the *Lawrence*, manning the sweeps with a steady rowing toward the sandbar. She glided smooth and straight for the narrow gap in the sandbar. Then she hit. The men lurched forward, slamming against the deck.

"She's fast aground, sir!"

"Thank you, Mister Taylor. We'll have to work fast to free her," Perry said. "Armstrong, you and Silhammer take the skiff. Tell Mr. Brown we'll have use of those camels now."

George and John got into the trailing skiff, rowed to the dockyard, and Noah Brown immediately summoned his work crews to the 40-foot wooden camels beached along the shore.

"Now we shall see how well the men have labored on these, George. Let's have them linked together with rope and tow them out to the *Lawrence*."

Several of the militiamen men strung lines between the two and like a long chain of wood, the crew, joined by another boat, rowed the skiffs out to the brig stuck fast on the sandbar. Other boats rowed out behind the skiff, Noah Brown leading the way. Captain Perry stood on the aft deck.

"Well, Mr. Brown, let's see how this Dutch invention works for us."

"It will work, Captain."

Brown instructed the crewmen, and they climbed into the water. It was then they discovered they were in more dire circumstance than they first believed, for the men stood around the hull of the *Lawrence* in water only to their armpits. Though stripped down, the *Lawrence* would yet have to be buoyed up to cross the sandbar. The weight of the few remaining cannon and minimal ordinance had been too much, and she was stuck fast. Together with Brown, the officers ordered the few carronades unloaded first. The massive effort would take hours, and none was willing to admit they would be sitting stationary targets if the British attacked. On orders, Daniel Dobbins brought the *Ohio* out alongside the ship. Lieutenant Augustus Conkling brought in the *Tigress* and placed her to the stern of the *Lawrence*.

Using winches, pulleys, ropes, block and tackle, and mighty determination, the men hoisted each carronade from its carriage, transferred to the *Ohio* and to the *Tigress* to await re-mounting. More men came out to the shore. Militia stacked their muskets, removed their boots, hunting frocks and shirts and waded out to the sandbar. It seemed an entire army was now in the water, shirtless men bobbing above the waterline, ready to raise the ship when its load was lightened.

Noah Brown stood in the skiff, ordered the men to push the two camels along each side of the ship. The *Ohio* brought out long heavy timbers cut and prepared for the operation. The sailors opened the camels' plugs, forcibly sinking them into the silt on either side of the ship. George and his carpenters slid the long poles over the side of the ship from the *Ohio* and pushed through the sweeps' ports. At the same time, the militia volunteers and seamen strung rope under the hull and lashed it to the camels like a cradle. It was late afternoon before the guns were safely off of the *Lawrence* and the sunken camels were ready to inflate and float to the surface, lifting the brig. With the brig's timbers thrust out over the camels, the men replaced the plugs, attached pipes and manned the pumps. Bubbles rose from the water as the displaced water rushed out and the camels filled with air. Slowly the hollow camels rose to the surface, lifting the *Lawrence* by the protruding timbers and the rope cradle. The men cheered the brig rising in the water until the tops of the camels stood well above the surface. George pitched the first heavy line into the water off the bow. Eagerly the men took the heavy line, stretched it out across the sandbar and pulled it tight. Another line fastened to the bow, another line tossed out and the men swarmed around it in a long line. Waist deep in water, the army of men began the haul, some singing a sea chantey to the rhythmic tug of the lines. The *Lawrence* slowly moved forward, and the men sang louder as the evening sun faded. But then it stopped. The singing faded and the men grunted and struggled. The *Lawrence* was fast again in a mere four feet of water. The singing had turned to oaths, but no matter how seasoned the words spewed out, the ship would not budge. They began to grasp the full meaning. They were indeed at the mercy of the British ships, and they must act without delay if they hoped to save the fleet. Surely the British would return under cover of night, and happily blow them out of the water. A sense of doom settled in, and Captain Perry saw it, ordered the men to sink the camels and start again, this time using huge blocks of wood brought out to place on the camels, filling the distance between the tops of the pontoons and the bottoms of the timbers. The men labored well into the night, scrounging large blocks of wood, sorting for just the right ones to block up the timbers. They waded from the shore to the ship and back again, a continuous stream of workers. Fatigue eventually took its toll, and the men tried to sleep in shifts on the deck while the frantic work continued around them. When at last all of the timbers on either side of the hull had been sufficiently blocked, once again the long process of pumping water out of the camels began. Early in the morning, as the summer sun lit the harbor, townspeople walked and drove their wagons, buggies, carts to gather at the hillside and view the night's work. There before them, all their hopes for victory still sat on the sand.

Port Dover, Canada
Monday, August 2, 1813

The *Queen Charlotte*'s crew slept. The sun had risen brightly, heralding another stifling hot day on the lake. Sabbath had gone too quickly for the men, and they slept on, attempting to coax a few more hours of rest from the morning. Another day dawned for supervising the laborers loading supplies from the dock stores to the three ships, and Jesse prepared the inventory ledgers, determined to drag out the business as long as he could get away with it. *Lady Prevost* and *General Hunter* lay at anchor in the dead calm harbor, rippled occasionally by a sudden burst on the surface, bass feasting on the shadflies dotting the water. A soldier slouched along the beach, his Brown Bess slung over his shoulder. It was a lazy morning. No workers had yet appeared, but a familiar figure strolled toward the wharf.

"Mornin' Jessie. A fine bright day, eh?"

"Good morning, John. Yes, it could be another hot one. The fish are feeding early."

"I saw you'd left early and wondered where you'd gone. The barracks are still silent, and only a few soldiers with guard duty are stirring about. Why are you here? No one's pushing any work today. The officers are all in town asleep, I reckon."

"Couldn't sleep. That's all." Jesse said vaguely.

Chapman looked around for prying eyes and ears. "You weren't planning on running today, were you?" he asked quietly.

"Hadn't even thought about it," Jesse said. "We've too much work to do in re-supplying the ships. I was merely trying to find a way to delay it a bit more. Maybe even add to the list a few items that we don't have in the storerooms so we'd have to search."

Chapman laughed. "Good plan. Think it'll work?"

"I don't know. I just want to delay going back across the lake."

"Well, you may not have to make that your concern. From what I hear, the captain was at a party last night for the officers and he's invited to a dinner in his honor tomorrow evening. We'll just have to wait on the officers' pleasure."

"That's good news, indeed."

"More good news, Jesse. When the *Chippewa* sailed, she was taking supplies to General Proctor at Malden. He apparently is planning to attack the forts along the Sandusky River. It's true, at least what I can gather. Men were talking last night, and they said they'd heard the officers talking about it. That's why soldiers of the 41st had gone on the *Little Belt*. They're planning on using the smaller gunboats to sortie up the river. We're too heavy and draw too much to aid them. We get to stay and blockade the fleet at Presque Isle. That is, after we get supplied," he said with a wink.

"If all that's true, then the later we get to Presque Isle, the better. The ships might just slip out and attack Proctor if we delay long enough."

"I thought so too, but one of the men said he overheard Lieutenant Stokoe say that if the American fleet were able to slip out, they'd come here to try to attack us. The spies from the states say that's what Perry is planning."

"Well, John, it's all speculation anyway. The water over the sandbar is too shallow for them to get out. That's why we haven't gone in. It looks like Captain Barclay is content to keep them quarantined in the harbor until Proctor can invade Ohio and sweep across to Erie."

"Lieutenant Irvine said Captain Barclay wants to sail across the lake in the next day or two. The wind has been south and the harbor is undoubtedly so shallow that the Americans will have run aground. He plans to blast them into kindling where they rest."

"Then by all means, we delay as much as possible. There will be no one to command us today if they're all on furlough. I'd say a fortuitous circumstance, wouldn't you?" Jesse said, a sardonic smile spreading across his lips.

"Fortuitous. Ha. Indeed, Jesse. Fortuitous."

Chapman walked up the dock, determined to get any more rumors chased down, anything that would aid them in the sabotage of the time schedule. Jesse adjusted the work schedule. He approved half of the workers to take furlough into town while he supervised the rest. He passed orders to the workers to return by two o'clock, knowing full well, they would use every last minute of time, thus slowing down the supply loading. The jack tars would take the brunt of the punishment for not having the supplies loaded, but at least he would escape punishment.

Presque Isle Bay
Tuesday, August 3, 1813

The oppressive haze of summer lay heavy-handed on the fleet and only the relief of standing in the water covering the sandbar cooled the workers. Twice more during the night the *Lawrence* had stuck fast again on the shallow bar. The nervousness circulated from the spectators who had first gathered with high hopes. The work continued, but the chances of moving the brig grew more and more remote. Polly had come to the shore with her mother, and like the rest of the town, had brought what food they could hastily collect for the exhausted workers. She found George asleep on the sand, gave him some breakfast, and distributed food to other waking workers.

At last George's crew began taking down the masts, a daunting, complex task. Floating these beside the vessel allowed them to raise the brig enough to attempt to haul her across the bar. The camels were re-filled with air, the blocks wedged high against the thick protruding beams, and the scores of soldiers, militia, citizens, seamen, tugged at the ropes, digging their toes into the sand and silt and pulled. The *Lawrence* began to move, now scraping, now skimming the sandbar. She was free, and the long line of workers pulled the two massive ropes until the tiller slipped across, plunging the men happily into the deeper water outside the harbor. Loud *huzzahs* echoed from the shoreline. The crowd that had gathered during daylight hours joined in a festive, yet uneasy celebration. Men who had left sleep aside to drag the brig across to open water collapsed wearily into the water and tried to cool themselves. Captain Perry was jubilant, had slept little in the 48 hours of non-stop effort, but began to drive himself and the men to the next task.

"George, your crew must begin at once to reassemble the masts. When the foremast is secure, we'll bring the guns aboard. I'll have the *Niagara* brought up without delay. She is lightened already with her guns removed. We'll use what we have learned on the first to speedily move the second."

George felt the energy leave him in a rush. No time to rest, just let the muscles continue to cramp up. The men had pushed themselves beyond exertion to fatigue, and some were showing signs of sickness. "Where does this man get his energy?" he muttered to no one in particular. He stood at the gunwale, watched Perry disappear over the side and slip into a rowboat, aiding two seamen in rowing toward the *Niagara* sitting high in the water some two hundred yards back in the harbor. She had been stripped of all excess weight except her anchor and masts.

And now a sense of urgency hung in the air like a storm cloud. The men called on all reserve energy from deep within and set about re-equipping the fleet, making ready for combat. In no short order, the men had raised the masts and began the rigging. The lines had raised the yards and men climbed out to begin raising the sails. Borrowed time was running out, and that incessant pendulum would soon cease. It drove the men on. More volunteers had arrived when word passed that the last brig was preparing to cross the bar. Now all available hands moved in a mass of humanity to the beaches. The efficiency of the seamen working the yard arms, tying lines, lifting the sails, re-rigging the ship was encouraging. As he stood on the deck of the *Lawrence* and pulled at the lines, George's admiration for these men grew. He sensed that history was being made here in Erie's harbor, and he was proud that he was a part of it.

A commotion of shouts on shore began and was picked up by the workers in the water. Finally, the cry reverberated from the cliff above. "Sail ho!" Dozens of voices echoed the cry. Perry stood up in the skiff carrying him to the docks from the *Niagara*. "Where away?"

"Two points nor'east!"

Perry quickly sat, the skiff turned and the men pulled mightily on the oars, carrying him back to the *Lawrence*. From the boat he called orders. The *Lawrence* had only one gun mounted and awaited the others to be brought up. "Everyone out of the water and to your posts!"

George saw that they were now merely sitting wood ducks. The men unfurled the sails on command, leaving them hang loosely to spill the

wind. The crew aboard the gunboats beyond the
harbor entrance moved to their battle stations. Perry
prepared to engage the British squadron with four
gunboats and a brig with only one working
carronade and no men to load it. To the stern and
just approaching the sandbar, the *Niagara* dropped
her lines into the water for the men to secure. Her
anchor was gone, her carronade gone, all of them
resting on timbers on the shore, some aimed toward
the lake, and much of her rigging gone in order to
lighten her for the crossing. She glided in slowly
and came to a lurching stop as she grounded on the
sandbar. If the British caught sight of her state, it
would take a few minutes to pound her into scrap
wood. The panic swelled like a rising tide and
George realized once again they would need a
blessing of Providence and a lot of luck to escape a
disaster.

Orders shouted all along the shoreline,
controlled commotion ruled as soldiers, militia, and
seamen all rushed to assigned duties and voluntary
positions, manning the three long 12-pounders near
the beach. The few men aboard the *Niagara* rushed
into action, giving a show of battle preparation. The
drummer beat to quarters, and those still in the
water pivoted the brig slowly on the sandbar to face
her bow to the enemy preventing them from seeing
her vacant gunports. To the enemy at a distance the
fleet looked ready to engage. It was a bluff, a very
daring bluff, George thought. And the risk was
great. The enemy ships continued forward, and
Perry ordered all the gunboats to prepare to sail. The
*Lawrence* sent men into the lofts and gave every

sign of organizing for a fight. All hands stood silent at their posts on the gunboats, preparing for the inevitable confrontation. Through the hailing trumpet the order passed to the gunboats to feign an attack. Lieutenant Packett raised the anchor, turned the *Ariel* directly toward the British fleet. The *Scorpion* followed. The guns all loaded, the wait for the firing range to close, dragged on. Then the long guns of the American gunboats belched fire and smoke, the thunderous report of the cannon, and four plumes of water fell far short of the *Queen Charlotte*. The sailors all watched the enemy ships, and at about four miles distant, they suddenly changed course and bore to the west. The men cheered as the squadron showed their sterns and sailed back toward the Canadian shore. The bluff had worked. The squadron was saved, and immediately *Ariel* and *Scorpion* turned back to their position, standing sentinel over the harbor. The men re-entered the water, stretched out the lines and the timbers, prepared to inflate the camels and raise the *Niagara* off the bar. Sliding back into the harbor's waters, George shook his head in disbelief. Providence again had smiled on their cause.

## Chapter Eighteen
## Erie, Pennsylvania
## Sunday, August 8, 1813

Early Friday morning the fleet had finally weighed anchor and the *Lawrence*, *Scorpion, Ariel* and *Somers* sailed for Long Point to scout the British position and pick a fight. By noon they came in sight of Long Point, but Barclay's squadron had moved on, seeking the safety of the Detroit River. George sailed on the *Lawrence*, still unsure of all of his duties when the battle would begin. Carrying powder for the guns seemed a good enough task for him and he was fully satisfied to be on the ship he helped build. He had to admit he was relieved finding the *Queen Charlotte* gone. The crews used the voyage across the lake to develop a routine and gain experience handling the brig. By afternoon they had completed a loop past Long Point again and, seeing no enemy sails, had returned in the evening to the safety of the shore guns at Erie. That night a heavy rain moved in and George spent the night alone at home, comfortably out of the elements. Saturday saw the arrival of more men from Black Rock, and Perry couldn't contain his joy in seeing anything resembling a seaman. The fleet was undermanned, but the bodies who came were a welcome sight and immediately put to work drilling with the cannons. Captain Perry had also begun recruiting militia, soldiers, anyone willing, with a promise of prize money upon the defeat of the British squadron. Many had signed on for thirty days and their terms were nearly up. Dobbins even tried his persuasive powers, but those who had served were ready to relinquish their slot on the ships to other men and return to their homes, their term of militia enlistment now expiring.

As George walked Polly home from the church, he turned it all over in his mind. The fleet would set sail during the week and he had decided that when the orders came, he would sail with them, go into the fray and do what he could in good conscience perform for the good of the ship. Hundreds of deckhands were still needed, he told her, and he had resolved to add his hands to the company. Finally a commander for the *Niagara* had been ordered to Erie. Lieutenant Jesse Elliott arrived from Black Rock with one hundred much needed officers and men to supply the *Niagara* and the remaining vessels. George still hated this officer who had tried to halt the project. In fact, George admitted to Polly that he never gave Elliott a chance to show his expertise or earn his respect. Didn't want him to try either.

Even the most casual observers saw the men Elliott brought with him were head and shoulders above the first arrivals from Chauncey's gleanings. When George saw Elliott smugly overseeing his men preparing the *Niagara* for the coming expedition, he respected him even less. One seaman had confided to George that if the lieutenant had known he was destined to command one of the brigs of Presque Isle, he would have chosen a better lot to send earlier. But for all the training, Elliott was, on the whole, happy with the crew of the *Niagara* and allowed they would give a good accounting in the coming fight, inviting comparisons between the new arrivals and the sickly specimens under Perry's command. But on the *Lawrence*, the captain drilled the men constantly, and they appeared to improve somewhat. George paid particular attention to the blacks aboard the ship. Weeks before, Perry had said he was disappointed in the selection afforded to him, yet as the men drilled at the guns, all of them did their duties without delay, without question. They were a remarkable lot. Most had shipped before on Lake Ontario and some from the Atlantic. George had known very few freedmen and worked alongside them with a fascinating interest. Polly saw his curiosity and approached him tactfully.

"What is your opinion of them," she asked at last.

"As far as sailors? Workers? What, Polly?"

"As inferiors. Some people still think they are," she said.

"They're remarkable workers, though I have known too few to make a judgment. I met Bennett aboard the *Lawrence*. He knows sailing better than I do. I think the captain was too rash in his first criticism. I see no one that is inferior, at least not due to color. There are many – white and black – who are just too sick to work. How can we face the enemy with the lake fever laying on most of the crew? Even the captain has had a bout of it already."

"You've managed to stay healthy."

"I have so far."

They continued awkwardly in the quiet, arriving at the blockhouse. Polly stopped by the blockhouse, staring out at the fleet resting at anchor. She turned, looked full at him, searching for the right words, then quickly looked away.

"I'm glad you're well, George," she said, looking again at the ships below.

"If you wish to say something Polly, say it. We haven't many hours left."

Polly looked down, studied the ground, avoided his gaze. George uneasily shifted from leg to leg, stepped away, walked to the rose trellis beside the Fulmer home. He stared at the flowers, inhaled deeply, caught their scent, impulsively snapped off a sprig of two blooms, held them out.

"Here."

Polly took the sprig, placed the blooms to her face, took a deep breath, then looked up and deeply into his eyes. "I forgive you, George."

In a quiet moment of release, she had emptied her resentment, and now he felt ashamed of his suspicions from so many months before.

"I want so much to be right with you, to mend what I tore from us. You say you forgive me, but how do I forgive myself, Polly?"

"Forgiveness is a needle that is used to mend. You must do what your conscience tells you to do. I realized that an unforgiving heart sets the cost of love too high. I wasn't willing to pay the price. What will an unforgiving heart cost you, George?"

George stared down at the ships, silently searching for an answer. "I don't know, Polly," he said at last.

"I hope you find out before too long, George. I don't want you to discover it for yourself out on the lake when it might be too late."

## Fort Malden, Canada
## Monday, August 9, 1813

The *Queen Charlotte's* crew lowered her sails and set out the sweeps, rowing the vessel into the harbor under the protection of Ft. Malden's guns. Jesse stood at the ship's wheel, bringing her into the harbor and close in to the wharf where they could tie up and load more provisions. The crew was noticeably deflated since missing the opportunity to engage the American squadron at Presque Isle. But the likelihood of facing Perry's fleet had diminished to a last gasp of hope. For there near the shore at the King's Yard, floated the *HMS Detroit*, no paint, no cannon, no masts, and consequently no rigging. Even more fortunate, very few workers were busy at their stations. The construction site looked abandoned. No materials lay about. Jesse guessed the naval yard had either run out of workers, run out of material, run out of impetus, or a combination of all. Without that ship, Barclay would surely not try to face the American fleet. Unfortunately, he might be in for a long stay at Malden.

Released from their duties, the men departed for Amherstburg, happily off the ship and away from danger, happier still to go into the village and enjoy the comforts of the community. John met Jesse at the shore, walked the path leading up to the fort, out of hearing.

"Another delay seems to have made its home with us, eh Jesse?"

"Yes, but for how long?"

"Did you get a good look at her, Jesse? She's not going to be ready for action any time soon. You can tell just by looking at her. No guns. No able seamen. She's absolutely powerless where she rests. We may have shore duty for a long stay this time."

"Unless they put us to work on building."

"They won't have us build. We're not ship's carpenters. They need experienced workers, and it doesn't look as though there are any to be found out here."

"Something else is missing, John. Where are the other ships? The gunboats that have been here in the harbor are all gone. This harbor is as naked as a newborn."

"They couldn't be on the lake. We would've encountered them on our return. They're too small to attack the American squadron alone."

"Well, they must be somewhere."

Chapman called to Lieutenant Stokoe as he passed. "Begging your pardon, Sir, but where is the fleet? We're not very well defended here with the gunboats missing, are we?"

"Nothing to concern yourself with, Private Chapman. They've gone up to Lake Huron and should return soon enough to assist us here."

But sir," Jesse broke in, "if the enemy should try to attack us here –"

"We have the guns of the fort to repel any attack, Mr. Harris. The *Queen Charlotte* and the *General Hunter* will be ready also. We'll give a good accounting and make them wish they hadn't been so foolish," the lieutenant said, and he dismissed their words with an indifferent wave of his hand as he walked on.

"Well, if he's not concerned, then why should we be, eh? Join me in Amherstburg, Jesse? Someone somewhere will have loose lips and we can learn more with a few mugs of rum."

"I'll try, John, but I want to call on Sara. I'm sure she has information she may readily share. I'll join you later or see you back aboard the ship."

Jesse walked the path up to the fort and passed below the fortifications toward the Hall residence. Enough time had passed since his departure for Long Point that he felt Sara would have recovered from his hasty departure. He could safely renew his friendship with her to learn any other details to which she might be privy. He stopped at the top of the hill, surveyed the harbor below, looked down onto the deck of the *Detroit*, could see no one aboard. She was completely abandoned. The sails of the *Little Belt* raised and Jesse watched her move out of the harbor, making for the river beyond. *Scout vessel*, he thought. *Captain Barclay needs eyes out on the lake to spy on the American squadron.* The Indian encampment around the fort had grown considerably since Jesse had left and he picked his way through the village, noted that they were primarily Shawnee. Suddenly he remembered the blue jacketed warrior. He searched warily about the camp, moving quickly beyond the perimeter and onto the dusty path toward Commodore Hall's house. He saw no sign of the brave, but was surprised to see Sara before the house, talking to a redcoat officer, laughing at something she had just said. She lay her hand on the crook of his arm and tucked her head against his chest and laughed as well. *Awkward timing*, he thought. Just for an instant she saw him, and then she quickly looked away. Or maybe it was his imagination. A pang of jealousy made him feel queasy, but only for an instant. He didn't care for her, he knew. But he had hoped she still carried a torch for him, at least until he could get more information from her. Resigned to gleaning no news this evening, he turned back to the path and made for the ship as the evening light began to fade. Esther's face was before him, and he felt more homesick than he had felt in months.

Presque Isle Bay
Thursday, August 12, 1813

George stood on the shore beyond the sandbar. The cutter ran onto the sand and fellow seamen, soldiers, militia climbed in. George hesitated. His feet seemed nailed to the shore. For an instant he lost all ability to move them. He heard a voice call his name. David Bunnell stood in the bow, his hand extended.

"C'mon, George, we can't wait all morning!"

He heard the voice, but he was detached, without power of movement, frozen. He wanted his legs to move, but he couldn't force them to step. He heard his name again, this time behind him at a distance. Stirred from his trance, he looked back, saw Polly halfway up the bank beside her mother. She raised her arm, a handkerchief in her hand, and she waved. He saw no tears, no sobbing, none of what he may have expected. She stood tall and proudly, a bright yellow bonnet framing her curls. He understood her wave, her brave stance.

"George. Get in," Bunnell said.

He stepped into the boat, found his seat and rode the vessel out to the anchored *Lawrence*. He looked back over his shoulder, saw Polly and her mother walking back up the hill to where many had gathered to watch the fleet sail out to destiny. He stood tall, saw her stop at the hilltop, waved to her broadly. Several spectators waved back. He wondered to himself if these same spectators would be there when the fleet returned. Then a sinking feeling. Would there be a fleet to return to Erie? He rode past the *Ohio*, caught sight of Daniel Dobbins at the rail. Dobbins tossed a salute and smiled. George weakly saluted back attempting a brave smile. Beside him, a young boy watched the shoreline fade. George had seen him before.

"What's your name, boy?"

"Ephraim."

"You're not from Erie, or I'd know you."

"No. I'm from Cleveland. I came here to be a ship's boy."

"A ship's boy? At your age?"

"I'm twelve years," he said proudly.

"This is dangerous work, Ephraim."

"Yes, but we get prize money!"

*How naive*, George thought. This was that boy he admired with his riding skills months ago. And here he would ride a different steed. He prayed silently that young Ephraim would live to see his prize money.

The ships set sail with a fair wind, turning west toward the open waters of Lake Erie. From the stern railing, George saw Polly, still on the bank even as the crowd wandered off. She waved broadly. The ships, ten in all, formed a formidable squadron, and they seemed to sail with arrogance. All the months of scraping, scrounging, borrowing, buying, and even the hard labor of cutting trees in a winter-blanketed wilderness had finally culminated in this crusading voyage, and it reflected on the faces of the officers and the eastern coast seamen. They had set sail as an armada to wrest control of the Upper Lakes and take the fight to the enemy. Once again he felt partner and witness to an historic event. He could only guess what Dobbins's mind-set was at this moment. All that he too had suffered since their capture last year rested here on the floating green wood of Presque Isle. Dobbins's smile spoke loudly. But was it worth the cost of all the misery, the losses of so many with the fever, the separation from family, the loss of his mother, of nearly losing Polly? George walked to the bow as the *Lawrence* crawled on through the light waves. Much had passed. Much lay ahead. And like Erie's open waters, George knew the winds could change in an instant, and their luck could change just as quickly.

By evening they had reached their first destination of Cleveland at the mouth of the Cuyahoga for the night. Sunday the fleet had passed through a steady rain on the lake and anchored among the islands off of Sandusky's shoreline. Two houses were visible on one island and George wondered what the inhabitants had done when war broke out. He had not seen these homes when he first arrived by the canoe last August, and as he scanned the island from the ship's deck, he saw no evidence of inhabitants now. Curious that the homes had not been set to the torch. The presence of a strong militia possibly saved the frontier, and the rumors of pillaging and savagery in the area seemed more now than ever just that, rumors.

Dozens of the crew had taken to their hammocks under the attack of lake fever. Even the surgeon's assistant, Usher Parsons had fallen victim. George had so far escaped the nausea and violent cramping that came with drinking Lake Erie's waters. In the heat of August weather, he quenched his thirst with water from the freshwater barrels in the hold, as did others. Unknowingly, some men still insisted on treating their fever by slinging buckets into the lake and drawing them back to the ship with the attached hemp lines where they would share the water out. More fell ill. Those that showed no vicious tremors, nonetheless walked about in a stupor, going about their duties, weakened with aching heads and nausea, often sending Lake Erie's waters violently back to her. It was during this abysmal anchorage off of Sandusky that the lookouts sighted sails on the horizon. Three British ships sailed to the north of the Bass Islands, giving every indication of movement to engage the Americans. George immediately saw the folly in it. Orders passed through the fleet, and soon the *Somers*, *Porcupine* and *Trippe* gave chase. The *Lawrence*, dreadfully undermanned, remained at anchor with her sickly crew. The British ships prudently turned and sailed back toward the Detroit River. Again a confrontation was avoided. None of the vessels resembled the *Queen Charlotte*, and George was relieved that if Jesse was still aboard, he had escaped the squadron's iron missiles. By nightfall the pursuers had returned, having exchanged no gunfire with the enemy. Once again the ten ships of the Lake Erie flotilla anchored in safe harbor as a blustery wind blew unabated all night. The ships tossed at their moorings, adding misery upon misery to the afflicted crew. George swung in his hammock until he drifted off to the worst stench he had ever experienced.

August 17 greeted the crew with a hot sun and thick humidity. Once again Lake Erie had calmed, having shaken off another of her fickle tempests. Tuesday at noon, the fleet weighed anchors and sailed back deeper into the harbor protected by the long island of Catawba. George stood on the deck and scanned the Ohio shore, lost in thought.

Lieutenant John Brooks came from behind. "Peaceful, eh?"

"Exactly what I was thinking, Sir. And beautiful."

"Well, we must break the tranquility, George."

"Sir?"

"We need seven charges of powder."

"Yessir," and he ran to the hold. No enemy. *Powder for what*? He returned to the deck, the bucket heavy with black powder bags. He passed them along to each carronade crew beginning their loading sequence. Captain Perry stood at the bow, directing the crews. They fired three guns, the report echoing across the water. In ten minutes, the final four fired in sequence. *A signal*, George thought. Within minutes, the beach showed movement, and a vessel made way to the *Lawrence*. Three officers and a guard of seven Indians climbed aboard.

"Indians aboard this ship?"

George turned to see David Bunnell. "At least they're not Shawnee," he said.

A tall major of the US Regulars saluted Perry. "General Harrison's compliments, sir. He asks that you have your ships moved off of Cunningham's Island and anchored there. The enemy fleet has sailed up the Detroit, probably to Malden. From your position in the lake, you'll have adequate view of their dispensation should they try to sail out for Long Point. He asks that you also consider the anchorage in the safe harbor of Put-in-Bay on South Bass Island and will meet with you to hear your opinion on that matter when he joins you tomorrow."

"My compliments to General Harrison, and tell him that we will make sail for Cunningham's Island within the hour and await his arrival there. I'll leave the *Ariel* in Sandusky for his convenience. Inform the general that I'll also consider his suggestion of South Bass Island."

The natives that gathered on the deck were more than a little curious and investigated the carronade that had made such a thunderous voice to call them in. Perry saw this.

"Lieutenant Brooks, have the larboard batteries loaded with powder charge only. A salute to our fellow soldiers and to General Harrison," Perry said.

"Yes sir," Brooks saluted. "Gun captains, to your posts. One round, blank fire!"

George hurried to get his charges for the four guns in the battery he serviced. Sponged, loaded, and primed, the carronade awaited the order and the slow match.

"One round blank fire salute. Fire!"

Eight carronade belched out the flaming orange-yellow of burning embers, and the concussion shook the deck. The Indian escort immediately cowered in place, drawing back in fearful wonder. Holding the smoking slow match in hand, Bunnell looked at the dazed party. "That certainly made an impression," he whispered.

"I think that was the intent," George said. "Might help them remember whose side they're fighting on."

The soldiers exchanged courtesies and climbed over the side of the boat, the Indian ceremonial guard passing them quickly in a rush for the small sailboat, warily staring up at the carronade that thrust through the gun port just over their heads. The vessel pushed off and the sail set, turning back to the harbor and General Harrison's encampment. Soon the fleet turned eastward and sailed for the safe anchor to the southwest of Cunningham's Island to await further orders.

Chapter Nineteen
Fort Malden, Canada
Tuesday, August 17, 1813

The wind that had blown heavily most of the night finally abated, and the gloriously sunny dawn greeted the ships in the harbor. The morning's brilliance contrasted the gloomy countenances in the officers' ranks and the ranks of the normal seamen. Jesse reported to the supply building to begin the provision requisitions for the *Queen Charlotte*. He took heart in the gloom surrounding him, a reassurance that freedom was yet closer. The rumors gained wings and flew from one crew to the next. It didn't take long for the rumors to grow. But the size of the crews did not. The seamen Barclay had long requested failed to arrive. Instead, in their place arrived apologies and rhetoric designed to instill pride in the flag, in the country, in the commander's gallantry, and nothing else. Military and naval stores ran dangerously low. The Shawnee and their brethren encamped around Amherstburg expected to be fed and cared for by the Great War Chief, General Proctor. Flour was no longer adequate to feed the fourteen thousand who had come to suckle at the breast of Fort Malden. General Proctor's troops had now joined the gathered force and further depleted the provisions.

In their miracle escape over the sandbar, the Americans abruptly gained the advantage, and now they nestled near the Bass Islands, fortifying them for an eventual Canada invasion. Barclay was distraught with the news reported by his scout vessels, but vexed even more with the news from Lake Ontario. No able-seamen would come. He prepared his ships with those few who had already seen duty on the lake, adding to their number a few merchant marines, soldiers of the 41st Regiment of Foot, some Canadian militia, many of whom only spoke French, and ultimately with Indian warriors who volunteered or were coerced with promises of scalps and whiskey. A patchwork quilt at best, it already started to separate at the seams.

All of Barclay's applications and pleadings to Sir James Yeo went unheeded. He would not receive any more able seamen to man the fleet. Correspondence informed him he would receive fifty extra men from General Proctor. However, when they arrived, Jesse blithely commented to anyone willing to listen that a British count of fifty was equal to an American count of only thirty-six, plus the two officers. These all came from Quebec, and consequently spoke abysmal English. Jesse noted the irony. The British navy had pressed American sailors to fill out the company on their ships, and now that war had started, they couldn't even get four men in a gun crew who could understand each other. Jesse marked off two crates as two Canadian militiamen prepared to load them on the cart bound for the docks.

"I don't know why we're havin' to take dese crates to de ships. I heard dem say de fleet would be burned radder den turned over to de Americans."

Jesse looked up quickly. "Burned? Who told that lie?"

"Is what dey're sayin', dat is, some of de officers."

"You believe that too?"

The French trapper seemed well informed, didn't give any indication that the two militiamen were joking with the others. He nodded to Jessie knowingly.

"Still," Jesse said, "until I hear the orders, I won't take much stock in it. Anyway, where would we go if we burned the fleet? That would be the last of the defenses."

"Some say dey burn de fleet, den dey burn de fort and move inland," said Rinaud.

"You mean retreat?"

"Some say."

A look passed between John and Jesse. This might be the opportunity. In the confusion, they could just slip away. Jesse read the unstated message in Chapman's eyes, eyes that grew a bit brighter with their prospects.

"Well, it's just hearsay anyhow, so I don't take much stock in it," Jesse said.

"Believe what ya' want," said the militiaman. "I know what I heard de officers say, and dat be good enough wit me."

"Dat Captain Barclay," said Rinaud, "he 's not gonna run. Too much honor dere. He likely take de fleet as it is and attack de Americans radder dan give in and tuck tail and run."

John spoke up, "One thing's for certain, we're puttin' provisions aboard for something. They're not going to burn a ship once they've loaded provisions on her."

"One more reason to discount the rumors," Jesse said.

"Sail ho!" the lookout on the topmast of the *Queen Charlotte* cried out.

The warning repeated from on the high banks and the parapet of the fort, and men scrambled up from the docks and raced for the fortifications. A mast appeared sailing up the Detroit River. Then another followed close behind. A brig appeared behind. Jesse saw the Stars and Stripes on the topgallant. The American fleet had waited long enough and had brought the fight to the British. He and John scurried for shelter, just as a cannon fired from the first American vessel, a small gunboat. The shot splashed into the water far short of the *Detroit*, sitting completely undefended in the harbor. Men's voices barked orders from behind them, and they ducked behind the embankments for cover from the American gunfire. A barrage of cannon fire thundered across the harbor, plumes of water leaping high into the air around the first gunboat and off the bow of the brig. In less than a minute, the sails dropped and the Americans stopped their assault and began to drift back down the river toward the lake. Another warning shot fired from the 24-pounder long gun just above Jesse's head, and another plume leapt into the air, dangerously close off the stern of the gunboat. The Americans retreated out of cannon range, letting the current carry them swiftly away from the fight. A lusty cheer came from the cannon emplacements on the walls, the militia and redcoats waving their hats and muskets in the air in celebration.

"Well, that was easy," John said quietly.

"Looks like they're trying to do what we tried at Presque Isle, John. Guess it'll be left to the open lake to settle accounts."

Put-In-Bay, South Bass Island
Saturday, September 4, 1813

Once the fleet anchored safely at the deserted island of Put-in-Bay, the crews spread out to forage the island for food, found little but did discover a large cave that held a reservoir of freshwater. George reported to Usher Parsons the discovery, and soon the general officers had followed the footpath to the cave. With nearly fifty men sick and the effective fighting force being gradually whittled down to a token crew, the water was a welcome sight. Perry himself was not well and joined many others in the sickbay. Even Parsons, sick himself, worked between long sleeping spells just to keep up with the treatment of the others. Soon all of the surgeons aboard the entire fleet took to bed, and Parsons was left as the only medical officer with enough strength to travel from vessel to vessel to minister to the men. George finally succumbed to the fever and lay in his hammock alternating between violent chills and fever until he couldn't sweat anymore. The clammy cold below deck made him delirious, and he wavered between consciousness and dream. And the dreams kept coming back to Polly, standing on the shore, a yellow bonnet framing her head, a pocket handkerchief in her hand and broadly waving, while the words whispered like a breeze across the harbor, "I forgive you," and "what will it cost, George?"

He had no idea how many hours, or was it days, that passed while he lay in the hammock with the other moaning, puking, sweating, apparitions surrounding him. He tried to speak, "Let me go with you," as the orders above him on the deck were handed down to Daniel Dobbins. He was to sail the schooner *Ohio* back to Presque Isle and retrieve more supplies for the fleet. Food, ammunition, and medicine were foremost on the orders of stores. George needed to see Polly, but too weak to even swing one leg out and tumble from his hammock he could only mutter, "let me go with you," and then darkness.

## Wednesday, September 8, 1813

The situation was critical. With the food dwindling, so would the fighting force surrounding Fort Malden. Captain Barclay summoned the crews to the fort early on Monday and immediately put them to work on the *HMS Detroit*. He had made his decision with General Proctor. No armament expected. No experienced sailors expected. No help from Admiral Yeo. They must fend for themselves. He read the decision to the assembly and work began in earnest. The men soon set to stripping Fort Malden of all its heavy guns, and moving these cannon onto the *Detroit*. If they couldn't arm both the fort and the ship, Barclay's chose to arm the ship.

"Quite a risky move, wouldn't you say, Lieutenant?" John asked.

Lieutenant Stokoe tried to hide his apprehension, but he didn't convince Jesse, who privately delighted in their sad state. "Not much of a risk at all, John. Those guns will easily outdistance the Americans. They have short range carronade. These long guns will keep them at bay when we encounter them. We come to blows and I should think we'll win the day rather quickly. "

"But, Lieutenant, if *they* should win the day, the fort is defenseless," Jesse added.

"In that case, Mr. Harris, I should think you'll be joining your American brethren and toasting your return on the smoldering embers of Fort Malden. But I wouldn't plan any celebratory meals just yet."

Jesse left quietly from the fort and circled through the Shawnee encampment, leaving John at his guard post on the parapet to avoid suspicion. In minutes he arrived at the Hall's home. Sara Hall met him, exchanging pleasantries.

"I hear rumors that you'll soon sail out to Port Dover. The need for supplies, isn't it?"

"Yes, Miss Hall. I'm not sure when we'll return. We must sail past the American fleet, and I doubt they'll be so accommodating. I wanted to pay my respects and say goodbye."

"Not goodbye, Mr. Harris. We'll see you when you get back. I'll say instead Godspeed."

Jesse instinctively reached out and for the first time embraced Sara fondly. For him, it was truly goodbye, for by one way or another, he would not return to Malden. Sara looked deeply into his eyes, troubled. Then she kissed him. He held her close and then silently turned to the path leading past the gate he had closed so many times before, walked on toward the Shawnee camp, closing another chapter in his life.

South Bass Island
Wednesday, September 8, 1813

George's head still was foggy, but the fever finally broke, and he ventured out onto the island to take a turn in the fresh air. Several of the Kentucky soldiers who had arrived compliments of General Harrison also took a turn about on the island. As they wandered through one woods, they found the remains of two homes recently been burned out by the Shawnee who had brought the war to the island. A scalped, decomposing body lay a few yards from the threshold of his home. The fleet had not arrived in time to save the sole inhabitant who had defended his home to the last.

A black sailor, Cyrus Tiffany, stood over the body for a moment. "He deserves burial," he said. "We'll bring back shovels and do the deed ourselves."

George and the others agreed, and went on to find apples fairly ready to fall from the several trees near the burned-out homestead. As they gathered what they could carry, George watched Cyrus. "You came with the captain from Rhode Island?"

"I did. Have been with him several years now."

"I don't know how to ask this, but being black, how do you –" He paused.

"How do I what? Serve as a black man on a white ship? I suppose because it's not a white ship. The Navy has never had any issue with black sailors serving."

"I haven't met many of color and I know that slavery is still practiced in the southern states and territories. But how do you justify serving the US Navy while others are held in bondage?"

"George, I've been free all my life. I don't really concern myself with others who aren't free like me. I s'pose, I should, but I just work to show that I'm as good, no better, no worse than the next man."

"But it doesn't bother you to serve the government that supports slavery? It would bother me. I just don't understand why you'd do it. I don't think I could."

"There are many of us black sailors in this fleet, as you've seen. We all do our jobs. Different reasons, I suppose, but we all do our duty. It might cost many of us, indeed all of us, our lives, but we pay it to show we're just as good. Word is you belong to the Society of Friends. Why do you fight along with us?"

"I don't fight. I'll assist the ship in whatever way I can, but I have to remain true to my principles. Do the men talk about me that much?" George asked.

Cyrus took a bite of an apple, puckered his lips from the tartness. Slowly he chewed, watching George. "Would it matter if they didn't?"

"I suppose I wouldn't care one way or the other," George said.

"Then I won't tell you one way or the other. Listen, all of the men who've joined us are willing to face death to win this fight and capture Lake Erie. Many are here for the prize money. Many are here for love of country. Some are here just to prove to others they can do it. Others to prove to themselves they can. You're here because you volunteered to be here, but it must run deeper than that. You have to think hard on why you're really here, George, because you'll need that to understand your duty in this here fight. If you don't have it settled, you can't effectively serve the ship."

The men returned to the *Lawrence*, passed out the fruit they gathered on their foraging expedition. Many of the men were still suffering from sickness, and in their weakened state, not one man could handle himself in a conflict. Even Captain Perry had succumbed to the fever again and had taken to bed when George settled in for the evening. He drifted off feeling healthier than he had for several days, but old Tiffany's words lay on him. And then Polly's words repeated in his head. What price was he willing to pay for his freedom?

## Chapter Twenty
## Amherstburg Naval Yard
## Friday, September 10, 1813

"All hands to the decks, away all anchors."

In the dark morning hours, the order passed and the soldiers, merchant marines, navy tars, and Six Nations warriors bustled about the decks, handling the lines, pulling sails, getting underway. Jesse joined Chapman at the larboard rail, pulling and securing stays.

"They won't let us slip by this time, John. The Americans are out there among those islands waiting for us. This'll be a death struggle soon," he said quietly.

"If we are captured, all the better, eh Jesse? Your release, and my imprisonment. But at least we'll both be free of this," he said, indicating the ship.

"John, stay away from me during the fight that's coming. No need to risk both of us on one shot from their guns. Promise me that you 'll get to her."

"Who?"

"Esther. If anything should happen, if I should fall here in the battle, find Esther and take care of her. You've been a good friend and I would want you to care for her."

"Jesse, this is not the time to talk of this. You and I will survive, and I expect you to have Esther introduce me to someone in New York. Remember that we're to work together after the war, eh?"

"Promise me, John." Jesse waited for John to assent. For his own peace of mind, he had to know she would be cared for. John looked full at Jesse, nodded and tugged at a line, tying it to the rail pin.

"Thank you, John. Now let's go about keeping ourselves alive this day."

The fleet turned into the blackness of the Detroit River. The *Queen Charlotte* followed Captain Barclay's *HMS Detroit*, with the *Lady Prevost* alongside within hailing distance. The wind from the southwest caught the sails and the fleet pushed forward, slowly navigating past Fort Malden where early morning campfires silhouetted scores of warriors. They stood on the banks, watching their fellow braves sail off to fight the Americans, to bring back scalps to hang on their lodging, share stories of the great battle, of the roaring cannon cutting down their enemy. They slowly sailed past Grosse Ile, a silhouette against the lightening sky, now catching the current, gaining speed. He stood at the prow, peering into the morning haze, searching intently for the fleet, hoped they would be at the mouth of the river. He could make a jump and swim the river, use the confusion to make his escape. But as the minutes passed and the morning sun brightened the sky, his tension grew. No sails appeared, no fleet to rescue him.

George sat on the platform of the main topsail. The warm air was still as death, Put-in-Bay's harbor quiet, broken by coughs coming from some souls still sick with the lake fever. His early watch had all but passed, and as the orange glow over the island lit the dawn, George stretched his legs, leaned back against the mast. Another day of boredom, waiting.

He would ask permission to accompany any party going on the island to its caves again to fetch fresh water. Just a chance to get off of the ship for a day, even half a day. It was nearly 6 in the morning, Friday, two days to Sabbath. Chaplain Breese would undoubtedly hold services then. Providence had sent him another glorious morning, and George took in the colors, scanned the water's surface. Behind him, Cunningham's Island, dark green against the morning's orange glow, before him Snake Island, almost white with the rising sun illuminating its rocks and shoreline. Just to starboard, in the distance the water lay flat calm, sparkling with white sails rising from the surface. Sails! White sails! He scrambled to his feet. It was indeed sails, several sails! *Barclay's fleet. This is it. Let them pass. No. Duty comes first.* His voice broke, tense, shaking as he strained to shout.

"Sail…." He coughed, cleared his throat. "Sail Ho!"

Below him Lieutenant Dulany Forrest, officer of the watch, ran to the mast and cupped his hands, yelled up, "Where away!"

"Off Snake Island," George yelled, and he pointed. "It's the whole fleet!"

Forrest ran to the hatch to alert Captain Perry, disappeared below deck. The clamor spread from ship to ship. Close by he saw John Silhammer aboard the *Ariel* pass the word to Lieutenant Packet. John saw George scramble down the ropes, grin and toss an eager salute.

Soon every ship swarmed with men taking their stations, pulling lines, raising sails, making every preparation to get underway. The boatswains' piercing whistles called all hands to their duty, though still weak from lake fever.

"All hands, up anchor!" The order passed from each vessel, the ropes raised the heavy iron from the muck of the bay, and the sweeps splashed into the water. The *Ariel* and *Scorpion* crews pulled together, the rhythm steady, rowing out of the harbor to where the southwest wind between South Bass Island and Snake Island could catch their sails and drive them into the fight.

The *Lawrence* struggled to get underway, the wind light, and the sails barely filled. Sailing Master Taylor, noted the time in the log, stood near the tiller watching the *Caledonia* moving slowly past, saluted Lieutenant Daniel Turner. *Scorpion* and *Ariel* cleared the harbor, passing Gibraltar Island. The *Niagara* followed behind, Lieutenant Elliott calling the commands to the deck hands, line pulling, sails unfurling. *Caledonia* moved into her position directly behind and nearly hugging the stern of the *Niagara*. As per the battle order, the *Lawrence* now swung slowly into position, trailing *Caledonia*, and putting George's ship directly in the middle of the battle group. He looked behind and watched the safety of the harbor growing smaller, the *Somers* moving in off the *Lawrence*'s stern. He saw George Senat bring *Porcupine* into the line. Remarkable. Only ten months earlier she had been piles of timber lying in the back of his wagon traversing the road from the forest to the little shipyard at the foot of Erie's escarpment. And out there beyond Snake Island sailed a warship preparing to convert her back into splintered timbers strewn over the lake. *What a waste*, he thought. *Tigress* and *Trippe* struggled to pull into line in the weak breeze, and the fleet, like a long disjointed snake, stretched out agonizingly slow, slithering toward its prey.

"Mister Taylor, it appears we lost the weather," Captain Perry's voice startled George, and he turned to see Perry fairly animated and gripping the starboard gunwale.

"It does so appear, sir. Wind sou'west, seven knots, sir. What are your orders?"

"We must gain the weather gauge and head west of Snake Island. Keep the island on the leeward, and we'll bring her about when we clear the island and chase down Barclay's ships! We'll have the wind on the starboard beam, and that'll bring us in to close action."

"Sir, west will take us into the teeth of the wind, we'll be at a dead standstill," Taylor said.

"Then we tack, Mr. Taylor. We tack."

"Aye, sir. But they have the weather gauge and we'll be exposed to their fire until we get close enough for the carronade to take effect. We're to the windward. Should we consider turning to the leeward and wait for more advantageous winds, sir?"

"To windward or leeward, Mr. Taylor, we will fight today!"

*There is no dissuading him*, George thought. Captain Perry paced along the deck, a caged lion, impatiently awaiting the winds to carry him to the fight. And there he would pounce. George tried to calm his own anxiety, watched the boulders jutting up from the water lapping Gibraltar's shore. Never took notice of boulders before, their many facets washed smooth from centuries of gales on the lake. Trees grew among them with no visible soil to hold their roots. Individual miracles dotting the shore. An eagle soared toward the *Lawrence*, passed over the topmast, turned and followed the ship, finally gliding into a treetop on the island. Perching on the topmost branch, it stretched out its wings, flapped them gracefully, and folded them to its sides. *An omen,* George thought. *But good or evil?* He watched the eagle in curious fascination, its form diminishing with the distance.

"Mr. Armstrong!"

George snapped back to reality, turned to face Captain Perry. "Yessir?"

"This would be the time to go about dressing the deck. We'll have need before too long."

"Yessir," George said, and he hurried to the stern where six buckets of sand stood in a row. Taking two up, he tossed their contents about the deck, the sand forming long low mounds. Charles Pohig, a seaman from Perry's Rhode Island contingent, scattered the mounds with his bare toes.

"George, it'll be of little use in clumps. Scatter it thinly about the deck. Cover the deck's entire surface well. We'll need to keep our footing soon enough."

"I'm sorry, Charles. I'm not very good at this sort of thing."

"Then it's time you learned."

The beauty of the island's trees, the rocks of the shore, the grace of the eagle, all were lost now to the business of preparing for bloodletting. His anxiety returned, and George went about the deck, scattering the sand near each gun crew, the men spreading the sand with their feet around their position. All buckets emptied, he passed them down into the hatch, another seaman taking them to refill. These would aid the first buckets in absorbing the blood, and they would help if a fire broke out on deck. The *Lawrence* continued to zigzag, catching any breeze that would propel it forward, while the men readied the eighteen carronades for battle. George brought the sand buckets back to the gun crews, retrieving six more at the bow. As he positioned these along the deck at intervals, he watched the men, some seated on the carronade platforms, some coating grease on the wooden slides of the gun carriages to aid the recoil of the gun. There was a somber methodical attitude among the men. Few of the gun crews had faced an enemy in combat; the only time they had fired the guns was in the training exercises at Presque Isle Bay. Regular soldiers on loan from General Harrison, Pennsylvania militia eager to earn a share of the prize money for winning this one battle, seamen from the east coast looking for glory on the upper lakes, Kentucky riflemen waiting to ascend to the sharpshooter's platforms at the topmast, all going about the business of preparing themselves mentally, spiritually for the coming conflict. George took it all in, listened to the emotions in the words traded between the men. Some asked for relief or aid for their families if they should fall, others exchanged small wrapped packs of letters, promises for delivery to loved ones. This too was a methodical preparation for battle. George had said his goodbyes, wanted to write something of value to leave for Polly, so many emotions, and no words to express them. Apology, promises, hopes? She would wait for him, he knew. He would tell her then. *Keep me alive through this fight*, he prayed. *Keep Jesse alive.* His mission was clear. Help the cause to win, and rescue him. The sails on the horizon were clear now, maybe three miles distant. What grace there was in the filled sails. The captain walked up to the prow, gazed through his telescope, dropped his arms, slammed the scope, collapsing it. George repeatedly caught himself holding his own breath, had to remind himself to work his lungs. *Why would anyone do that?* He felt his legs tremble. Caught Perry's gaze, smiled self-consciously. Something had happened. Agitated, Perry walked along the deck past him. Then George saw it. The wind had completely died. The *Ariel* had cleared, and the *Scorpion* now passed Snake Island, but immediately they came to a standstill. At first, the wind spilled from the sails and the fleet sat at the mercy of the on-coming British squadron. But then something else garnered the captain's attention. The wind suddenly switched its course, and Providence had come to Perry's aid. The American fleet now gained the wind gauge and the British fleet began the turn to position themselves for battle.

"Mister Taylor," Perry called.

"Aye, Captain?"

"The trumpet, if you please."

Sailing Master Taylor retrieved the hailing trumpet for Perry, who now stood at the prow of the *Lawrence*, called ahead to the *Caledonia*, ordering Lieutenant Turner to pass word to the *Niagara* to drop sail. The order relayed, Jesse Elliott's ship drifted to a standstill as the *Lawrence* passed on the larboard side of *Caledonia*, gliding alongside the leading brig. US Army officer Captain Henry Brevoort stood at the stern of *Niagara*.

"Captain Brevoort, the battle line has changed," Perry called. "Am I correct that the *Detroit* is now in the van?"

"It is," the captain called.

"Very well," Perry answered. "The *Lawrence* will engage Captain Barclay, and you and Captain Elliott will engage the *Queen Charlotte* as previously ordered. Engage each your designated adversary, in close action, at half cable's length! But we must close in rapidly. They still outgun us until we can close into carronade range."

"Yes sir," Brevoort called.

George heard the urgency in Perry's voice, not a command, but more a desperate entreaty to bring the guns to bear on the enemy quickly. At 300 feet! *This doesn't bode well for the ship,* he thought. The swagger and confident air had slipped away, and George saw a man moved to create an advantage where there was none.

The order repeated for clarification aboard the *Niagara*, and Perry affirmed the order as his new battle line. There was no mistaking the tone of voice shouted through the trumpet in questioning the order. The commanders of the *Niagara* were displeased with its new position, the honor of leading the battle now falling upon the *Lawrence*. George would happily resign the van to any other ship in the fleet. But the order now repeated to all hands on the *Lawrence*, and the crew scrambled to their posts at the lines, hauling the sails up, preparing to sail into the maelstrom. Perry disappeared below deck.

The order passed in succession, first to the *Niagara*, and then to the commanders of the remaining gunboats. The squadron sluggishly changed its order of battle. As the orders passed through the hailing trumpets, George saw the British fleet also re-aligning their positions. The new ship, *HMS Detroit*, sporting a fresh bright coat of paint turned to take the van. The *Lawrence* now took the lead to engage Commander Barclay's ship, relegating the *Niagara* to fall into order of battle behind the *Caledonia*, and engage the *Queen Charlotte*. The *Ariel,* out in front by a mile, would soon sail in range of the leading British gunboats. The signal flags raised, prepare to engage. The seamen read the order flying from the halyards and explained the flags' message to the landsmen at the guns, and the entire crew grew quiet. The waiting began.

Then Captain Perry, who had discarded his officer's uniform, quickly emerged from the berth deck wearing the blue woolen jacket of a normal seaman. Under his arm, he carried a large black cloth with white letters.

"George Armstrong!"

"Here, sir," he called.

"Your hands, if you please."

George walked to the mast, grasped the cloth. Hosea Sergeant laid his musket aside, took one fold of the cloth. The three of them stretched out the large black cloth. His heart began to race, for there lay the flag that Polly had told him about, the cloth she had helped Margaret Stewart and her daughters sew, the banner they had kept in strictest secrecy. The black coarse material bore the large white letters Polly had cut. Her handiwork accompanying him on what may very well be his last hour on earth. Sewn onto the black field, the dying words of the hero of the *USS Chesapeake*, Captain James Lawrence: *DONT GIVE UP THE SHIP,* exclaimed their resolve.

"Here are the words of the valiant Captain Lawrence. Shall I run 'er up, boys?" Perry called down the length of the ship.

The cheers echoed across the deck, and Perry hooked the battle flag's grommets to each clasp of the halyard. The men held the flag as Perry grasped the rope and swiftly pulled, sending the flag to the top of the mast. The cries of "*Huzzah!*" carried across the water, men aboard each ship in the line cheering the flag hanging loose in the light wind, barely fluttering.

"This flag does not come down today!" More cheers from the men on deck, and even George for a moment forgot his fear and felt that flutter in his chest, the pride in this ship he helped build. The wind picked up on the stern, and the black battle flag now fluttered, outstretched. He heard the snap of the cloth far above the quieted deck around him. Perry clasped his hands behind his back, calmly paced to the bow, and studied the approaching British fleet. His demeanor now one of quiet confidence, he had changed in that short moment in time. George thought how mercurial the man was. But in this captain now charging them into battle, George observed again what the men had revealed to him. He was also the luckiest man they had ever sailed with. He had sailed the ships from Buffalo in a fog right under the noses of the British fleet. He had escaped entrapment on the sandbar at Presque Isle and cleared the defenseless brigs while in sight of the British. He had received powder to arm the cannon when it seemed there was little to be had. He escaped the guns of Fort Malden and then set the trap for Barclay among the Bass Islands. And now he had sailed out into an unfavorable wind, only to have it change and grant him the weather gauge he desperately needed to defeat Barclay. Providence, it seemed, smiled on the American squadron. Perry's luck. George hoped it would hold.

Perry turned to the starboard gun crews, paused, looked into their faces. "Well, you boys of the *Constitution* know how to beat 'em, don't you?"

"Yes sir," one young sailor yelled out. His eager shout brought a laugh from the gun crew.

"That's it, lad," he said. "Let 'em hear what we're made of. Look at these Newport boys. They know how to do their duty, I warrant."

"Aye," the men called out.

George saw how each man prepared himself for battle – for death, wished that he were as brave as these. Or did they just mask their fears better than he did? The silence was oppressive, and he simply wished for the thing to begin. He wanted to shout. He wanted to just scream across the lake so that if Jesse were still aboard, he would hear him and take courage. *Courage for what? To face the iron the Lawrence would soon use to batter his ship?* What could he tell Jesse that his cousin didn't already know? He wanted to apologize for suspecting him, congratulate him on his betrothal. Shake his hand. Bear hug him. Tell him how they would move to Ohio together. Start a business. The *Lawrence* was about to engage Jesse's prison. He hoped that maybe they had mistrusted him, had given him some minor inconsequential duty where he could be below deck, out of harm's way. Nature hushed. George listened intently to hear the slightest slap of the waves against the bow. Even the waves whispered in anticipation.

Aboard the *Queen Charlotte* Jesse watched the tiny flag flow to the top of the second brig, preparing to do battle. The American squadron would have had a hard job catching up, as the wind had blown in the *Queen Charlotte's* favor. Possibly Barclay had planned to outrun them, glide safely into the harbor at Long Point, take shelter at Port Dover, and the American fleet would have to lay outside the harbor, out of reach of the long guns. That would suit him perfectly. Get off the ship at Long Point and make his way to the fort, find a way to escape. He had waited long enough. But then the ship's bell sounded, 10am. He looked up at the Union Jack, fluttering proudly. Then it suddenly dropped limp. Erie displayed her fickle temperament. The flag fluttered, only this time the wind had backed around nearly 45 degrees. Jesse saw it immediately. Barclay had lost the wind gauge, and the US fleet would fill their sails and bear down on them. He would not see Long Point this day. Captain Barclay passed orders through the hailing trumpet. Captain Finis called hands to the rails. In the light wind, the *Queen Charlotte* turned slowly and began to follow the *Lady Prevost*. Captain Barclay now turned to place the *Detroit* in the van. No time to maneuver, just get the ships into battle formation. How would the Americans react? At the same instant, he saw it. The *Niagara* had dropped sail, as did the *Caledonia*, and Jesse saw the second brig under full sail come alongside the *Niagara*. Each fleet now maneuvered for the advantage, and it would be a few short hours until the fleet would be upon them. He hoped to soon be a prisoner of war, freed from impressment. "Come quickly," he whispered.

He watched the *Detroit* now in its position, saw provincial marines in uniform leading a dark object, the black bear. This day's mascot, destined to be slaughtered for the celebration meal was now led to the hatchway, out of harm's way. *Strange*, he thought. *This bear is brought along to be slaughtered, and now taken below the deck for safety. And the men hoping to survive for the feast, now preparing to expose themselves to the slaughtering fire of the American fleet. Oh, the irony,* he thought.

"Mr. Harris!" Sergeant McDonough barked from across the deck.

"Yes, Sergeant McDonough?"

"To your gun!"

Jesse took his place beside John at the bow chaser, grabbed the sponge ramrod, and dunked it into the water bucket. He swabbed out the barrel, returned the rammer to the floor at the gunwale. The blue jacket warrior, his face painted for battle, loaded the powder bag into the barrel, and Jesse rammed it to the breech. Chapman poured powder from the horn into the vent. With no slow match for the cannon, the time had come to improvise. Lieutenant Stokoe strode across the deck.

"Use your pistol, mister," he ordered.

The young gunner loaded his pistol's pan with black powder, tightened the flint, pulled the hammer back to half-cock and took his place to the side of the cannon, the firearm alongside his leg. The wait began. McDonough marked their target.

"That second brig in line, the large ship trailing the *Caledonia.* That is our adversary. Hold your fire until she's in range, and then unleash hell on them!"

"That brig is not engaging, Sergeant," the gunner said.

"It will."

"She's brailed her top sails and is losing speed. The *Caledonia* has backed off as well."

"Captain Finis will give us our orders. We maintain the position in the line until we are ordered otherwise, understood?"

They could do nothing but helplessly wait for the enemy to close the distance and fall into their range. Finally the lead brig turned and slowly headed directly toward the line, following the two smaller gunboats. These two sailed straight toward engaging Masters Mate Campbell's schooner *Chippewa*, at the van of the British squadron. The brig flying the black flag from its topmast crept closer, exposing her bow to raking fire from the *Detroit*. But still her guns remained silent. Jesse felt the sweat in his palms, wiped them on his shirt, watched the closing brig point its bow at him. He judged it to be about two miles distant. The quiet settled on the ship and the men stood to their guns, presenting the full broadside toward the Americans. Still the brig came on. The sound of a bugle pierced the stillness. Jesse could barely see the bugler on the quarterdeck of the *Detroit* calling to battle stations, while a small group of blue uniformed men gathered around him. All the crewmen peered ahead of the *Queen Charlotte* toward the sound. The bugle call to stations stopped, a roll of drums, and then the 41st regiment's military band in the blue uniforms began. Across the lake resounded the regal notes of "Rule Britannia." The men came to attention, faced the music. Jesse could only look off to the larboard beam and watch the American brig closing. It wasn't his anthem. He had no anthem. He had only the hopes of a quick surrender of this ship to his countrymen.

The music ended, and the lake once again fell silent but for the rustle of the sails in the wind. Then a flash of fire from the *Detroit*'s bow brightened the side of the ship. In that instant a white cloud belched out. Within that same instant, a deep boom traveled across the water. A tall plume of water shot high into the air just before the bow of the approaching American brig. Still the ship charged on. Two minutes later, another flash, another cloud of white smoke, and the echoing boom sounded again.

On the *Lawrence*, George stood agape as the *Detroit*'s flash in the distance burst toward him a second time. He had no time to think, for a rapid low buzz became a thudding crash, showering the deck with whirling spears of timber and wood chips. Three men at the bow chaser collapsed into a heap. George instinctively rushed upon them to find two rising to their hands and knees, stunned by the concussion. The third gunner lay on the deck, already red with his blood from a wood plank imbedded in his neck. No moan, no scream, only a lifeless form, the first victim of the day's bloody business. George's stomach churned. Impulsively, he kicked sand over the red puddle.

Perry called the order, the crew tugged the ropes, and the *Lawrence* luffed hard to larboard, presenting her full starboard broadside of 32-pounder carronades at the British fleet. "Fire!" The nine slow matches touched nine vents and nine carronades erupted in fire and smoke. Through the haze, George saw nine plumes of water where nine iron balls had fallen short. Wasted shots. Captain Perry immediately called the helm up, and the *Lawrence* swung gradually to starboard and advanced on the British line, painfully deliberate in closing the distance to effective carronade range.

"Mr. Taylor, signal the *Ariel* and *Scorpion* to engage!"

"Aye, Captain!" The signal flags linked to the halyard now rushed up the mast.

George looked to the mast, saw the pennants, when immediately his attention was wrenched back to the ship by exploding timbers before him. Seaman John Shrouder was thrown to the deck, his shirt torn asunder and his right arm dangling in a bloody string. In that same impact, a splintered board cart-wheeled toward George just as he dove aside. Two men rushed to Shrouder, wrapped a bandage from the bloody shirt remnant, and supported him walking to the steps down to the berth deck. The men watched with grim resignation as the suffering man passed, dripping blood on the deck. Another crash and George quickly hunched over as the yard on the foremast broke in two, dropping cloth and trailing hemp lines, dropping the Kentucky sharpshooter from his perch, never having fired his rifle on the enemy.

"Steady," Perry called calmly. He casually walked behind the gunners. "Remember to take careful aim, boys. Don't waste shots."

"Waste shots?" George stood, muttered to himself, "We can't even fire our shots."

Another flash of fire, the echoing boom from the *Detroit*, and the ensuing splash of the iron ball sent a plume of water up over the *Lawrence's* bow. The shot had fallen short, but George's fear flooded over him. The next ball could be the last pain he felt on earth. No place to hide. No place for skulking. The terror gripped him and he stooped over, stunned, his stomach coming into his mouth, and he watched the gunners crouch with the smoldering lint stocks, anxiously waiting to bring their own carronade to life again.

A young sailor positioned on the bow chaser blew on the rope, the burning glow brightening. He touched the lintstock to the vent hole. The 12-pounder long gun roared to life, kicking the carriage back, the ship's wall engulfed in white smoke, and the violent shudder rocked George into the capstan. An echo of returning cannon fire reported across the water. In an instant, the prow exploded into hundreds of wood splinters. The concussion knocked him to his knees, peppered with wood chips and freckled with blood. Before him, on his side, lay the young sailor, lintstock still in hand, blood gushing from his chest, a long spear of Presque Isle oak pointing out his back. He spoke one word, "George."

"Steady, boys. We're not yet in range. Hold your fire, and let us close in and lay alongside and then unleash fury on them," Perry called. Two sailors rushed to the lifeless form, pulled the spear out and grasped the hands and feet, dragged him to the hatchway, handing him down to Usher Parsons's assistants. Two others quickly pulled the body of the rifleman from the tangle of lines and trailing sail cloth and dragged him to the stairs.

"Mr. Yarnell, raise the flag. All ships engage!" Perry called. "Mr. Taylor, bring the helm over and bear alongside the enemy. Pistol shot range!"

Another explosion of wood showered the deck with splinters, and the *Lawrence* continued to close in, painfully slow, opening the ship to devastating fire. At 100 yards, the *Lawrence* still tried to close, the seaman at the tiller brought her hard to starboard, trying to close the gap. The flash of all the guns on the broadside of the *Detroit* were followed in an instant by the thunder of their voices.

Again the long gun on the bow roared to life, the concussion shaking the deck. "George! More powder, and be quick about it!"

"Hold your fire, you men on the carronades. Be patient. Not yet!" Perry called.

George spread out his legs, braced himself, as the roar shook again. He grabbed the shoulder of one soldier, steadied himself, rushed to the hatch, a hand reaching up through the entrance, lifting a bag of powder, then another. George dropped them into the leather cartridge pouch, struggled to keep his feet, walked to the first gun, handed the powder bag to the first soldier of the gun crew. Then on to the next carronade. From here it was automatic, no thinking, just scurry to the hatch, receive the bags of powder, return to the next gun, and then the next, and the next. Another crash above the deafening roar. Showers of wood chips and spear-like wooden beams, pummeled the deck. And then the blood came. As the red wave spread across the deck, one black seaman dumped a bucket of sand on the flood. And still the gunners had not engaged. *How much more pounding can we take,* George thought. *We are being beaten into sawdust.* He wanted to see the men turn the carronade on the British now, unleash *their* roar, quiet *their* cannons.

At the order, the *Lawrence* luffed again, turned to larboard. More shot thundered from the *Detroit*, langrage scattered in a wave of hundreds of small splashes, rattling wooden sides, and tearing gaping holes in the sails, slashing the rigging, and maiming men on the deck.

"Now you Yankee men, let them taste it!" Perry yelled above the roar.

Seven remaining guns roared to life, and the *Detroit*'s sides showered wood splinters into the air, tumbling into the lake and over the deck. George caught sight of just that one blast through the smoke and then methodically began his run to the hatch, fetching more powder in the leather pouch. Each time he returned to a gun, the deck had grown slick with blood and tissue, ripped from the seamen. The *Lawrence*'s death struggle had begun, trading blast for blast. The roar of the cannon made his ears ring. One seaman stood aside his gun with his sponge rammer, revealing blood streaming from his ears. George grasped some torn shirt pieces lying wet on the deck, pinched them and stuffed them into his own ears. It merely amplified the ringing, but the concussive explosions were diminished. Then more explosions sounded from the British flotilla. Over the roar, he could not distinguish the other American guns as he ran the powder to the carronades. It seemed as though his ship was the only one fighting now. He looked off the stern as he ran along the deck. The *Caledonia* had drifted away from the fight, firing her long 24's in the general direction of the *General Hunter* and the *Queen Charlotte*, but he saw no effect from the guns. Yet even more disturbing, the *Niagara* had also lagged far behind, firing her bow-chaser ineffectually. He reached for more powder, tucked the bags into the leather, ran to the leading carronade near the starboard bow.

Charles Pohig took the black powder and thrust the bag into the cannon bore. "George! Where is the *Niagara*?"

"There," he said pointing into the smoke to a distant mast, "behind the *Caledonia*!"

"Why does she tarry?"

"I don't know, Charles, but it appears we're left to fend for ourselves!"

"Captain!" Pohig yelled above the din. "The *Niagara*! Why does she hang back so?"

Perry looked to the stern, obviously agitated. "Do your duty, men! They will engage."

Just as he spoke, another crash hit the side of the ship, the carronade tossed askew from its carriage. Pohig collapsed on top of the barrel, a bloody gash in his face, nose broken, long splinter wedged in his right arm and the left hanging useless at his side. "George, help me," he called, looking down at his body. "I think they are broken," he said.

George grasped his arm around Charles for support and walked him to the hatch, stepping over long shards of metal and wood strewn across the red-stained deck sand. Another loud thump nearby, and George saw David Bunnell, covered with the blood from the collapsed headless gunner beside him. George helped Pohig down the steps. On the berth deck below, the wardroom served as Usher Parsons's surgery where he toiled at the business of triage. He patched up bloodied and bruised sailors, militia, soldiers with limited supplies and limited help. George helped Pohig onto a hammock to sit and wait his turn on the operating table. Parsons concentrated on stitching a wounded arm on the young midshipman Henry Laub. "Will this do, Mr. Parsons?" George called.

More wounded came down the steps. Parsons did not look up. "Wherever there is space."

Pohig called to George above the groans of the wounded, "Take care of yourself, George."

George looked to where the surgeon was helping Laub up from the table, then to Pohig, "You do the same. I'll see you after—"

A crushing screech of wood blew into the operating area of the wardroom, and in an instant, a hole had appeared in the hull. In that same instant, the cannonball had ripped half of Henry Laub from the surgeon's grasp, had carried his torso away, and buried itself deep into the wall beside Pohig who immediately collapsed in a heap on the floor. George's stomach retched and he grabbed the handrail, pulling himself up to the deck. He came face to face with the disoriented Perry.

"George, I need anyone who can man a gun! Ask Doctor Parsons to send any wounded who can still fire a gun. At once!" he shouted over the roar.

George repeated the order, and several wounded and maimed sailors limped up the stairs, leaning on each other for support. He followed behind them, carrying more powder cartridges, handed them to the three gun crews still in action, and then he stopped, gazed on the carnage. Blood and other matter scattered and sprayed across the decks, on the men's uniforms. Captain Perry stood with Lieutenant John Brooks near two guns, still directing their fire. Delaney Forrest had left the helm, had joined another gun crew. Lieutenant John Yarnall directed the third gun, the rest on the starboard side having been effectively dismounted from their gun carriages by direct fire. Yarnall created a sight with his bandage wrapped around his head and loose feathers from a mattress in the berth deck stuck to the bandage. George thought he was every bit the vision of a plucked chicken, and the men laughed at his appearance, what small humor they could find in this butchery. Then another cannonball burst through the bulwark, and Brooks collapsed in agony, the left side of his hip ripped apart. The scream that exploded from him shook George more than any of the others he had witnessed in these two gruesome hours. Perry bent over his friend, tried to comfort him.

"Oliver," Brooks cried weakly. He grimaced, gritted his teeth and reached for the pistol in Perry's belt, tugged at it. Perry pushed his hand gently away, laid his hand on the top of Brooks's head.

"No, John. I can't."

Aboard the *Queen Charlotte*, Jesse gave silent thanks that the second brig had not engaged. But now the fire directed entirely on the *Lawrence*, the lone brig in the attack. This was Perry's flagship, the men said, and they were all too willing to take the fight to the American commander. Knock his ship out of the fight, and the odds would lay heavily in British favor. Stokoe directed the fire onto the *Lawrence*, bearing the black battle flag. Jesse manned the swivel gun on the starboard bow, as yet with no adversary to engage. Even in the din of the roaring guns, he held onto the quiet consolation that he would not be delivering death to any fellow countrymen. The smaller brig *Caledonia* had broken away from the battle line and now used the freshened wind to close in for action against the *Queen Charlotte*. The *General Hunter* had slipped back along the leeward side soon to fall behind the *Charlotte* as the ship moved in for the kill on the *Lawrence*. Then a long gun found its range. The report of the *Caledonia's* 24-pounder thundered across the water. The ball splintered apart the railing, struck Captain Finis in the face and continued into the chest of Lieutenant Garden, impaling both onto the opposite bulwark, and spraying Jesse's face with blood and brain matter. On convulsive impulse, he swiped his sleeve over his face, his lips, spat on the deck, tried to rid himself of the mass. They were his enemy, yet his heart sickened for the two young officers.

Lieutenant Stokoe immediately assumed command of the ship, and ordered her to run toward the *Detroit* which had been under the heavy fire of the *Lawrence's* 32-pounders. Jesse saw the wood tossing in the air with each explosion of the carronades. The commodore's ship was inflicting heavy damage, no doubt, but now the *Charlotte's* guns, combined with the Commodore Barclay's *Detroit,* could decimate the brig.

"Mr. Harris, it looks like we will soon win the day!"

"Sergeant McDonough, I hope you won't live to see it," Jesse called.

"No chance of you escaping this time, eh? I'll have you trussed up with all the other Americans we capture this day. Finally I have had my fill of you." McDonough stood with the Brown Bess at the ready, fixed bayonet poised to impale anyone just as soon as he could join the boarding party to take possession of the *Lawrence.*

"Be careful you don't hurt yourself with that bayonet there, Sergeant," Jesse yelled mockingly above the roar of the cannon. A thunderous crash sounded overhead and the yard cracked, tumbling down mainstay, rigging, and wooden beams. Jesse looked up to see the exploding wood shards and ship tackle let loose. A block landed directly on McDonough's head, crushed the tall shako flat, and sent him sprawling onto the deck, motionless. Jesse walked calmly to the sergeant, kicked his leg. No movement. Jesse rolled him aside and saw the bayonet buried in his heart.

"Clear this deck," an officer yelled. Jesse and Chapman grabbed the sergeant's feet, dragged him to a gaping hole in the gunwale, and unceremoniously shoved him into Lake Erie. No words were spoken. Jesse felt no anger, no satisfaction, no triumph. Providence once again had acted, and he was merely an observer. He now attended to only the duties he felt obligated to perform. Across the deck, he watched two Provincial Marines drag the bloodied corpse of one of the Shawnee warriors to an opening and toss him overboard. *Doing their best to keep a ship cleared for battle,* Jesse thought. Another tremendous crash hit the ship and wood beams tossed like so much cordwood tumbled on the deck, breaking legs and decapitating a soldier. Stokoe called above the noise, "Harris, fetch Lieutenant Irvine!"

Jesse looked to the voice and saw Stokoe leaning heavily against the capstan, a long spear of wood imbedded in his shoulder. He had liked Stokoe, and now to see another good officer go down with a wound made him shudder.

"Lieutenant Irvine! Lieutenant Stokoe is down, sir!"

Irvine left the larboard side bow chaser, rushing to the stern. "Aye, sir," he said staring at the grotesque bloodied wood point protruding from Stokoe's armpit.

Stokoe gritted his teeth against the pain. "All are down but you. Take command. Stay close to the *Detroit.* Don't allow them to rake us!" He grimaced and exhaled heavily. Another crash against the bulwark, and more splinters whirled past his head.

"Harris! Take the lieutenant below and report to me at once!"

Jesse glanced quickly at Chapman, nodded his farewell, and then supported the officer, as he stumbled to the main hatchway. Below decks, the carnage was immeasurable. One doctor labored with his tools to amputate limbs or treat dozens of men, as the moans and shrieks of wounded muffled the sound of the guns above. Shawnee and Ojibwa warriors, brave fighters on their own lands now cowered below the decks, covering their ears and jumping at every crash. *Braves,* Jesse thought. The blue jacketed warrior looked at Jesse, humiliated by his fear. Jesse looked him in the eye, sneered, shook his head in exaggerated disbelief and scorn and climbed back to the deck. The ship's cannon still fired, but now diminished. Two cannon lay dismounted with no one left to man the larboard bow chaser.

He yelled above the confusion. "What are your orders, sir?"

"Take the helm, Mr. Harris. Steady the course and keep close on the *Detroit.* That other brig, the *Niagara* is under sail now and looks to break the line. Don't let her come between us!"

"Yes sir. Close on the *Detroit.* No gap. I'll hold her to that." He firmly gripped the ship's wheel. *How strange indeed are the ways of Providence,* he thought. Commodore Hall's prediction had come true. He was now piloting *His Majesty's Ship Queen Charlotte.* If Sara Hall could just see him now. He smiled. If only *Esther* could see him now.

George looked over the last larboard carronade, "Captain Perry, sir! It's the *Niagara!*"

Perry's calm demeanor had maintained the crew's respect for two hours, but it now abated as he saw Elliott's tardy ship sailing to the windward side of the helpless *Lawrence.* The fierceness in his eyes intensified, and George witnessed a horrific desperation about them. Perry stared at the *Niagara*, and then seemed to stand taller, determined.

"Lieutenant Yarnall! We can no longer fight this ship. I'll transfer to the *Niagara* as she comes up. Armstrong, ready the boat!" George leaned over the stern, tugged on the rope that had towed the boat behind the ship, out of harm's way. He hauled on the line with all his might, pulling the boat along the windward side. Another crash against the ship, and one more cannon pivoted off its carriage. Now only one gun remained. Perry held the slow match, touched the vent. The carronade erupted in one more defiant blast. George tied the rope to a long splintered beam on the gunwale, took a deep breath and gazed on the destruction. The decks literally ran red with blood. Few men remained on deck, and most of those were wounded, placed there to relieve the crowded surgery below. *So much waste of life*, he thought. *So, this is what father had seen. This is what had shaped his principles.*

"Lieutenant, I leave it to your discretion to strike or not, but the American colors must not be pulled down over my head today. The boys have done all that I have asked. If this battle is to be won, *I* will win it!" Perry turned to the few remaining men still able to stand. "I need four lads with strength enough left for one more duty. Mr. Armstrong, will you handle an oar?" Perry called.

"Yes sir," George said. *Anything to get clear of this vessel*, he thought. He climbed over the side, and down into the rowboat, holding onto the *Lawrence's* undamaged side. Two more sailors climbed in, followed by Captain Perry. The last seaman, Cyrus Tiffiny, pushed away. George held the tiller for the captain and then saw the black battle flag come down from the topmast.

"Hold there!" a voice shouted.

Private Hosea Sergeant gathered up the large flag and tossed it into the boat. One of the men stuffed it into a corner, stopping up a leak which had sprung from a cannon shot. The *Niagara* continued past the ship to her windward. A determined fierceness on Perry's face once again, he yelled, "Row, lads. Put your backs into it!"

Chapter Twenty-One
Near West Sister Island
September 10, 1813
2:45PM

"She's surrendered! Look there! The flag's struck!" The cheering *huzzah*'s went up from the *Queen Charlotte*, and were echoed by the *Detroit*. The cannons silenced and the men watched a small rowboat rapidly crossing the gap between the wrecked *Lawrence* and the *Niagara*, now dropping sail to take in its passengers.

"Are we to board her?" one of the soldiers of the 41st regiment called out.

"We have no boarding vessels left. They're all broken into scrap by *Caledonia's* guns. She's still active. See how she's coming to our stern?"

"If we can't board and take possession, is she still in the fight?" one marine called.

"I reckon she is," Jesse smiled.

"Yes, but her captain isn't," said Irvine looking through his telescope. "That's Perry in the boat. Gunners! Load and fire on that skiff! Mr. Chapman, take careful aim and sink that cutter!"

The few active cannon left on the windward side fired toward the small craft, showering the boat with spumes of water. John aimed his cannon directly at the cutter, looked at Jesse, winked, and fired his pistol flint at the touch hole. The shot burst true toward its mark – a yard behind the escaping cutter. The white fog of smoke cleared, and Jesse saw the boat continue its pace, and he looked back at Chapman with a subtle smile. The crewmen reloaded, trained the guns on the skiff, fired again. More plumes of water cascaded over the boat, and still they rowed on, one figure standing and then quickly sitting again as the shots narrowly missed. *That's one lucky boat*, Jesse thought. More shots boomed across the water. The *Caledonia* had moved in for the kill, and turned her long guns on the *Charlotte*, firing chain shot entangling the top sails on the mainmast. The *Queen Charlotte* had lost the wind and now had become harder to steer, another shot hitting her rudder. Jesse felt the sluggishness on the wheel, decided not to report it. The advantage had slipped away, and fortunately time was finally running out. Ahead of him, the *Detroit* began to change course, but devastated by the *Lawrence's* firing, now moved lethargically. Only a few of her windward guns fired, and these could not reach the *Niagara* now using the *Lawrence's* surrendered, battered hulk as a screen. Jesse saw the escaping boat had reached the *Niagara*, which had all sails dropped. *Lawrence* struck her colors and belonged to the British squadron. But no boats remained to carry a boarding party to take possession. The prize of war continued to drift out of reach.

Alongside the *Niagara*, George reached out for a rail to hold. The men steadied the vessel and Captain Perry immediately stood to climb the ship's ladder. George grabbed the battle flag from the hole in the hull, draped it over his shoulder and climbed behind the captain. On the deck, Elliott and other officers met Perry, who stood before them, a dazed look on his face, spattered with blood and dirtied with black powder burns. Elliott saluted.

"Captain Perry, how goes the day?"

Perry stood, stupefied by the question. "Badly."

"What are your orders?"

"I fear we may have lost the day. The *Lawrence* can no longer render fire on the enemy. Without the gunboats engaging, we are outgunned."

"I'll put off and bring up the *Somers* and the other gunboats if you will take the *Niagara*. We may yet take the victory," Elliott said.

Perry looked back to the schooners which now had full sails in the freshening wind, attempting to close in on the British line, fragmenting into individual fighting sections. He turned to Elliott, "Do so at once!"

Elliott brushed past George, quickly climbed down into the skiff, four of the *Niagara*'s crew joining him to take the oars. The *Lawrence*'s three crewmen climbed aboard the *Niagara* and joined the gun crews loading the carronades. George attached the battle flag to the halyard and pulled swiftly, sending it to the top. A cheer rose across the deck. "Full sail! Load with double shot, lads!" Perry yelled. George joined the number eight gun crew whose shot man had left with Elliott. He hefted a 32-pound shot from the rack and pushed it into the barrel. He grabbed a bag of langrage, the cloth bag holding bits of the scrap iron sewn in during the spring months for this purpose. The ball rammed down and seated against the powder cartridge, George fed the bag of metal shards into the barrel. It too was rammed down to the breach. The gunner shoved a metal rod into the vent, puncturing the cloth. A quill loaded with the priming powder followed, and the crew stood at the ready. At the same time, the deckhands had raised the sails driving the *Niagara* ahead of the British line and turning hard to starboard. She positioned to breach the line, "cross the *T,*" heading straight for the gap between the *Detroit's* bow and *Lady Prevost's* stern. With three ships to larboard, three ships to starboard, the *Niagara* now prepared all eighteen carronade to rake the British line from close quarters. The tension left George weakened and he leaned on the gunwale, anticipating the guns to roar to life again. Closer they came, and he could see the British soldiers moving quickly on the deck, trying to turn the guns, turn the ship to face the threat. Some had climbed into the tangle of ropes, chopping at the mass with boarding axes. But the ship didn't respond to their exertions. And he was close enough to see the faces of the enemy. The *Detroit* was a sitting duck, and the *Niagara*, the hunter. Off the stern, the rowboat carrying Captain Elliott and his oarsmen had pulled to the *Somers,* far out of the range of the *Queen Charlotte* which tossed feeble shots in its direction, the plumes rising ineffectually. The *Caledonia* now closed on the line to cross the stern of the *Charlotte* and rake her decks from the aft. The two brigs, the main power of Barclay's fleet, had no escape.

"George," Perry yelled. "To your station! Service the guns!"

"Mr. Harris," Irvine called. "That brig is about to break the line! Put her helm up and come leeward of the *Detroit*!"

Jesse gripped the wheel. The order meant they would continue the fight, have the fresh guns on the leeward ready for the *Niagara* when she cleared within range. He saw the blue jacketed warrior approaching him on the deck. In his hand, he carried a boarding ax. No threat made to Jesse, he methodically paced, appearing to ready himself for hand to hand fighting. Now the bowsprit aimed directly at the mizzen mast of the *Detroit*, and failure to turn her hard to starboard would skewer the *Detroit* where she sat. The wheel still was sluggish. *End it now,* he thought. In an instant he turned the wheel hard to larboard, used up precious time, then turned her hard over, and watched the bow aim directly for *Detroit's* rigging.

"Harris, hard to starboard!" Irvine yelled.

"Aye, sir!" Jesse yelled.

It was too late. The *Queen Charlotte* fell onto the *Detroit*, running the bowsprit and jib into the mizzen, hopelessly tangling the lines. The shock lurched Jesse forward, slamming himself against the wheel. The sudden shock sent the men tumbling forward. The warrior was thrown against the main mast, dropping his axe. A thunder of cannon followed, and the *Caledonia* sent a shot into the stern, throwing splinters across the deck, a ragged board slamming into Jesse's back and knocking the breath out of him. Dazed, he stood up, took a deep breath, saw Irvine gaze at him. No anger, no hatred, only a simple questioning look delivered to Jesse –

why? Jesse left his position, walked away from the destruction trained at the stern. The warrior stood erect, grasped the axe, looked directly into Jesse's eyes, that all too familiar look of intense hatred. He limped toward Jesse, his intention clear. Jesse had nowhere to hide. John stood at the number six gun, saw the brave pass. He turned quickly to stop him. The warrior's axe raised overhead, another resounding boom from off the stern, and in an instant the warrior's arm was gone, spirited away with its raised axe, and carried into Lake Erie. The warrior stumbled forward, blood spewing from his shoulder. Jesse and John converged on him, and in one swift motion hurled him into the lake.

Another blast hit the *Charlotte*, and then another. Screams carried across the deck and Jesse became conscious of the direction of the assault. For in the confusion and white cannon smoke covering the scene, he saw the bow of the *Niagara* passing the bow of the *Detroit*, close enough to hurl rocks at each other. *Niagara* raked the *Detroit* fore to aft with langrage and canister. Small iron balls blasted out, tearing holes in sails and seamen. Then the horror emerged as the *Niagara* passed the helpless flagship and reloaded her guns for the *Queen Charlotte*. Irvine spotted the break-through, ordered the few gunners still standing to the starboard batteries. Jesse stood immobile, no insolence, only unable to join the gun crews aiming at the *Niagara*.

On the *Niagara* George ran to the hatch, powder cartridges handed up by the young black seaman below, and he returned them to the first three starboard gun crews. Then back to service the next. The carronade erupted, raking the *Detroit*, slicing into the sails, toppling the lines. The entire ship shuddered in extremis, a sharpshooter firing down on the *Niagara* plummeted into the tangle of ropes to be caught and hang limply in the lower shrouds. George stared at the figure, close enough to read the agony of his face, then he immediately ran back, retrieving more powder bags. As the ship cleared past the bow, the *Queen Charlotte* now was in range. Orders passed, the *Niagara* came about, fired the larboard guns into the *Lady Prevost*, ripping down her sails. The starboard guns reloaded, the gun captains ordered a broadside. From fifty yards distance, *Niagara* unleashed the full weight of the broadside into the *Queen Charlotte* with bar shot, canister, langrage, all guns double-shotted. Through the smoke George saw men tossed across the deck to collapse in grotesque forms. Then one redcoat grabbed a rope and the Union Jack quickly flew down to the deck. On the *Detroit*, a seaman scrambled up the mast which had been shattered in half. He pulled hard at the flag which was nailed to the mast, and threw it to the deck.

"Cease your firing!" the gun captains shouted along the line. A cheer arose from the *Niagara* and was repeated by the *Caledonia's* crew. Two small gunboats broke away from the battle group and set sail for the Detroit River and the safety of Fort Malden. Captain Perry signaled the *Scorpion* and *Ariel* to chase them down. More guns fired. Their long guns threw cannonballs across the bows of the two gunboats and they dropped their sails. George leaned back against the main mast, roughened with splinters and embedded scrap iron, breathed deeply, coughed from the smoky haze hanging over the deck. Ears still ringing from the roaring, he pulled out the cloth ear stops, tossed these blood stained shirt fragments to the deck.

A crew prepared the longboat to row to the *Queen Charlotte*. George shook his head, cleared the numb sensation. "Captain Perry, sir, may I go with the boarding party?"

Perry searched George's face. "Are you certain that you want to?"

"Do I have your permission, sir?" George asked.

"Of course. Report to me after, and I will assist you anyway I can."

George climbed into the boat with the other twelve, and they pulled to the *Queen Charlotte*. A boat from the *Somers* rowed steadily toward Commodore Barclay's *Detroit*. In it sat Jesse Elliott, prepared to accept the formal surrender of the British fleet. Three hours of cannon firing had finally silenced, and across the calm lake waters echoed another sound. George heard it immediately. Moans from the wounded strewn on the decks of the ships, bloodied fighters writing in agony, oblivious to the enemy, oblivious to anything but their own suffering. The chorus of pain unnerved George, and he fought back the nausea and forming tears.

The boat pulled alongside the *Queen Charlotte*, and George sprang up, stepping past the others and drawing protests. He climbed the ladder, was met on the deck with a scene of carnage nearly equal to what he witnessed on the *Lawrence*. Lieutenant

Irvine stood before him with his sword in hand, the hilt offered forward in surrender.

He swept the sword aside. "Sir, is Jesse Harris aboard this ship?" he said.

Irvine stepped aside, pointed to the gunwale. Jesse sat propped up against the bulwark, his arm bloodied, his face pale, puffed-up, nose swollen and broken. A soldier kneeling beside him attempted to dress the gash under his right eye.

"Jesse!"

"George," he said weakly. "Sorry I can't stand to greet you." Then a feeble smile through bloodied teeth, "You look well enough."

"Well enough, Jesse. Polly sends her love –" his voice broke.

Jesse shifted his weight and moaned. "And Esther? Have you heard from her?"

"She is well, Jesse."

"George, this is John Chapman. He's my friend. Could you – could you find work for him in Ohio?"

George wiped a tear away with a dirty sleeve. "Work enough for all of our friends, Jesse. Mr. Chapman, since you're now our prisoner, can you help me help him?"

"It would be an honor," Chapman said.

The two lifted Jesse to his feet, helped him to the boat. Another boat came alongside to assist with wounded prisoners. The men rowed toward the battered hulk of the *Lawrence*, once again flying the Stars and Stripes. Ahead of them, another boat neared the wreckage. Captain Perry stood up in the vessel as it reached the side. He climbed the steps, and as George's skiff reached the side, he looked to see the black flag once again rise on the broken mast.

"Don't give... don't give up the ship. Good words," Jesse said, reading the frayed standard as it fluttered overhead.

Jesse and the other wounded were lifted up to the *Lawrence* and laid out on the deck where Usher Parsons labored over each, administering what aid he could. Captain Perry, emerged from the wardroom, wearing his officer's uniform, blood still spattered on his white trousers. He quietly walked to a dismounted carronade, sat on it, laid his commodore's hat on his lap. He unfolded an envelope and began to write. George watched him; Perry paused, stared about at the bloodied deck, finished writing and folded the envelope.

"Captain Perry, sir. I found Jesse, sir."

"I pray he is well, George."

"He's well enough. When we're permitted, I'd like to accompany him back to Erie."

"When Mr. Dobbins returns with the *Ohio*, I'll allow you to accompany him. I'll have Purser Hambleton sign your release. George, I'm not insensitive to your convictions. I want to say you handled yourself admirably, and you're a credit to your family. I would that I had more men of your courage.

"Thank you, sir, but I was anything but courageous. I only wanted it to end. I don't believe I could ever do it again."

"George, we never know what manner of men we are until we're tried in the crucible. Tomorrow, next month, even years from now, then you'll understand who you are. For now, we've much work to do. I've signaled the *Ariel* to rejoin the fleet. I'm sending this message to General Harrison at Sandusky. You'll see to it he receives it?"

"I'd be honored." George carried the envelope to the bow of the *Lawrence*. Jesse lay exhausted, grimacing in pain. Chapman sat by his side, holding a wooden canteen. A prisoner of war yes, but no longer the enemy.

"I have to leave for awhile. Take care of him, John."

"George?"

"Here, Jesse."

"Thank you."

George walked to the steps, climbed over the side. Two crewmen sat in the skiff, waiting to row him to the *Ariel*. He sat and unfolded the envelope, discreetly peered into the message:

*U.S. brig Niagara, off the Western Sister, head of Lake Erie, Sept. 10th, 1813, 4 P.M*

*Dear general – We have met the enemy – and they are ours. Two ships, two brigs, one schooner, and one sloop.*

*Yours, with great respect and esteem,*

*O.H. Perry.*

*Understatement*, he thought, as he folded the envelope again. The captain has stated the outcome so simply. Yet there was nothing simple in this fight. By luck or by Providence, he had made it through unscathed. A second chance with Polly, while on the deck Jesse clung to life. He'd never do battle again. The government had what it wanted. The Army had what *it* wanted. Mr. Dobbins had what *he* wanted. The last roar of the cannon had died, and George sat blood-stained and weary in the skiff's bow, riding the waves toward the *Ariel*. He leaned forward on his arms, folded across his knees and with a sobbing release, closed his eyes at last and contemplated the cost.

## Afterward

The country honored Oliver Hazard Perry as the hero of the battle and shared the accolades with Jesse Elliott. But dissension followed the battle and the controversy of Elliott's conduct continues in debate to this day. After public exchanges and accusations became an embarrassment to the government, President Monroe ordered Elliott east to captain other vessels, eventually including the *USS Constitution*. Perry took the position of a diplomat and, while on a mission to Venezuela aboard the *USS Nonesuch*, he contracted malaria. He died on his 34th birthday. Buried in Port of Spain, Trinidad, his body eventually was returned to the family plot in Newport, Rhode Island.

George married Polly and ultimately fulfilled his dream of starting his own business venture in Ashtabula, Ohio. He kept his friendship with Daniel Dobbins and through that friendship, he joined the *Underground Railroad* movement, helping escaped slaves journey to Canada. He died in Ashtabula, Ohio. His legacy is the subject of *A Bit of Colored Ribbon*, the second book of the trilogy.

Daniel Dobbins returned to his shipping merchant livelihood after the war, transporting trade goods to Canada. He became actively involved with helping escaped slaves in their quest for freedom. Today, Dobbins Wharf and Dobbins Landing in Erie, Pennsylvania, still bear his name. He lobbied for the establishment of a *US Revenue Cutter Service* station in Erie. This forerunner of the US Coast Guard in time established a USCG office which remains in Erie to this day. He died in 1856 and is buried in the Erie Cemetery.

John Chapman of the 41st Regiment of Foot was captured with the *Queen Charlotte* and taken with other prisoners to the POW camp at Chillicothe, Ohio. After the war, when the prisoners were paroled to return home, he remained in Twinsburg, Ohio, and is buried there. No record exists of his work there.

James Bennett received a fatal wound during the battle, most probably plugging the holes in *Lawrence's* hold. He was one of 83 causalities on board *Lawrence*, a loss rate of 55 percent. Splinters, contusions, and fractures all contributed to this significant loss rate. His widow, Sarah, spent decades fighting to receive part of the prize money or pension for his service during the *Battle of Lake Erie*; however the Senate rejected her appeal.

Jesse recovered from his wounds and returned to Buffalo, New York, married Esther and lived the rest of his days there, working as a carpenter like his cousin, George.

Robert Barclay, commander of the British fleet, recovered from his wounds and returned to Great Britain. The ensuing court-martial exonerated him of any wrong-doing in losing his fleet to the Americans. It was the only time in history that an entire British fleet surrendered to a foreign power.

The American sailors who died in the fight were buried in the lake, laced up in their hammocks and rest near West Sister Island. A US Coast Guard buoy close to the island marks the approximate location of the end of the battle.

The officers of both sides, under the administration of Chaplain Thomas Breese, were buried in a joint ceremony on land: South Bass Island, Ohio. A pyramid of cannonballs in the village of Put-in-Bay marks the original burial spot. One hundred years later, many of the bones that could be recovered were placed in a singular catafalque. During a combined British, Canadian and American ceremony in 1912, the former enemies placed the catafalque under the floor of the rotunda of *Perry's Victory and International Peace Memorial* on South Bass Island, Ohio. The memorial is administered by the National Park Service.

Commodore Perry's famous battle flag that Margaret Forster Stewart and the women of Erie sewed from black dress material was kept by the US Navy and today hangs on display at the US Naval Academy at Annapolis, Maryland. Over the years it has faded and some of the attempts to restore the tears and deterioration have given it a brown and somewhat blue tint. For this reason, nearly all reproductions are made from blue cloth. But it was originally black with white sewn-on lettering showing the misspelled word, *Dont*. The reproduction *Flagship Niagara* today sails from her home port in Erie, Pennsylvania, flying the blue reproduction flag.

## Appendix

aft – at, near, or toward the stern of a ship

boatswain – a ship's officer in charge of equipment and crew

bow-chaser – One of a pair of long guns mounted forward in the bow to fire directly ahead.

brig – a sailing vessel with two square-rigged masts

carronade – a powerful, short, smoothbore cast iron cannon used at short range as an anti-ship and anti-personnel weapon.

frigate – a full-rigged ship that is square-rigged on all three masts, lighter armament and built for speed.

gunwale – the top edge of the hull of a ship

halyard – a rope used to hoist a ladder, sail, or flag

impressment – the taking of men by force to serve in a  military force, usually without notice.

jib – a triangular sail set ahead of the foremast

keel – the bottom-most longitudinal structure on the ship

larboard – the ship's left side as the observer faces forward toward the bow. The name changed to Port in the 1840s due to its confusion with Starboard, the right side in shouted orders.

langrage – nails, scrap metal, nails, and even pottery shards sewn into a cloth bag to fire from a cannon.

lintstock (also linstock) – a staff to hold a lighted slow-match (cotton rope as a wick) to discharge a cannon.

luff – a ship steers far enough toward the direction of the wind (windward) disrupting the airflow and the sail flaps or "luffs."

mizzen – the aft-most mast of a ship, typically shorter than the foremast at the front.

prow – the forward part of the ship's bow above the waterline.

ratlines (pronounced "rattlins") – lengths of thin rope tied between the shrouds to form a ladder.

schooner – a type of ship defined by its fore and aft rigging on all of two or more masts.

skiff – term used for small row boats, sometimes using a sail on coastal areas and rivers.

starboard – right side of the ship as an observer aboard faces the front, toward the bow.

stern – the back or aft-most part of the ship.

sweep – long oar for moving a ship in slight wind. Each rower has only one oar or sweep and must pair with a rower on the opposite side.

trenail (pronounced trunnel) – a wooden peg, pin, or dowel used to fasten pieces of wood together by boring a hole in the wood and pounded into the hole.

# ABOUT THE AUTHOR

Craig S. Whitmore is a former English/Creative Writing/ Dramatics teacher from Ohio. After retirement, he joined the National Park Service as a seasonal Park Service Ranger. His duties as an interpretation ranger at *Perry's Victory and International Peace Memorial* at Put-in-Bay, Ohio, led him to write this first novel, *The Last Roar* about the *Battle of Lake Erie* during the *War of 1812*. *A Bit of Colored Ribbon* is the sequel to that story and includes events from the battles for Chattanooga where Craig worked for the National Park Service at *Chickamauga and Chattanooga National Military Park* in Fort Oglethorpe, Georgia. He researched Ohio's workers in the Underground Railroad prior to and at the beginning of the American Civil War and developed the story of Nat, the escaped slave. His final novel in the series, *Bridge to Beulah*, completes the trilogy about the fictional Armstrong family.